EMBASSYTOWN

ALSO BY CHINA MIÉVILLE

King Rat

Perdido Street Station

The Scar

Iron Council

Looking for Jake and Other Stories

Un Lun Dun

The City & The City

Kraken

CHINA MIÉVILLE

EMBASSYTOWN

MACMILLAN

First published 2011 by Macmillan
an imprint of Pan Macmillan, a division of Macmillan Publishers Limited
Pan Macmillan, 20 New Wharf Road, London N1 9RR
Basingstoke and Oxford
Associated companies throughout the world
www.panmacmillan.com

ISBN 978-0-230-75076-0 HB
ISBN 978-0-230-75431-7 TPB

1 3 5 7 9 8 6 4 2

A CIP catalogue record for this book is available from
the British Library.

Typeset by SetSystems Ltd, Saffron Walden, Essex
Printed in the UK by CPI Mackays, Chatham ME5 8TD

To Jesse

I'm very grateful to
Mark Bould, Mic Cheetham, Julie Crisp,
Andrea Gibbons, Chloe Healy, Deanna Hoak,
Simon Kavanagh, Peter Lavery, Amy Lines, Farah Mendlesohn,
David Moench, Tom Penn, Max Schaefer, Chris Schluep,
Jesse Soodalter, Karen Traviss, Jeremy Trevathan,
and all at Macmillan and Del Rey.

"The word must communicate *something* (other than itself)"

Walter Benjamin,
"On Language as Such and on the Language of Man"

THE CHILDREN of the embassy all saw the boat land. Their teachers and shiftparents had had them painting it for days. One wall of the room had been given over to their ideas. It's been centuries since any voidcraft vented fire, as they imagined this one doing, but it's a tradition to represent them with such trails. When I was young, I painted ships the same way.

I looked at the pictures and the man beside me leaned in too. "Look," I said. "See? That's you." A face at the boat's window. The man smiled. He gripped a pretend wheel like the simply rendered figure.

"You have to excuse us," I said, nodding at the decorations. "We're a bit parochial."

"No, no," the pilot said. I was older than him, dressed up and dropping slang to tell him stories. He enjoyed me flustering him. "Anyway," he said, "that's not . . . It is amazing though. Coming here. To the edge. With Lord knows what's beyond." He looked into the Arrival Ball.

THERE WERE other parties: seasonals, comings-out, graduations and yearsends, the three Christmases of December; but the Arrival Ball was always the most important. Dictated by the vagaries of trade winds, it was irregular and rare. It had been years since the last.

Diplomacy Hall was crowded. Mingling with the embassy staff were security, teachers and physicians, local artists. There were delegates from isolated outsider communities, hermit-

1

farmers. There were very few newcomers from the out, in clothes the locals would soon emulate. The crew was due to leave the next day or the one after; Arrival Balls always came at the end of a visit, as if celebrating an arrival and a departure at once.

A string septet played. One of the members was my friend Gharda, who saw me and frowned an apology for the unsubtle jig she was halfway through. Young men and women were dancing. They were licensed embarrassments to their bosses and elders, who would themselves, to their younger colleagues' delight, sometimes sway or turn a humorously stilted pirouette.

By the temporary display of children's illustrations were Diplomacy Hall's permanent hangings: oils and gouaches, flat and trid photographs of staff, Ambassadors and attachés; even of Hosts. They tracked the city's history. Creepers reached the height of the panelling to a deco cornice, spread into a thicket canopy. The wood was designed to sustain them. Their leaves were disturbed by thumb-sized vespcams hunting for images to transmit.

A security man I'd been friends with years before waved a brief greeting with his prosthesis. He was silhouetted in a window metres high and wide, which overlooked the city and Lilypad Hill. Behind that slope was the boat, loaded with cargo. Beyond kilometres of roofs, past rotating church-beacons, were the power stations. They had been made uneasy by the landing, and were still skittish, days later. I could see them stamping.

"That's you," I said, pointing them out to the steersman. "That's your fault." He laughed but he was only half-looking. He was distracted by pretty much everything. This was his first descent.

I thought I recognised a lieutenant from a previous party. On his last arrival, years before, it had been a mild autumn in the embassy. He'd walked with me through the leaves of the high-floor gardens and stared into the city, where it had not been autumn, nor any other season he could have known.

I walked through smoke from salvers of stimulant resin and said goodbyes. A few outlanders who'd finished commissions were leaving, and with them a tiny number of locals who'd requested, and been granted, egress.

"Darling, are you weepy?" said Kayliegh. I wasn't. "I'll see you tomorrow, and maybe even the day after. And you can . . ." But she knew that communication would be so difficult it would end. We hugged until she, at least, was a little teary, and laughing too, saying, "You of all people, you must know why I'm off," and I was saying, "I know, you cow, I'm so jealous!"

I could see her thinking, *You chose*, and it was true. I'd been going to leave, until half a year before, until the last miab had descended, with the shocking news of what, who, was on the way. Even then I'd told myself I'd stick to my plan, head into the out when the next relief came. But it was no real revelation to me when at last the yawl had crossed the sky and left it howling, and I'd realised I was going to stay. Scile, my husband, had probably suspected before I did that I would.

"When will they be here?" asked the pilot. He meant the Hosts.

"Soon," I said, having no idea. It wasn't the Hosts I wanted to see.

Ambassadors had arrived. People came close to them but they didn't get jostled. There was always space around them, a moat of respect. Outside, rain hit the windows. I'd been able to ascertain nothing of what had been going on behind doors from any of my friends, any usual sources. Only the top bureaucrats and their advisors had met our most important, controversial newcomers, and I was hardly among them.

People were glancing at the entrance. I smiled at the pilot. More Ambassadors were entering. I smiled at them, too, until they acknowledged me.

The city Hosts would come before long, and the last of the new arrivals. The captain and the rest of the ship's crew; the attachés; the consuls and researchers; perhaps a few late immigrants; and the point of all this, the impossible new Ambassador.

Proem

THE IMMERSER

0.1

WHEN WE WERE YOUNG in Embassytown, we played a game
with coins and coin-sized crescent offcuts from a workshop. We
always did so in the same place, by a particular house, beyond
the rialto in a steep-sloping backstreet of tenements, where
advertisements turned in colours under the ivy. We played in
the smothered light of those old screens, by a wall we christened
for the tokens we played with. I remember spinning a heavy
two-sou piece on its edge and chanting as it went, *turnabout,
incline, pig-snout, sunshine,* until it wobbled and fell. The face
that showed and the word I'd reached when the motion stopped
would combine to specify some reward or forfeit.

I see myself clearly in wet spring and in summer, with a
deuce in my hand, arguing over interpretations with other girls
and with boys. We would never have played elsewhere, though
that house, about which and about the inhabitant of which
there were stories, could make us uneasy.

Like all children we mapped our hometown carefully,
urgently and idiosyncratically. In the market we were less
interested in the stalls than in a high cubby left by lost bricks in
a wall, which we always failed to reach. I disliked the enormous
rock that marked the town's edge, which had been split and set
again with mortar (for a purpose I did not yet know), and the
library, the crenellations and armature of which felt unsafe to
me. We all loved the college for the smooth plastone of its
courtyard, on which tops and hovering toys travelled for metres.

We were a hectic little tribe and constables would frequently challenge us, but we need only say, "It's alright sir, madam, we have to just..." and keep on. We would come fast down the steep and crowded grid of streets, past the houseless automa of Embassytown, with animals running among us or by us on low roofs, and while we might pause to climb trees and vines, we always eventually reached the interstice.

At this edge of town the angles and piazzas of our home alleys were interrupted by at first a few uncanny geometries of Hosts' buildings; then more and more, until our own were all replaced. Of course we would try to enter the Host city, where the streets changed their looks, and brick, cement or plasm walls surrendered to other more lively materials. I was sincere in these attempts but comforted that I knew I'd fail.

We'd compete, daring each other to go as far as we could, marking our limits. "We're being chased by wolves, and we have to run," or "Whoever goes furthest's vizier," we said. I was the third-best southgoer in my gang. In our usual spot, there was a Hostnest in fine alien colours tethered by creaking ropes of muscle to a stockade, that in some affectation the Hosts had fashioned like one of our wicker fences. I'd creep up on it while my friends whistled from the crossroads.

See images of me as a child and there's no surprise: my face then was just my face now not-yet-finished, the same suspicious mouth-pinch or smile, the same squint of effort that sometimes got me laughed at later, and then as now I was rangy and restless. I'd hold my breath and go forward on a lungful through where the airs mixed—past what was not quite a hard border but was still remarkably abrupt, a gaseous transition, breezes sculpted with nanotech particle-machines and consummate atmosphere artistry—to write *Avice* on the white wood. Once on a whim of bravado I patted the nest's flesh anchor where it interwove the slats. It felt as taut as a gourd. I ran back, gasping, to my friends.

"You touched it." They said that with admiration. I stared at my hand. We would head north to where aeoli blew, and compare our achievements.

A QUIET, well-dressed man lived in the house where we played with coins. He was a source of local disquiet. Sometimes he came out while we were gathered. He would regard us and purse his lips in what might have been greeting or disapproval, before he turned and walked.

We thought we understood what he was. We were wrong, of course, but we'd picked up whatever we had from around the place and considered him broken and his presence inappropriate. "Hey," I said more than once to my friends, when he emerged, pointing at him behind his back, "hey." We would follow when we were brave, as he walked alleys of hedgerow toward the river or a market, or in the direction of the archive ruins or the Embassy. Twice I think one of us jeered nervously. Passersby instantly hushed us.

"Have some respect," an altoysterman told us firmly. He put down his basket of shellfish and aimed a quick cuff at Yohn, who had shouted. The vendor watched the old man's back. I remember suddenly knowing, though I didn't have the words to express it, that not all his anger was directed at us, that those tutting in our faces were disapproving, at least in part, of the man.

"They're not happy about where he lives," said that evening's shiftfather, Dad Berdan, when I told him about it. I told the story more than once, describing the man we had followed carefully and confusedly, asking the dad about him. I asked him

why the neighbours weren't happy and he smiled in embarrassment and kissed me good night. I stared out of my window and
didn't sleep. I watched the stars and the moons, the glimmering
of Wreck.

I CAN DATE the following events precisely, as they occurred on
the day after my birthday. I was melancholic in a way I'm now
amused by. It was late afternoon. It was the third sixteenth of
September, a Dominday. I was sitting alone, reflecting on my
age (absurd little Buddha!), spinning my birthday money by the
coin wall. I heard a door open but I didn't look up, so it may
have been seconds that the man from the house stood before
me while I played. When I realised, I looked up at him in
bewildered alarm.

"Girl," he said. He beckoned. "Please come with me." I
don't remember considering running. What could I do, it
seemed, but obey?

His house was astonishing. There was a long room full of
dark colours, cluttered with furniture, screens and figurines.
Things were moving, automa on their tasks. We had creepers
on the walls of our nursery but nothing like these shining black-
leaved sinews in ogees and spirals so perfect they looked like
prints. Paintings covered the walls, and plasmings, their movements altering as we entered. Information changed on screens
in antique frames. Hand-sized ghosts moved among potted
plants on a trid like a mother-of-pearl games board.

"Your friend." The man pointed at his sofa. On it lay Yohn.

I said his name. His booted feet were up on the upholstery,
his eyes were closed. He was red and wheezing.

I looked at the man, afraid that whatever he'd done to Yohn,
as he must have done, he would do to me. He did not meet my
eyes, instead fussing with a bottle. "They brought him to me,"

he said. He looked around, as if for inspiration on how to speak to me. "I've called the constables."

He sat me on a stool by my barely breathing friend and held out a glass of cordial to me. I stared at it suspiciously until he drank from it himself, swallowed and showed me he had by sighing with his mouth open. He put the vessel in my hand. I looked at his neck, but I could not see a link.

I sipped what he had given me. "The constables are coming," he said. "I heard you playing. I thought it might help him to have a friend with him. You could hold his hand." I put the glass down and did so. "You could tell him you're here, tell him he'll be alright."

"Yohn, it's me, Avice." After a silence I patted Yohn on the shoulder. "I'm here. You'll be alright, Yohn." My concern was quite real. I looked up for more instructions, and the man shook his head and laughed.

"Just hold his hand then," he said.

"What happened, sir?" I said.

"They found him. He went too far."

Poor Yohn looked very sick. I knew what he'd done.

Yohn was the second-best southgoer in our group. He couldn't compete with Simmon, the best of all, but Yohn could write his name on the picket fence several slats farther than I. Over some weeks I'd strained to hold my breath longer and longer, and my marks had been creeping closer to his. So he must have been secretly practising. He'd run too far from the breath of the aeoli. I could imagine him gasping, letting his mouth open and sucking in air with the sour bite of the interzone, trying to go back but stumbling with the toxins, the lack of clean oxygen. He might have been down, unconscious, breathing that nasty stew for minutes.

"They brought him to me," the man said again. I made a

tiny noise as I suddenly noticed that, half-hidden by a huge ficus, something was moving. I don't know how I'd failed to see it.

It was a Host. It stepped to the centre of the carpet. I stood immediately, out of the respect I'd been taught and my child's fear. The Host came forward with its swaying grace, in complicated articulation. It looked at me, I think: I think the constellation of forking skin that was its lustreless eyes regarded me. It extended and reclenched a limb. I thought it was reaching for me.

"It's waiting to see the boy's taken," the man said. "If he gets better it'll be because of our Host here. You should say thank you."

I did so and the man smiled. He squatted beside me, put his hand on my shoulder. Together we looked up at the strangely moving presence. "Little egg," he said, kindly. "You know it can't hear you? Or, well . . . that it hears you but only as noise? But you're a good girl, polite." He gave me some inadequately sweet adult confection from a mantelpiece bowl. I crooned over Yohn, and not only because I was told to. I was scared. My poor friend's skin didn't feel like skin, and his movements were troubling. The Host bobbed on its legs. At its feet shuffled a dog-sized presence, its companion. The man looked up into what must be the Host's face. Staring at it, he might have looked regretful, or I might be saying that because of things I later knew.

The Host spoke.

Of course I'd seen its like many times. Some lived in the interstice where we dared ourselves to play. We sometimes found ourselves facing them, as they walked with crablike precision on whatever their tasks were, or even ran, with a gait that made them look as if they must fall, though they did not. We saw them tending the flesh walls of their nests, or what we thought of as their pets, those whispering companion animal things. We would quieten abruptly down in their presence and move away from them. We mimicked the careful politeness our shiftparents showed them. Our discomfort, like that of the adults we learned it from, outweighed any curiosity at the strange actions we might see the Hosts performing.

We would hear them speak to each other in their precise tones, so almost like our voices. Later in our lives a few of us might understand some of what they said, but not yet, and never really me.

I'd never been so close to one of the Hosts. My fear for Yohn distracted me from all I'd otherwise feel from this proximity to the thing, but I kept it in my sight, so it could not surprise me, then when it rocked closer to me I shied away abruptly and broke off whispering to my friend.

They were not the only exoterres I'd seen. There were exot inhabitants of Embassytown—a few Kedis, a handful of Shur'asi and others—but with them, while there was strangeness of course there was never that abstraction, that sheer remove one felt from Hosts. One Shur'asi shopkeeper would even joke with us, his accent bizarre but his humour clear.

Later I understood that those immigrants were exclusively from species with which we shared conceptual models, according to various measures. Hosts, the indigenes, in whose city we had been graciously allowed to build Embassytown, were cool, incomprehensible presences. Powers like subaltern gods, who sometimes watched us as if we were interesting, curious dust; and who provided our biorigging, and to which the Ambassadors alone spoke. We were reminded often that we owed them courtesy. Pass them in the street and we would show the required respect, then run on giggling. Without my friends, though, I couldn't camouflage my fear with silliness.

"It's asking if the boy'll be alright," the man said. He rubbed his mouth. "Colloquially, something like, *will he run later or will he cool?* It wants to help. It *has* helped. It probably thinks me rude." He sighed. "Or mentally ill. Because I won't answer it. It can see I'm diminished. If your friend doesn't die it'll be because it brought him here.

"The Hosts found him." I could tell the man was trying to speak gently to me. He seemed unpractised. "They can come here but they know we can't leave. They know more or less what we need." He pointed at the Host's pet. "They had their engines breathe oxygen into him. Yohn'll maybe be fine. The constables'll come soon. Your name's Avice. Where do you live, Avice?" I told him. "Do you know my name?"

I'd heard it of course. I was unsure of the etiquette of speaking it to him. "Bren," I said.

"Bren. That isn't right. You understand that? You can't say my name. You might spell it, but you can't say it. But then I can't say my name either. *Bren* is as good as any of us can do. *It . . .*" He looked at the Host, which nodded gravely. "Now, it can say my name. But that's no good: it and I can't speak anymore."

"Why did they bring him to you, sir?" His house was close to the interstice, to where Yohn had fallen, but hardly adjacent.

"They know me. They brought your friend to me because though as I say they know me to be *lessened* in some way they also recognise me. They speak and they must hope I'll answer them. I'm . . . I must be . . . very confusing to them." He smiled. "It's all foolishness, I know. Believe me I do know that. Do you know what I am, Avice?"

I nodded. Now, of course, I know that I had no idea what he was, and I'm not sure he did either.

The constables at last arrived with a medical team, and Bren's room became an impromptu surgery. Yohn was intubated, drugged, monitored. Bren pulled me gently out of the experts' way. We stood to one side, I, Bren and the Host, its animal tasting my feet with a tongue like a feather. A constable bowed to the Host, which moved its face in response.

"Thanks for helping your friend, Avice. Perhaps he'll be fine. And I'll see you soon, I'm sure. *'Turnaround, incline, piggy, sunshine'*?" Bren smiled.

While a constable ushered me out at last, Bren stood with the Host. It had wrapped him in a companionable limb. He did not pull away. They stood in polite silence, both looking at me.

AT THE NURSERY they fussed over me. Even assured by the officer that I'd done nothing wrong, the staffparents seemed a little suspicious about what I'd got myself into. But they were decent, because they loved us. They could see I was in shock. How could I forget Yohn's shaking figure? More, how could I forget being quite so close up to the Host, the sounds of its voice? I was haunted by what had been, without question, its precise attention on me.

"So somebody had drinks with Staff, today, did they?" my shiftfather teased as he put me to bed. It was Dad Shemmi, my favourite.

Later in the out I took mild interest in all the varieties of ways to be a family. I don't remember any particular jealousy I, or most other Embassytown children, felt at those of our shiftsiblings whose blood parents at times visited them: it wasn't in particular our norm there. I never looked into it, but I wondered, in later life, whether our shift-and-nursery system continued social practices of Embassytown's founders (Bremen has for a long time been relaxed about including a variety of mores in its sphere of governance), or if it had been thrown up a little later. Perhaps in vague social-evolutionary sympathy with the institutional raising of our Ambassadors.

No matter. You heard terrible stories from the nurseries from time to time, yes, but then in the out I heard bad stories too, about people raised by those who'd birthed them. On Embassytown we all had our favourites and those we were more scared of, those whose on-duty weeks we relished and those not, those we'd go to for comfort, those for advice, those we'd steal from, and so on; but our shiftparents were good people. Shemmi I loved the most.

"Why do the people not like Mr. Bren living there?"

"Not Mr. Bren, darling, just Bren. They, some of them, don't think it's right for him to live like that, in town."

"What do you think?"

He paused. "I think they're right. I think it's . . . unseemly. There are places for the cleaved." I'd heard that word before, from Dad Berdan. "Retreats just for them, so . . . It's ugly to see, Avvy. He's a funny one. Grumpy old sod. Poor man. But it isn't good to see. That kind of wound."

It's disgusting, some of my friends later said. They'd learnt this attitude from less liberal shiftparents. Nasty old cripple should go to the sanatorium. *Leave him alone*, I'd say. *He saved Yohn*.

Yohn recovered. His experience didn't stop our game. I went a little farther, a little farther over weeks, but I never reached Yohn's marks. The fruits of his dangerous experiment, a last mark, was metres beyond any of his others, the initial letter of his name in a terrible hand. "I fainted there," he would tell us. "I nearly died." After his accident he was never able to go nearly so far again. He remained the second-best because of his history, but I could beat him now.

"How do I spell Bren's name?" I asked Dad Shemmi, and he showed me.

"*Bren*," he said, running his finger along the word: seven letters; four he sounded; three he could not.

0.2

WHEN I WAS seven years old I left Embassytown. Kissed my shiftparents and siblings goodbye. I returned when I was eleven: married; not rich but with savings and a bit of property; knowing a little of how to fight, how to obey orders, how and when to disobey them; and how to immerse.

I'd become fair-to-good at several things, though I excelled, I thought, at only one. It wasn't violence. That's an everyday risk of port life, and over my time away I'd lost only a few more fights than I'd won. I look stronger than I am, I was always quickish, and like many middling scrappers I'd become good at insinuating more skill than I had. I could avoid confrontations without obvious cowardice.

I was bad at money but had amassed some. I couldn't claim that marriage was my real skill, but I was better at it than many. I'd had two previous husbands and a wife. I'd lost them to changes of predilection, without rancour—as I say, I wasn't bad at marriage. Scile was my fourth spouse.

As an immerser I progressed to the ranks I aspired to—those that granted me a certain cachet and income while keeping me from fundamental responsibilities. This is what I excelled at: the life-technique of aggregated skill, luck, laziness and chutzpah that we call floaking.

Immersers, I think, created the term. Everyone has some floaker in them. There's a devil on your shoulder. Not everyone crewing aspires to master the technique—there are those who want to captain or explore—but for most, floaking is indispensable. Some people think it mere indolence but it's a more active and nuanced technique than that. Floakers aren't afraid of effort: many crew work very hard to get shipboard in the first place. I did.

When I think of my age I think in years, still, even after all this time and travel. It's bad form, and ship-life should have cured me of it. "Years?" one of my first officers shouted at me. "I don't give two shits about whatever your pisspot home's sidereal shenanigans are, I want to know how *old* you are."

Answer in hours. Answer in subjective hours: no officer cares if you've slowed any compared to your pisspot home. No one cares which of the countless year-lengths you grew up with. So, when I was about 170 kilohours old I left Embassytown. I returned when I was 266Kh, married, with savings, having learnt a few things.

I was about 158 kilohours old when I learnt that I could immerse. I knew then what I'd do, and I did it.

I answer in subjective hours; I have to bear objective hours vaguely in mind; I think in the years of my birth-home, which was itself dictated to by the schedules of another place. None of this has anything to do with Terre. I once met a junior immerser from some self-hating backwater who reckoned in what he called "earth-years", the risible fool. I asked him if he'd been to the place by the calendar of which he lived. Of course he'd no more idea of where it was than I.

As I've grown older I've become conscious of how unsurprising I am. What happened to me didn't happen to many Embassytowners—that's surely the point—but the *story* of its happening is classic. I was born in a place that I thought for thousands of hours was enough of a universe. Then I knew quite suddenly that it was not, but that I wouldn't be able to leave;

and then I could leave. You hear the same all over the place, and not only among the human.

Here's another memory. We used to play at immersing, running up behind each other in a little *I'm invisible* crouch, then shouting "Emerge!" and grabbing. We knew very little about immersion, and that play-acting was, I would come to learn, not much more inaccurate than most adult descriptions of the immer.

Irregularly throughout my youth, scheduled between incoming ships, miabs would arrive. Uncrewed little boxes full of oddments, steered by 'ware. Plenty were lost en route: became hazards forever, I later learned, in variously strange corroded forms, in the immer they'd been built to travel. But most reached us. As I got older my excitement at those arrivals became coloured by frustration, envy of them, until I realised I would, in fact, get out into the out. They became hints, then: little whispers.

When I was four and a half years old I saw a train hauling a just-touched-down miab through Embassytown. Like most children and many adults, I always wanted to witness their arrival. There was a little gang of us there from the nursery, watched and lightly corralled by Mum Quiller, I think it was, and we ourselves roughly looked out for our much younger shiftfriends. We were able to lean up over the railings mostly uninterrupted and chatter at each other and the arrival.

As always the miab was laid on a colossal flatbed, and the biorigged locomotor that hauled it through the wide cut of Embassytown's industrial rails was heaving, putting out temporary muscular legs to strain along with its engine. The miab on its back was bigger than my nursery's hall. A very real container, snub-bullet-shaped, moving through light rain. Its surface sheened with saft that evanesced out from its crystal shielding in threads that degraded to nothing. The authorities were irresponsible, I know now, not to have waited for that immer-stained surface to calm. This wasn't the first miab they'd brought in still damp from its journey.

I saw a building dragged. That's what it looked like. A big train wheezing with effort, its enginarii cajoling it through a gash. The enormous room was tugged uphill towards the Ambassadors' castle, surrounded by Embassytowners, cheering and waving ribbons. It had an escort of centaurs, men and women perched at the front of quadruped biorigged conveyances. Some of the town's few exots stood by their Terre friends: Kedis frills rose and flushed colours, Shur'asi and Pannegetch made their sounds. There were automa in the crowd: some staggering boxes, some with persuasive-enough Turingware that they seemed enthusiastic participants.

Inside the unmanned vessel would be cargo, presents to us from Dagostin and perhaps beyond, import things we coveted, bookware and books, newsware, rare foods, tech, letters. The craft itself would be cannibalised, too. I'd sent things out in return myself, yearly, when our own much smaller miabs were dispatched. They contained hardy goods and the paraphernalia of official duties (all carefully copied before dispatch—no one would assume any miab would reach its destination), but a little space was retained for children to correspond with pen-pal schools in the out.

"Miab, miab, message in a bottle!" Mum Berwick would sing as she gathered our letters up. *Dear Class 7, Bowchurch High, Charo City, Bremen, Dagostin,* I remember writing. *I wish that I could come with my letter to visit you.* Brief catch-up epistolary flurries every rare often.

The miab passed by one of the waterways we called rivers, which are small canals, under Stilt Bridge. I remember that there were Hosts there, with a delegation of Embassy Staff, looking down through the bridge's coloured-glass portals, flanked by our security on biorigged mount-machines.

It was out of my sight when the stowaway emerged from the miab, but I've seen recordings. The tracks were overlooked by tenements on the east side and the animal gardens on the west when cracking first became audible. Had it been a kilometre farther, into the rookeries and under the bridgepaths in the Embassy's close vicinity, it would have gone much worse.

You can see from the newsloads that some in the crowd knew what was happening. There were shouts as the noise grew, people trying to warn people. Some of those who understood simply ran. Us kids mostly just stood I think, though Mum Quiller would have done her best to get us out of there. There's the sound of the miab's ceramic case straining in anti-Newtonian ways. People are peering over the railings to see; more and more are getting out of there.

The miab splits, sending blades of hull matter viciously airborne. Something from the immer comes out.

Taxonomy is imprecise. Most experts agree that what emerged on that day was a minor manifestation, one I'd later learn to call a stichling. It was an insinuation at first, composing itself of angles and shadows. It accreted itself from its surrounds, manifesting in the transient. The bricks, plastone and concrete of buildings, the energy of the cages and the flesh of the captive animals from the gardens spilled toward and into the swimming thing, against physics. They substanced it. Houses were unroofed as their slates dripped sideways into a presence growing every moment more physical, more suited to this realness.

IT WAS PUT DOWN quickly. They hammered it with sometimes-guns, that violently assert the manchmal, this stuff, our everyday, against the always of the immer. It was banished or dispatched after minutes of shrieking.

Thankfully no Hosts were harmed. But the emergence left scores of others dead. Some were killed in the explosion; some were lessened, had partially poured away. From then on, when retrieving miabs, Staff obeyed the protocols of care that they had been letting slip. Our trids showed repeated debates, fury and angst. Whoever it was in Staff who was sacked in disgrace was a scapegoat for the system. A young, dashingly ill-disciplined Ambassador DalTon more or less asserted that on cam, in anger, which I remember the parents talking about. Dad Noor even told me the disaster would be the end of the pomp of arrival. He was wrong about this, of course. He was always a lugubrious man.

Of course my friends and I were obsessed with the tragedy. Within a very short time we were playing it as a game, making immer-bubbling and cracking-shellcase noises, firing finger-guns and sticks at those of us temporarily monsters. I conceived of the stichling as some sort of slayed dragon.

THERE'S A STORY told, sort of a traditional view, that immersers never remember their childhoods. That's obviously not true. People say it as a way to stress the strangeness of the immer; the implication being that there's something in that foundational altreality that plays buggery with human minds. (Which it can do, certainly, but not like that.)

It's not true, but it is the case that I, and most of the immersers I've known, have casual, or vague, or discombobulated memories of when we were small. I don't think it's a mystery: I think it's a corollary of our mindsets, the way we think, those of us who want to go into the out.

I recall episodes very well, but episodes, not a timeline. The most relevant times, the definitional ones. The rest of it's disorganised in my head, and mostly I don't mind. Here: one other time in my childhood, I was in the company of Hosts. One morning in the third monthling of July I was called to a meeting.

It was Dad Shemmi they sent to fetch me. He squeezed my shoulder as he pointed me in to one of the nursery's scruffy paperwork-and-datspace-filled offices. It was Mum Solfer's room, and I'd not been in it before. Mostly Terretech, though a boxy biorigged bin was quietly eating her rubbish. Solfer was older, kind, distracted, knew me by name, which she did not all my shiftsiblings. She beckoned me, obviously uneasy. She stood, glanced around as if for a sofa, which the room was without, sat again. Behind her desk with her—not unamusing, in retrospect, it was smallish and too cramped for them—was Dad Renshaw, a relatively new, thoughtful and teacherly shiftfather, who smiled at me; and to my astonishment the third person waiting for me was Bren.

It had been almost a year, nearly 25Kh, since Yohn's accident, since I or any of us had returned to that house. I'd grown, of course, and more than many of my siblings, but as soon as I entered, Bren smiled recognition. He looked unchanged. They might have been the same clothes he had on as before.

Mum shifted. Though she sat with the others on one side of the desk while I, on the stiffly adult chair to which she directed me, was on the other, the way she moved her eyebrows at me I felt suddenly that she and I were together in whatever this oddness was.

I'd be paid for this, she said (an uploading of no little size, it turned out); it was quite safe; it was an honour. She didn't make very much sense. Dad Renshaw gently interrupted her. He turned to Bren and motioned for him to speak.

"You're needed," Bren said to me. "That's all this is." He

opened his hands palm up, as if their emptiness were evidence of something. "The Hosts need you and again for some reason it's ended up going through me. They're trying to prepare something. They're having a debate. A few of them are convinced they can make their point clearly by . . . by comparison." He watched to see if I followed. "They've . . . sort of thought of one. But the events it describes haven't happened. Do you understand what that means? They want to make it speakable. So they need to organise it. Quite precisely. It involves a human girl." He smiled. "You see why I asked for you." I suppose he didn't know any other children.

Bren smiled at the way my mouth was moving. "You . . . want me to . . . perform a *simile*?" I said at last.

"It's an honour!" Dad Renshaw said.

"It is an honour," Bren said. "I can see you know that. 'Perform'?" He wagged his head in a sort of *well, yes and no* way. "I won't tell you lies. It'll hurt. And it won't be nice. But I promise you'll be alright. I promise." He leaned toward me. "There'll be money in it for you, like your Mum was saying. *And*. Also. You'll have the thanks of the Staff. And the Ambassadors." Renshaw glanced up. I wasn't so young as to not know what that gratitude was worth. I'd an idea of what I hoped to do when I was old enough, by then, and the goodwill of Staff was something I wanted very much.

I ALSO SAID YES to the request because I thought it would take me into the Host city. It did not. The Hosts came to us, to a part of town to which I'd hardly ever been. I was taken there in a corvid—my first flight, but I was too nervous to enjoy it— escorted not by constables but Embassy SecStaff, their bodies subtly gnarled with augmens and tecs.

Bren escorted me, with no one else, no shiftparents, though

he had no official role in Embassytown. (I didn't know that then.) That was a time, though, before he withdrew from the last of such informal Staff-like roles. He tried to be kind to me. I remember we skirted Embassytown's edges and I saw for the first time the scale of the enormous throats that delivered biorigging and supplies to us. They flexed, wet and warm ends of siphons extending kilometres beyond our boundaries. I saw other craft over the city: some biorigged, some old Terretech, some chimerical.

We came down in a neglected quarter that no one had been bothered to take off-grid. Though it was almost empty its streets were lit by lifelong neon and trid spectres dancing in midair, announcing restaurants long-since closed. In the ruins of one such, Hosts were waiting. Their simile, I had been warned, required me to be alone with them, so Bren gave me into their authority.

He shook his head at me as he did, as if we were agreeing that something was a little absurd. He whispered that it wouldn't be long, and that he would be waiting.

WHAT OCCURRED in that crumbling once-dining room wasn't by any means the worst thing I've ever suffered, or the most painful, or the most disgusting. It was quite bearable. It was, however, the least comprehensible event that had or has ever happened to me. I was surprised how much that upset me.

For a long time the Hosts didn't pay attention to me, but performed precise mimes. They raised their giftwings, they stepped forward and back. I could smell their sweet smell. I was frightened. I'd been prepared: it was imperative for the sake of the simile that I act my part perfectly. They spoke. I understood only the very basics of what I heard, could pick out an occasional word. I listened for the overlapping whisper I'd been told meant *she*, and when I heard it I came forward and did what they wanted.

I know now to call what I did then disassociating. I watched it all, myself included. I was impatient for it to finish; I felt nothing growing, no special connection between me and the Hosts. I was only watching. While we performed the actions that were necessary, that would allow them to speak their analogy, I thought of Bren. He could of course no longer speak to the Hosts. What was happening had been organised by the Embassy, and I supposed Bren's erstwhile colleagues, the Ambassadors, must have been glad for him to help organise it. I wonder if they were giving him something to do.

After I was done, in the youthmall, my friends demanded all details. We were roughnecks like most Embassytowner children are. "You were with the *Hosts*? That's *import*, Avvy! Swear? Say it like a Host?"

"Say it like a Host," I said, appropriately solemn for the oath.

"No *way*. What did they *do*?" I showed my bruises. I both did and didn't want to talk about it. Eventually I enjoyed the telling and embellishing of it. It gave me status for days.

Other consequences were more important. Two days later, Dad Renshaw escorted me to Bren's house. It was the first time I'd been there since Yohn's accident. Bren smiled and welcomed me, and there within I met my first Ambassadors.

Their clothes were the most beautiful I'd seen. Their links glinted, the lights on them stuttering in time to the fields they generated. I was cowed. There were three of them, and the room was crowded. The more so as, behind them, moving side to side, whispering to Bren or one or other Ambassador, was an autom, computer in segmented body, the woman's face it gave

27

itself animated as it spoke. I could see the Ambassadors trying to be warm to me, a child, as Bren had tried, without having any practise at it.

An older woman said, "Avice Benner Cho, is it?" in an amazing, grand voice. "Come in. Sit. We wanted to thank you. We think you should hear how you've been canonised."

The Ambassadors spoke to me in the language of our Hosts. They spoke me: they said me. They warned me that the literal translation of the simile would be inadequate and misleading. *There was a human girl who in pain ate what was given her in an old room built for eating in which eating had not happened for a time.* "It'll be shortened with use," Bren told me. "Soon they'll be saying you're *a girl ate what was given her.*"

"What does it mean, sirs, ma'ams?"

They shook their heads, they moued. "It's not really important, Avice," one of them said. She whispered to the computer and I saw the created face nod. "And it wouldn't be accurate anyway." I asked again with another formulation, but they would say nothing more about it. They kept congratulating me on being in Language.

Twice during the rest of my adolescence I heard myself, my simile, spoken: once by an Ambassador, once by a Host. Years, thousands of hours after I acted it, I finally had it sort-of explained to me. It was a crude rendering, of course, but it is I think more or less an expression intended to invoke surprise and irony, a kind of resentful fatalism.

I didn't speak to Bren again the whole rest of my childhood and youth, but I found out he visited my shiftparents at least one other time. I'm sure it was my help with the simile, and Bren's vague patronage, that helped get me past the exam board. I worked hard but was never an intellectual. I had what was needed for immersion, but no more than several others did, and less than some who didn't pass. Very few cartas were granted, to civilians, or those of us with the aptitudes to traverse the immer out of sopor. There was no obvious reason that a few months later, after those tests, even with my facilities acknowledged, I should have been given, as I was, rights to de-world, into the out.

0.3

EACH SCHOOL YEAR, the second monthling of December was given over to assessments. Most investigated what we'd learnt from our lessons; a few others checked more recherché abilities. Not many of us scored particularly highly in these latter, in the various flairs prized elsewhere, in the out. In Embassytown we started from the wrong stock, we were told: we had the wrong mutagens, the wrong equipment, a lack of aspiration. Many children didn't even sit the more arcane exams, but I was encouraged to. Which I suppose means my teachers and shift-parents had seen something in me.

I did perfectly fine in most things; well in rhetoric and some performative elements of literature, which pleased me, and in readings of poetry. But what I stood out in, it transpired, without knowing what it was I was doing, were certain activities the purposes of which I couldn't divine. I stared at a query-screen of bizarre plasmings. I had to react to them in various ways. It took about an hour and it was well designed, like a game, so I wasn't bored. I proceeded to other tasks, none testing knowledge, but reactions, intuitions, inner-ear control, nervousness. What they gauged was potential skill at immersing.

The woman who ran the sessions, young and chic in smart clothes borrowed, bartered or begged from one of the Bremeni staff, in fashion in the out, went over my results with me, and told me what they meant. I could see she was not unimpressed. She stressed to me, not cruelly but to avoid any later upset, that this concluded nothing and was just stage one of many. But I knew as she explained this that I would become an immerser, and I did. I'd only started to feel the smallness of Embassytown by then, to grumble in claustrophobia, but with her readings came impatience.

I finagled, when I was old enough, invitations to Arrival Balls, and hobnobbed with women and men from the out. I enjoyed and envied the seeming insouciance with which they mentioned countries on other planets.

It was only kilohours or years later that I really understood how not-inevitable my trajectory had been. That many students with more aptitude than me hadn't succeeded; that I truly might have failed to leave. My story was the cliché, but theirs was by far the more common, the more true. That contingency had made me feel sick, then, as if I might fail still, even though I was out.

Even people who've never immersed think they know— more or less, they might grant—what the immer is. They don't. I had this argument once with Scile. It was the second conversation we ever had (the first was about language). He started in with his opinions, and I told him I wasn't interested in hearing what the landstuck might think about immer. We lay in bed and he teased me as I went on about his ignorance.

"What are you talking about?" he said. "You don't even believe what you're saying; you're too smart for this. You're just spouting immerser bullshit. I could do this stuff in my sleep. 'No one understands it like us, not the scientists, not the politicians, not the bloody public!' It's your favourite story, this. Keeps everyone out."

He made me laugh with his impression. Still, I told him, still: the immer was indescribable. But he wouldn't let me have that either. "You're fooling no one with this stuff. You think I haven't listened to how you talk? I know, I know, you're not one for the gab, you're just a floaker, blah blah. As if *you* don't read your poetry, as if you take language for granted." He shook his head. "Anyway, you'll do me out of a job with talk like that. 'It's *beyond words*,' indeed. There's no such thing."

I put my hand over his mouth. That was just how it was, I told him. "Now, granted," he continued through my fingers, performing the same teacherly tone, now muffled, "words can't actually *be* referents, *that* I grant you, there's the tragedy of language, but our asymptotic efforts at deploying them aren't nothing, either." Hush up, you, I told him. It's all true, I said, I say it like a Host. "Well then," he said, "I withdraw, in the face of truth."

I'd studied the immer a long time, but my first moment of immersion had been as impossible to describe as I insisted. With the handful of other carta-passed new crew and emigrants, and Bremeni Embassy Staff who'd finished their commissions, I'd come by ketch to my vessel. My first commission was with the *Wasp of Kolkata*. It was quasi-autonomous, a cityship, immersing under the flag of itself, subcontracted by Dagostin for this run. I remember I stood with all the other greenhorns in the crow's-nest, Arieka a wall across the sky through which we moved, with beautiful care, toward our immersion point. Somewhere beneath the world's static-seeming cloud was Embassytown.

The steersperson took us close to Wreck. It was hard to see. It looked at first like lines drawn across space, then was briefly, shabbily corporeal. It ebbed back and forth in solidity. It was many hundreds of metres across. It rotated, all its extrusions moving, each on its own schedule, its coagulated-teardrops-and-girder-filigree shape spinning complexly.

Wreck's architecture was roughly similar to *Wasp*'s, but it was antiquated, and it seemed many times our dimensions. It was like an original of which we were a scale model, until abruptly it altered its planes and became small or far off. Occasionally it wasn't there, and sometimes only just.

Officers, augmens glimmering under their skins, reminded us first-timers what it was we were about to do, of the dangers of the immer. This, Wreck, showed that and why Arieka was an outpost, so hard to reach, so underdeveloped, satelliteless after that first catastrophe.

I would have been professional. Yes I was about to immerse for the first time, but I would have done anything I was ordered and I think I'd have done it well. But the officers remembered what it was like to be a rookie, and they had us, the handful of new immersers, at a viewing place. Where we could react as we had to, the skills we'd practised never a guarantee that the first time wouldn't sicken you. Where we could take a moment with our awe and experience it however we experienced it. There are currents and storm fronts in the immer. There are in the immer stretches it takes tremendous skill and time to cross. Those were among the techniques I now knew, along with the somatic control, the mantric thoughtfulness and instrumentalised matter-of-factness that made me an immerser, allowed immersers to stay conscious and intentional when we immersed.

On a map, it's not so many billions of kilometres from Dagostin or other hubs. But those Euclidian star charts are used only by cosmologists, by some exoterres whose physics we can't work, by religious nomads adrift at excruciating sublux pace. I was scandalised to first see them—maps were discouraged on Embassytown—and anyway such charts are irrelevant to travellers like me.

Look instead at a map of the immer. Such a big and tidal quiddity. Pull it up, rotate it, check its projections. Examine that light phantom every way you can, and even allowing that it's a flat or trid rendering of a topos which rebels against our accounting, the situation is visibly different.

The immer's reaches don't correspond at all to the dimensions of the manchmal, this space where we live. The best we can do is say that the immer *underlies* or *overlies*, *infuses*, is a *foundation*, is *langue* of which our actuality is a *parole*, and so on. Here in the everyday, in light-decades and petametres, Dagostin is vastly more distant from Tarsk and Hodgson's than from Arieka. But in the immer, Dagostin to Tarsk is a few hundred hours on a prevailing wind; Hodgson's is in the centre of sedate and crowded deeps; and Arieka is very far from anything.

It's beyond a convulsion where violent streams of immer roll against each other, where there are shallows, dangerous juts and matterbanks of everyday space in the always. It sits alone at the edge of known immer, so far as the immer can be known. Without expertise and bravery, and the skill of the immersers, no one could get to my world.

The stringency of the final exams I'd sat makes sense when you see those charts. Raw aptitude was hardly enough. Certainly there were politics of exclusion, too: of course Bremen wanted to keep careful control of us Embassytowners; but only the most skilled crew could safely come to Arieka in any case, or could leave it. Some of us were socketed to link us to ship routines, and immerware and augmens helped; but none of that was enough to make an immerser.

The way the officers explained it made it seem as if the ruins of the *Pionier*, which I had to stop calling Wreck now it was no longer a star to me but a coffin for colleagues, were a warning against carelessness. As a parable that was unfair. The *Pionier* had not been so horribly beached between states by officers or crew *underestimating* the immer: it was precisely care and respectful exploration that had destroyed it. Like other vessels across various *tracta cognita* in the early hours of it all, it had been lured. By what it had thought a message, an invitation.

When immernauts first breached the meniscus of everyday space, among the many phenomena that had astounded them was the fact that, even on their crude instruments, they had received signals, from somewhere in the ur-space. Regular and resonant, clear evidence of sentience. They had tried to go to the sources. For a long time they'd thought it was lack of skill, neophyte immersion, that kept bringing their ships to disaster on those searches. Again and again they wrecked, bursting ruinously half-out of the immer into the corporeal manchmal.

The *Pionier* was a casualty of that time, before explorers had understood that the pulses were put out by lighthouses. They were not invitations. What the ships had striven toward were warnings to stay away.

So THERE ARE lighthouses throughout the immer. Not every dangerous zone is marked by the beacons, but many are. They are, it seems, at least as old as this universe, which isn't the first there's been. The prayer so often muttered before immersion is one of thanks to those unknown who placed them. *Gracious Pharotekton watch over us now.*

I didn't see the Ariekene Pharos that first time out, but thousands of hours later. To be precise I've never seen it, of course, nor could I; that would require light and reflection and other physics that are meaningless there. But I've seen representations, rendered by ships' windows.

The 'ware in those portholes depicts the immer and everything in it in terms useful to crew. I've seen pharoes like complex clots, like crosshatching, contoured and shaped into information. When I returned to Embassytown, the captain, in what I think was a gift to me, had the screens run tropeware: as we approached gnarls of immer into the dangerous buffetings that surround Arieka, I saw a beam in the fractal black, a pointing arm of light as a lamp seemed to turn. And when the pharos came into view, floating in the middle of the unplace, it was a brick lighthouse topped with bronze and glass.

I TOLD HIM about these things when I met him, and Scile, who would later be my husband, wanted me to describe my first immersion. He'd been through immer, of course—he wasn't indigene to the world on which we slept together—but as a passenger of modest income and no particular immunities, he'd remained in sopor. Though he had, he told me, once paid to be woken a little early, so he could experience immersion. (I'd heard of people doing that. A crew shouldn't allow it, and surely only would in shallow shallows.) Scile had been violently immersick.

What could I tell him? Protected by the everyday-field, that first time the *Wasp* splashed through and immersed it wasn't even as if I had immer against my skin. Truth was you could say I'd felt more directly connected to the immer as a trainee in Embassytown, when I'd socketed to a scope that worked on the immer like the flat bottom of a glass pushed down on water. I'd seen right into it then, up close, and that had changed me. Don't ask me to describe *that*, I'd have said.

The *Wasp* went in hard. I was inexperienced but I could easily grit through the nausea that, despite my training, I felt. Even cosseted in that manchmal-field I felt all the tugs of strange velocity, as we moved in what were not really directions, and the misleading gravity bubble we'd brought with us did its best. But I was much too anxious not to disgrace myself to give in to awe. That came only later, after our indulgence was ended, after we'd been put to initial frantic duties and then after those were finished, when we'd reached a cruising depth of immersion.

What we do, what we can do—immersers—is not just keep ourselves stable, sentient and healthy in the immer, stay able to walk and think, eat, defecate, obey and give orders, make decisions, judge immerstuff, the paradata that approximate distances and conditions, without being crippled with always-sick. Though that's not nothing. It isn't only that we have, some say (and some refute), a certain flatness of imagination that keeps the immer from basilisking us out of usefulness. We've learnt its caprices, to travel it, but knowledge can always be learnt.

Ships while still in the manchmal—Terre ones, I mean, I've never been on any exot vessels that abjure the immer and I know nothing about the ways they move—are heavy boxes full of people and stuff. Immerse, into the immer, where the translations of their ungainly lines have purpose, and they're gestalts of which we're part, each of us a function. Yes, we're a crew working together like any crew, but more. The engines take us out of the sometimes, but it's we who do the taking, too; it's we who push the ship as well as it that pulls us. It's us tacking and involuting through the ur-space, the shifts in it we call tides. Civilians, even those awake not puking or weeping, can't do that. The fact is a lot of the bullshit we tell you about the immer is true. We're still playing you, when we tell you: the story dramatises, even without lying.

"This is the third universe," I told Scile. "There've been two others before this. Right?" I didn't know how much civilians knew: this stuff had become my common sense. "Each one was born different. It had its own laws—in the first one they reckon light was about twice as fast as it is here now. Each one was born and grew and got old and collapsed. Three different sometimes. But below all that, or around it, or whatever, there's only ever been one immer, one always."

He did know all that, it turned out. But to be told these everyday facts by an immerser made them something new, and he listened like a boy.

WE WERE in a bad hotel on the outskirts of Pellucias, a small city popular with tourists because of the gorgeous magmafalls it straddles. It's the capital of a small country on a world the name of which I don't remember. In the everyday, it's not in our galaxy, it's off somewhere light-aeons away, but it and Dagostin are close neighbours via the immer.

By then I was seasoned enough. I'd been to many places. I was between commissions, when I met Scile, spending a couple of local weeks on self-granted shore leave before I went for another job. I was picking up rumours—of new immertech, exploration, dubious missions. The hotel bar was full of immersers and other port life, travellers recovering, and, this time, academics. I was pretty familiar with all but the last of these types. In the lobby was an ad for a course in The Healing Power of Story, at which I made rude noises. A trid of turning and altering words floated the corridors, welcoming guests to the inaugural meeting of the Gold and Silver Circuits Board; to a convocation of Shur'asi philosopher-bureaucrats; to CHEL, the Conference of Human Exoterre Linguists.

I was drunk in the bar with a bunch of temporary stopover friends, all now thoroughly hazy memories. We were being obnoxious. I went from half-heartedly flirting with a bartender to mocking a table of scholars from CHEL, no less drunk or boisterous than we. We'd eavesdropped on them, then told them with immerser swagger that they didn't know anything about life or even languages in the out, and so on.

"Go on then, ask me something," I said to Scile. That was the first thing I ever said to him. I know exactly how I'd have looked: leaning back in my high chair, turned so resting my back against the bar top, my head back so I could look down at him. I was surely pointing at him with both hands and smiling a bit pinch-mouthed so as to not yet give him any satisfaction. Scile was the least gone at his table, and he was refereeing the teasing on both sides. "I know all about weird languages," I told him. "More than any of you buggers. I'm from *Embassytown*."

When he believed me, I've never seen a man so astonished, so delighted. He didn't stop playing but he looked at me very differently, the more when he discovered none of my companions were my compatriots. I was the only Embassytowner, and Scile loved it.

It wasn't just his attention I liked: I was pleased with how this compact, tough-looking guy fenced with me, and kept everyone raucously amused while asking questions with actual content. We stumbled off after a while and spent a night and a day trying to enjoy sex together, sleeping, trying again, several times, with good-humoured lack of success. After that over breakfast he badgered and blandished and begged me; and I, pretending disdain and having a lovely time, acquiesced, and let him take me, tired but, as I teased him, not sore enough, to the conference.

He presented me to his colleagues. The CHEL was for the Terre study of all exot languages, but it was those generally considered most strange that fascinated its members. I saw slapdash temporary trids advertising sessions on cross-cultural chromatophore signalling, on touch communication among the unseeing Burdhan, and on me.

"I'm working in Homash. Do you know it?" said one young woman to me, apropos of nothing. She was very happy when I told her no. "They speak by regurgitation. Pellets embedded with enzymes in different combinations are sentences, which their interlocutors eat."

I noticed my own trid in the background. *Embassytowner guest! On life among the Ariekei.* "That's wrong," I told the conference organisers, "they're Hosts." But they told me: "Only to you."

Scile's colleagues were eager to talk to me: no one there had met Embassytowners before. Nor Hosts, of course.

"They're still quarantined," I told them, "but in any case they've never asked about coming out. We don't even know if they could take immersion."

I was willing to be a curio but I disappointed them. I'd warned Scile I would. The discussion became vague and socio-logical when they realised that I wouldn't be able to tell them almost anything about Language.

"I hardly understand any," I said. "We only learn a tiny bit, except Staff and Ambassadors."

One participant pulled up some recordings of Hosts speak-ing, and ran through some vocabulary. I was pleased to be able to nuance a couple of the definitions, but honestly there were at least two people in the room who understood Language better than I did.

Instead I told them stories of life in the outpost. They didn't know about the aeoli, the air-sculpting that kept a breathable dome over Embassytown. A few had seen some bits of exported biorigging, but I could talk them through the out-of-date trids they had of the vaster infrastructure, the herds of houses, time-lapse of a young bridge maturing from its pontoon-cell to link city regions for no reasons I could give. Scile asked me about religion, and I told him that so far as I knew the Hosts had none. I mentioned the Festivals of Lies. Scile was not the only one who wanted to pursue that. "But I thought they couldn't," someone said.

"That's sort of the point," I said. "To strive for the impossible."

"What're they like, those festivals?" I laughed and said I'd no clue, had never been to one, of course, had never been into the Host city.

They began to debate Language among themselves. Wondering how to repay their hospitality in anecdote, I told what had happened to me in the abandoned restaurant. They were attentive all over again. Scile stared with his manic precision. "You were in a simile?" they said.

"I *am* a simile," I said.

"You're a story?"

I was glad to be able to give Scile something. He and his colleagues were more excited at my having been similed than I was.

SOMETIMES I teased Scile that he only wanted me for my Hosts' language, or because I'm part of a vocabulary.

He'd finished the bulk of his research. It was a comparative study of a particular set of phonemes, in several different languages—and not all of one species, or one world, which made little sense to me. "What are you looking for?" I said.

"Oh, secrets," he said. "You know. Essences. Inherentnesses."

"Bravo on *that* ugly word. And?"

"And there aren't any."

"Mmm," I said. "Awkward."

"That's defeatist talk. I'll cobble something together. A scholar can never let mere wrongness get in the way of the theory."

"Bravo again." I toasted him.

We stayed together in that hotel much longer than either of us had planned, and then I, having no plans and no commission, sought work on the vessel taking him a trade route home. I was experienced and well-referenced, and getting the job wasn't hard. It was only a short trip, 400 hours or somesuch. When I realised how bad was Scile's reaction to immersion I was very touched that he chose not to travel in sopor that first time together. It was a pointless gesture—he endured my shifts in lonely nausea, and despite meds could hardly even speak to me when I was off-duty. But even irritated at his condition, I was touched.

From what I gathered, it wouldn't have taken very much for him to tidy up his last few chapters, the charts, sound files and trids. But Scile suddenly announced to me that he was not going to hand in his thesis.

"You've done all that work and you won't jump the last hoop?" I said.

"Sod it," he said, flamboyantly unconcerned. He made me laugh. "The revolution stalled!"

"My poor failed radical."

"Yeah. Well. I was bored."

"But, hold on," I tried to say, more or less, "but are you serious? Surely it would be worth—"

"It's done, it's old news, forget it. I have other research projects anyway, simile. What are you *like*?" He bowed at that bad joke, clicked his fingers and moved us, thematically, on. He kept asking about Embassytown. His intensity was exciting, but he diluted it with enough self-mockery that I believed his sometimes obsessive demeanour was partly performance.

We didn't stay long in his parochial university town. He said he'd follow me and pester me until I gave in and took him

I-knew-where. I didn't believe any of this, but when I got my next commission he took transit with me, as a passenger.

Once on that trip, when we were in shallow, calm immer, I brought Scile out of sopor to see a school of the immer predators we call hai. I've spoken to captains and scientists who don't believe them to be anything like life, only aggregates of immer, their attacks and jackknife precision just the jostles of an immer chaos in which our manchmal brains can't learn to see the deep random. Myself, I've always thought them monsters. Scile, fortified with drugs, and I watched our assertion-charges shake the immer and send the hai darting.

When we emerged wherever we emerged, wherever our vessel had delivery or pickup, Scile would register at local libraries, picking at old research and starting his new project. Where there were sights we saw them. We shared beds but fairly quickly we gave up on sex.

He learnt languages wherever we were, with his ferocious concentration, slang if he already knew the formal vocabulary. I'd travelled far more than he had, but I spoke and read only Anglo-Ubiq. I was pleased by his company, often amused, always interested. I tested him, taking jobs that hauled us through immer for hundreds of hours at a time, nothing cruelly long but long enough. He finally passed, according to my unclear emotional accounting, when I realised that I wasn't only watching to see if he'd stay, but was hoping he wouldn't leave.

We were married on Dagostin, in Bremen, in Charo City, to where I'd sent my childish letters. I told myself, and it was true, that it was important for me to emerge in my capital port sometimes. Even at the dragged-out pace of interworld letter-exchanges, Scile had corresponded with local researchers; and I, never a loner, had contacts and the quick intense friendships that come and go among immersers; so we knew we'd have a reasonable turnout. There in my national capital, which most Embassytowners never saw, I could register with the union, download savings into my main account, amass news of Bremen jurisdiction. The flat I owned was in an unfashionable but pleasant part of the city. Around my house I rarely saw anyone accoutremented with the silly luxury tech imported from Embassytown.

Being married under local law would make it easier for Scile to visit any of Bremen's provinces or holdings. I responded for a long time to his pestering fascination, never the joke he at first pretended, with the information that I'd no intention of returning to Embassytown. But I think by the time we married I was ready to give him the gift of taking him to my first home.

It wasn't wholly straightforward: Bremen controlled entry to some of its territories almost as carefully as it did egress. We were intending to disembark there, so I wasn't just signing up on a merchant run. At Transit House, perplexed officials sent me up a chain of authority. I'd expected that but I was mildly surprised at how high, if my reading of office furniture as evidence wasn't on the fritz, the buck-passing went.

"You want to go *back* to Embassytown?" a woman who must presumably have been only a rung or two down from the boss said. "You have to realise that's . . . unusual."

"So everyone keeps telling me."

"You miss home?"

"Hardly," I told her. "The things we do for love." I sighed theatrically but she didn't want to play. "It's not as if I relish the idea of being stuck so far from the hub." She met my look and did not respond.

She asked me what I planned to do on Arieka, in Embassytown. I told her the truth—to floak, I said. That didn't amuse her either. To whom would I be reporting on arrival? I told her no one—I was no one's subordinate there, I was a civilian. She reminded me that Embassytown was a Bremen port. Where had I been since entering the out? Everywhere, she stressed, and who could remember that? I had to go through my cartas and all my old dat-swipes, though she must have known that at plenty of places such formalities of arrival were slapdash. She read my list, including terminuses and brief stops I didn't remember at all. She asked me questions about the local politics of one or two at which I could only smile, so ill-equipped was I to answer; and she stared at me as I burbled.

I wasn't sure what she suspected me of. Ultimately, as a carta-carrying Embassytown native immerser, crewing and vouching for my fiancé, it only took tenacity to get him the rights to entry, and me to reentry. Scile had been preparing for his work there, reading, listening to recordings, watching what few trids and vids there are. He'd even decided on what the title of his book would be.

"One shift only," I told him. "We're only going until the next relief." In Charo City, in a cathedral to Christ Uploaded, which to my surprise he asked for, I married Scile according to Bremen law, in the second degree, registering as a nonconnubial love-match, and I took him to Embassytown.

Part One

INCOME

Latterday, 1

DIPLOMACY HALL was jammed. It was usual for every ball, every greeting of leaving visitors, to be busy, but not like that night. It was hardly surprising: there'd been extraordinary anticipation. However much the Staff might have insisted to us all that this was a regular arrival, they didn't even attempt to sound as if they believed it.

I was jostled among the dress-clothes. I wore jewels and I activated a few augmens that sent a corona of pretty lights around me. I leaned against the wall in the thick leaves.

"Well don't you look good?" Ehrsul had found me. "Short hair. Choppy. Like it. Did you say goodbye to Kayliegh?"

"I thank you, and I did indeed. I still can't believe she got the papers to leave."

"Well." Ehrsul nodded to where Kayliegh hung onto the arm of Damier, a Staffwoman partly responsible for cartas. "I think she may have made a horizontal application." I laughed.

Ehrsul was autom. Her integument was adorned that night with acrylic peacock feathers, and trid jewellery orbited her. "I'm so tired," she said. She made her face crackle as if static interrupted it. "I'm just waiting to see our new Ambassador in action—how can I not, really?—then I'm gone."

She only ever used one corpus, according to some Terrephile sense of politesse or accommodation. I think she knew that having to relate to someone variably physically incarnate would trouble us. She was import, of course, though it wasn't clear where she'd come from, or when. She'd been in Embassytown for longer than the lifetime of anyone I knew. Her Turingware was way beyond local capabilities, and more than the equal of any I'd seen in the out. Spending time with most automa is like accompanying someone brutally cognitively damaged, but Ehrsul was a friend. "Come save me from the village idiots," she sometimes said to me after downloading updates alongside other automa.

"Do you joke to yourself when no one's watching?" I had asked her once.

"Does it matter?" she had said at last, and I felt scolded. It had been rude and adolescent to raise the question of her personality, her apparent consciousness, of whether it was for my benefit. It was a tradition that none of the few automs whose behaviour was human enough to prompt the question would answer it.

She was my best friend, and somewhat well known, oddity that she was. When I met her I was certain I had seen her before. I couldn't place it, at first; then when I realised what I thought the situation had been I asked her abruptly (as if I could startle her): "What did they want you there for? At Bren's place, ages ago, when the Ambassadors recited my simile to me? That was you, wasn't it? Remember?"

"Avice," she had said, gently reproving, and made her face shake as if disappointed. That was all I ever got from her on the matter and I didn't push it.

We huddled together by the indoor ivy and watched little cams flit around the room, recording. Decorative biorigging shed colours from carapaces.

"Have you met them, then?" Ehrsul said. "The esteemed intake for whom we wait? I haven't."

That surprised me. Ehrsul had no job, wasn't under the obligation of any tithe, but as a computer she was valuable to Staff, and often acted for them. I would have said the same about me—

that my inside-outside status had been useful to them—until I fell from favour. I'd have expected Ehrsul to be part of whatever discussions had been ongoing, but since the new Ambassador had arrived, apparently, the Staff had retreated into clique.

"There's tussling," Ehrsul said. "That's what I've heard." People told Ehrsul things: perhaps it was because she wasn't human, but was almost. I think she also tapped into the localnet, broke encryption on enough snips to be a good source of information to friends. "People are worried. Though I gather some have rather taken a shine ... Watch MagDa. And now Wyatt's been insisting on getting involved."

"Wyatt?"

"He's been citing old laws, trying to brief the Ambassador alone, thank you very much. That sort of thing."

Wyatt, the Bremen representative, had arrived with his small staff on the previous trade vessel, to relieve Chettenham, his predecessor. He was scheduled to leave in one more tour's time. Bremen had established Embassytown somewhat more than two megahours ago. We were all juridically Bremeni: protectees. But the Ambassadors who governed formally in Bremen's name were born here, of course, as were Staff and we who made up their canton. Wyatt, Chettenham and other attachés on their lengthy postings relied on Staff for trade information, for suggestions, for access to Hosts and tech. It was rare for them to issue orders other than "Carry on." They were advisors to Staff, too, useful for gauging the politics in the capital. I was intrigued that Wyatt was now interpreting his remit in so muscular a fashion.

This was the first time in living memory that an Ambassador had arrived from the out. Had the party not forced their hands—the ship was leaving and the ball couldn't be delayed—I suspected the Staff would have tried to quarantine the new arrivals longer, and continued with whatever their intrigues were.

"CalVin's here," Ehrsul warned quietly, her displayed face glancing over my shoulder. I did not look round. She looked at me and made a little *what?* face, telling me without words that she'd still like to know what had happened there, sometime. I shook my head.

Yanna Southel, Embassytown's senior research scientist, arrived, and with her an Ambassador. I whispered to Ehrsul, "Good, it's EdGar. Time to schmooze. I'll report back in a bit." I made it slowly through the crowd into the Ambassador's orbit. There in the middle of laughter and buffeted a little by those dancing, I raised my glass and made EdGar face me.

"Ambassador," I said. They smiled. "So," I said. "Are we ready?"

"Christ Pharos no," said Ed or Gar. "You ask as if I should know what's going on, Avice," said the other. I inclined my head. EdGar and I had always enjoyed an exaggerated flirtation. They liked me; they were garrulous, gossips, always giving up as much as and a little more than they should. The dapper older men glanced side to side, raised eyebrows in theatrical alarm as if someone might swoop in and stop them speaking. That conspiratorialism was their shtick. They had probably been warned off me in the last few months, but they still treated me with a chatty courtesy I appreciated. I smiled but hesitated when I realised that despite their party faces, they seemed genuinely unhappy.

"I wouldn't have thought it were . . ." ". . . possible," EdGar said. "There's things going on here . . ." ". . . that we don't understand."

"What about the rest of the Ambassadors?" I said.

We looked around the room. Many of their colleagues had arrived now. I saw EsMé in iridescent dresses; ArnOld fingering the tight collars wedged uncomfortably below their links; JasMin and HelEn debating complexly, each Ambassador interrupting the other, each half of each Ambassador finishing their doppel's words. So many Ambassadors in one place made for a dreamish feel. Socketed into their necks and variously ornamental, according to taste, diodes in their circuited links staccattoed through colours in simultaneous pairs.

"Honestly?" said EdGar. "They're all worried." "To various degrees." "Some of them think we're . . ." ". . . exaggerating. RanDolph thinks it'll all be good for us." "To have a newcomer, to shake us up. But no one's sanguine."

"Where's JoaQuin? And where's Wyatt?"

"They're bringing the new boy along. Together." "Neither's been letting the other out of their sight."

Staff were making space in front of the entrance to the hall, preparing for JoaQuin, the Chair of the Ambassadors, for Wyatt the Bremen attaché, and for the new Ambassador. There were people I didn't recognise. I'd lost sight of the pilot, so couldn't ask if they were crew, immigrants or temporaries.

At most of these balls the newly arrived—permanent or single-tour—would be surrounded by locals. They wouldn't lack company, sexual or conversational. Their clothes and accoutrements, their augmens, would be like grails. What 'ware they had would be pirated, and for weeks the localnet would be twittering with exotic new algorithms. This time, no one cared about anything but the new Ambassador.

"What else arrived? Anything useful?" Ambassador JasMin was in earshot, and I made a point of asking them, rather than EdGar. JasMin didn't like me so I spoke to them when I could to let them know they didn't intimidate me. They didn't answer and I walked, greeted Simmon, a security officer. We hadn't been close for years, but we liked each other sincerely enough that there was little awkwardness, though I was present as a guest, and an out-of-favour one at that, while he was working.

He shook my hand with his biorigged right limb, which he'd worn since a gun had burst on a target range and taken off his own flesh version.

I went through the crowd, talked to friends, watching the glimmer of augmens interact, hearing snatches of immer slang and turning to the immersers who spoke them with a word or two in the same dialect, or a hand held in the fingerlock that told them what ship I'd last served on, to their delight. I might touch their glasses, and I'd go on.

Mostly, like everyone else, I was watching for the new Ambassador.

AND THEN they came, in a moment that could only have been an anticlimax. It was Wyatt who opened the doors, more careful and hesitant than usual. JoaQuin smiled beside him, and I admired how well they hid the anxiety they must have felt. Conversation hushed. I was holding my breath.

There was some little commotion behind them, a moment of dispute between the figures who followed. The new Ambassador stepped forward past their guides, into Diplomacy Hall. That was a palpable moment.

One of the two men was tall and thin, with hair receding—a blinking, shyly smiling, sallow man. The other was stocky, muscular and more than a hand shorter. He grinned. He was looking around. He ran his hand through his hair. He wore augmens in his blood: I could see the shine of them around him. His companion seemed to have none. The shorter man had a Roman nose, the other a snub. Their skins were different colours, their eyes. They didn't look like or at each other.

They stood, the new Ambassador, smiling in their very different ways. They stood there mooncalf and quite impossible.

Formerly, 1

KILOHOURS BEFORE, as we prepared for our travel, Scile came to some arrangement with his employers-cum-supervisors. I never made much effort to understand his academic world. So far as I could gather, he had arranged a very extended sabbatical, and technically his residence in Embassytown was part of a project minutely funded by his university. They were paying him a peppercorn retainer and keeping his access accounts live, with a view to ultimately publishing *Forked Tongues: The SocioPsychoLinguistics of the Ariekei.*

Researchers had come to Embassytown before, particularly Bremen scientists fascinated by the Hosts' biological contrivings: there were one or two still there, waiting for relief. But there hadn't been outsider linguists on Arieka in living memory, not since the pioneers who had striven to crack Language, nearly three and a half megahours before.

"I can stand on their shoulders," Scile told me. "They had to work out how it worked from scratch. Why we could understand the Ariekei but they couldn't understand us. Now we know that."

While we prepared to arrive in Embassytown on what he called our honeymoon, Scile searched the libraries in Charo City. With my help he tried to tap into immerser-lore about the place and its inhabitants, and finally when we arrived he hunted in our own archives in Embassytown, but he found nothing systematic on his topic. That made him happy.

"Why's no one written on it before?" I asked him.

"No one comes here," he said. "It's too far. It's—no offence—stuck out in the middle of nowhere."

"Lord, none taken."

"And dangerous nowhere, as well. Plus Bremen red tape. And to be honest, none of it makes much sense, anyway."

"The language?"

"Yes. Language."

Embassytown had its own linguists, but most, carta-denied if they even bothered to apply, were scholars in the abstract. They learnt and taught Old and New French, Mandarin, Panarabic, spoke them to each other as exercises like others played chess. Some learnt exot languages, to the extent that physiology allowed. The local Pannegetch forgot their native languages when they learnt our Anglo-Ubiq, but five Kedis languages and three Shur'asi dialects were spoken in Embassytown, four and all of which respectively we could approximate.

Local linguists didn't work on the language of the Hosts. Scile, though, was unaffected by our taboos.

HE WASN'T FROM Bremen, nor from any of its outposts, nor from another nation on Dagostin. Scile was from an urban moon, Sebastapolis, which I'd vaguely heard of. He grew up very polyglot. I was never quite sure which language, if any, he considered his first. While we travelled I was envious of the blitheness, the sheer uninterest with which he ignored his birth home.

Our route to Embassytown was roundabout. The ships we took were crewed by immersers from more places than I'd ever see. I knew the charts of Bremen's crowded *immer cognita*, could once have told you the names of nations on many of its core worlds, and some of those I served with on my way home were from none of them. There were Terre from regions so far off that they teased, telling me the name of their world was Fata Morgana, or Fiddler's Green.

Had I ship-hopped in other directions, I could have gone to regions of immer and everyday where Bremen was the fable. People get lost in the overlapping sets of knownspace. Those who serve on exot vessels, who learn to withstand the strange strains of their propulsion—of swallowdrives, overlight foldings, bansheetech—go even farther with less predictable trajectories, and become even more lost. It's been this way for megahours, since women and men found the immer and we became *Homo diaspora*.

Scile's fascination with the Hosts' language was always a bit of a titillation to me. I don't know if, as an outsider not only to Embassytown but to Bremen space itself, he could appreciate the frisson he produced in me every time he said "Ariekei" instead of the respectful "Hosts," every time he parsed their sentences and told me what they meant. I'm sure it's some kind of irony or something that it was through my foreign husband's researches that I learnt most of what I know about the language of the city in a ghetto of which I was born.

ACL—ACCELERATED CONTACT LINGUISTICS—was, Scile told me, a speciality crossbred from pedagogics, receptivity, programming and cryptography. It was used by the scholar-explorers of Bremen's pioneer ships to effect very fast communication with indigenes they encountered or which encountered them.

In the logs of those early journeys, the excitement of the ACLers is moving. On continents, on worlds vivid and drab, they record first moments of understanding with menageries of exots. Tactile languages, bioluminescent words, all varieties of sounds that organisms can make. Dialects comprehensible only as palimpsests of references to everything already said, or in which adjectives are rude and verbs unholy. I've seen the trid diary of an ACLer barricaded in his cabin, whose vessel has been boarded by what we didn't then know as Corscans—it was first contact. He's afraid, as he should be, of the huge things battering at his door, but he's recording his excitement at having just understood the tonal structures of their speech.

When the ACLers and the crews came to Arieka, there started more than 250 kilohours of bewilderment. It wasn't that the Host language is particularly difficult to understand, or changeable, or excessively various. There were startlingly few Hosts on Arieka, scattered around the one city, and all spoke the same language. With the linguists' earware and drives it wasn't hard to amass a database of sound-words (the newcomers thought of them as words, though where they divided one from the next of the Ariekei, might not recognise fissures). The scholars made pretty quick sense of syntax. Like all exot languages it had its share of astonishments. But there was nothing so alien that it trumped the ACLers or their machines.

The Hosts were patient, seemed intrigued by and, insofar as anyone could tell through their polite opacity, welcoming to their guests. They had no access to immer, nor exotic drives or even sublux engines; they never left their atmosphere, but they were otherwise advanced. They manipulated life with astonishing finesse, and they seemed unsurprised that there was sentience elsewhere.

The Hosts did not learn our Anglo-Ubiq. Did not seem to try. But within a few thousand hours, Terre linguists could understand much of what the Hosts said, and synthesised responses and questions in the one Ariekene language. The phonetic structure of the sentences they had their machines

speak—the tonal shifts, the vowels and the rhythm of conson-
ants—were precise, accurate to the very limits of testing.

The Hosts listened, and did not understand a single sound.

"How MANY OF YOU get away?" Scile asked me.

"You make it sound like a prison-break," I said.

"Well, come on. As I recall, you've said to me more than
once that you *made it out*. As I recall you may have told me
that, ahem, you'd never go back." He looked a sly look.

"Touché," I said. We were about to start on the last leg to
Embassytown.

"So how many of you?"

"Not a whole lot. You mean immersers?"

"I mean anyone."

I shrugged. "A couple of non-immersers must get cartas
every so often. Not that many people bother applying, even if
you do pass the tests."

"You in touch with any of your classmates?"

"Classmates? You mean the immersers in my batch, who
left with me? Hardly." I made finger motions to indicate our
dispersal. "Anyway. There were only three others. We weren't
close." Even had the practicalities of miab-hauled letters not
made it near impossible, I wouldn't have tried and nor would
they. A classic unspoken agreement among escapees from a
small town: don't look back, don't be each other's anchors, no
nostalgia. I wasn't expecting any of them to return.

On that journey to Embassytown, Scile had had his sopor
amended, spiked with gerons so he would age while under. It's
an affecting gesture, to ensure that the sleep of travel doesn't
keep you young while your working partner grows older.

In fact he didn't spend all his time under. With the help of medicines and augmens, he spent a little of the journey awake and studying, where immer allowed, breaking off to retch or fend off panic with chemical prophylactics as necessary. "Listen to this," he read to me. We were at the table, passing through very calm immer shallows. In deference to his always-sickness I was eating dried-up fruit, a nearly odourless food. "'You are of course aware that every Man has two mouths or voices.' In this"—he prodded what he was reading—"they have sex by singing to each other." It was some antique book about a flat land.

"What's the point of that nonsense?" I said.

"I'm looking for epigraphs," he said. He tried other old stories. Looking for invented cousins to the Hosts, he showed me descriptions of Chorians and Tucans, Ithorians, Wess'har, invented double-tongued beasts. I couldn't share his enthusiasms for these grotesques.

"I could have Proverbs 5:4," he said, staring at his screen. I didn't ask for an explanation: we used to joust like that sometimes. Instead I uploaded a Bible when I was alone, to find: "But in the end she's bitter as wormwood, sharp as a sword with two mouths."

The Hosts aren't the only polyvocal exots. Apparently there are races who emit two, three or countless sounds simultaneously, to talk. The Hosts, the Ariekei, are comparatively simple. Their speech is an intertwining of two voices only, too complexly various to be pegged as "bass" or "treble." Two sounds—they can't speak either voice singly—inextricable by the chance co-evolution of a vocalising ingestion mouth and what was once probably a specialised organ of alarm.

The first ACLers listened and recorded and understood them. "Today we heard them talk about a new building," the bewildered figures on the old trid told Scile and me. "Today they were discussing their bio-work." "Today they were listing the names of stars."

We saw Urich and Becker and their colleagues, neither of them yet famous at the time we spied on, mimicking the noises of the locals, repeating their sentences to them. "We know that's a greeting. We *know* it is." We watched a long-dead linguist play sounds to a waiting Ariekes. "We know they can hear," she said. "We know they understand by hearing each other; we know that if one of its friends said *exactly what I just played*, they'd understand each other." Her recording shook its head at us and Scile shook his.

Of the epiphany itself, there's only Urich and Becker's written testimony. In the way of these things, others from their party later denounced the record as misrepresentative, but it was the Urich-Becker manuscript that became the story. I'd seen the children's version long ago. I remembered the picture of the moment; Urich's features a delight to the caricaturist, him and subtler-faced Sura Becker both rendered with pop-eyed exaggeration, staring at a Host. I'd never read the unbowdlerised manuscript till Scile pulled it up for me.

We knew a great number of words and phrases [I read]. We knew the most important greeting: $\frac{suhaill}{jarr}$. We heard it every day and we repeated it every day—the latter without effect.

We programmed our voxware and had it speak the word repeatedly. And repeatedly the Ariekei ignored it again. At last in frustration we looked at each other and screamed half the word each like a curse. By chance they were simultaneous. Urich yelled "suhaill," Becker "jarr," at once.

The Ariekes turned to us. It spoke. We didn't need our 'ware to make sense of what it said.

It asked us who we were.

It asked what we were, and what we had said.

It had not understood us, but it had known that there was something to understand. Before, it had always heard the synthesised voices just as noise: but this time, even though our shouts were much less accurate than any 'ware renditions, it knew that we had tried to speak.

I've heard versions of that unlikely story many times. From that moment, or from whatever really happened, via misjudgements and wrong directions, within seventy-five kilohours, our predecessors understood the language's strange nature.

"Is it unique?" I asked Scile once, and when he nodded I, for the first time, really felt astonishment at it, as if I were an outsider, too.

"There's nothing like this anywhere," he said. "*Eh, nee, where.* It isn't about the sounds, you know. The sounds aren't where the meaning lives."

There are exots who speak without speaking. There are no telepaths in this universe, I think, but there are empathics, with languages so silent that they may as well be sharing thoughts. The Hosts are not like that. They're empaths of another kind.

For humans, say *red* and it's the *reh* and the *eh* and the *duh* combined, those phonemes in context, that communicate the colour. That's the case whether I say it, or Scile does, or a Shur'asi, or a mindless program that has no sense that it's speaking at all. That is not how it is for the Ariekei.

Their language is organised noise, like all of ours are, but for them each word is a funnel. Where to us each word *means* something, to the Hosts, each is an opening. A door, through which the thought of that referent, the thought itself that reached for that word, can be seen.

"If I program 'ware with an Anglo-Ubiq word and play it, you understand it," Scile said. "If I do the same with a word in

Language, and play it to an Ariekes, *I* understand it, but to them it means nothing, because it's only sound, and that's not where the meaning lives. It needs a mind behind it.''

Hosts' minds were inextricable from their doubled tongue. They couldn't learn other languages, couldn't conceive of their existence, or that the noises we made to each other were words at all. A Host could understand nothing not spoken in Language, by a speaker, with intent, with a mind behind the words. That was why those early ACL pioneers were confused. When their machines spoke, the Hosts heard only empty barks.

"There's no other language that works like this," Scile said. "'The human voice can apprehend itself as the sounding of the soul itself.'"

"Who was that?" I said. I could tell he was quoting.

"I can't remember. Some philosopher. It's not true anyway and he knew it."

"Or she."

"Or she. It's not true, not for the human voice. But the Ariekei . . . when they speak they *do* hear the soul in each voice. That's how the meaning lives there. The words have got . . .'' He shook his head, hesitating, then just using that religiose term. "Got the soul in them. And it has to be there, the meaning. Has to be true to be Language. That's why they make similes."

"Like me," I said.

"Like you but not just like you. They made similes long before you lot ever touched down. With anything they could get their hands on. Animals. Their wings. And that's what that split rock's for."

"Split-and-fixed. That's the point."

"Well quite. They had to make it so they could say 'It's like the rock which was split and fixed.' About whatever it is they say that about."

"But they didn't make as many similes, I thought. Before us."

"No," Scile said. "That is . . . No."

"I can think things which aren't there," I said. "And so can they. Obviously. They must, to plan the similes in the first place."

"Not . . . quite. They've no what-ifs," he said. "At best, it must be like a pre-ghost in their heads. Everything in Language is a truth claim. So they need the similes to compare things to, to make true things that aren't there yet, that they need to say. It might not be that they can think of it: maybe Language just demands it. That soul, that soul I was talking about's what they hear in Ambassadors, too."

Linguists invented notation like musical score for the interwoven streams of Hostspeak, named the two parts according to some lost reference: the Cut and the Turn voices. Their, our, human version of Language was more flexible than the original of which it was a crude phonetic copy. It could be sounded out by 'ware, it could be written, neither of which forms the Hosts, for which Language was speech spoken by a thinker thinking thoughts, could understand.

We can't learn it, Scile said. All we can do's teach ourselves something with the same noises, which works quite differently. We jury-rigged a methodology, as we had to. Our minds aren't like theirs. We had to misunderstand Language to learn it.

When Urich and Becker spoke together with shared, intense feeling, one the Cut and the other the Turn, a flicker of meaning was transmitted, where zettabytes of 'ware had failed.

Of course they tried again, they and their colleagues practising duets, words that meant *hello* or *we would like to speak*. We watched their recorded ghosts. We listened to them learn their lines. "Sounds flawless to me," said Scile, and even I recognised phrases, but the Ariekei did not. "U and B had no shared mind," Scile said. "No coherent thoughts behind each word."

The Hosts didn't react with quite the same blankness with which they had heard synthesised voices. They were uninterested in most, but listened hard to a few of these stuttering couples. They didn't understand it, but they seemed to know that something was being said.

Linguists, singers, psychospecialists had investigated those pairs who had the most obvious impact. Scientists had striven to work out what they shared. That was how the Stadt Dyadic Empathy Test was created. Attain a certain threshold together on its steep curve of mutual understandingness, fire up machines to connect various brainwaves, synching and linking them, and a particular pair of humans might just be able to persuade the Ariekei that there was meaning to their noises.

Still communication remained impossible, for megahours after contact. It was a long time after those early revelations that researches into empathy got us anywhere. Very few pairs of people scored well on the Stadt scale, scored highly enough to mum a unified mind behind the Language they ventriloquised. That was the minimum it would take to speak across the species.

What the colony needed, someone had joked, were single people split in two. And to put it like that was to suggest a solution.

The first interlocutors with the Hosts were exhaustively trained monozygote twins. Few such siblings could make Language work any better than the rest of us, but those that could were a slightly larger minority than in any control group.

They spoke it horribly, we now know, and there were innumerable misunderstandings between them and the Ariekei, but this meant trade, too, at last, and a struggling to learn.

In my life, I'd met one other pair of idents, non-Embassytowners I mean, in a port on Treony, a cold moon. They were dancers, they did an act. They were blood-born, of course, not made, but still. I was absolutely stunned by them. By how they looked like each other, but only so far. That their hair and clothes were not precisely the same, that they spoke in distinguishable voices, went to different parts of the room, talked to different people.

On Arieka, for lifetimes, the last two megahours, our representatives hadn't been twins but doppels, cloned. It was the only viable way. They were bred in twos in the Ambassador-farm, tweaked to accentuate certain psychological qualities. Blood twins had long been outlawed.

A limited empathy might be taught and drugged and tech-linked in between two people, but that wouldn't have been enough. The Ambassadors were created and bought up to be one, with unified minds. They had the same genes but much more: it was the minds those carefully nurtured genes made that the Hosts could hear. If you raised them right, taught them to think of themselves right, wired them with links, then they could speak Language, with close enough to one sentience that the Ariekei could understand it.

The Stadt test was still taken in the out, by students of the psyche and of languages. It had no practical use, now, though— we grew our own Ambassadors in Embassytown, and didn't have to find each precious potential one among very young twins. As a way to source speakers of Language, the test was obsolete, I had thought.

Latterday, 2

"PLEASE JOIN ME"—I couldn't see who it was who spoke loudly, announcing the arrivals to Diplomacy Hall—"in welcoming Ambassador EzRa."

They were immediately surrounded. In that moment I saw no close friends, had no one with whom to share my tension or conspiratorial look. I waited for EzRa to do the rounds. When they did, how they did so was another indicator of their strangeness. They must have known how it would seem to us. As JoaQuin and Wyatt introduced them to people, Ez and Ra separated, moved somewhat apart. They glanced at each other from time to time, like a couple, but there were soon metres between them: nothing like doppels, nothing like an Ambassador. Their links must work differently, I thought. I glanced at their little mechanisms. They each wore a distinct design. I shouldn't have been surprised. Disguising their unease with functionaries' aplomb, JoaQuin led Ez and Wyatt Ra.

Each half of the new Ambassador was at the centre of a curious crowd. This was the first chance most of us had had to meet them. But there were Staff and Ambassadors whose fascination for the newcomers had clearly outlasted their own initial meetings. LeNa, RanDolph and HenRy were laughing with Ez, the shorter man, while Ra looked bashful as AnDrew asked him questions, and MagDa, I realised, stayed close enough to touch his hands.

The party bustled about me. I caught sight of Ehrsul's rendered eyes at last and winked as Ra approached me. Wyatt made an *aaah* noise, held out his hands, kissed my cheeks.

"Avice! Ra, this is Avice Benner Cho, one of Embassytown's
... Well, Avice is any number of things." He bowed as if
granting me something. "She's one of our immersers. She's
spent a good deal of time in the out, and now she offers
cosmopolitan expertise and an invaluable traveller's eye." I liked
Wyatt, and his little power plays. You might say we tended to
twinkle at each other.

"Ra," I said. A hesitation too short for him to notice, I think,
and I held out my hand. I shouldn't call him "Mr." or "Squire":
legally he was not a man, but half of something. Had he been
with Ez I'd have addressed them as "Ambassador." I nodded at
AnDrew, at Mag, at Da, who watched.

"Helmser Cho," Ra said quietly. He after his own hesitation
took my hand.

I laughed. "You've promoted me. And it's Avice. Avice is
fine."

"Avice."

We stood silent for a moment. He was tall and slim, pale,
his hair dark and plaited. He seemed slightly anxious but he
pulled himself together somewhat as we spoke.

"I admire you being able to immerse," he said. "I never
get used to it. Not that I've travelled a lot, but that's partly
why."

I forget what I replied, but whatever it was, there was a
silence after it. After a minute I said to him, "You'll have to get
better at it, you know. Small talk. That's what your job is, from
here on in."

He smiled. "I'm not sure that's quite fair," he said.

"No," I said. "There's wine to drink and papers to sign, too."
He seemed delighted by that. "And for that you came all the
way to Arieka," I said. "For ever and ever."

"Not for ever," he said. "We'll be here seventy, eighty

kilohours. Until the next relief but one, I think. Then back to Bremen."

I was astounded. My blather stopped. Of course I should not have been taken aback. An Ambassador leaving Embassytown. Nothing about this situation made sense. An Ambassador with somewhere else to return to was a contradiction in my terms.

Wyatt was muttering to Ra. MagDa smiled at me from behind them. I liked MagDa: they were one of the Ambassadors who hadn't treated me differently since my falling out with CalVin.

"I'm from Bremen," Ra told me. "I'd like to travel like you have."

"Are you Cut or Turn?" I asked.

It was obvious he didn't like the question. "Turn," he said. He was older than me but not by very much.

"How did all this happen?" I said. "You and Ez? It takes years . . . How long have you been training?"

"Avice, really," Wyatt said from behind Ra. "You'll hear all about that—" He raised his eyebrows in a rebuke, but I raised mine back. There was a moment between him and Ra, before Ra spoke.

"We'd been friends a long time," he said. "We got tested years ago. Kilohours, I mean. It was a random thing, part of an exhibition about the Stadt method." He stopped as the noise in the room grew louder. Mag or Da said something, laughing, moved between me and Ra demanding the attention he politely turned on them.

"He's tense," I said to Wyatt quietly.

"I don't think this is his favourite thing," he said. "But then, would it be yours? Poor man's in a zoo."

"'Poor man,'" I said. "Very, very strange to hear you speak of him like that."

"Strange times." We laughed over a swell of music. There was a strong smell of perfume and wine. We watched EzRa, who were not EzRa, not really, who were Ez and Ra, separated by metres. Ez was bantering with facility and pleasure. He caught my eye, excused himself to his interlocutors and approached.

"Hi," he said. "I see you met my colleague." He held out his hand.

"Your *colleague*? Yes, I met him." I shook my head. JoaQuin were at Ez's elbows, one on each side like elderly parents, and I nodded at them. "Your colleague. You really are just determined to scandalise us, Ez," I said.

"Oh, please. No. Not at all, not at all." He grinned an apology at the doppels escorting him. "It's . . . well, I suppose it's just a slightly different way of doing things."

"And it'll be invaluable," said Joa, or Quin, heartily. The two spoke in turn. "You're always telling us we're too . . ." ". . . stuck in our ways, Avice. This will be . . ." ". . . good for us, and good for Embassytown." One of them slapped Ez on the back. "Ambassador EzRa's an outstanding linguist and bureaucrat."

"You're going to say they're a 'new broom,' aren't you, Ambassador?" I said.

JoaQuin laughed. "Why not?" "Why not indeed?" "That's exactly what they are."

WE WERE RUDE, Ehrsul and I. We'd stick together, whispering and showing off, at all these sorts of events. So when she waved a trid hand to attract my attention I joined her expecting to play. But when I reached her she said to me urgently, "Scile's here."

I didn't look round. "Are you sure?"

"I never thought he'd come," she said.

I said, "I don't know what . . ." It was some time since I'd seen my husband. I didn't want a scene. I bit a knuckle for a moment, stood up straighter. "He's with CalVin, isn't he?"

"Am I going to have to separate you two girls?" It was Ez again. He made me start. He'd extricated himself from JoaQuin's anxious stewarding. He offered me a drink. He flexed something inside himself, and his augmens glimmered, changing the colour of his vague halo. I realised that with the help of his innard tech he might have been listening to us. I focused on him and tried not to look for Scile. Ez was shorter than me, and muscular. His hair was cut close.

"Ez, this is Ehrsul," I said. To my astonishment he looked at her, said nothing and looked back at me. The rudeness made me gasp.

"Having a good time?" he said to me. I watched tiny lights move across his corneas. Ehrsul was moving away. I was going to go with her and blank him haughtily, but behind his back she flashed a quick display: *Stay, learn*.

"You're going to have to do a lot better than that," I said to him quietly.

"What?" He was startled. "What? Your—"

"She's not mine," I said. He stared at me.

"The autom? I apologise. I'm sorry."

"It isn't me you owe that to." He inclined his head.

"What are you monitoring?" I said to him after a silence. "I can see your displays."

"It's just habit. Temperature, air impurities, ambient noise. Mostly pointless. A few other things: I worked for years in situations that . . . well, I got used to checking for trid, cameras, ears, that sort of thing." I raised an eyebrow. "And I tend to run translationware as a default."

"No!" I said. "How exciting. Now, tell me the truth. Got 'ware in your ears? Are you running a soundtrack?"

He laughed. "No," he said. "I grew out of that. I haven't done that for . . . a good week or two."

"Why are you running translation programs? You . . ." I put my arm on his and looked suddenly exaggeratedly stricken. "You *do speak* Language, don't you? Oh dear, there's been a terrible misunderstanding."

He laughed again. "Oh, I can *get by* in Language, that's not it." More seriously: "But I don't speak any of the Shur'asi or Kedis dialects, or . . ."

"Oh, you won't find exots here tonight. Apart from Mine Host, obviously." I was surprised he didn't know this. Embassytown was a Bremen colony, under Bremen laws that restricted our few exots to guestworker status.

"What about you?" he said. "I don't see augmens. So you speak Language?"

For a moment I really didn't understand what he meant. "No. I let my sockets close up. I had a few bits and pieces once. They can be useful for immersion. And also," I said, "yes, you know, I can see how a bit to help make sense of what the Hosts say is . . . useful. But I've seen them, they're too . . . It's intrusive."

"That's sort of the point," he said.

"Right, and I can put up with that if it's any use, but Language is beyond it," I said. "Get them, when you hear a Host speak you get a whole eyeful or earful of nonsense. *Hello slash query is all well? parenthesis enquiry after suitability of timing slash insinuations of warmness sixty percent insinuations of belief that interlocutor has topic to be discussed forty percent* blah blah." I raised an eyebrow. "It was pointless."

Ez watched me. He knew I was lying. He must have known that the notion of using translationware for Language would be, to an Embassytowner, profoundly inappropriate. Not illegal, but an appalling impertinence. I didn't even know quite why I had said all that.

"I've heard of you," he said. I waited. If EzRa were even slightly good at their job they'd have prepared something personal to say to most of the people they might meet, tonight. What Ez said next, though, astonished me. "Ra reminded me where we'd heard your name. You're in a simile, aren't you? And I gather you've been to the city? Outside Embassytown." Someone brushed past him. He didn't stop looking at me.

"Yes," I said. "I've been there."

"I'm sorry, I think I've ... Sorry if I've ... It's not my business."

"No, it's just, I'm surprised."

"Of course I've heard of you. We do our research, you know. There's not many Embassytowners who've done what you've done."

I didn't say anything. I felt I don't know what, to hear that I featured in the Bremen reports on Embassytown. I inclined a glass at Ez, said some goodbye, and went to find Ehrsul manoeuvring her chassis through the crowd.

"So what's their story?" I said. Ehrsul gave her display shoulders a shrug.

"Ez is a charmer, isn't he?" she said. "Ra seems better but he's shy."

"Anything online?" She'd probably been trying to hack into data floating around.

"Not much," she said. "It's some kind of coup for Wyatt that they're here. He's crowing so hard hens everywhere are getting randy. That's why the Staff are so tense. I decrypted the tail end of something ... I'm pretty sure Staff made EzRa *sit a test*. I suppose, you know, it's the first time in Christ-knows-how-long there's been an Ambassador from the out, and they queried whether anyone who didn't grow up speaking Language could possibly get the nuances. They must resent this appointment."

"*They're* all technically appointees too, don't forget," I said. It was something that rankled with Staff: on his arrival, Wyatt, like every attaché, had had to formally license all the Ambassadors to speak for Bremen. "Anyway, they can speak Language? EzRa?"

She shrugged again. "Wouldn't be here if they'd failed," she said.

Something happened in the room. A feeling, a moment when, conviviality notwithstanding, it was suddenly imperative to focus. It was like that every time the Hosts came into a room, as they had just come into Diplomacy Hall.

THE PARTYGOERS tried not to be rude—as if it were possible for us to be rude to them, as if the Hosts considered politesse on axes that would make any sense to us. Nonetheless, most of us kept up our chitchat and did not ogle.

An exception was the crew, who stared frankly at the Ariekei they had never seen before. Across the room I saw my helmsman and I saw the expression on his face. Once I had heard a theory. It was an attempt to make sense of the fact that no matter how travelled people are, no matter how cosmopolitan, how biotically miscegenated their homes, they can't be insouciant at the first sight of any exot race. The theory is that we're hardwired with the Terre biome, that every glimpse of anything not descended from that original backwater home, our bodies know we should not ever see.

Formerly, 2

I WASN'T SURE how Embassytown would be for Scile. He can't have been the first settler from the out to be brought back by a returnee, but I'd never known others.

I'd spent a long time on ships in the immer, or in ports on planets with diurnal durations inimical to humanity's. My return was the first time for thousands of hours that I'd been able to dispense with circadian implants and settle into actual solar rhythms. Scile and I acclimatised to the nineteen-hour Ariekene days by traditional means, spending most of our time outside.

"I warned you," I told him. "It's a tiny place."

Now I remember those days with real pleasure. Still. I kept telling Scile about my sacrifice in returning to that little place—to come back from the out! to funnel back down!—but I was happier than I'd imagined I would be when I emerged from the sealed train in the aeolian zone, and breathed Embassytown smells. It felt like being a child again, though it was not. Being a child is like nothing. It's only being. Later, when we think about it, we make it into youth.

My early days back in Embassytown, with savings and an outsider, immerser chic. I swaggered. I was welcomed back in delight by those who'd known me, who had never thought to see me again, who'd doubted the news of my return in the preceding miab.

I wasn't rich by any real standard, but my savings were in Bremen Eumarks. This was the foundation currency of Embassytown, of course, but one rarely seen: with thirty or more kilohours between visits from the metropole—more than an Embassytown year—our little economy was self-standing. In deference to the Eumark, like all Bremen's colonies, our currency was called the Ersatz. All those Ersatzes were incommensurable, each its own and worthless beyond its polity's bounds. That portion of my account I'd downloaded and had with me, a few months' life in Bremen, was enough for me to live in Embassytown until the next relief, perhaps even the one after that. I don't even think people much resented it—I'd earned my money in the out. I told people that what I was doing with it now was floaking. That was inaccurate—there being no commands for me to get away with minimally obeying, I was simply not working—but they were delighted with the immer slang. They seemed to consider my idleness my right.

Those of my shiftparents still working had a party for me, and I was a bit startled by how happy it made me to go back, to be in the nursery, to kiss and hug and shout and re-greet these kind men and women, some now disconcertingly old, some seeming unchanged. "I told you you'd come back!" Dad Shemmi kept saying as I danced with him. "I told you!" They unwrapped the Bremen gewgaws I'd brought them. "This is too much, my love!" Mum Quiller said of some bracelet with aesthetic augmens. The dads and mums were shyly welcoming to my husband. He stood with a game smile all evening in the streamer-decorated hall while I got drunk, and he answered the same questions about himself repeatedly.

A few of those I'd grown up with crossed paths with me again, like Simmon. Though I slightly expected to, I never saw Yohn. I made other friends, from unfamiliar strata. I was invited to Staff parties. Though these had not been my circles before I left, there hadn't been room enough in little Embassytown for me, an immerser-in-training, not at least to get near them.

People, Staff, Ambassadors I'd known by sight and reputation in those days were abruptly acquaintances, and more. Some that I had expected to meet, however, were gone.

"Where's Oaten?" I asked about a man who had mouth-pieced often for Staff on our Embassytown trid. "Where's Dad Renshaw?" "Where are GaeNor?" about that elderly Ambassador, one of whom, when recruiting me to Language, had said "Avice Benner Cho, is it?" with a cadence so splendidly stilted it had become part of my internal idiolect, so whenever I introduced myself by my full name, a little *is it?* trailed the words in my head, in her voice. "Where're DalTon?" I said, of the notorious Ambassador, men with reputations for cleverness and intrigue, who had been less concerned to hide disputes with colleagues than was customary, and whom I had been looking forward to meeting since I learnt it was they who had shown public anger when that miab had broken, back in my childhood.

Oaten had retired on his modest local riches. Renshaw had died. Young. I was sad at that. GaeNor had died, one then almost immediately the other, of linkshock and loss. DalTon, I gathered—after continuing dissidence and some hinted-at final impatience with their colleagues, some ostentatiously opaque Staff internecine strife—had disappeared or been disappeared. Intrigued, I prodded at that, but got nothing more. I had enough licence as a returnee to ask such questions about Ambassadors directly, rather improperly, but I could gauge how far to push it and when not to.

I have no doubt that this was fallacious, but it felt to me as if I was quicker, better at sarcasm, wittier, because of my time in the out. People were kind to Scile and fascinated by him. He was fascinated back. He'd been on several worlds but emerged into Embassytown as if through a door in a wall. He explored. Our status wasn't a secret. Nonex marriages like ours were known of but rare in Embassytown, which made us a titillation. We were spending most of our time together, still, but gradually less, as he expanded his own circles.

"Careful," I told Scile, after one party where a man called Ramir had flirted with him, using augmens to make his face provocative, according to local aesthetics. I'd never known Scile show interest in men, but still. Homosex was a little bit illegal, I told him. Except for Ambassadors.

"What about that woman, Damier?" he said.

"She's Staff," I said. "Anyway it's only a little bit illegal."

"How quaint," he said.

"Oh yes, it's just darling."

"So do they know you were once married to a woman?"

"I've been to the out, my love," I said. "I can do anything I bloody want."

I showed him where I'd played. We went to galleries and exhibitions of trid. Scile was fascinated by the tramp automa of Embassytown, melancholy-seeming mendicant machines. "Do they ever go into the city?" he said. They did, but even could he corner them their artminds were too feeble to describe it to him.

It was Language that he was there for, of course, but he wasn't blinkered to other strangenesses. Ariekene biorigging astonished him. At the houses of friends, he would stare like an appraiser at their quasi-living artefacts, architectural filigrees, their occasional medical tweak, prostheses and similar. With me, he would stand at the edge of the aeolian breath, on balconies and viewbridges in Embassytown, watching the herds of power plants and factories graze. Yes, he was staring into the city at where Language was, but he was looking at the city itself as well. Once, he waved like a boy, and though the far-off things can't have seen us, it seemed as if one station twitched its antennae in response.

Near the heart of Embassytown was the site of the first archive. The field of rubble could have been cleared but it had been left as it was for lifetimes, since it fell: over one and a half megahours, more than half a local century. Our early town-planners must have thought that humans need ruins. Children still came, as we had, sometimes, and the overgrown dereliction was busy with Terre animals and those local lives that could tolerate the air we breathed. They, too, Scile spent a long time watching.

"What's that?" A red simian thing with a dog's head, shinning up a pipe.

"A fox, it's called," I said.

"Is it an altered?"

"I don't know. Way back, if so."

"What's that?"

"A jackdaw." "A stickleback-cat." "A dog." "Some indigene, I don't know its name."

"That's not what we call a dog where I come from," he'd say, or "Jack, daw," carefully repeating names. It was unfamiliar indigenous Ariekene things that interested him most.

Once we spent hours in a very hot sun. We sat talking about things, then not talking, holding hands long enough and still enough that the animals and abflora forgot we were alive and treated us as landscape. Two creatures each the size of my forearm wrestled in the grass. "Look," I said, quietly. "Shh." Some way from the animals a clumsy little biped was edging away, its rear a fringe of blood.

"It's injured," Scile said.

"Not exactly." Like every Embassytowner child, I knew what

this was. "Look," I said. "That's the hunter." A ferocious little altbrock, its black-and-white fur spattered. "What it's fighting's called a trunc. As is that thing running away. I know they look like different animals. You see how the tail end of that one over there's all ragged? And the head of the one getting into it with the altbrock's torn, too? That's the brainhalf and that's the meathalf of the same animal. They tear apart when the trunc's attacked: the meathalf holds off any predators while the brain end runs off looking for a last chance to mate."

"It doesn't look anything like other local stuff," Scile said. "But . . . I don't think it's Terre?" The meathalf of the trunc was winning, grinding the altbrock down. "Before it tore apart it would have had eight legs. There weren't any octopodes on Terre, were there? Maybe underwater, but . . ."

"It's not Terre *or* Ariekene," I said. "It was brought in by accident kilohours ago, on a Kedis ship. They're little gypsies. They must smell good or something: loads of things attack them. Even though if they then win, eating trunc-flesh makes them puke, or kills them. Poor little refugees."

The brainhalf of the autotruncator was in the shadow of long-fallen stone and circuitry, watching the triumph of its erstwhile hind limbs. It teetered like a meerkat or a little dinosaur. The brainhalf had taken the trunc's only eyes, and the meathalf circled in blind pugnacity, sniffing for more enemies from which to protect its escaped mind.

In an act of obscure sentimentality, Scile, with some effort, evaded the trunc meathalf's claws—no small achievement, given that all it was driven to do by its remaining scrag-end thoughts was to fight—and brought it home. He kept it alive for several days. In the cage he rigged he put down food, and the trunc circled it and snatched mouthfuls as it continued its unending vigilant rounds, though it had no brain to protect. It tried to fight any brushes or cloths that we dangled near it. It died, and broke down very fast like a salted slug, leaving only mess for us to dispose of.

At the coin wall, I told Scile about that first encounter with Bren. I'd found myself hesitating to take him there or tell him the story, and that piqued me, so I made myself. Scile looked lengthily at the house.

"Is he still there?" I asked a local stallholder.

"Don't see much of him but he's still there." The man made a finger-sign against bad luck.

All this beckoning Scile through my childhood. Out at breakfast late one morning, at the end of the square in which we sat, I saw, and pointed out to Scile, a little group of young trainee Ambassadors, on one of their controlled, corralled, protected expeditions into the town for which they would one day intercede. There were five or six of them, it looked like, all from the same batch, ten or twelve children, a few kilohours off puberty, escorted by teachers, security, two adult Ambassadors, a men and a women, whom I could not identify at this distance. The apprentices' links winked frenetically.

"What are they doing?" he said.

"Treasure hunt. Lessons. Don't know," I said. "Showing them round their demesne." To my mild embarrassment and the amusement of other diners, Scile stood to watch them go, still chewing the dense Embassytown toast he claimed to love (too ascetic now for me).

"Do you see that often?"

"Not really," I said. Most of the few times I'd seen such groups was as a child myself. If it happened when I was with my friends, we might try to catch the eyes of one or other of the not-yet-Ambassadors, giggle and run off if we succeeded, chased or not by their escorts. We'd play mocking and somewhat nervous games in their wake, for a few ostentatious minutes. I paid attention to my breakfast and waited for Scile to sit.

When he did he said, "What do you think about kids?"

I glanced in the direction the young doppels had taken. "Interesting chain of thought," I said. "Here, it wouldn't be like . . ." In the country he'd been born in, on the world he'd been born on, children were mostly raised by between two and six adults, connected to them and each other by direct genetics. Scile had mentioned his father, his mother, his auntfathers or whatever he called them, more than once and with affection. It was a long time since he had seen them: such ties mostly attenuate in the out.

"I know," he said. "I just . . ." He waved at the town. "It's nice here."

"Nice?"

"There's something here."

"'Something.' I can tell words are your business. Anyway we're going to pretend that I didn't hear you. Why would I inflict this little place . . ."

"Oh stop it, really." He smiled with only a little prickle in his voice. "You got out, yes, I know. You don't mind it here half as much as you pretend to, Avice. You don't like me *that* much, to come here if it was purgatory for you." He smiled again. "Why would you mind it, anyway?"

"You're forgetting something. This isn't the out. In Bremen they consider most of what we do here—biorigging aside, and that we get out of the good graces of you-know-who—thuggish field medicine. And that includes sex-tech. You do remember how kids get made? You and I don't exactly . . ."

He laughed. "Point," he said. He took my hand. "Compatible everywhere but between sheets."

"Who said I wanted to do it between sheets?" I said. It was a joke, not a seduction.

It all feels like prelude, now I reflect on it. The first time I saw exots of species I'd not grown up with was in a rowdy town on a tiny world we called Sebzi. I was introduced to a group of hive-things. I've no idea what they were, or from where their race originated. I've seen none of their kind since. One came forward on a pseudopod, leaned its hourglass body toward me and from a tiny snag-toothed ventricle said, in perfect Anglo-Ubiq, "Ms. Cho. It's a pleasure."

Scile reacted to Kedis and Shur'asi and Pannegetch, I don't doubt, with more aplomb than I had that time. He gave talks in Embassytown's east, about his work and travels (I was impressed by how he was able to tell the truth but make his life sound coherent, precisely arced). A Kedis troika approached afterwards, colourcells winking in their frills, and the shemale speaker thanked him in her curious diction, shaking his hand with her prehensile genitalia.

He introduced himself to the Shur'asi shopkeeper we knew as Gusty—Scile ostentatiously and with pleasure told me its actual namestring—and cultivated a brief friendship. People were charmed to see them about town, Scile with a companionable arm around Gusty's main trunk, the Shur'asi's cilia scuttling it at Scile's pace. They'd swap stories. "You go on about the immer," Gusty would say. "Try travelling by whorl-drive. Blimey, that was a journey." I was never able to decide if his mind really was as like ours as the shape of his anecdotes suggested. Certainly he performed our small talk well, even once mimicking the poor Anglo-Ubiq of a Kedis neighbour, in a complicated joke.

Of course Scile wanted to meet the Ariekei. It was the

Ariekei he studied nightly, when he stopped being social. It was they who eluded him.

"I still can't find out almost anything about them," he said. "What they're like, what they think, what they do, how they work. Even stuff written by Ambassadors describing their work, their, you know, their interactions with the Ariekei, it's all . . . incredibly empty." He looked at me as if he wanted something. "They know what to do," he said, "but not what it is they're doing."

It took me moments to make sense of his complaint. "It's not the Ambassadors' job to *understand* the Hosts," I said.

"So whose is it?"

"It's no one's job to understand them." I think that was when I first really saw the gap between us.

By now we knew Gharda and Kayliegh and others, Staff and those close to them. I had become friends with Ehrsul. She teased me about my lack of profession (she, unlike most Embassytowners, had been au fait with the term "floaker" before I introduced it), and I teased her right back about the same thing. As autom, Ehrsul had neither rights nor tasks, but so far as it was understood an owner, a settler of some previous generation, had died intestate, and she'd never become anyone else's property. There were variants of salvage laws by which someone might theoretically have tried to claim her, but by now it would have seemed abominable.

"It's just Turingware," Scile said when she wasn't there, though he allowed that it was better such than he'd seen before. He was amused by how we related to her. I didn't like his attitude, but he was as polite to her as if he did think her a person, so I didn't pick a fight with him about it. The only real interest he ever showed in Ehrsul was when it occurred to him that, because she did not breathe, she would be able to go into the city. I told him the truth: that she said to me when I asked her about it that she never did or would, that I could not say why, and, given how she'd said it, I wasn't minded to ask.

She was sometimes asked to tinker with Embassytown's artminds and automa, which would bring her into close contact with Staff: we were often at the same official soirées. I was there because I had uses, too. I'd been out more recently than any of my superiors: only a few Staff had ever left for official business to Bremen and returned. I was a source, could tell them about the recent politics and culture in Charo City.

When I'd first left Embassytown, Dad Renshaw had taken me to one side—literally, he'd steered me to the edge of the room in which I was having a farewell party. I'd waited for fatherly homilies, spurious rumours about life in the out, but what he had told me was that if I ever came *back*, Embassytown would be very interested in information on the state of things in Bremen. It was so polite and matter-of-fact it took me a while to assure myself I'd been asked to spy. I was only amused, was all, at the unlikeliness. Then I was ruefully amused again when, thousands of hours later, back in Embassytown, I realised I was making myself useful just as I'd been asked to.

Scile and I would have been objects of interest whatever we did—he, an intense and fascinated outsider, was a curio; I, part of Language, and a returned immerser, a minor celebrity. But purveying facts about Bremen as I did, I, a commoner, and my commoner husband were welcomed into Staff circles even more smoothly than we would otherwise have been. Our invitations continued after Embassytown's little media stopped running interviews with and stories about the prodigal immerser.

They approached me very soon after I returned. Not Ambassadors, of course, but some viziers and high-level muck-a-mucks, requesting my presence at a meeting where they said things so vague I didn't parse their purpose for a minute, until abruptly I remembered Dad Renshaw's intercession, and understood that the muted questions about *some of the trends in Bremen and associated powers* and *possible attitudes to dependencies and their aspirations* were requests for political intelligence. And that they were offering payment.

That last seemed silly. I took no money for telling them what little I could. I waved into silence someone's diplomatic explanations of their political concerns: it didn't matter. I showed them newspipes, downloads, gave them perhaps a tiny sense of the balance of power in Bremen's ruling Cosmopolitan Democratic party. Bremen's wars, interventions and exigencies had never fascinated me, but perhaps to those more focused on them, what I told them might give insights into recent vicissitudes. Honestly I doubt any of it was stuff their artminds and analysts wouldn't have predicted or guessed.

It was hardly high espionage drama. A few days later I was introduced to Wyatt, then Bremen's new man in Embassytown, whom my Staff interlocutors had mentioned to me in obliquely warning fashion. He immediately teased me about that earlier meeting. He asked if I had a camera in his bedroom, or something like that. I laughed. I liked it when we crossed paths. He gave me a personal number.

It was in circles such as this, Embassytown society, that I met Ambassador CalVin and became their lover. One of the things they did for me was give Scile an opportunity to meet the Hosts.

CalVin were tall, grey-skinned men, a little older than me, with a certain playfulness, and the charming arrogance of the best Ambassadors. They invited me, and, at my request, Scile, to functions, and would come in turn into the town with us, where an Ambassador walking the streets without a Staff retinue was uncommon enough to attract attention.

"Ambassador," Scile worked up courage to ask them, at first cautiously, "I have a question about your . . . exchanges with the Hosts." And then into some minutely specific, arcane enquiry. CalVin, earning at that time my gratitude, were patient, though their answers were doubtless disappointing.

In CalVin's company I saw, heard and intuited details about aspects of Embassytown life I never otherwise would have. I picked up on my lovers' momentary references, hints and asides. They wouldn't always answer me when I pressed them—they might say something about colleagues gone astray, or Ariekene factions, and then refuse to elaborate—but I learnt even just from overhearing.

I asked them about Bren. "I don't see him often," I said. "He doesn't seem to come to gatherings."

"I'd forgotten you've a connection with him," CalVin said, both eyeing me, though in slightly different ways. "No, Bren's rather self-exiled. Not that he'd ever *leave*, you understand." "That wouldn't fit with what he thinks he is, to the rest of us." "And he had the chance. He *could* have left." "After he was cleaved." "Instead . . ." They laughed. "He's sort of our licensed misery." "He knows most of what goes on. And further afield, too—he knows things he really shouldn't." "You couldn't call him loyal. But he's useful." "But you really couldn't call him loyal, anymore, if he ever was." Scile listened avidly to them.

"What's it like?" Scile asked me. "I mean, I've been with two people before and I'm sure you have too, but I don't think that's—"

"No, Pharoi, no. Lord, you're *terrible*. It's not the same at all." I was adamant at the time: now I have doubts.

"Do they both concentrate on you?" he said. We giggled, he at the silly prurience, me at what felt almost like blasphemy.

"No, it's all very egalitarian. Cal, me and Vin, all in it together. Honestly, Scile, it's not like I'm the only person an Ambassador's ever—"

"You're the only one I've got access to, though." By then I wasn't sure that was true. "I thought homosex isn't approved of," he said.

"Now you're just showing off," I said. "That's not what they do together. Them or any of the Ambassadors. You know that. It's ... masturbation." That was the common if scandalous description, and it made me feel like a kid to say it. "Imagine what it's like when two Ambassadors get together."

Scile spent hours, many hours, listening to recordings of Ariekei speaking, watching trids and flats of encounters between them and the Ambassadors. I watched him mouth things to himself and write illegible notes, one-handedly input into his datspace. He learnt fast. That was no surprise to me. When at last CalVin invited us to an event at which the Hosts would be present, Scile understood Language pretty much perfectly.

It was to be one of the discussions Ambassadors held with Hosts every few weeks. Interworld trade might come only every few thousand hours, but it was backed by and built on exhaustive, careful negotiation. With the arrival of each immership, terms agreed between Staff and Hosts (with the imprimatur of Bremen's representative) were communicated, the vessel would leave with those details and Ariekene goods and tech, returning on its next round with whatever we had promised the Ariekei in return. They were patient.

"There's a reception," one of CalVin told us. "Would you like to come?"

We were not allowed into the actual negotiations, of course.

Scile regretted this. "Why do you care?" I said. "It'll be dull as hell. Trade talks? Really? How much of this, what do you want of that . . ."

"I want to know, that's exactly it. What is it they want? Do you even know what we exchange with them?"

"Expertise, mostly. For AI and artminds and things. That they can't make . . ."

"I know, because of Language. But I'd love to hear how they *relate* to that tech, when they get hold of it."

An Ariekes couldn't type into an artmind, of course: writing was incomprehensible to them. Oral input was no better: as far as any exopsych specialists could discern, the Hosts couldn't ken interacting with a machine. The computer would speak back to them in what we heard as flawless vernacular, but to the Ariekei, with no sentience behind them, those words were just noises.

So our designers had created computers that were eaves-droppers. We built them from the simple loudhailer- and telephone-animals the Ariekei biorigged. They could—though no one made sense of how—understand each other's voices (and those of our Ambassadors) through speakers or even recorded: so long as what was or had been said had that sentience, a genuine mind speaking it, neither distance nor time degraded its compre-hensibility, its meaningness, what Scile had provocatively called the "soul". We took those little mediators and upgraded, altered and sometimes ultimately replaced them with communication tech the Hosts could not have created. We routed their voices through artminds.

The programs were designed to work between interlocutors, to create their own instructions by insinuation. The Ariekei spoke to each other as they always had, and if their conversations took certain theoretical turns, the 'ware would listen in, make calculations, alter production, perform automated tasks. Just what the Ariekei understood to be occurring was of course beyond me, but they knew, I was told, that we had given them something—they paid for it, after all.

"And what do we get?" Scile said.

CalVin indicated a chandelier above us, tugging itself with slow grace into the darker areas of the room, extruding and reabsorbing tendril-end lights. "Biorigged stuff, of course," they said. "You know that." "You've seen it in Bremen, too. A lot of our food. And some gems and bits and pieces." Like most Embassytowners I was rather vague on the details of the barters they were describing. "And gold."

They were on duty, but CalVin hosted well, that first party. Scile stood by the table of delicacies, human and Ariekene, waiting. "Fraternising with the locals, at last?" Ehrsul had come quietly up behind me. She spoke suddenly, made me start and laugh.

"He's so well behaved," I said, nodding in Scile's direction.

"Patient," she said. "But then, you don't have to be, you've already met the Hosts."

She was only passing through, she said, supposedly on some upgrading errand. She swivelled and rolled past Scile with a whispered word, and he greeted her and watched her go. "You know what CalVin told me?" he said quietly to me. He gestured with his glass towards Ehrsul's retreating form. "She can speak it. It sounds flawless. All the Ambassadors know exactly what she's saying. But if she tries it with the Hosts, they don't get a word." He met my eyes. "She's not really speaking Language at all."

He continued his effort to cover his impatience—he was, at least, not rude about it. CalVin made sure to introduce him to those Staff and Ambassadors present he didn't know. And of course, finally, when they arrived, with that usual shift in the room, to the Hosts.

It was the first time for thousands of hours I'd seen them so close. There were four. Three were in prime, in their third instar, and their tall outlines quivered with whiskers. The last was in finis—its dotage. Its abdomen was massive and pendulous and its limbs spindled. It walked firmly but was mindless. Its siblings had brought it as a kind of charity. It followed them under instinct, by sight and chemical trail. It was an evolutionary strategy on Arieka shared by more than one phylum that an animal's last incarnation was as a food store for the young. They could gnaw at the nutritional swathings of its abdomen for days without killing it. Our Hosts had done so, in their early history, but they had given the practice up generations before as, we inferred, a barbarism. They mourned when their fellows entered their penultimate form, when their minds died, and respectfully shepherded the ambulatory corpses till they fell apart.

The undead thing bumped the table, upsetting wine and canapés, and HenRy, LoGan, CalVin and the other Ambassadors laughed politely as if at a joke.

"Please," CalVin said, and brought Scile forward, towards the honoured indigens. I could not read Scile's face. "Scile Cho Baradjian, this is Speaker—" and then in Cut and Turn at once they said the lead Host's name.

It looked down at us from its jutting coralline extrusion, each random bud studded with an eye.

"$\frac{kora}{shahundi}$," CalVin said, together. Only Ambassadors could speak Host names.

Waving on a stalk-throat by its neck, its Cut-mouth terribly like human lips, the Host muttered: and at the level of our chests, where its body swelled, its Turn-mouth opened and coughed, emitting little rounded vowel sounds, *tao dao thao*.

It wore the organs of tiny animals coiled about its neck. Something wound between its stiletto feet, a companion animal. One accompanied all the Ariekei but the brain-dead old-timer. It was the size of a baby, a grub-thing with stump legs and filigree antennae, its back punctuated with holes, some ringed with inlaid metal. Its locomotion was between a scamper and a convulsion. It was a zelle, a biorigged battery-beast, into which leads and wires could be slotted, and out of which, depending on what its owner fed it, different power would flow. The Ariekene city was full of such sources.

$\frac{kora}{shahundi}$ stepped forward on four legs a little like a spider's, long, too-jointed, dark-haired, and extended its wings: from its back its auditory fanwing, in many colours; from its front, from below its larger mouth, its limb of interaction and manipulation, its giftwing.

We would like to shake your giftwing with our hands, CalVin said in Language, and Scile, his face still closed to me, only pursing his lips a tiny bit, held out his hand. The Host clasped my husband's hand in a greeting that would have made no sense to it, and then it clasped mine.

So Scile saw Language spoken. He listened. He asked quick questions of CalVin between their exchanges with the Host, which they, to my surprise, put up with.

"What? Is he insinuating that you couldn't agree . . . ?"

"No, it's . . ." ". . . more complicated than that." "Hold on."

Then CalVin would speak together. "$\frac{suhaish}{ko}$," I heard them say at one point; they were saying *please*.

"I got almost all of it," Scile told me afterwards. He was very excited. "They shift tenses," he said. "When they mentioned the negotiations they—the Ariekei, I mean—were in present discontinuous, but then they shifted into the elided past-present. That's for, uh . . ." I knew what it was for, I assured him. He'd told me already. How could you not smile at him? I'd listened to him with affection, if not always with interest, over hundreds of hours.

"Does it ever occur to you that this language is impossible, Avice?" he said. "*Im, poss, ih, bul.* It makes no sense. They don't have polysemy. Words don't signify: they *are* their referents. How can they be sentient and not have symbolic language? How do their *numbers* work? It makes no sense. And Ambassadors are twins, not single people. There's *not* one mind behind Language when they speak it . . ."

"They're not twins, love," I said.

"Whatever. You're right. Clones. Doppels. The Ariekei think they're hearing one mind, but they're not." I raised one eyebrow and he said, "No they're not. It's like we can only talk to them because of a mutual misunderstanding. What we call their words aren't words: they don't, you know, *signify*. And what they call our minds aren't minds at all." He didn't laugh when I did. "You have to wonder," he said. "Don't you? What it is they do— Staff I mean—to make two people think they're one."

"Yeah but they're *not* two," I said. "That's the point about Ambassadors. That's where your whole theory falls down."

"But they could have been. Should have been. So what did they do?"

Unlike monozygots', even doppels' fingerprints were moulded and made identical. On principle. Every evening and morning Ambassadors corrected. Artmind microsurgery found whatever tiny marks and abrasions each half of each pair had uniquely picked up over the preceding day or night, and if they couldn't be eradicated, they were replicated in the untouched half. Scile meant that, and more. He wanted to see the children: young doppels in the crèche. He could still scandalise me with stuff like that. Not that such requests got responses. He wanted to watch how they were raised.

STAFF AND AMBASSADORS went into the city regularly, but only the young or gauche would ask for details. As naughty children we hacked communications and found pictures and reports we thought were secret (that of course weren't very), that gave us insinuations of what occurred.

"Sometimes," CalVin told us, "they call us in for what we call moots. They chant—not words, or words we don't know." "And when they're done, one by one we take a turn, singing to them."

"What's it for?" I asked, and simultaneously CalVin replied, "We don't know," and smiled.

Everyone was in his or her best again, for another event. Very different from any previous. I wore a dress studded with oxblood jade. Scile wore a tuxedo and white rose. The flyer that came for us was a biorigged mongrel, Ariekene breed-techniques but its quasi-living interior tailored to Terre needs, and piloted by our artminds.

It had been a huge shock to us when CalVin had told us we could accompany them. This wasn't a party in the Embassy. We were going into the Host city, to a Festival of Lies.

I'd spent thousands of hours in the immer. I'd been to ports on tens of countries on tens of worlds, had even experienced that travellers' shock we floakers called the retour, when after preparations for the alterity of a new world, one walks a quite inhuman capital and stares at intricate indigens, and starts to suspect that one has been there before. Still, the night Scile and I dressed to go into the city, I was nervous as I had not been since I left Arieka.

I watched through boat windows as we flew over the ivy and roofs of my little ghetto city. I breathed out when we crossed over the zone where the architecture went from the brick and ivied wood of my youth to the polymers and biorigged flesh of the Hosts, from alley-tangles to street-analogues of other topographies. Building-things were coming down and being replaced. Construction sites like combined slaughterhouses, puppy farms and quarries.

There were about twenty of us: five Ambassadors, a handful of Staff, and we two. Scile and I smiled at each other through our masks and breathed in the exhalations of our little portable aeoli. Quickly, very quickly, we were touched down on a roof, and followed our companions out and down and into an edifice, in the city.

A complex, many-chambered place the angles of which astonished me. Everyone who had ever talked about my *poise* would have laughed to see me literally stagger backwards in that room. Walls and ceilings moved with ratcheting mechanical life like the offspring of chains and crabs. A kind Staff member steered Scile and me. Our party walked without Ariekene chaperone. I wanted to touch the walls. I could hear my heart. I heard Hosts. Suddenly we were among them. More than I'd ever seen.

The rooms were alive, cells rainbowing as we entered. Ariekei were speaking in turn, and the Ambassadors sung in alien politeness. Through a swallowing corridor, several Hosts in their final instars milled in dignified mindlessness. A bridge whistled to us.

For the first time in my life I saw Host young: steaming nutrient broths effervesced with elvers. Further off was the fight-crèche, where the savage little second instars played with and killed each other. In a hall crisscrossed with walkways on tendons and platforms on muscular limbs were hundreds of

Ariekei, giftwings extended, fanwings pretty with inks and nat-
ural pigments, gathered for the Festival of Lies.

FOR HOSTS, speech was thought. It was as nonsensical to them
that a speaker could say, could claim, something it knew to
be untrue as, to me, that I could believe something I knew
to be untrue. Without Language for things that didn't exist, they
could hardly think them; they were vaguer by far than dreams.
What imaginaries any of them could conjure at all must be
misty and trapped in their heads.

Our Ambassadors, though, were human. They could lie as
well in Language as in our own language, to the Hosts' unending delight. These eisteddfods of mendacity had not existed—
how could they?—before we Terre came. The Festivals of Lies
had occurred almost as long as Embassytown had existed: they
were one of our first gifts to the Hosts. I'd heard of them, but
never expected to see one.

Our Ambassadors went among the hundreds of whickering
Ariekei. Staff, Scile and I—we who couldn't speak here—
watched. The room was punctured with ventricles: I could hear
it breathing.

"They're welcoming us," Scile told me, listening to all the
voices. More. "It's saying that, uh, they'll see, I think, miracles,
now. He's asking our first *something* to step forward. It's a
compound, wait, uh . . ." He sounded tense. "Our first *liar*."

"How do they make that word?" I said.

"Oh you know," he said. "Sayer-of-things-that-are-not, that
sort of thing."

Furniture was extruding in the room as it self-organised
into a vague amphitheatre. Ambassador MayBel, elderly, styl-
ish women, stood before an Ariekes, which raised what looked

96

like a big fibre-trailing fungus in its giftwing. It inserted the dangles into the sockets of the zelle jigging by its legs, and the mushroom-thing made a sound and glowed quickly changing colours, cycling to a nacreous blue.

The Host spoke. "It says: 'describe it,'" Scile whispered. MayBel answered, May in the Cut, Bel the Turn voice.

The Ariekei stepped up and down, a sudden unanimity. A tense excitement. They tottered and chattered.

"What did they say?" I said. "MayBel? What did they—?"

Scile looked as if in disbelief at me. "They're saying 'It's red.'"

MayBel bowed. The Ariekene hubbub continued while Ambassador LeRoy took their place. The Ariekes stroked its zelle, and the object attached to it changed shape and colour, altered into a great green teardrop. "Describe it," Scile translated again.

LeRoy glanced at each other and began. "They said: 'It's a bird,'" Scile said. The Ariekei muttered. The noun was shorthand for a local winged form, as well as meaning our Embassytown birds. LeRoy spoke again and several Ariekei shouted, out of control. "LeRoy says it's flying away," Scile said into my helmet. I swear I saw Hosts crane their eye-corals up as if the lifeless plasm might have taken off. Le and Roy spoke together again. "They say . . ." Scile frowned as he followed. "They say it's become a wheel," he said, over the strange pandemonium of the audience.

One at a time every Ambassador lied. The Hosts grew boisterous in a fashion I'd never seen, then to my alarm seemed intoxicated, literally lie-drunk. Scile was tense. The room was whispering, echoing the furore of its inhabitants.

It was CalVin's turn. They declaimed. "'And the walls are disappearing,'" Scile translated. "'And the ivy of Embassytown is winding about our legs . . ." Hosts examined their limbs. ". . . and the room's turning to metal and I'm growing larger and the room and I are becoming one.'"

That's enough, I thought, and someone must have agreed, and whispered to CalVin. They bowed and stepped away.

The Ariekei slowly calmed. I thought it was over. But then, as we stared, a few Host came forward.

"It's a sport," said Cal, or Vin, who approached, sweating, as they saw my surprise. "An extreme sport," said the other. "For— oh for years now, they've been trying to mimic us." "A few are getting not-too-bad at it." I watched.

"What colour is it?" the Ariekes holding the target object asked the competitors, as it had the Terre. One by one each Host would try to lie.

Most could not. They emitted croons and clickings that were effort.

"Red," Scile translated. The bulb was red, and the speaker double-whined in what I presumed was disappointment. "Blue," said another, also truthfully; the object changed each time. "Green." "Black." Some made noises that were only noises, clicks and wheezes of failure, not words at all.

Every tiniest success was celebrated. When the object was a yellow, the Host trying to lie, an Ariekes with a scissor-shape on its fanwing, shuddered and retracted several of its eyes, gathered itself, and in its two voices said a word that would have translated as something like "yellow-beige." It was hardly a dramatic untruth, but the crowd were rapturous at it.

A group of Hosts approached us. "Avice," Cal or Vin said politely. "This is . . ." and they started to say names.

I never saw the point of these niceties between the likes of me and Ariekei. Understanding only Language-speakers to have minds, they must have thought it odd when Ambassadors carefully introduced them to speechless amputated half-things. As if an Ariekes insisted on one politely saying hello to its battery animal.

So I thought, but it didn't turn out that way. The Ariekei shook my hand with their giftwings when CalVin asked them to. They had cool dry skin. I shut my mouth to obscure whatever emotion was rising in me (I'm still not sure what it was). The Ariekei registered something as the Ambassadors told them my name. They spoke, and Scile quickly translated into my ear.

"They're saying: 'This?'" he told me. "'This is the one?'"

Latterday, 3

THERE ARE WAYS to tell Hosts apart. There's the fingerprint-unique patterning on each fanwing (any observation of this fact was generally followed by the tedious mention of the fact that Embassytown was the only place where Terre fingerprints were *not* all unique). There are subtleties of carapace shading, of spines on limbs, of eye-antler shape. These days I rarely bothered to pay attention, nor with a few exceptions did I learn the names of the Ariekei I met. So I couldn't say if during that first or any later visit to the city, I had previously met any of the Host delegation that joined us all those kilohours later, in Diplomacy Hall, to greet EzRa, the impossible new Ambassador.

So far as I could tell all were in middle age, in their third instar, and therefore sentient. Some wore sashes indicating incomprehensible (to me) rank or predilections; some were studded with ugly little jewels where their chitin was thick. The most senior of the Ambassadors, MayBel and JoaQuin, were walking them slowly through the room, giving each of them a glass of champagne—carefully rigged to be palatable to them. The Hosts held them daintily and sipped with their Cut mouths. I saw Ez watch them.

"Ra's coming," Ehrsul said.

"What do we call him?" I said. "What are he and Ez to each other? They're not doppels."

Wherever in the room he was, and with whom, Scile, I knew, would be as tense at the strangeness of all this as I. Ez and Ra approached each other, changing how they held themselves, getting into another mode.

How could it have happened?

All those structures in place, for all those thousands of hours, years. Embassytown years, the years I grew up with, long months named in silly nostalgia for an antique calendar, each many dozen-day weeks long. For almost an Embassytown century, since Embassytown was born, structures had been in place. Clone farms had been run; careful and unique child rearing had raised doppels into Ambassadors, with the skills of governance they would need. It was all under Bremen's aegis of course: they were our home power; our public buildings all displayed clocks and calendars in Charo City time. But so far out here in the immer, everything should have been under Staff control.

CalVin once told me that Bremen's original expectations of Arieka's reserves, of luxuries and oddities and local gold, had been over-optimistic. Ariekene bioriggery was valuable, though, certainly. More elegant and functional than any of the crude chimeras or particle-spliced jiggery-pokery any Terre I knew of had ever managed, these Ariekene things were moulded from fecund plasms by the Hosts with techniques we could not merely not mimic, but that were impossible according to our sciences. Was that enough? In any case, no colony is ever wound down.

How and why had Charo City trained this impossible Ambassador? I'd heard, like we all had, the story of the experiment and the freak result, the empathy reading spiking off the Stadt scale. But even if these two random friends did have such a connection, for whatever contingent psychic reason, why would they become Ambassadors?

"Wyatt's excited," Ehrsul said.

"They all are." Gharda had approached, her music shift

over, her instrument folded away. "Why wouldn't they be?" she said.

"Ladies and gentlemen." Augmens relayed JoaQuin's voices to hidden speakers. JoaQuin and MayBel went into encomia to their Ariekene guests. When that was done, they welcomed the new Ambassador.

I'd been to comings-out when Ambassadors came of age (strange, arrogant, charming young doppels greeting the crowd). But this of course was nothing like those appointments.

JoaQuin said, "This is an extraordinary time. We find ourselves with the task..." "... the *enviable* task, the *strange* task..." "... of coming up with a new kind of welcome. Perhaps some of you had heard that we have a new Ambassador?" Polite laughs. "We've spent a good deal of time with them over the last few days..." "... got to know them, and they us." "These are unusual times." *Hear hear*, said RanDolph. "It's a privilege to be here, at an event I hope you will indulge us..." "... if we describe as history. This is an historic moment." "Ladies and gentlemen..." "... Hosts..." "... all our guests. It's our very great pleasure to welcome to Embassytown..." "... Ambassador EzRa."

As the applause died, JoaQuin turned to the Hosts who stood beside them, and said our new Ambassador's name accurately, in Language. "$\frac{ez}{ra}$," they said. The Hosts craned their eye-corals.

"Thank you, Ambassador JoaQuin," Ez said. He conferred quietly with Ra. "It's a great pleasure to be here," Ez continued. He said a few standard, gracious things. I was watching the other Ambassadors. Ra's self-introduction was brief, little more than his own name.

"We want to stress what an honour this is for us," Ez said. "Embassytown's one of the most important outposts of Bremen, and a vibrant community in its own right. We're more grateful than we can say for your wonderful welcome. We look forward to becoming a part of the Embassytown community, working together for its future, and working together for Bremen's." There was applause of course. Ez waited.

"We look forward to working with you," Ra said. Some Staff and Ambassadors were trying to hide nervousness. Some, I thought, eagerness.

"We realise that you must have questions," Ez said. "Please don't be shy about them. We realise we're an . . . *anomaly*, for now . . ." He smiled. "We're happy to talk about it, though to be honest we don't really know why or how we can do what we do, either. We're a mystery to us as well as to you." The laugh he waited for and got was brief. "Now we'd like to do something we've trained very long and hard to do. We are an Ambassador— I'm very proud to say that—and we have a job to do. What we would like to do is to greet our gracious Hosts." This applause seemed genuine.

The vespcams swarmed and wallscreens showed images, from scores of angles, of Ez and Ra coming together, ushered by their new colleagues toward the Hosts. The Ariekei stood in a semicircle. I've no idea what their conception was of what was happening. If nothing else, they knew that this was an Ambassador and that it was called $\frac{ez}{ra}$.

EzRa conferred together like any other Ambassador did, whispering, preparing their words. The Hosts craned their eyes. Every Terre in the room seemed to lean in, to hold her or his breath. With great theatre, EzRa turned and spoke Language.

Ez was the Cut, Ra the Turn. They spoke well, beautifully. I had heard enough of it to tell that. Their accent was good, their timing good. Their voices were well suited. They said to the Hosts that it was an honour to meet them. $\frac{suhail}{shurasuhail}$, they said. Good greetings.

That was the moment everything changed. EzRa looked at each other, smiled. Their first official pronouncement. If it hadn't been an absurd faux pas I think we would all have clapped. I'm sure many people hadn't really thought them capable.

We were busy listening to them speak, and gauging their abilities. We didn't notice everything change. I don't think any of us at that moment noticed the reactions of the Hosts.

Part Two

FESTIVALS

Latterday, 4

WE WERE ALL WATCHING the new Ambassador.

Ez hunkered down into a slightly pugnacious pose. He opened and closed his fists. I could tell he enjoyed what he was doing. He looked up at the Hosts from below a gathered brow.

Ra watched them sidelong. He pulled himself up, so tall and straight that he seemed to teeter slightly. The two of them were so absurdly distinct it was like a joke that erred in overdoing it. I was reminded of Laurel and Hardy, of Merlo and Rattleshape, of Sancho Panza and Don Quixote.

When they were done speaking, a wave of something went through all of us in Diplomacy Hall so palpably it was as if it rippled the ivy. I turned to Ehrsul and raised my eyebrows. We all knew this had been momentous, but there were perhaps a full five seconds before any of us realised that anything bad had happened.

THE HOSTS were swaying as if they were at sea. One spasmed its giftwing and its fanwing, another kept them unnaturally still. One opened and closed its membranes several times in neurotic repetition.

Three were plugged into their zelles by flesh skeins that bled in chemicals or energy, and by I suppose feedback the untoward behaviour of the Hosts infected their battery-beasts. The little ambulatory generators staggered, emitted sounds unlike any I'd heard them make before.

In very slow and unnerving unison, the Ariekei emerged

from their trance. Their eye-corals drooped toward us, and at last focused. They straightened and unstiffened their legs, as if coming out of sleep.

EzRa were frowning. They whispered to each other, and spoke again.

Are the bodies and/or brains of our Hosts troubled by invading biological entities or an allergic reaction to an environmental factor? they said, I later learnt. That is they said, *Has something happened to make you suboptimal?* They said, *Are you alright?*

Their words sounded as if Ez said some stuttering poem while Ra mimicked birds. As they spoke the Ariekei jerked again, again in that ugly simultaneity, the linked zelles snapping back with them. They were lost back to their glaze. This time one made a noise, a moan from its Cut-mouth.

JoaQuin and MayBel conferred in agitation. MayBel approached the Ariekei. The Hosts came gradually again, very gradually, out of what had taken them. CalVin saw me. We stared at each other, across the room, for the first time in some time. I saw in their eyes nothing but fear.

STAFF RALLIED, Ambassadors stepped in, bustled and led the Hosts away. As the Ariekei woke from whatever this was, they started declaiming, talking across each other, loud and chaotically. They were asking for the new Ambassador. *Where is $\frac{ez}{ra}$?* they kept saying. *Where is $\frac{ez}{ra}$?* I understood enough Language to know that.

"Ladies and Gentlemen, please," one of JoaQuin said. Someone from Staff must have spoken to the musicians on duty, because their playing started again. I'd not even realised they had stopped. Waiters recirculated. I saw security officers going somewhere, Simmon among them, controlled but in obvious urgency.

"Excuse us, ladies and gentlemen," JoaQuin said. "Our guests, the Hosts, have been . . ." JoaQuin paused and conferred. "There's been a small misunderstanding . . ." ". . . absolutely nothing to be concerned about . . ." I saw LoGan, CharLott, LuCy, AnDrew crowding the Hosts away. "Nothing at all important and entirely our own fault . . ." The two of them laughed. "We're rectifying things now." "There's absolutely no reason to concern yourselves!" "The party continues. Please join us in raising your glasses."

Many locals were eager to be reassured. Newcomers and temporary guests didn't know how concerned they should be. We raised our glasses.

"To the captain and crew of the immership *Tolpuddle Martyrs' Response* . . ." said JoaQuin, ". . . to our most welcome immigrants, new citizens . . ." ". . . and above all, to Ambassador EzRa. May they have a long and happy career here in Embassy-town." "To EzRa!"

We all said it. The recipients of our toast raised their own drinks in reciprocation. They looked at the door through which the Hosts had been taken. It was to the credit of Staff that the party didn't die. Within ten minutes most people were behaving more or less as they had been before.

"What the fuck was that?" I said quietly to Gharda.

"No bloody idea," she said.

I couldn't see Scile. There were several Ambassadors still in the room, along with Staff. I approached EdGar, but to my shock they turned away from me. I said their name in such a way that they couldn't pretend not to have heard, and they glanced and said, "Not now, Avice."

"You don't even know what I want," I said.

"Really, Avice." "Not now." They interspersed their words with smiles of greeting to those who passed them.

The crowd parted a moment and as if by plan revealed Cal or Vin. He still stared right at me. I was so startled I stopped moving. I couldn't see my watcher's doppel. The party concealed him again.

Gharda reappeared, with the pilot on her arm. She saw me and hesitated, looked a query at me. I waved, *by all means*. It mattered not at all how much more travelled I was than my city's rulers, how airily I'd given them knowledge, how eagerly they'd received it. As EdGar walked away, I was nothing. It was they and the other Ambassadors who would, in closed session, decide what had happened, and what would happen now. They made law.

Formerly, 3

A LONG TIME AGO I performed a strange unpleasant ritual in the shell of a restaurant. For that I was, Ambassadors and Staff had occasionally told me, feted by the Ariekei in my absence. That had meant nothing until the moment in the hall, at the festival, after the lying, when the Hosts discovered who I was.

They spoke rapidly, craned their eye-corals. They spoke me every day, Scile told me afterwards. That was what they said to CalVin. *I do not know*, one Host said to CalVin, about me, *how I did without her, how I thought what I needed to think*.

Her? This was the question that we called the Tallying Mystery: did the Hosts consider each Ambassador one mind, double-bodied people? And if so, did they think the rest of us half-things, irrelevances, machines? A city full of the Ambassadors' marionettes? When they knew me as simile, they asked for me to come back, but I was never sure if I was guest, exhibit, or something else. When we went, the Hosts took care of us, whether or not they understood that we were people.

I accepted their invitations because Scile could always come with me. A present to him, for which he was effusive, though I think he wanted to talk, to debrief, after the events more than I would. We would be ushered to the Hosts' halls. There were usually Ambassadors and viziers and others there too, and these glimpses of secrets that had gone on all my life, the toing and froing of Staff in the Host city, were almost as disturbing to me as anything else that happened. I'd keep spotting Ambassadors walking flesh corridors in conversation with Ariekei, places I couldn't imagine any human having a purpose.

These events, to which they had no in, were titillations to most of my friends. "A festival? Of lies?" Gharda said at a party after the first one. "The Hosts *asked* for you?" They were all gathered around me demanding to know what the city was like, and I laughed because someone said *That's import!* exactly as we had when we were children.

My occasional presence in the city was troubling, I could tell, to the Ambassadors. They didn't like seeing me there. This was their mystery. Staff debriefed me exhaustively after each of these trips, asking what I'd seen, what I'd understood.

The second time I entered the city, into another hall with a crowd of Hosts, I was left near a collection of obscure objects and anaesthetised Ariekene animals, and with four other humans, enzymatic lights bowing in the curves of their aeoli helmets. Two were Ambassador LeNa, who ignored me. The other two were young men, commoners like me.

"Hello," said one. He smiled enthusiastically and I did not smile back. "I'm Hasser: I'm an example. Davyn's a topic. You're Avice, aren't you? You're a simile."

NEITHER THIS, nor any of the other times I went in, was an event the same as the first gathering I'd attended. They were more chaotic, and, I learnt, less focused. There had for a while been a vogue among the Hosts for what were, more or less, conventions. Celebrations of Language, with broader remits than just the rare lies. They would gather as many of us necessary constructed facts as they could in one place, as many enLanguaged elements as possible—animate, inanimate, sentient and not—and come to look at us, use and theorise us, without consensus. We sat polite through wheezing, stuttering, sung arguments around and about us. I found it less compelling than the devoted lying I'd first seen.

I was lulled by the roar and whisper of the Cut- and the Turn-mouths, while Scile tried to translate. Hosts stamped back and forward, disagreeing in factions. Something like a polemic, I gathered, went on between those who thought me a useful figure of speech, and those who did not.

It was a crippled, strange debate, I think. There were those Hosts who thought something better could have been said and better thoughts therefore thought, had I only been made to do other things than I had. That I could have been a better simile for those in need of one to speak precisely; to speak about those somethings other than me that I was—they would have asserted—like. But those critics of course couldn't say what those thoughts would have been, because they could not have them.

"But . . ." said Scile. He was unhappy.

"They must be in the back of their minds, those thoughts," I said. "Is that why they're angry? They've been denied them."

"Hold on," he said. "One of them's saying about you: 'It's a comparison, and . . . it is something new.' I don't understand. I don't understand."

"Alright, my love, just . . ."

"Hey," Scile whispered. "They're using the other figures of speech." He indicated our Embassytown companions, at whom the Hosts stared. He turned his head in surprise. "If I understand them . . . that man Hasser—he lied to us. He's not an example: he's a simile, like you."

Whatever the question marks over my efficacy, I must have had my uses: for the several weeks these events were in vogue, the Hosts kept bringing me back.

*

113

SOMETHING SOURED between CalVin and me. For weeks during our sex I'd teased them that I could tell the difference in the way they touched me: they probably knew there was a little truth to it. When we'd first got together I'd been immaturely excited that I was *sleeping with an Ambassador*. But that rather performed giddiness didn't last long.

I remember the feel of them, the cool of their links in their necks, minimalist jewellery amplifying their thoughts into each other. I remember watching them touch each other—peculiar, unique erotics. Afterwards, I might grin salaciously when I distinguished them, but it was an edgy game. "Cal," I would say, pointing at one, then the other. "Vin. Cal . . . Vin." They might smile, might look away. I could sometimes, especially in the mornings, see differences. The marks of night-time—a face imprinted by a pillow, particular bags below eyes. CalVin never left long before ablutions, locking the door to the correction chamber and emerging with all those tiny differences effaced or copied.

They didn't like that I was being asked back to the conferences and conventions. But Staff would hardly turn down Host requests like that. Once one of CalVin told me in sudden fury, apropos of nothing I'd noticed, that Ambassadors had no bloody power at all, that the other Staff and viziers and the rest made all the bloody decisions, that he and his doppel had less say than anyone.

I argued with them, now, sometimes. After one really unpleasant altercation I swear I did not start, Cal or Vin stayed for seconds in the doorway staring at me, with an expression I couldn't read, while his doppel walked away. Perhaps I wouldn't have liked it if they could immerse, I supposed. I doubted I would have cared, though.

"It's not the same," I said to the one still there. "You speak Language. I am it."

THERE WERE HOSTS who favoured my simile above all others, and came to every event at which I was present. They extolled my uses, over all the allegories or rhetorical devices embedded in varying ways in men and women and other things present. "You have fans," Scile said. These were my months of simile fame.

I saw Hasser several other times; we would stand and wait while we were deployed in harsh arguments. There were Language dissidents, urging a reconception of what I and the other similes might have been. From the reactions of the other Hosts, this thought-experiment was in bad taste. After one such, I asked Scile if he'd heard the Hosts speak to Hasser, and if so what he was about.

Scile understood Language as well as an Ambassador, but "I don't know how you bloody things work," he said. "I never see any relation between what you mean and what they're talking about, what they compare you with and use you for. So are you asking what do they *think* with Hasser? I've no idea."

"That isn't what I mean."

"You mean *literally* what does he mean?"

"Right. Like, foundation-fact, like I mean *girl who ate* . . . well, you know."

Scile hesitated. "I'm not sure," he said, "but I think it was, is . . . what they said was *it's like the boy who was opened up and closed again.*" We stared at each other.

"Oh God," I said.

"Yes. I can't be sure, so don't . . . but, yes."

"Jesus."

In the corvid, being hauled back to Embassytown, I said to Hasser, "Why didn't you tell me you were a simile?"

"Sorry," he said. "Overheard, then?" He smiled. "It's complicated. It's something I think about a lot, being simile. But I don't know how you feel about it . . . For some of us, if you're . . . If you want to talk about this stuff," and he sounded guarded but excited, "there are a few of us who think it's important."

"Similes?" I said. "You, what, hang out?"

Well. They knew other tropes and Language moments too, of course, he explained. But it was certain of the similes in particular who had found a community with each other. I despised them instantly he told me.

"I don't know how we missed you," he said. "I know they say you, but how did the Hosts miss you for these events all this time? How did you miss us?"

"I suppose being Language was never the main thing in my life," I said. I think I accidentally showed my contempt. If I'd not learnt to immerse and hadn't got into the out, I reminded myself, I might have spent my days in the bars and halls and drink houses where these similes gathered. It must be a strange kind of life and notoriety, but it was something. I wanted to apologise for showing my sneer. I asked him what it all meant to him. After an initial guardedness, he said, "To be part of it! Language."

Latterday, 5

Nᴏɴᴇ ᴏꜰ ᴜs with any nous believed the party was really back to normal. "Ehrsul." I whispered to her and made motions, but when, winding her long chassis precisely she pathed her way to me, it was to tell me she couldn't hack any coms to work out what was happening.

I found a couple of the last Ambassadors in the room, MagDa and EsMé. "What's going on?" I said to them. "Hey. MagDa. Please."

"We have to . . ." one of EsMé said. "It's . . ." "Everything's under control."

"MagDa. What's going on?"

Mag and Da and Es and Mé looked as if they were going to say something. EsMé had never liked me, had a common Ambassador opinion of the returned outgoer, immerser, floaker, and so on, but still, they hesitated.

To my great shock Scile appeared beside us. He met my eyes, either without emotion or hiding it. "MagDa," he said. "You have to come and talk to Ra."

They nodded and I lost that moment. As the five of them walked away, I grabbed Scile's arm. I kept my face impassive, and he looked back at me similarly. It hardly surprised me that he was closer to whatever was happening than I. He'd been working with Staff, he'd been in cahoots with Ambassadors. They'd always been so focused on using Language they weren't used to learning about it, and as things had shifted in Embassy-town, and it had become useful to think about such questions, they had, I understood, been fascinated with his theories. His work had made him useful. He had certainly been to more Staff functions than I had.

"So?" I said. I was only slightly surprised at my brazen self. Floakers did what they had to. "What's going on?"

"Avvy," he said. "I can't tell you."

"Scile, do you know what's happening?"

"No. I don't. I'd a . . . I really don't. This isn't what I expected." Near us two people touched wine glasses like little bells. The musicians were drunk now and the music was veering. This was the single chance many locals would have to meet the immerser crew, and they were taking advantage. Seeing pairs and little groups leave the party, I remembered that borrowed sex appeal of immer. I'd benefited from it myself on my return: it had been a heady few weeks.

"I have to go," Scile said. "They need me."

Es took one of his arms, Mé the other. They surely knew relations were bad between Scile and me, and perhaps even why. I doubt they were sleeping with him. Scile's assignations were brief and occasional. Though all Bremen marriages were legal in Embassytown, locals tended to invoke exclusive, property-based models. I *was* jealous of Scile, of course, but at what he'd become, and what secrets he knew.

IT WAS HALF an hour to my flat. Ehrsul came with me. In a lot of countries I've been in the populace all have personal vehicles. All but the largest streets of Embassytown were too narrow, and often too steep, for that. There were altanimals and some biorigged carriages to take certain routes, which switched from wheels or treads to legs where necessary, but most people went on foot.

Embassytown was a small and crowded place, our population

growth limited by the edge of the aeoli breath. It was surrounded by the Host city, except at the very northern point, where Ariekene plains started. Semilegal urban growth was tolerated, jury-rigged rooms sutured to walls, looming over alleys like eaves, thrown up on roofs, always ready to be abandoned. Most Staff tacitly approved of such enterprising space-maximisation. Here and there were half-trained biorigged bits and pieces, some backstreet-crossbred with Terretech and holding together through luck, tended aspects of domesticity.

Arced over Embassytown was the Embassy itself, edging up to those plains. At something over a hundred metres it was the tallest building we had. A fat pillar, studded with horizontal boughs and landing pads, to and from which, even so late, bioluminescent corvids moved. Like something melted, the Embassy spread out at its base and became part of the streets that surrounded it. Staff neighbourhoods were half-covered, as much the innards of the Embassy itself as alleyways. Ehrsul and I descended by panelled lift, through walkways, corridors that became things between corridors and streets, arcades half-open, with unglazed windows, and then into the streets proper, and the breeze.

"God, it's nice to get outside," I said.

"We're not, not really," Ehrsul said. "We're all always in the aeoli breath." A room of air.

It made me think about her, that she didn't leave Embassytown, though she could have. She wasn't programmed to be interested in the city, I supposed. I shied away from that. In my rooms I sipped more wine, and Ehrsul companionably made trid visions of a similar glass, made her trid head drink from it. She patched into my station but could find out nothing about the evening's occurrences on the localnet.

"I'll try again when I get home," she said. "No offence but your machine . . . you'd have more luck banging rocks together."

I'd been to her home several times. It was tiny, and sparse, but there were pictures on the walls, a kitchen, furniture for human and other guests (one beautiful, obscene-looking Shur'asi stool). Her flat and its tasteful accoutrements were perhaps for my and others' benefits: her pictures, her coffee table, her imported rug elements of an operating system, designed to make her user-friendly. These ruminations felt disgraceful. I wondered about EzRa.

Formerly, 4

HASSER BUZZED ME. "How did you get my number?" I said.

"Please," he said. He didn't sound particularly intimidated, though I was deploying my best fuck-you immerser swagger. "It's not hard to track you down. Come and have a drink."

"Why would I come and have a drink?"

"Please," he said. "There are people you should really meet."

The similes met in an amiably collapsing part of Embassytown, near our young ruins. I took a long route, walking for most of the morning, past many ignored and homeless automa. I even passed the coin wall and as I always did glanced at the door.

There are slums on Charo City, and I've spent more time than I'd like in their environs. Many of the ports at which I've docked are in or by such areas: it's as if slumism is an infection carried by ships. When in the course of Embassytown parties, members of reformer factions started mouthing, I tended to interrupt them. "Slums?" I'd say. "Believe me, my friend, I've seen slums. You know where I've been? I know from slums. We don't have slums."

In Embassytown there were no rag-draped children playing with paper boats in stinking water, in potholes; no people selling themselves for food to immersers and people from the out, nor hawking bits of their DNA or flesh to bioccaneers; wattle-and-daub huts didn't shake as ships rose and descended overhead, didn't collapse every few landings. Our social graphs were pretty flat: differentials of money and power were minor. Excepting Staff, and Ambassadors.

The wallscreens and projectors in our unkempt areas were on forgotten loops, their cycles degraded. Some advertised discontinued products, or luxuries from the out of which I knew there had been none left for a long time. Here as elsewhere in Embassytown the walls were overgrown with ivy and altivy, and specked with a local moss-analogue, so the light from those advertisements and crude public art was dappled with leaf-shadows.

There were places where, pushed through the foliage, embedded in bricks and plastone, pipes siphoned information from or fed illicit and troublemaking opinions to the screens. I walked in the glimmer of hacked denunciations of Bremen, threats of violence to Wyatt and his small staff. A demagogic trid ghost muttered about freedoms, democracies and taxation. Even Wyatt would hardly have been very concerned about this half-hearted radical's display, though I'm sure he would have excoriated the constabulary for failing to take such graffiti offline.

I was in a shopping street specialising in leather and altleather. I smelt tanning and guts by a shop where ripe purses were being harvested from a biorigged tree. The butchers cut them with skill, making a slit to which they would attach a clasp, scooping out innards and readying the skins for sealing. In the rear was a crop of immature umbrellas, silly luxuries weakly flexing their vespertilian canopies. The altleather goods were simple, mouthless, arseless things which couldn't have lived: the viscera that slopped in the shop's gutter were vague and meaningless.

At least a dozen similes were gathered in the wine-café called The Cravat, to where I'd been directed. Its trid sign stalked endlessly in front of it, a figure failing to do up its neckpiece. I stepped through it (an unexpected flourish of tridware making it look up as if startled before reverting to its loop) and inside.

"Avice!" Hasser was delighted. "Introductions . . . Darius, who wore tools instead of jewellery; Shanita, who was kept blind and awake for three nights; Valdik, who swims every week with fishes." He went round the room like that. "This is Avice," he said, "who ate what was given to her."

OF COURSE we were hardly all the similes the Ariekei spoke. Some were animal or inanimate: there was a house in Embassytown out of which, many years before, the Hosts had taken all the furniture, then put it back, to allow some figure of speech. The split stone, made so they could speak the thought, *it's like the stone that was split and put together again*. Most, though, were Terre men and women: there was something in us that facilitated.

Many similes, of course, were uninterested in their status. There were I gathered one or two among Staff. Even Ambassadors. They never came.

"They don't like being Language," Hasser said. "It makes them feel vulnerable—they like *speaking* Language, not being it. Plus they'd have to hobnob with commoners." He spoke with the complicated amalgam of respect and resentment I'd heard before and would again, many times.

We talked about Language, and what it meant to be what we were. They talked: mostly I listened. I tried to keep the irritations their blather raised to myself. I'd come, after all. A disproportionate number of the similes seemed, to varying degrees, to be independencers. They said this and that about Bremen's benighted hand and ruthless agents. Having met Wyatt, this in particular made me snort.

"I don't see any of you turning down anything from the miab," I said.

"No," someone answered, "but we should *trade*, instead of handing over bloody taxes and aid."

Hasser gave me sotto voce information about my interlocutors as they spoke, like a vizier in the ears of an Ambassador. "She's just bitter because she doesn't get called very often. Her simile's too recondite." "He's less a simile than an example, honestly. And he knows it." When I went home I was peppery about them all. I told Scile how ridiculous a scene it was. But I went back. I've thought a lot about why I did. Which does not mean I could explain it.

On my second trip, Valdik, who every week swam with fishes, told the story of his similification. He was an ongoing: his status depended not on something that he had done or had done to him, but on something he had to continue to do. *It's like the man who swims with fishes every week*, the Hosts might want to say, to make whatever obscure point it was, and to allow them that, it had to be true that he did. Hence his duty.

"There's a marble bath in Staff quarters," Valdik said. Glanced up at me, back down. "They shipped it years ago, all the way through the immer. They put little altfish in with me, which can take the chlorine. I swim every Overday." I suspected he spent the eleven days between each such trip preparing for the next. I did not know what efforts were made to ensure such activities were ongoing, the tenses of the Hosts' similes accurate. I wondered if that was part of the Ambassadors' slight unease with us: the possibility of a simile strike.

When it was my turn, I told my new companions about the restaurant, and the things I ate, and it was unpleasant enough, what had happened, that I accrued some credibility. Some of them stared at me; one or two, like Valdik, were avoiding looking at me at all. "Welcome home," said someone quietly. I hated that and stopped policing my expressions, made sure they could see that I hated it. And I hated that when he took his own turn, described terrible things done to enLanguage him, Hasser, who had been opened and closed again, modulated his voice and timed his delivery and turned it, true as it was, into a story.

Latterday, 6

A CITIZEN WHO didn't spend much time at the Embassy might not have seen that anything was wrong: the checkpoints were manned; Staff and Staff-apprentices were around; signs still appeared in trid and flatscreen glowing information. Disquiet, though, was palpable, since the party, to those who knew.

No ship had ever left with such an unfocused valedictory as our last arrival. Of course sufficient pomp had been attempted. Soon enough after the Arrival Ball that some were still cheerfully dishevelled, the immerser crew had been seen off on their boat by a gathering of Ambassadors, Staff and people like me, Embassytowners holding their breath until, left alone, they could deal with whatever it was that was happening. In fact, they, we, didn't deal with it at all. There were those among the Staff, I picked up later, who had tried to insist that the ship not leave.

I, Avice Benner Cho, immerser, first a lover then an ex of CalVin (some Embassytowners probably thought it a lie, that, but it was part of me and was also true), advisor to Staff on out-business, had my entry to the state offices blocked by a nervous constable. In the end it didn't take much. A little floaking—*I think you've made a mistake, Officer,* a moment's *But that's precisely why I'm here, they wanted my help*—and I was passed. I had no illusions about my real stock to insiders. But to have to go through that simply to get into the hallways?

Inside there wasn't even a pretence at calm. I jostled past Staff whispering arguments with each other. I looked for EdGar, or someone I knew would talk to me. "What are you *doing* here?" said Ag or Nes of AgNes, her doppel shaking her head. They were rather *grandes dames*, and paid no attention to my muttered response. "I'd get going, girl." "You'll only be . . ." ". . . in the way." Others were less dismissive—RanDolph gave me smiles and mimed exhaustion, a high-ranking vizier I'd once got drunk with even winked at me—but AgNes were right, I was an obstruction.

In a top-floor teahouse, overlooking our roofscape and its segue into the outlines of the city, I found Simmon, from Security, and cornered him. After obligatory protestations that he knew nothing, that he couldn't tell me anything, he said, "I've not seen Ambassador EzRa since the party. I don't know where they've gone. According to the original schedule they were due to be part of a meet-and-greet half an hour ago, but they never turned up. Mind you they weren't the only ones. Plans have mostly gone to shit. Where in hell are the Hosts?"

Good question. Discussions of major issues between Embassytown and the Hosts—mining rights, our farms, technology barter, Language celebrations—were only occasional, but every day, there were minutiae that had to be agreed. There were always a few Ariekei in the corridors, for one or other negotiation. The Embassy was toughly floored, to withstand their point-feet.

"They're not here," Simmon said. He massaged the odd flesh of his biorigged arm. "None of them. We've had generations to compromise with them on what constitutes an appointment, so we know fine bloody well that several were supposed to be here this morning, and would normally have been, and they're not. They're not returning any of our buzzes. They're not communicating with us at all."

"We must have offended them pretty badly," I said at last.

"Looks like it," he said.

"How, do you think?"

"Pharotekton bloody knows how. Or EzRa knows." Neither of us said anything for a moment. "Do you know someone called Oratee?" he said. "Or Oratees?"

"No. Who's that?" It hadn't sounded like an Ambassador: a strange name with no ghost-stress halfway through it.

"I don't know. I heard CalVin and HenRy talking about them, sounded as if they'd know what's going on. I thought you might know them. You know everyone." It was nice of him, but I didn't have it in me to play that up. "AgNes and a couple of other Ambassadors blame Wyatt for this, you know."

"For what?"

"For whatever. For whatever it is that happened. I heard them. 'This is all down to him and Bremen,' they were saying. 'We always knew they were undermining us, well here we are . . .'" Simmon made his prosthetic hand move open-closed to show a talkative mouth.

"So they know what's going on, then?" He shrugged.

"Don't think so, but. You don't have to understand something to blame someone for it," he said. "They're right, anyway. This has to be a . . . manoeuvre, no question. EzRa . . . some Bremen weapon."

What if AgNes were right? If so, and I played the particular last contact-card I had, it would be, I supposed, a betrayal of Embassytown. CalVin and Scile came to my mind and I overcame any hesitation. I buzzed Wyatt. As I connected I tried to think strategically, to work out where and how he was professional, where likely to bend, trying to work out what to say that might actually gain me some insight, persuade him to divulge something. The payoff to all this skulduggery was sheer bathos.

"Avice," Wyatt shouted when I got through. "Thank God

you called. I can't get anyone to pick up over there. For fuck's sake, Avice, what's going on?"

HE WAS MORE CUT OFF even than me. He and his few assistants had offices in the heart of the Embassy, of course, but some Staff blamed him, others wanted to keep him out of whatever was happening, and all agreed they should caucus without him. They managed to do so never quite breaching the law that placed him, their Bremen overseer, above them.

They had circulated, as they were obliged to, a list of all that day's many meetings. Wyatt had sent officers to all those in main halls, and had gone himself to one titled "Emergency Organisation" to discover that all these were sideshows, anxious extemporised discussions between mid-level Staff over issues such as stationery acquisition. The real debates, post-mortems on the party, hypotheses about the Hosts' silence, had happened already, during the Any Other Business sessions of meetings of the Public Works Committee.

"It's a fucking outrage, Avice!" he said. "That's exactly the kind of thing that has to stop, that is *exactly* the sort of thing we've been sent to put an end to. They have *conspired* to keep me out. I'm their bloody superior! Not to mention what they're doing to EzRa—these men are their colleagues, and they're ostracising them. It's a disgrace."

"Wyatt, wait. Where are EzRa?"

"Ra's in his room, or he was when I buzzed him. Ez I don't know. Your colleagues—"

"They're not my—"

"Your colleagues are freezing them out. I'm sure they'd arrest them if they could. Ez's not answering, and I can't find him . . ." The notion of an Ambassador having separate rooms, doing different things, still reeled me.

"Do they know what's going on?"

"Don't you think they'd tell me?" he said. "It's not *everyone* here who tries to cut me out, you realise, just your bloody Ambassadors. Whatever it is they're hatching . . ."

"Wyatt calm down. Whatever's going on, you can see Staff aren't in any more control than you." He must have known the Embassy had had no contact of any kind from the city, since that night. "The Hosts aren't saying anything. I think . . ." I said carefully, "I think EzRa . . . or we . . . must have accidentally done something that offended them . . . badly . . ."

"Oh, bullshit," Wyatt said. I blinked. "This isn't one of those stories, Avice. One moment of cack-handedness, Captain Cook offends the bloody locals, one slip of the tongue or misuse of sacred cutlery, and bang, he's on the grill. Do you ever think how self-aggrandising that stuff is? Oh, all those stories pretend to be *mea culpa*s about cultural insensitivity, *oops we said the wrong thing*, but they're really all about how ridiculous natives overreact." He laughed and shook his head. "Avice, we must have made *thousands* of fuckups like that over the years. Think about it. Just like *our* visitors did when they first met our lot, on Terre. And for the most part we didn't lose our shit, did we? The Ariekei—and the Kedis, and Shur'asi, and Cymar and what-have-you, pretty much all the exots I've ever dealt with— are perfectly capable of understanding when an insult's intended, and when it's a misunderstanding. Behind every Ku and Lono story, there's . . . pilfering and cannon-fire. Believe me," he added wryly. "It's my job." He made thieving-fingers motions. It was because he would say things like that that I liked him.

"There's always argy-bargy, Avice," he said, and leaned toward the screen. "Job like mine. I've not shown bad form, have I?" He said this suddenly almost plaintively. "But this . . .

Avice, there are limits. JoaQuin and MayBel and that lot—they need to remember what I represent."

Bremen was a power, so always at war, with other countries on Dagostin, and on other worlds. What if enemies sent battleships in *our* direction? Kicked Bremen in the colonies? What, were we going to raise our rifles, our biorigged cannons, aim at the skies? Any comeback for a little genocide like that, which they could offhandedly commit, would have to come from Bremen itself, if it calculated it worth it. Mêlées in the vacuum of sometimes-space, or terrible strange firefights in the immer. That threat, and Arieka's isolation in rough immer—and, though it went unspoken, our lack of importance—were the deterrents against attacks at that level. But there were other factors in Bremen's martial calculations.

The Ariekei were not pacifists. They sometimes conducted obscure internecine murders and feuds, I had been told; and whatever Wyatt said, whatever the reasons, there had been violent confrontations, deaths, between our species, in the early years of contact. Protocols between us were very firm, and for generations, there'd been no trouble in relations. So it felt absurd to imagine the Ariekei, the city, ever turning against Embassytown. But we were some thousands, and they were many many times that, and they had weapons.

Wyatt was more than a bureaucrat. He represented Bremen, officially our protector; and as such, he must be armed. His staff were suspiciously athletic for office workers. It was well known that there were weapon caches in Embassytown, to which Wyatt alone had access. The hidden silos were rumoured to contain firepower of a different magnitude from our own paltry guns. There for our benefit, of course, the claim was. Bremen officials arrived with the keys deep-coded in their augmens. It was impolitic and a little frightening of Wyatt to state so blatantly, even to me, an outsider of sorts and a friend of his, of sorts, that his staff were soldiers, with access to arms, and he their CO.

It was true that he was patient. He ignored Embassytown's minor-to-moderate embezzlement when the miabs came, and every few years when Bremen taxes were collected. He encouraged his officers to mix with Staff and commoners, and even sanctioned the occasional intermarriage. Like all colonial postings, his was a difficult job. With communication with his bosses so occasional, initiative and flexibility were vital. We'd had officious women and men in his post before, and it had made ugly politics. In return for his softly-softly stance Wyatt felt owed. That the Ambassadors were unfair.

I liked Wyatt but he was naïve. He was Bremen's man, when the lights went out. I understood that and what it meant, even if he did not.

Formerly, 5

HOSTS WOULD SOMETIMES bob into view, alone or in small groups, zelles at their feet, walking their slowed-down scuttle through our alleyways. Who can say what their errands were? Perhaps they were sightseeing, or taking what, according to odd topographies, were shortcuts, into our quarter and out again. Some came deep into the aeoli breath, right into Embassytown neighbourhoods, and of these some were looking for the similes. These Ariekei were fans.

Every few days one or two or a little conclave would arrive with dainty chitin steps. They would enter The Cravat, their fanwings twitching, wearing clothes for display—sashes fronded with fins and filigrees that each caught the wind with a particular sound, as distinct as garish colours.

"Our public demands us," someone said the first time I saw such an approach. Despite the faux-weary joke anyone could tell that this audience meant a great deal to the similes. The one time I persuaded Ehrsul to come with me, ostensibly to store up anecdotes so we could later laugh at my new acquaintances, the arrival of some Hosts seemed to discombobulate her. She ignored my whispers about the Ariekei, did not speak much except in brief polite non sequiturs. I'd been with her in Hosts' company before, of course, but never in so informal a setting, never according to their unknown whims, not terms requested by Embassytown panjandrums. She never came back.

The owners and regular clientele of The Cravat would courteously ignore the Hosts, which would murmur to each other. Their eye-corals would crane and the tines separate, looking us over as we looked back. Waiters and customers stepped smoothly around them. The Hosts would talk quietly as they examined us.

"Says it's looking for the one who balanced metal," someone would translate. "That's you, Burnham. Stand up, man! Make yourself known." "They're talking about your clothes, Sasha." "That one says I'm more useful than you are—says he speaks me all the time." "That's *not* what it says, you cheeky sod . . ." So on. When the Hosts gathered around me, sometimes I had to suppress a moment of memory of child-me in that restaurant.

I didn't find it hard to recognise repeat visitors, by that configuration of eye-corals, those patterns on the fanwing. With the exhilaration of minor blasphemy we christened them according to these peculiarities: Stumpy, Croissant, Fiver. They, it seemed, recognised each of us as easily.

We learnt the favourite similes of many. One of my own regular articulators was a tall Host with a vivid black-and-red fanwing, just enough like a flamenco dress for us to call it Spanish Dancer.

"It does this brilliant thing," Hasser said to me. He knew I was hardly fluent. "When it talks about you." I could see him groping for nuances. "'When we talk about talking,' it says, 'most of us are like the girl who ate what was given to her. But we might *choose* what we say with her.' It's virtuoso." He shrugged at my expression and would have left it, but I made him explain.

In the main my simile was used to describe a kind of making do. Spanish Dancer and its friends, though, by some odd rhetoric, by emphasis on a certain syllable, spoke me rather to imply potential change. That was the kind of panache that could get Hosts ecstatic. I had no idea whether many of them had always been so fascinated by Language, or whether that obsession resulted from their interactions with the Ambassadors, and with us strange Languageless things.

Scile always wanted details of what had happened, who had said what, which Hosts had been there. "It's not fair," I told him. "You won't come with me, but you get annoyed if I can't repeat every tedious thing anyone said?"

"I wouldn't be welcome and you know it." That was true. "Why do you keep going if it's so dull?"

It was a reasonable question. The excitement with which the other similes reacted to the Host visitors, and the range, or its lack, of what they talked about when there were no Hosts there, irritated me, greatly, every time. I think I had, though, a sense that this was where things might occur, that this was important.

THERE WAS A HOST who often accompanied Spanish Dancer. It was squatter than most, its legs gnarled, its underbelly more pendulous, as it approached old age. For some reason I forget we named it Beehive.

"I've seen it before," said Shanita. It spoke incessantly, and we listened, but it seemed a mixture of half-sentences. We could make no sense of what it said. I remembered where I knew it from: my first-ever journey into the city. It had competed at that Festival of Lies. It had been unusually able to misdescribe that untruth-target object. It had called the thing some wrong colour.

"It's a liar," I said. I was clicking my fingers. "I've seen it before too."

"Hm," said Valdik. He looked rather suspicious. "What's it saying now?" Beehive was circling, watching us, scratching at the air with its giftwing.

"'Like this, like this,'" Hasser translated. He shook his head,

I've no idea. "'Like, they are, similar, different, not the same, the same.'"

The Cravat wasn't the only place we met, but it was by far the most common venue. Occasionally we might get together in a restaurant near the shopping districts, or the canalside benches of another parlour, but only when planned in advance and only from some vague sense of propriety, of not being hidebound. The Cravat, though, was where the Hosts had come to know they might find us, and being so found was very much the point.

The similes thought of themselves as a salon of debate, but only a certain range of dissidence was permissible. Once a young man tried to engage us with arguments that turned from independence to seditionism, anti-Staffist stuff, and I had to intervene to save him from a beating.

I took him outside. "Go," I told him. A crowd of the similes were gathered, jeering, shouting at him to come back and try impugning the Ambassadors one more time.

He said, "I thought they were supposed to be radicals." He looked so forlorn I wanted to give him a hug.

"That lot? Depends who you ask," I said. "Yeah, they'd be traitors according to Bremen. But they're more loyal to *Staff* than the Staff are."

Plebiscite politics were absurd in Embassytown. As if any of us could speak to Hosts! And for The Cravat crew, even ignoring the fact of Embassytown's inevitable collapse in the event of their absence, without Ambassadors, who would speak these men and women so proud of being similes to the Hosts?

Latterday, 7

THE ARIEKEI didn't respond to any attempts at contact. In those incommunicado hours, I more than once considered buzzing CalVin, or Scile, to demand information: they would be more likely than anyone else I knew to have some. It wasn't the confrontation that stopped me, but the conviction that I wouldn't be able to shame or bully anything out of them.

It was a spring in Embassytown and the chill was dissipating. From high in the Embassy I looked over the roofscape of the city, to animalships and blinking architecture. Something was changing. A colour or its lack, a motion, a palsy.

A corvid rose from an Embassy landing pad, moved through the sky to the city's airspace, edged from place to place, hovering, looking for somewhere to land; defeated, it returned. The Ambassadors aboard must have sent messages down to the various housebodies they overflew, without response.

There were probably still plenty of Embassytowners who didn't yet know anything was wrong. The official press were loyal or inefficient. But there had been many people at that party, and stories were spreading.

THE SUN still rose, and the shops sold things, and people went to work. It was a slow catastrophe.

I called the number Ehrsul had given me, which she had extracted from a newly and imperfectly upgraded net, which she had told me was Ez's. He—or whomever it was I'd called—

137

didn't answer. I kept swearing, as quietly as I could make myself, and tried again, again without result.

Later I learnt that that day, in desperation, Ambassadors went into the city on foot. Pairs of desperate doppels accosted the Hosts they met, speaking Language at them through the transmitters of their aeoli helmets and receiving polite non-answers, or incomprehension, or unhelpful intimations of disaster.

Someone came to my house. I opened the door and it was Ra, standing there on my threshold. I stared at him in silence for long seconds.

"You look surprised," he said.

"Understatement," I said. I stepped aside for him. Ra kept taking his buzzer out and making as if to switch it off, then leaving it on. "They trying to reach you?" I said.

"Only Wyatt," he said.

"Really? No one else? No Ambassadors? You not being followed?"

"How are you?" he said. "I was thinking . . ." We sat for a long time on chairs facing each other. He looked over his shoulder, behind himself, more than once. There was nothing there but my wall.

"Where's Ez?" I said.

He shrugged. "He's gone out."

"Shouldn't you be together?" He shrugged again. "In the Embassy? Look, Ra, how did you even get out? I'd have thought they'd have you on bloody lockdown." If it had been me in charge, I would have incarcerated EzRa, to control the situation, or contain it, whatever the situation was. Perhaps they had tried. But if Ra was telling the truth, both the new Ambassador had got away.

"Yeah, well," he said. "You know. Needs must. I just wanted

to . . . Had to split." I had to laugh a second at that. There had to be quite a story there.

"So," I said eventually. "How do you like our little town?" He laughed in turn.

"Jesus," he said. As if he'd seen something good and unexpected. Outside, gulls sounded. They veered, headed constantly for the sea they glimpsed kilometres away, were turned back constantly by sculpted winds and aeoli breath. It was very rare that any broke out into the proper local air, and died.

"You have to help me," he said. "I need to know what's going on."

"Are you *joking*?" I said. "What do you think I know? Jesus, this is a comedy of errors. What do you think I've been trying to find out, for God's sake? Why have *you* come to *me*?"

"I've spoken to everyone I could find who was at that party—"

"Didn't try very hard, did you, if you only just got to me . . ."

"All the Staff, I mean, and other people from the Embassy. The higher-up ones wouldn't say anything to me, and the rest . . . A couple of them told me to talk to you."

"Well, I don't know why. I thought you were in the middle of it all, I thought you'd . . ."

"Whoever up there does know something, they're not telling me. Us. But these others, they just . . . They said you know people, Avice. Ambassadors. And that people tell you things."

I shook my head. "That's just bloody outsider-chic," I exhaled. "You thought you could go a roundabout way, get something through me? They're just saying that because I'm immerser. And because I was sleeping with CalVin, for a while. But not for months. Local months, not Bremen months. My own damn *husband's* a foreigner and he knows more than me, and he won't even talk to me." I stared at him. "You seriously telling me you've got no idea what's happening? Does Wyatt know you're here?"

"No. He helped me slip away, but . . . And neither does Ez. It's not their business." He bit his lip. "Well, officially it is, I mean . . . I just wanted . . ." After a silence, Ra met my eye. He stood. "Look," he said, all of a sudden calm. "I need to find out what's going on. Wyatt is worse than useless. Ez's trying to pull rank. We'll see how far that gets him. And I hear you might know people who know things." In that moment he seemed not like Ez's luggage, but an officer and an agent of a colonial power.

"Tell me," I said at last. "What you *do* know. What's been going on. What you've heard, suspect, anything."

The Hosts had come back. Two days of silence, and then they had been at the Embassy, a troupe of heavy presences swaying across a landing pod. "At least forty of them," he said. "Christ knows how they fit into their vessel. They were asking for me and Ez."

The way he told it, the Ariekei had barely responded to Ambassadors' questions and greetings. They demanded, repeatedly and with strange rudeness, to speak to EzRa.

"I trained for this," Ra said. "I've studied them, I've studied Language. You saw the first group meet us at the party? That wasn't normal, was it? I knew it wasn't. This was the same, only more. They were . . . agitated. Talking nonsense. I was there already, but then Ez came in and *then* they recognised us. Started saying: 'Please, good evening Ambassador EzRa, please, please, yes.' Like that.

"Some of the others—like your friends CalVin—tried to get in our way. Telling us no. We'd *said too much*." He shook his head. "And the Hosts are edging closer and closer. We've got nowhere to go, and they're huge. It's feeling . . . So we just . . . raised our voices and spoke Language. Ez and I. We said good evening. Told them it was an honour. And when we did—"

When they spoke the same thing happened as had before, but this time to a larger little multitude. I might have been able to track down footage or trid of the occurrence—there must have been vespcams there—but Ra told me and I could easily imagine it. The crowd of Hosts stiffening; some staggering; maybe tumbling in carapace piles. Sounds, the double-calls of Ariekene distress, becoming something unfamiliar, counter-points. Were they swooning? Their noises went up and down in complex relation to EzRa's voice. "We tried to keep going," Ra said. "To keep talking. But in the end Ez just petered out. So I did too." When they did, the Host in front rebudded open its eyes and craned them backwards at its companions, without turning its body, and said to them: "I told you."

The Ariekei had staggered in the wood-walled stateroom, with the concrete of Embassytown beyond, and the sky dusted with birds in their air-cage. The Ambassadors and Staff were left standing half to attention and bewildered.

We thought of Ariekei in terms of stuff from an antique world—we looked at our Hosts and saw insect-horse-coral-fan things. Those were chimeras of our own baggage. There they were, the Hosts, humming polyphonically in reveries that were utterly their own.

"They left. Some Ambassadors were trying to stop them but short of actually getting in their way, what could they do? They were shouting at them to stay, to talk. EdGar and LoGan were screaming, JoaQuin and AgNes were . . . trying to be more persuasive. But the Hosts just marched back out. Me and Ez were saying what should we do, and CalVin and ArnOld were saying we'd done quite enough." He held his head in his hands.

"Now not even MagDa'll talk to us. I haven't seen them for days. Don't you *want* to know what's going on?"

"Of course," I said. "Don't be absurd."

"There was a lot of shouting."

"Who's Oratees?" I said.

"I don't know," he said. "Why?"

"CalVin and HenRy mentioned them," I said. Simmon's half-heard insight. "I think they might be who to find. I thought you might know . . ."

"You mean Oratees, or CalVin, or HenRy might be who to find?"

"I don't know," I said. ". . . Yes." I shrugged, *Yes, why not?*

"I thought you could help," he said. "People have a lot of faith in your abilities."

"Did they tell you I can floak?" I said. "I wish I'd never told them that fucking word. They think I can do anything now. Except they don't, really: they just want the opportunity to say 'floak'."

"They're talking to the exots." Ra said. "The Ambassadors have to let the Kedis and the others know something's happening. They were obviously hoping they'd have things under control, but . . ." My doorbell sounded again. "Wait," he said, but I was already up and out of the room.

I opened my door to constables and Security officers. Some were men younger than me, looking shy.

"Ms. Benner Cho?" one said. "Sorry to disturb you. I believe, uh, is Ra here?" He stumbled over the lack of honorific.

"Avice, where is he?"

I knew that voice. "MagDa?" I said. I'd not seen them behind the escort.

The Ambassador pushed their way to the front. "We need to talk to them." "Urgently."

"Hello." It was Ra, come up behind me. I didn't turn.

"Ra." I thought they'd be furious, but Mag and Da looked just relieved to see him. Emotional. "There you are." "You have to come back."

"You need *protective custody*, sir," an officer said. MagDa seemed exasperated by that, in fact, but they didn't interrupt. "For your safety. Until we've got things under control. Please come with us."

Ra stood up tall. The officer met his eye. Ra nodded to me, after a moment, and let them take him. I nodded back. I was vaguely disappointed in him.

When they led him away they didn't lock his hands together. They walked respectfully beside him, like what they said they were, a protective corps. It was a sort of courtesy, I suppose, though I don't think anyone with a passing understanding of Embassytown politics wouldn't have known he was more or less under arrest. I watched him go, to join Ez, and perhaps Wyatt, in what I was sure would be scrupulously well-kept rooms, locked and guarded from the outside.

Formerly, 6

IN ITS RELIGIOUS LAWS Embassytown was a cutting from Bremen. There was no established church, but as with many smaller colonies, its founders had included a reasonable minority of faithful. The Church of God Pharotekton was as close as we came to an official congregation. Its lighthouse towers jutted through Embassytown roofs, their beacons spinning, rotating spokes of light at night.

There were other congregations: tiny synagogues; temples; mosques; churches, mustering a few score regulars. A handful of ultra-orthodox in each tradition stood firm against ungodly innovations, attempting to maintain religious calendars based on Bremen's thirty-seven-hour days, or according to insane nostalgia on the supposed days and seasons of Terre.

Like the Hosts, the Kedis of Embassytown had no gods: according to their professed faith the souls of their ancestors and of their unborn were united in a never-ending jealous war against them, the living, but they mostly displayed a far less bleak and embattled outlook than that theology would suggest. There were religious Shur'asi, but only dissidents: most were atheist, perhaps because apart from through accident, they didn't die and were very rarely born.

Embassytowners were free not to believe. I wasn't used to thinking about evil.

BEEHIVE'S NAME was $\frac{surl}{tesh\ echer}$, we gleaned from its conversations with other Hosts. I told CalVin, mangling the name with my monovoice, saying the Cut and Turn one after the other. "Can you find out when it's competing at another Festival of Lies?" I said. "It's a loyal fan of mine, and I'd like to . . . return the favour."

"You want to go . . ." ". . . to another festival?"

"Yeah. Me and another couple of the similes." It had occurred as a whim, mere curiosity about my observer, but having thought of it I could not let the idea go. When I'd mooted it to Hasser and a couple of the others, they'd been enthusiastic. "Do you think we could do that? Think you could get us in again?" It had been a while since we'd been summoned to any Languagefests, and though I was alone among them in being more intrigued by the lying than by my own deployment, the other Cravateers would hardly say no to any entry.

CalVin did pursue this, though not with the best grace. I wondered at the time why they were indulging me at all. One or the other always behaved with surliness to me. The differences in their demeanours were tiny, but I was used to Ambassadors and could sense them. I thought that they were taking turns to be colder and warmer, in a variant of traditional police procedure.

In The Cravat, conversations between the Hosts illuminated disagreements. They had camps, constituted by theories and arcane politics. Some seemed to love us—of course I shouldn't use that word—as spectacle. Some rated our various merits: we called them the critics. *The man who swims with the fishes is simple*, one said. *The girl who ate what was given to her is like more things*. Valdik laughed but wasn't happy to hear that the trope of him was trite. Beehive, which I started to call "Surl Tesh-echer", a failure closer to its name, was the guru of another group. Champion liar.

It had regular companions: Spanish Dancer; and one we called

Spindle; and one Longjohn—it had a biorigged replacement hoof. Of what any of us understood it's hard to approximate what they said in Anglo-Ubiq: think of people circling an exhibit in a gallery, staring at it, from time to time uttering a single word or short phrase, like "Incomplete", or "Potential", or "Intricacies of fact and uncertainties of expression", and occasional longer opaque things.

"'The birds circle like the girl who ate what was put in front of her,'" Hasser translated. "'The birds are like the girl who ate what was put in front of her and are like the man who swims with fishes and are like the split stone . . .'"

The other Ariekei, those not of $\frac{surl}{tesh\ echer}$'s party, loudly answered these garbled claims. They responded to the presence of $\frac{surl}{tesh\ echer}$ and its companions with excitement or agitation. Contrariwise, $\frac{surl}{tesh\ echer}$, Spanish Dancer and the others didn't acknowledge the critics at all, that I could tell. We called $\frac{surl}{tesh\ echer}$'s group the Professors.

$\frac{surl}{tesh\ echer}$ stretched the logic of analogy—the birds were *not* like me, having eaten the food given to me, as far as most of the other Ariekei could see. "They think it's being disrespectful when it says they are," Hasser said. He looked unhappy. *The birds are like the girl who ate what she was given*, one of the Professors said again. It stuttered as it spoke, it mangled its words, had to stop and start and try again.

AN EARLY winter day I came to The Cravat—still attending, I noted wryly—dirty with leaf-muck and cold dust from Embassytown alleys. Valdik was the only other simile there. He was uncomfortable with me, less talkative even than usual. I wondered if perhaps he'd had some bad news about his outside life, of which I knew and wanted to know nothing. We sat in silence that was not companionable.

After one coffee I was ready to leave, when Shanita and Darius came in together. She was a taciturn simile I'd always sensed was a bit intimidated by me; he was frank and ingenuous, not very smart. They greeted me pleasantly enough.

"Why was Scile here?" Darius said as he sat. I was aware of Valdik sitting still and not reacting.

"Scile?" I said.

"He was here again, earlier," Darius said. "A Host was here. Being really weird. Your husband, not the Host. He walked around putting little . . ." He fingered the air for the words. "Little nuts and bolts on all the tables. Wouldn't tell me why."

"Again? Here *again*?"

He had come once before when I was not there, it seemed, late at night, with three Hosts present. Darius hadn't seen it but Hasser had, and told him. That time Scile had been strangely dressed, in clothes all one colour. Shanita nodded at the anecdote. Scile had, she said, while Valdik said nothing, laid down the same objects that first time, too.

"What's that all about?" Darius said.

"I don't know," I said. I spoke carefully.

I suspected from his stillness that Valdik had an idea, in fact, as I did, what this might have been. That Scile, by these unnatural attention-getting rituals, was trying to stick in the mind. Trying to be good to think with, to be suggestive. To become a simile.

What the hell did he think he might mean? I thought, but corrected myself: that wouldn't matter.

A CORVID DROPPED us deep in the city, in astonishing rooms, catacombs in skin, alcoves full of house's organs sutured in place.

The hall was full of the interplaited cadences of Language.

147

I'd never seen so many young, just woken into their third instar and Language. They matched their parents in size and shape, but they were children and you could tell by the colour of their bellies and the way they were given to swaying. They were avid spectators while the liars tried to lie.

Most of the competitors could only be silent, failing in their struggle to say something not true. I was with Hasser, Valdik and a few others chosen from among our regulars I don't know how. We were chaperoned by ArnOld. They were there to perform and made it clear that they resented this babysitting duty. Hosts greeted them by their correct name: "$\frac{old}{arn}$".

Scile was with me. He was talking, tentatively, with my simile companions. It had been a fair time since he'd seen Language in its home; it was for him I'd asked for this: he knew it, had been shy with gratitude. We were not nearly so close as we'd been at the time of our first festival, and I think the present surprised him. I hadn't heard of any more efforts to enLanguage himself. I'd said nothing about any of them to him.

Before now the humans came. A Host, a lie-athlete, one of the Professors, I realised, was speaking.

Before the humans came we were . . . and it stalled. One of its companions continued. *Before the humans came we didn't speak so much of certain things.* A sensation went through the audience. It was followed by another speaker: *Before the humans came we didn't speak so much . . .*

I'd learnt enough to know this trick, a collaborative faux-mendacity: the last was repeating the previous sentence but dropping its voices to near nothing at the final clause. *Of certain things* was said, but so quietly the audience couldn't hear it. It was showmanship, fakery, a crowd-pleaser, and the crowd were pleased.

ArnOld stiffened and said together: " $\frac{surl}{tesh\ echer}$."

Beehive. It was swaying. Its giftwing circled, its fanwing stretched. It stepped up to the lying ground.

THERE WERE two main ways the few Ariekei who could lie a little could lie. One was to go slow. They would try to conceive the untrue clause—near-impossible, their minds reacting allergically to such a counterfactual even unspoken, conceived without signification. Having prepared it mentally, however successfully or un-, they would pretend-forget it to themselves. Speak each of its constituent words at a certain speed, at a beat, separated, apart enough in the mind of a speaker that each was a distinct concept, utterable with and as its own meaning; but just sufficiently fast and rhythmic that to listeners, they accreted into a ponderous but comprehensible, and untrue, sentence. The liars I had thus far seen with any success were slow-liars.

There was another technique. It was the more base and vivid, and by far harder. This was for the speaker to collapse, in their mind, even individual word-meanings, and simply to brute-utter all necessary sounds. To force out a statement. This was quick-lying: the spitting out of a tumble of noises before the untruth of their totality stole a speaker's ability to think them.

$\frac{surl}{tesh\ echer}$ opened its mouths.

Before the humans came, it said in ornery staccato, *we didn't speak*.

There was a long quiet. And then a convulsion, a riot.

I wished very much that I had any understanding of Ariekene body language. $\frac{surl}{tesh\ echer}$ might have been exuding triumph, patience, or nothing. It hadn't whispered the second half of any truth; or trudged sound-by-metronome-sound through a constructed-unconstructed sentence. What $\frac{surl}{tesh\ echer}$ had said was unquestionably a lie.

The audience reeled. I reeled.

THE HOSTS woke in their third instar suddenly fluent, Language a direct function of their consciousness. "Millions of years back there must have been some adaptive advantage to knowing that what was communicated was true," Scile said to me, last time we'd hypothesised this history. "Selection for a mind that could only express that."

"The evolution of trust . . ." I started to say.

"There's no need for trust, this way," he interrupted. Chance, struggle, failure, survival, a Darwinian chaos of instinctive grammar, the drives of a big-brained animal in a hard environment, the selection out of traits, had made a race of pure truth-tellers. "This Language is miraculous," Scile had said. I was somehow repulsed by it, in fact. It was astonishing, given what Language needs to do, that the Ariekei had survived. That, I decided, was what Scile must have meant, so I agreed.

If evolution was morality they would be unable to hear lies, too, like two-thirds of the fabular monkeys, but it's more random and beautiful, so that was only the case for those few who managed to speak them, of their own little untruths. Unbacked by signifieds, the lies of Language were just noises to their own liar. Biology's lazy: if mouths speak truth, why should ears discriminate between it and its opposite? When what was spoken was, definitionally, what was? And by this hole in adaptation, though or because they were not built to say them, the Hosts *could* understand lies. And either believe them—belief being a meaningless given—or, where the falsity was ostentatious and the point, experience them as some giddying impossible, the said unthinkable.

It's me who's monomaniacal, here: it's unfair to insinuate that all Hosts cared about was Language, but I can't fail to do so. This is a true story I'm telling, but I am telling it, and that entails certain things. So: the Hosts cared about everything, but Language most of all.

RADICAL AND cussed, $\frac{surl}{tesh\ echer}$ got that lie out into the world, a vomit of phonemes, against its own mind.

The public were rapturous. We'd witnessed a rare perform-ance. I was delighted. Ambassador ArnOld was astonished. Hasser was bemused. Valdik and Scile were aghast.

Latterday, 8

KEDIS AND SHUR'ASI were being escorted to the Embassy. The newscasts' little vespcams saw them.

Midlevel Staff gathered troikas and quads from the Kedis community, a few Shur'asi think-captains. Vehicles arced over our roofs, antennas and the girders of our construction, over the white smoke from our chimneys. One shot recurred on the bulletins: a young Staff member swatting at the cam through which we saw. He must have been very tense to be so unprofessional.

The newscasts, voice and text, were flummoxed. Perhaps to most locals there'd been no sense of crisis until this ingathering of our exots. The pods that took them to the Ambassadorial explanations flocked with birds, and fist-sized cams that rose and fell among them.

Beyond Embassytown, the oddness of angles and movements that had touched the city seemed to be spreading.

I BUZZED Ehrsul, RanDolph, Simmon, but could get through to no one. After a hesitation I tried Wyatt, but he didn't answer either.

My handset still contained Hasser's number, and Valdik's, and several other similes'. It had been a long time. I considered calling one. *What does it matter now?* I thought, but I didn't do it.

I'm sure I wasn't the only one doing so, but I'd begun to prepare, for whatever it was. I was copying what data I thought precious, hiding treasured objects, packing essentials into a shoulder bag. I'd always been fascinated at how my body ran things sometimes. While I felt like I was agonising, my limbs did what was needed.

Night would come without my noticing, and the aeoli-breath was still cool. Then at this crucial change-moment I remember there were night-bird noises and the gibbering of local animals. It wasn't yet so late there was no traffic. I wasn't tired at all. It was hard to make sense of the shots from Embassytown that I was watching. The newsware was still processing. A human commentator said, "We're not sure what . . . we . . . we're seeing something from the city . . . ah . . . movement from . . ."

The figures in cam-view were Ariekei. The Ariekei were moving. On my screen and through my window, I saw corvids frantic in several directions in the air. I heard things. I was already leaning out of my house and I saw their source. The Hosts were coming out of their city into Embassytown.

I RAN TO the interzone between Embassytown and the city. Lights came on as people woke to the noise, but though I was joined by more and more blinking citizens I didn't feel part of anything. I passed under light globes whispering where moths touched them. Below arches I'd known all my life, and, tasting the thinning air, I knew I was only a street or two from the edge of the city. I was in Beckon Street, which swept downhill out of our enclave.

It was an old part of Embassytown. There were plaster griffins at the edges of the eaves. Not far away, our architecture was overcome, the ivy that tugged it smothered by fronds of fleshmatter and Ariekene business. The biorigging probed plastone and brick in a rill of skin.

The Hosts filled the road, jostling each other with odd motion. A single Host had grace but en masse they were a herd, in slow stampede. I'd never seen so many. I could hear the slide of their armour, the tap-tapping of thousands of their feet. Zelles scuttled.

As they came into the human reach the streetlamps and the colours of our displays made them a psychedelia. Rumpled women and men in nightclothes lined the walkways, so the Ariekei entered Embassytown with us either side as if to greet them, as if this were a parade. Cameras darted overhead, little busybodies.

There were Hosts in all their sentient stages, from the newly conscious to those about to slip into mindlessness. Hundreds of fanwings fluttered, and I wanted to be above looking down at that, a camouflage of shuddering colours. They passed me, I followed them.

Many Terre watching could understand Language, but of course none of us could speak it. Some couldn't restrain asking in Anglo-Ubiq: "What are you doing?" "Where are you going?" We trailed the Ariekei north, climbing the incline toward the Embassy, on the roadways and verges, crabgrass and our debris. Constables had arrived. They waved their arms as if moving us on, as if they were protecting our aging walls. They said things that had no meaning at all: "Come on now!" or "Move away there!"

Human children had come to stare. I saw them play Ambassador, dueting nonsense noises and nodding wisely as if the Ariekei were responding. The Hosts took us a coiled route, amassing onlookers, cats and altfoxes bolting before the aliens. We came past the ruins.

Several Ambassadors—RanDolph, MagDa, EdGar, I saw—emerged from the dark, constables and Staff around them. They shouted greetings, but the Hosts didn't pause or acknowledge them.

The Ambassadors said, "$\frac{ursh}{hesser}$!" Stop. Wait. Stop.

Friends, they shouted, *tell us what we can do, why are you here?* They retreated at the head of the Ariekene crowd, ignored. Someone had turned on the light of a church, as if it were Utuday, and its beam rotated overhead. The Hosts began to speak, to shout, each in their two voices. A cacophony at first, a mix of speech and sounds I think weren't speech, and out of that came a chant. Several words I didn't know, and one I did.

"$\frac{ez}{ra}$ · · · $\frac{ez}{ra}$ · · · $\frac{ez}{ra}$ · · ·"

THE ARIEKEI spread out before the black stone steps of the Embassy. I walked among them. The Hosts let me in, moving to accommodate me, glancing with eye-corals. Their spiky fibrous limbs were a thicket, their unbending flanks like polished plastic. My littleness was hidden, and unobserved I watched the Ambassadors panicking. "$\frac{ez}{ra}$," the Hosts kept saying. The people of Embassytown were saying it as best they could, too—"EzRa . . ." An undeliberate chant of the same word in two languages, the name.

JoaQuin and MayBel debated in furious whispers. Behind JasMin and ArnOld and MagDa I saw CalVin. They looked stricken. Staff were bickering too, and the constables around them looked close to panic, their carbines and geistguns dangerously at ready.

A Host stepped forward. "$\frac{du\ kora\ eshin}{u\ shahundi\ qes}$," it said: *I am* $\frac{kora}{shahundi}$. One of those that had greeted EzRa, at the Arrival Ball.

Hello, $\frac{kora}{shahundi}$ said. *We are here for* $\frac{ez}{ra}$. *Bring* $\frac{ez}{ra}$. And on. JoaQuin tried to speak, and MayBel, and the Host paid no attention. Others joined in with it, its demand. They came slowly forward, and it was impossible not to have a sense of their bigness, the sway of their shell-hard limbs.

"*. . . we have no choice!*" I heard Joa or Quin, and I thought it was to MayBel but saw with shock that it was to Quin or Joa. The Ambassadors unhuddled, and stepping out from among them, coming forth as if in a conjuring trick, was EzRa.

Ez LOOKED anxious; Ra was cardsharp blank. As their colleagues parted for them Ez gave them a look of hatred. At the top of the stairs EzRa looked down at the congregation.

The Ariekei spread the tines of their antlers of eyes wide to take in the two men.

"$\frac{ez}{ra}$ · $\frac{kora}{shahundi}$" spoke again. The Language-fluent among us meant what it said was quickly communicated.

EzRa, it said. *Talk.*

EzRa will speak to us or we will make it speak.

"You can't do this," someone from Staff or Ambassadorial ranks shouted, and someone else answered, "What *can* we do?" EzRa looked at each other and murmured a preparation. Ez sighed; Ra's face remained set.

Friends, they said. Ez said "curish" and Ra "loah"—*friends*. There was a snap of Ariekei thoraxes and limbs.

Friends, we thank you for this visit, EzRa said, and the Ariekei reeled, buffeting me. *Friends, we thank you for this greeting*, EzRa said, and the ecstasy went on.

Ra continued to mutter occasionally but Ez had gone silent, so Language decomposed. The Hosts hubbubbed. Some flailed their giftwings and wrapped themselves within them, some entwined them with others'.

$\frac{kora}{shahundi}$ shouted *speak* and $\frac{ez}{ra}$ spoke again. They said pleasantries, emptinesses, polite variants of *Hello, hello.*

The Ariekei concentrated, as if asleep or digesting. Around the plaza I saw hundreds of Embassytowners, and soundless hovering cams.

"You stupid, stupid bastards," someone said on the Embassy steps. The words were as ignored as the ivy. Everyone was looking at the Hosts. They were coming back from whatever it was that had happened to them.

Good, said one. It wasn't $\frac{kora}{shahundi}$. *Good*. It turned. $\frac{kora}{shahundi}$ did so too. The Ariekei all turned back the way they had come.

"Wait! Wait!" It was MagDa. "Pharos!" "We have to . . ." One of them gestured to Ez and Ra: *Don't speak again.* MagDa conferred and shouted in Language. *We must speak*, they said.

Whether out of pity, courtesy, curiosity or whatever, $\frac{kora}{shahundi}$ and other leaders, if that's what they were, of the gathering craned their eye-corals, twisted them backwards, looking behind them. I heard someone say, "Put it down, Officer. Christ, man . . ."

We have much to discuss, MagDa said. *Please join us. May we ask you to enter?*

Constables and SecStaff came through the crowd. "Go." One stood before me. She held a stubby gun. She spoke to me rapidly, the same spiel she was giving everyone. "Please clear the streets. We're trying to bring this under control. Please."

Like everyone else, I obeyed my orders slowly. The Ariekei had arrived in strange coherence. Now most of them straggled away at random, leaving their scent and unique marks in the dirt. An urgent-faced boy in a constable's uniform whispered to me to *please fuck off right now*, and I sped up a little. The Ambassadors were trying to usher a few Hosts, those which had hesitated, into the Embassy. They didn't seem to be succeeding.

Part Three

LIKE AS NOT

Formerly, 7

AFTER THE FESTIVAL, Scile disappeared. He wouldn't answer my buzzes, or did so only with terse comments and promises to return. Wherever he was he might be blanking me, but he had conferred, I suspected, with unlikely people. I was with Valdik and Shanita a day after the festival when Valdik was buzzed; when he'd answered he shut up and glanced at me with wide-open eyes. I had been abruptly sure that Scile was on the line.

After a couple of days my husband came back to our rooms and we had the fight that had been simmering for a long time. As with most such, the specifics are uninteresting and largely beside the point. He was surly, and pissy, and made little quips about how I passed my time, barbs at least as anxious as they were nasty, not that I was in the mood to care about that. I'd had enough of his recent predilection for gnomic pronouncements, and his bad temper.

"Who do you think arranged that trip, Scile?" I shouted. He wouldn't answer or look at me, and I didn't put my hand on my hips or gesticulate, I folded my arms and leaned back and stared down my face at him like I had the first time I'd met him. "Some people might think thanks were in order, not days of this sulky shit. What makes you think you can behave like this? Where did you fucking go?"

He made some reference that made it clear he had been with Ambassadors. I stopped at that, halfway through a riposte. *What in immer?* I remember thinking. *Who buggers off to high-level meetings when they're having a hissy fit?*

"Listen," Scile said. I could see him deciding something, trying hard to calm our altercation. "Listen, will you please listen." He waved a paper. "I know what it's trying to do. Surl Tesh-echer. It practises, and it preaches, to its coterie. This is what it's been saying." He didn't say how he'd got the transcript. "You, similes . . ." he said. "The Hosts aren't like us, okay: it's not exactly most of us who'd get excited to meet a . . . an adjectival phrase or a past participle or whatever. But it's no surprise some of *them* would want to meet a simile. You help them think. Someone with reverence for Language would love that.

"But who'd want to *lie*? A punk, is who. Avice, listen. There are fans, and there are liars. And only Surl Tesh-echer and its friends are both." He smoothed out the paper. "Are you ready to listen to me? You think I've just been sitting in a cupboard for the good of my health? This is what it's been saying."

"'BEFORE THE HUMANS came we didn't speak so much of certain things. Before the humans came we didn't speak so much. Before the humans came we didn't speak." He glanced at me. "We didn't walk on our wings. We didn't walk. We didn't swallow earth. We didn't swallow." Scile was reading nervously, quickly.

"'There's a Terre who swims with fishes, one who wore no clothes, one who ate what was given her, one who walks backwards. There's a rock that was broken and cemented together. I differ with myself then agree, like the rock that was broken and cemented together. I change my opinion. I'm like the rock that was broken and cemented together. I wasn't not like the rock that was broken and cemented together.

"'I do what I always do, I'm like the Terre who swims with fishes. I'm not unlike that Terre. I'm very like it.

'I'm not water. I'm not water. I'm water.'"

No translations I'd ever seen of Host pronouncements were properly comprehensible, but this read different. I realised a counter-intuitive affinity. For all its strangeness it sounded a little, a tiny bit, more like, less unlike Anglo-Ubiq than most Language did. It didn't have the usual precise and nuanced exactnesses.

"It's not like most competitors, trying to force out a lie," Scile said. "It's more systematic. It's *training* itself into untruth. It's using these weird constructions so it can say something true, then interrupt itself, to lie."

"It didn't perform most of these," I said.

"It's been practising," he said. "We've always known the Hosts need you, right? You and the rest of you. Like the split rock, like they need those two poor cats they stitched into a bag. They need similes to say certain things, right? To think them. They need to make them in the world, so they can make the comparison."

"Yes. But . . ." I looked at the paper. I read over it. $\frac{surl}{tesh\ echer}$ was teaching itself to lie.

"'I'm like the rock that was broken,'" Scile said, "then 'not not it.' It can't quite do it, but it's trying to go from 'I'm *like* the rock' to 'I *am* the rock.' See? Same comparative term, but different. Not a comparison anymore."

He showed me old books in hard or virtua: Leezenberg, Lakoff, u-senHe, Ricoeur. I was used to his odd fascinations, they'd helped charm me ages ago. Now they and he made me uneasy.

"A simile," he said, "is true because you say so. It's a persuasion: this is like that. That's not enough for it anymore. Similes aren't enough." He stared. "It wants to make you a kind of lie. To change everything.

"Simile spells an argument out: it's ongoing, explicit, truth-making. You don't need . . . *logos*, they used to call it. Judgement. You don't need to . . . to link incommensurables. Unlike if you claim: 'This *is* that.' When it patently is not. That's what *we* do. That's what we call 'reason', that exchange, metaphor. That *lying*. The world becomes a lie. That's what Surl Tesh-echer wants. To bring in a lie." He spoke very calmly. "It wants to usher in evil."

"I'm worried about Scile," I said to Ehrsul.

"Avice," she said to me at last, after I'd tried to explain to her. "I'm sorry but I'm not sure what you're saying to me." She did listen: I don't want to give the impression that all she did was tell me not to tell her. Ehrsul listened but I'm not sure to what. I was hardly exact, I couldn't be.

"I'M WORRIED about Scile," I said to CalVin. I tried them instead. "He's gone a bit religious."

"Pharotekton?" one of them said.

"No. Not church. But . . ." I'd gleaned more scraps of Scile's emergent theology. I call it that though he was adamant it had nothing to do with God. "He wants to protect the Ariekei. From changing Language." I told CalVin about the temptation, what Scile thought $\frac{surl}{tesh\ echer}$ planned. "He thinks a lot's at stake," I said.

I still love this man and I'm afraid of what's happening, I was saying. *Can you help me? I don't understand why he's doing what he's doing, what's making him afraid, how he's able to make it even get to me.* Something like that.

"Let me talk to him," CalVin said. The one who hadn't spoken looked with raised eyebrows at his doppel, then smiled and looked back at me.

Formerly, 8

CALVIN, as they'd promised me, spent time with Scile. My husband's research was intense, antisocial, his memos to himself were everywhere and mostly not comprehensible, his files scattered across our datspace. The truth is I was a little scared. I didn't know how to react to what I saw in Scile now. The fervour had always been there, but though he tried to disguise it—after that one conversation he didn't talk about his anxieties to me—I could see it was growing stronger.

That he tried to hide it confused me. I wondered if he thought his concerns were the only appropriate ones to the shifts in some Hosts' practice, and if the lack of such anxiety from the rest of us was devastating. If he thought the whole world mad, forcing him into dissimulation. I went through those of his thesis notes, appointment diaries, textbook annotations I could access, as if looking for a master code. It gave me a better sense, if still partial and confused, of his theories.

"What do you think?" I asked CalVin. They looked put out by my uncharacteristic pleading. They told me there was no question that Scile was looking at things in an unusual way, and that his focus was, yes, rather intense. But overall, not to worry. What a useless injunction.

TO MY SURPRISE Scile started coming to The Cravat with me. I'd thought we would do less, not more, in each other's company. I didn't tell him I knew he'd been previously, on his own. I saw no evidence of more efforts to persuade the Hosts to speak him. Instead, he began to exercise a subtle pull on some of the similes. He took part in the discussions, would imply certain of his theories, especially those according to which similes represented the pinnacle and limit of Language. Communication *making* truth. Slightly to my surprise, no one made him, unsimile outsider, other than welcome. The opposite, really. Valdik wasn't alone in listening. Valdik wasn't an intelligent man and I was worried for him.

I mustn't exaggerate. I think Scile seemed himself, only perhaps more focused than previously, more distracted. I no longer thought we could stay together, but I wanted to know that he was alright.

These were in other ways not bad times for me. We were between reliefs. It was always deep in those days that Embassytown became most vividly itself, neither waiting for something, nor celebrating something that had happened. We called these times the doldrums. Of course we knew the more conventional use of the term, but like a few other uncanny words, for us it meant itself and its own opposite. During those still, drab days, cut off on our immer outskirt, without contact, a long time after and before any miabs, we turned inwards.

Fiestas and spectaculars, on the spareday at the end of each of our long months, our crooked alleys interwoven with ribbons and full of music. Children would dance wearing trid costumes, their integuments of light overlapping and crystalline. There were parties. Some formal; many not; some costume; a few naked.

This doldrums culture was part of our economy. After a visit, we had luxuries and new technology to invigorate our markets and production: when one was due there was a rash of spending and innovation, out of excitement and the knowledge that our commodities would soon change, that new-season goods would be in expensive vogue. Between, in the doldrums, things were static, not desperate but pinched, and these fetes were punctuations, and meant small runs on certain indulgences.

One night I was in bed with CalVin. One of them was asleep. The other was stroking my flank, whispering conversation. It was a rare thing, to be with one doppel only. I felt a strong urge to ask his name. I think now I know which it was. I was running my finger over the back of his neck, the link in him, beautifully rendered in the hollow below his skull's overhang. I looked at its twin, on the sleeping half of the Ambassador.

"Should I be worried about Scile?" I said. The sleeper shifted and we were still a second.

"I don't think so," my companion whispered. "He's onto something, you know."

I didn't understand. "I'm not worried that he's *wrong*," I said. "I'm worried that he's . . . that . . ."

"But he's *not* wrong. Or at least—he's pointing out something."

I sat up. "Are you saying—?" I stood and paced, and the sleeping doppel woke and looked at me mildly. Cal and Vin conferred in whispers, and it didn't sound like simple agreement. "What *are* you saying?" I said.

"There are some persuasive elements to what he says." It was the newly woken doppel who spoke.

"I can't believe you're telling me—"

"I'm not. I'm not telling you anything." He spoke impassively. His doppel looked at him and then at me, uneasily. "You asked us to keep a watch on him, and we are, and we have. And we're looking into some of the things he's saying. An eccentric he may be, but Scile's not stupid, and there's no question that this Host . . ." He looked at his doppel and together they said, " $\frac{surl}{tesh\ echer}$." The half of CalVin who had been talking continued: ". . . is definitely pursuing some odd strategies."

I stood naked at the edge of the bed and watched them: one lying back and looking up at me, the other with his knees drawn.

I ADMIT DEFEAT. I've been trying to present these events with a structure. I simply don't know how everything happened. Perhaps because I didn't pay proper attention, perhaps because it wasn't a narrative, but for whatever reasons, it doesn't want to be what I want to make it.

IN THE STREETS OF Embassytown, a congregation was forming. Valdik appeared to be at its centre. It was Valdik who expounded the theories, now. My husband was a canny man, even in his obsessions.

"Valdik Druman's at the centre of it now?" CalVin said. "Valdik? Really?"

"I know it sounds unlikely . . ." I said.

"Well, he's an adult, he's making his own choices."

"It's not that simple." I knew CalVin were right and wrong at the same time.

Most Embassytowners did not know or care about any of these debates. Of those who did, most would consider them pretty unimportant, secure—and there was security in it—in the certainty that Hosts could not lie, whatever a few agitated similes insisted. For those who knew about the festivals, a few Hosts determined to push at the boundaries of Language was too obscure a phenomenon to be any kind of problem, let alone a moral one. That left only a tiny number of Embassytowners, disproportionately the credulous. But their number was growing.

Valdik speechified at The Cravat on the nature of the similes and the role of Language. His arguments were confused but passionate and affecting.

"There's nothing like this anywhere," Valdik said. "No other language anywhere in the universe. Where what's said is truth. Can you imagine what it would be to lose that?"

"It isn't fair what you're doing to Valdik," I told Scile, on one of his rare visits to what had been our home.

"He's not a fucking child, Avice," Scile said. He was collecting clothes and notes. He did not look at me as he rummaged. "He decides what he wants."

WALKING NEAR the ruins I was handed a flyer on cheap nantech paper that flashed a trid as I unfolded it. It made me start: it was Valdik's face, apple-sized, in my hand.

DRUMAN, it said, ON THE BATTLE AGAINST THE LIE. A time and place, not The Cravat but a little hall. With it brought to my attention, I noticed details of that and similar meetings guerrilla-coded into wallscreens, hacked nuisance trids. I went. I'd thought I'd find Scile, but no. I stayed at the back of the room.

Valdik wore a projector, and trids of him appeared throughout the temple, random and staticky. At the front of the room I saw Shanita, Darius, Hasser and other similes and tropes. Valdik preached. He was still a middling speaker. I don't know how this mediocrity amassed a following—something about the doldrums. He expounded religiose foolishness—"two voices but one truth, because what is the truth but dual, bifurcated, not in conflict but two forms of one truth" and so forth.

The place wasn't a quarter full. It contained indulgent friends, the curious, refugees from other cults. A convocation of the hopeless and bored. When I got home, Scile was speaking down the line. He smiled an unconvincing greeting at me as I came in, turned so that I couldn't hear him nor see his mouth move. I wondered whether, if Valdik were removed from this self-appointed office, with what I was convinced was Scile's instrument confiscated, his mania would dissipate.

"What should we do?" CalVin said. "These meetings aren't illegal."

"You can do anything you want."

"Well . . ." "We could have Druman taken for Administrative Detention . . ." ". . . but do you really want that?"

"Yes!" I said, but of course I didn't, and of course they wouldn't do it.

"Listen," they said. "Don't worry." "We'll watch Scile." "We'll keep him safe." That they did, though neither in the way, nor from what, I'd assumed.

Formerly, 9

SOMEONE RELEASED a viral 'ware into the vagrant automa of Embassytown that gave them Valdik's mania. It made them preachers in his new church. Their eloquence depended on the sophistication of their processors: most were little more than ecstatics, but a few were sudden theologians. They ambled as they always had but now accosted us and exhorted us to defend prelapsarian language, Language, we poor sinners (the rhetoric was kitsch), doomed forever ourselves to speak with a deep structure of lie but at least granted service to the double-tongue of truth, and more like that.

Patches were programmed and released and did their job but the infection was tenacious, and for weeks these tramp priests proselytised us, their catechisms changing as their 'ware degraded and threw up protestant, variant sects. "We are the stewards of the angels," I was told by one machine that staggered like a supplicant. "We are the stewards of the speaking angels, of God's language." The virus shut down when its resultant theories strayed too far from emergent Drumanian orthodoxy.

I asked Ehrsul if she was concerned, if she'd felt the tickling of virtual germs. She dismissed the other automa as mental weaklings and told me that yes, though she'd felt it, she'd hardly been in danger herself. Of course Valdik and his radical similes were suspected, but no one could prove who had programmed it, and though it was a nuisance that was all it ultimately was.

I knew Scile didn't have the expertise to program, or I'd have thought it his doing.

WHEN I WENT back to The Cravat, now, I did so for socially diagnostic reasons. Many previous regulars no longer drank there: alienated by Valdik's vatic pronouncements, they set up refusenik simile salons. Others had taken their place. I went to hear Valdik speak, out of what I told myself was a pornography of doomed causes, and maybe to listen for grounds to demand some intervention. He hymned the Ambassadors (in his model, interceding hierophants); expressed gratitude at being simile, truths, Language in flesh.

$\frac{surl}{tesh\ echer}$ was there, with Spanish Dancer and others, at the last of Valdik's gatherings I went to. The Host had amassed more followers, too, so I thought it must be improving its technique, a better and better liar. They watched each other. Valdik glowered. I didn't know if the Hosts felt his hostility. Hasser was there—one of the few who retained friends on both sides of the emergent simile split. He acknowledged me, his face displaying an emotion for which I've no name; it reminded me of my own. An unease, is as close as I can get to it.

"Aren't you worried?" I asked Ehrsul.

"I told you," she said, "I'm immune."

"No I mean . . . what do you reckon? Do you ever think about it? I mean, does it ever make you feel anything one way or the other, that some of the Hosts are learning . . . well, can talk their way around truth, now?" She said nothing, so I said: "Can lie."

We were in a bar in one of Embassytown's shopping streets. Ehrsul in her minor notoriety was being glanced at by slightly moneyed youth. We spoke quietly under music and the clatter of glasses. Ehrsul did not answer me. "Something's changing. Which may or may not be a good thing," I said finally.

She looked at me with a projected face that, by design or a coincidence of ambiguous stimuli-responses in her 'ware, was inscrutable. She said nothing. I grew more and more uncomfortable in that enigmatic silence, until I talked about something else, to which she responded as normal, with all the exaggerated intimacies of our friendship.

It never meant that much to me one way or the other that I was simile; I didn't care what Valdik preached. *It's Scile,* I said to myself: but no, though I was worried for him that wasn't all. I never really knew what else it was.

"So what's being done?" I asked CalVin. Even the Ambassadors were concerned, now, I gathered. The new philosophy couldn't have had more than a score or two of serious devotees, but fervour unnerved us in Embassytown. The Hosts must surely have picked up some atmosphere: I'd seen more Ariekei than usual in the aeolian breath of our quarter.

"We're talking to the Hosts," CalVin said. "We're going to organise . . ." ". . . a festival." "Here, in Embassytown." "To stress that it's theirs too, to speak in."

"Okay," I said slowly. I'd never heard of an Ariekene event in Embassytown. "But is that supposed to . . . What are you doing about Valdik?"

One of CalVin stared at me, the other looked away. I was angry and I tried to work out with whom. Scile was ensconced somewhere, with radical similes or the Staff, and would never respond to me now, and that seemed to concern no one. There I was, between cliques and secrets. I couldn't tell if I was perspicacious or paranoid.

"It's the doldrums, Avvy," Ehrsul said to me later. "This is what happens. You're talking as if it's end-time. I think . . ." She paused. "You're upset because of Scile. You care about him, and he's gone from you." She stumbled exactly like someone who thought would.

ARIEKEI REPRESENTATIVES came in flyers, to plan this hybrid festival. I was often in the Embassy, floaking, and I came to know them all. One tall and thickset Ariekes had a mark on its fanwing like a bird in a canopy of leaf, so I called it Pear Tree.

"This is what we need," CalVin said. "We're all too tense." "There'll be a parade, and stalls and games for Terre . . ." ". . . and a Festival of Lies for the Hosts."

"What about Valdik?" I said again. "And what about Scile?"

"Valdik's nothing." "Scile we've not seen for a couple of weeks."

"So where *is* he . . . ?"

"Don't worry." "It'll be okay." "Honestly, this event'll put paid to a lot of these problems."

I thought it was absolutely absurd. No one agreed with me. In all my life I've never felt so alone.

The festival was to take place in a piazza near the southern edge of Embassytown. It was christened the Licence Party: a pun on Lies and Sense, I was told. I never got what the "sense" referred to. Signs went up displaying that idiot name, and a necessary explanation.

VALDIK LIVED in Embassytown's east. There was a balcony in front of his door overlooking a leisure canal, and a garden full of flowers and birds, altbirds, local fauna.

"Avice," he said, slowly, when he opened the door to me. If he was surprised he hid it.

"Valdik," I said. "Can you help me? I need to find Scile."

His relief was visible. "Is everything alright . . . ?" he said.

"Yes," I said. "No. I just . . . I haven't seen him for days . . ."

My hesitation was real, though my main reason for being there was not Scile, but to assess Valdik and his theology. He let me in and I saw the trappings of his new beliefs. Papers everywhere, all the crazy cabbala and misplaced rigour of a sect.

"Me neither," he said. "I'm sorry. I don't know. I think he's still with CalVin and the others."

"They haven't seen him for weeks," I said.

"No, they were with him a few days ago." That silenced me. "He was at The Cravat and they came for him," Valdik said.

"When?" I said. "Who?"

"CalVin and some Staff."

"CalVin?" I said. "Are you sure?"

"Yes." Valdik didn't sound like a prophet. I had to leave: I could hardly focus on his beliefs at that moment.

WHEN FINALLY CalVin next said they had time to see me, I was careful to be good company. We ate together. They spoke mostly about the Licence Party. One day, one night, half another day. CalVin emerged from their ablutions equalised. Their accrued blemishes were gone or replicated. I said nothing.

I watched them sleep, watched their skins take on differential marks from cotton and the unconscious motion of their hands. When one or other would half-wake, I would be waiting. I would try to murmur-talk to them: gauge what Cal or Vin said. It was strange, trying to do something I'd not known could even occur to me.

He on my left, I decided, at last, murmured my name with a care I recognised, smiled with something really warm. It was desperately hard to tell with only these night-fuddled moments. But he on my left, I decided at last, Cal or Vin, was the one who liked me more. I put my fingers to his lips, made him wake without sound. He opened his eyes.

"Cal," I whispered. "Or Vin. Tell me. I know he won't." I indicated the sleeping other. "I know you've seen Scile. I *know*. Where is he? What's happening?"

I saw my mistake. I saw it the instant I moved my hands.

"You," he said, and though he was quiet I could hear his outrage. That I'd try to find out secrets, and that I'd do so by this blasphemy. My expression was frozen in misplaced intimacy. "How *dare* you . . ."

I cursed. He sat up. His doppel shifted.

"You have some bastard nerve, Avice," the man I'd woken said. "How *dare* you. If we've seen Scile it's not your business . . ."

"He's my husband!"

"It's *not* your *business*. We're *taking care* of things. Like you begged us to. And you come here and treat us . . . like this . . . do this . . . ?"

Beside us the newly woken doppel was rising. I looked at him and felt shame. How could I have mis-seen it? There it was, that thing I'd thought I detected in his brother.

"You thought he was me . . . ?" he said. I saw hurt, and other emotions.

"How could you?" he said. His doppel added: ". . . *do* this?"

The raging one stood, sheets puddling on the floor. "Get out," he said. "Leave. You are damned . . . *fucking* lucky we don't pursue this."

"I can't believe you did that," said the other quietly.

"This is over," the standing one, Cal or Vin, said, and his doppel, the man I should have woken, looked up at him, looked at me, shook his head, turned away. I left the room having ruined my own plan.

On my way home, through the night, I cursed myself. I passed a little tour of Ariekei murmuring in Language as they looked like curators at our lamplit dwellings.

Formerly, 10

AT VARIOUS FAIRS and events in Embassytown, I'd been asked to tell stories of the immer. I'd shown trids and images of my hours in the out, supposedly for children, though there were always many adults in the audience. The immer was and is full of renegades and refugees. They emerge where they can and do what they can get away with. I'd tell the stories. I had transported most things to most places: jewellery; immer-miserable livestock; payloads of organic garbage to a trash planet-state run by pirates. I'd save the best for the end, a changing display of the pharos that marks the edge of the known always: here, right beside Arieka. I'd show it through various filters, culminating in the tropeware that made it a lighthouse, a beacon in murk.

"See? That's what you see. That's right here. Beyond us there's nothing charted. We live at the end of the light." I was amazed at how addictive the spook and thrill was. My presence wasn't requested this time, for the Licence Party.

"What happened between you and CalVin?" Ehrsul asked me. I didn't tell her, or anyone.

THE MICROCLIMATES over the city and those over Embassytown were rigged according to a complex algorithm I'd never bothered to decode. I was always vaguely charmed by planets in thrall to their tilt, with seasons that were more or less predictable. In Embassytown, I noticed particular weathers, of course, but didn't ever expect them.

It grew warm. It was apparently time for us to have a summer.

I went to the Licence Party alone. When I realised that she was expecting us to go together I had to tell Ehrsul no. From her silence I know I hurt her, or spurred the subroutine of her Turingware that manifested as if that were so. But I couldn't be there with anyone. I wasn't punishing her—because this had not been Ehrsul's only silence recently—but I needed to be alone for whatever would happen. I knew that something would as certainly as if this was a last chapter.

THERE WERE game rooms, food halls, massage houses, places for sex; and there were zones designed for our Hosts. They came in large numbers, informed by their networks, the tech like town criers that we had helped to automate. I'd never seen so many Hosts in Embassytown.

Fortune-tellers and performers were on the streets. Trid caricatures of passersby flashed in and out of existence. We came in through security: Terretech detectors of metals and energy flows, and biorigged proscenia that snuffled as we came through, tasting for the telltales of weapon compounds. There were constables in the crowd.

With night the humans and Kedis grew more drunk or drugged. Children ran on frenetic missions. Automa wandered in. I saw a pod of adolescent Shur'asi, a lone Pannegetch casting dice. The Hosts spectated as we played our shovepenny games. They looked with tourist fascination, listened to the songs our singers sung, titillated by our harmonics. I couldn't find Scile.

I don't think the Ariekei ever empathised with our predilection for symmetry and hinge-points: solstices, noon. But the

Licence Party was ours as well as theirs, and the Festival of Lies started at midnight.

The marquee was the size of a cathedral: in places the biorigged skin hadn't finished growing, and decorative gauze or plastic were woven over the holes. There was theatrical seating for Terre around the arena, and standing places for exots and for the Hosts. I saw people I knew. They shouted my name. I saw Hasser, and he raised his hand. He looked afraid. He was gone too fast for me to reach him. By the main performance space was a large group of Ambassadors. CalVin was there, and CharLott, JoaQuin and MagDa and JasMin and others, conferring with Staff. Ariekei were near them, one or two I recognised. Pear Tree, and others that perhaps I might call leaders. Beyond them performers waited, Host and Ariekei.

$\frac{surl}{tesh\ echer}$ was there, with Spanish Dancer and the others of its entourage. It wasn't hard to recognise.

There was a hush, whispered Terre excitement when the lights went down and a few coloured illuminations fired. In a strong, projected doubled voice, Ambassador CharLott stepped into the centre of the spectators, spoke Language. A translator shouted to us locals theatrically, "'It's raining in here,' the Ambassador says! 'It's raining liquor on us!'"

It sounded as though they were trying to excite Embassytowners with these feeble falsities as if we were Host, and I thought it absurd. But, over the delighted noises of the Ariekei looking up to find the rain that wasn't there, came the shrieks of Terre, my neighbours yelling delight at each new untruth from the Ambassador. As if none of them could lie.

I reached the front as CharLott came to the end of their set. Other Ambassadors performed. They were building an arc for the listeners, I realised. For us. Here were lies that were a comic interlude, here a ratcheting-up of tension, here a moving moment.

When after long heady minutes they were done, Hosts stepped up in their place. Each Ariekes spoke only one or two short lies. Most did it by verbal trickery like a whispered final clause. Each success was marked with Terre cheers and Ariekene approval. Many competitors stumbled and said something true. The Host audience responded with what could have been scorn or could have been pity.

I stand, I don't stand.

This before me is not red.

$\frac{surl}{tesh\ echer}$ stepped forward at last, for a scheduled confrontation. Opposite it was an Ambassador, LuCy, moving like pugilists, swinging their arms as if limbering. I realised I was surprised, that when I'd read about this contest I had thought it would be CalVin representing Embassytown. Ambassador and Host squared. This was some blasphemy, I thought. Who could have allowed this? There was cheering, but I heard a man beside me, as if channelling my opinion, muttering, "This is not right."

Before the humans came we didn't speak so much of certain things, $\frac{surl}{tesh\ echer}$ said.

The MC was shouting the rules of the stand-off. *Before the humans came we didn't speak so much of certain things,* $\frac{surl}{tesh\ echer}$ said again, and shucked its wings. Whatever alien feelings it was feeling, they looked to us like bravado. The two women of the Ambassador and that intricate big beast the Ariekes stared at each other. The Ambassador opened their mouths. Before they spoke, $\frac{surl}{tesh\ echer}$ said, *Before the humans came we didn't speak so much.*

Ruckus. *Before the humans came,* the Host went on, and I knew what the lie would be, *we didn't speak.*

It said it clearly. There was a moment, then the Ariekei

stuttered in their ecstasy of reception. Even the Terre knew that we had heard something extraordinary. There was noise everywhere. Some shouted argument. I saw jostling in the crowd.

"Not true!" someone was shouting. "Not true!"

Men and women were got suddenly, violently, out of someone else's way. They screamed and parted. I could see the man coming, and it was Valdik.

"Not true!" he said. He ran and shouted and brought a cudgel down on the ground, and I felt a spasming report. There was energy in his weapon. So much for security. He faced $\frac{surl}{tesh\ echer}$. Valdik shouted that it was not true. He raised his weapon. Eye-corals strained. People were running toward us. Valdik shouted, "Fucking snake!" $\frac{surl}{tesh\ echer}$ watched him, its coral spreading wide as horns. I heard the bark of a weapon and Valdik went down, his club scorching the floor. Constables grabbed him. He was beaten down.

"He went for a *Host*?" people were gasping.

I could hear Valdik still shouting: "The devil! He'll fucking destroy us! Don't let it lie!"

None of the Ariekei made a sound. The officers hauled Valdik upright finally, blood-smeared and ragged, hardly conscious. They began to drag him, his feet scratching on the floor, out of the grounds. Tens of seconds had passed since his attack. In that whole hall, I think I was the only person watching CalVin and their silent colleagues, one of the very few not staring at the battered would-be assassin being taken away.

I saw Scile. He was with them, among the Ambassadors and Staff. That was it; that was where to look. They were looking not at Valdik but at $\frac{surl}{tesh\ echer}$, and beyond it at Pear Tree and its group of Ariekei. I was one of very few in that hall who saw what happened then.

Pear Tree moved. From behind it stepped Hasser. He

walked quickly. Even $\frac{surl}{tesh\ echer}$ was still looking at Valdik. No constables saw Hasser coming, or were there to intervene. They were busy, suckers to the oldest feint. I moved.

One of $\frac{surl}{tesh\ echer}$'s eyebuds glimpsed something and the whole coral arced backward, to stare. I saw Spanish Dancer, heard it calling, its giftwing moving in alien distress. Hasser aimed a biorigged thing. A ceramic carapace, a pistolgrip that gripped him back. He fired. No one was there to stop him.

He fired and the gun-animal opened its throat and howled. He blasted $\frac{surl}{tesh\ echer}$ across the lying ground, spraying mud-coloured Host blood.

It broke apart as it flew. Hasser didn't stop firing. The assault tore $\frac{surl}{tesh\ echer}$'s giftwing from its body. Its legs dyingly scuttled, so insectile it was appalling. It gushed from everywhere.

Then Hasser was snatched out of my sight himself by a constable's bullet. By the time screaming started again I was beside him. I trembled. I struggled for breath as if I were beyond the aeoli. Hasser stared without sight. I heard the rattle of scute from $\frac{surl}{tesh\ echer}$'s posthumous fitting.

Spanish Dancer traced shapes with its wings. Its colours flushed. I'd never before seen Ariekene grief. I looked at Pear Tree, which looked down at me. I ignored the commotion and all the wails in the room, and watched Pear Tree, and CalVin, and Scile. I remember I moaned every time I exhaled. They were looking at Hasser's body without expression. They must have seen me.

THAT IS HOW the most virtuoso liar of the Ariekei was murdered.

The days after that were as you'd imagine. Chaos, fear, excitement. No Host had been harmed by an Embassytowner for hundreds of thousands of hours, for lifetimes. Suddenly we felt we existed on sufferance. Staff imposed a curfew, gave the constabulary and SecStaff extraordinary powers. In the out, I'd spent time in cities and colonies under dictatorships of various forms, and I knew that what we had was a quaint approximation of martial law; but for Embassytown it was unprecedented.

I HAD SO MUCH sadness in me. I cried, only when I was alone. I was so sorry for Hasser, silly secret zealot; and for Valdik who I still believe never knew he'd been a distraction, and whose loyalty to Scile was such that, after that night, he went to his execution denying that anyone else had had any hand in his plan.

So sorry for $\frac{surl}{tesh\ echer}$. I never knew what emotion would have been appropriate for an Ariekene loss, so I settled for sadness.

For a day I turned off my buzz and did not answer when anyone came to my door. The second day I kept the buzz off, but I did answer the knocking. It was an autom I'd never seen before, a whirring anthropoid outline. I blinked and wondered who'd sent this thing and then I saw its face. Its screen was cruder than any I'd seen her rendered on before, but it was Ehrsul.

"Avice," she said. "Can I come in?"

"Ehrsul, why'd you load yourself into . . . ?" I shook my head and stepped back for her to enter.

"The usual one doesn't have these." She swung the thing's arms like deadweight ropes.

"Why do you need them?" I said. And Pharotekton bless her she grabbed hold of me, just as if I'd lost someone. She did not ask me anything. I hugged her right back, for a long time.

I WENT BACK once more to The Cravat. Set my expression, walked a floaker walk. None of the similes were there, nor, I think, did any ever come back. I let my show drop. But the owner, a man whose name I had never bothered to learn, referring to him only by the vernacular slang handle we'd granted him that I now cannot remember, hurried up to me in agitation, as if I could help him. He told me that Ariekei were still coming: Spanish Dancer; one we'd known as Baptist; others of the Professors. They'd been staring at where the similes used to sit.

"Surl Tesh-echer used to come here all the time," I said. "Maybe they're coming to be where their friend used to be."

The owner was terrified the Hosts would commit reprisal for $\frac{surl}{tesh\ echer}$'s death. Most people were. I was not. I'd seen Pear Tree step aside for Hasser and say something to him on his way. I'd seen CalVin and the others waiting for that. $\frac{surl}{tesh\ echer}$ had been murdered but it also had been executed, publicly, by its peers. For heresy, $\frac{surl}{tesh\ echer}$ had been sentenced to Death by Human.

Embassytown couldn't know, and would not. The situation must be made to look to most people, and did, like a bloody mess, rather than the careful juridical moment it also was.

Ariekei traditioners had decided they could not tolerate $\frac{surl}{tesh\ echer}$, would not brook its experiments. A lie was a performance; a simile was rhetoric: their synthesis, though, the first step in their becoming quite another trope, was sedition. I would never assume I understood the motivations of any exot, and I had grown up knowing the thinking of the Hosts was beyond me. Whatever drove the Ariekene powers to their brutal decision might, might not, be comparable to the calculations that had also gone on behind Embassy doors. The Ariekene resistance to these innovations might have been ethical, or aesthetic, or random. It might have been religious or a game. Or instrumental, an expression of some cool, cynical calculation, a power-jostling among cliques.

I remembered Cal or Vin's anxiety, when they'd told me that some of Scile's ideas about $\frac{surl}{tesh\ echer}$ made sense. The Ambassadors, as much as its Ariekene judges, had seen in it an approaching danger. I never thought CalVin saw whatever that coming badness was as my husband had, but where there's commitment and dissent there might be change, and perhaps that was enough. There'd been a catastrophe on its way that, together, Ariekei and Terre had staved off. A problem they had solved.

Who could I tell? If I could prove anything, so what? Not everyone would think any of this the slightest crime. And what would I bring on myself? I'd no idea how many of the Ambassadors knew, or if they would disapprove if they did, or what they would do to me if I complained. I can't have been the only one who worked out what had happened. There were enough snatches of information. But Staff asserted horror and shock and stressed to Embassytowners that they had apologised to our Hosts, and that Hasser and Valdik had both been brought to justice. They unleashed harsh policing against the remnants of the Druman cult.

Scile moved at last into the Embassy, became Staff. One day all his possessions were gone from my home. Among his flaws wasn't cowardice. I think he was avoiding me; perhaps he wanted to spare me his rage.

I NEVER STOPPED being appalled by the sentencing I'd seen. But months passed—and our months are long—and we were out of the doldrums, and Valdik and Hasser were long dead. I still wouldn't speak to CalVin or Scile, but though I didn't know which Staff and Ambassadors were complicit in what had happened I couldn't spurn them all forever. I couldn't live in Embassytown like that. It felt not like compromise but survival.

Even CalVin and I came wordlessly to a way of being in the same room, if we so found ourselves. We might, I eventually came to accept, one day even exchange brief cool words.

I remembered those elements in Scile, the little opacities that had always been present, that I'd always been intrigued by, that now seemed to have come to constitute all of him. I didn't know what fears the rest of the complicit Staff had had of $\frac{surl}{tesh\ echer}$, but I thought they must have been political. I was never sure about Scile, though, for all that he was Staff too now, and had for a long time been of their party. For all his consummate manipulation of the credulous simile zealots. He worked as apparatchik, but I wondered if he really was a prophet.

Many months after those horrible events, the first crisis, as Embassytown geared into a different kind of time, as the arrival of the next ship grew closer, as the time I've called "formerly" ended, the Hosts apparently made Scile a simile. I heard that from Ehrsul.

She couldn't find out exactly what he'd had to do. He was part of Language but I never heard him used and in various, I hoped untraceable, eavesdropping ways, I did try. By contrast the similes Hasser and Valdik, changed as they were by the events, were invigorated. *It's like the boy who was opened and closed again and is dead. It's like the man who swam weekly with the fishes and is dead.* The Ariekei found new uses for these new formulations.

Ehrsul was a good friend to me in what was a pretty bleak time, though I wouldn't risk telling her everything that I knew had happened. I told myself that I was just waiting. I was immerser. When the relief came, I'd go into the out, away from this place. Then the miab arrived, with details of what would be arriving next, and news of our impossible Ambassador.

Wasn't I going to stay to see what would happen? Everything

after this was latterday, and it's the only story remaining. Wasn't I eager for Embassytown to change?

Later, the scale of the crisis that unfolded made this, retrospectively, a guilty memory, but when first I realised that things were not going quite to plan, the first time I met EzRa at the Arrival Ball, when I sensed that they were spreading some unexpected chaos in Embassytown, it had made me happy.

Part Four

ADDICT

9

PEOPLE WANDERED through streets in a kind of utopian uncertainty, knowing that everything was different but unsure in what sort of place they lived now. Adults were talking and children playing games. "I'm minded to be careful," I heard one man say, and I could have laughed in his face. Minded, are you? I could have said. Minded how? What will you do? How will you be careful?

We'd always lived in a ghetto, in a city that didn't belong to us but to beings far more powerful and strange. We'd lived among gods—little tiny gods but gods compared to us, considering what was at their and our disposal—and ignored the fact. Now they'd changed, and we had no way to understand that, and all we could do was wait. Embassytowners' foolish discussions were as meaningless right then as the sounds of birds.

Our news figures said things to me from screens and tridflats like: "The situation is being closely monitored." We were trying to find language to make sense of a time before whatever came after. I walked through the tiny Kedis district. The ruling troikas there had heard about the killing, knew enough Terre psychology that all our fears were rubbing off on them, and they were very anxious, too.

I couldn't persuade Ehrsul to come to join me in the agitation and rush of Embassytown main, in the hilltop districts where people massed, following rumours that taught them nothing, staring, powerless spectators, into the city moving as opaquely as ever but differently opaquely now. We could all

191

see it. I went to her apartment. Ehrsul was subdued, but then we all were.

She spiked me a coffee with one of the edgers many of us were taking. She moved backwards and forwards on her treads. Her mechanisms were smooth, but inevitably with that repetition tiny infelicitous noises in the machine of her became audible, then irritations.

"Have you found anything out?" I said.

"About what's going on? Nothing. Nothing."

"What about on the . . . ?"

"I said, nothing." She made her face blink. "There's all kinds of blather all over the nets, but if anyone out there understands what's happened or knows what's about to happen, they're talking about it below what I can tap."

"EzRa?"

"What about them? Do you think I'm just neglecting to tell you important bits? Christ." I was embarrassed at her tone. "I don't know where they are any more than you. I haven't seen them since the party either." I didn't say that I'd seen Ra more recently. "Oh, there's plenty of *rumours*: they're in the out, they're taking control, they're preparing an invasion, they're dead. Nothing I'd stake a rep on. If your channels to the Embassy haven't netted anything, why would my pitiful little searchware?" We regarded each other.

"Alright," I said slowly. "Come with me . . ."

"I'm not going anywhere, Avice," she said, and her voice foreclosed argument. I was not, this one time, wholly disappointed at that.

I WENT TO the coin wall. The return to anywhere you last visited as a child is difficult, especially when it's a door. Your heart beats harder when you knock. But I knocked, and Bren answered.

I was looking down when he opened the door, to give myself a second. I raised my head to him. He looked much older to me, because his hair was grey. That was all, though: he was hardly collapsing. He recognised me. Before I met his eyes, I'm sure.

"Avice," he said. "Benner. Cho."

"Bren," I said. We stared at each other, and eventually he made a sound between a sigh and a laugh, and I smiled if sadly and he stepped aside for me to enter the room I remembered so extraordinarily well, which hadn't changed at all.

He brought me a drink and I joked about the cordial he'd given me the first time I was there. He remembered the chant we'd used when spinning coins, and recited it to me, imperfectly. He said something or other, something that meant *you went into the out, you're an immerser!* A congratulations. I felt like thanking him. We sat looking at each other. He was still thin, wore what could have been the same smart clothes I remembered.

"So," he said. "You've come here because the world's ending." A muted screen behind him played out the confusion of Embassytown.

"Is it?" I said.

"Oh I think so. Don't you?"

"I don't know what to think," I said. "That's why I'm here."

"I think it's the end of the world, yes." He sat back. He looked comfortable. He drank and looked at me. "Yes I do. Everything you know's finished. You know that, don't you? Yes, I can see you do." I saw his affection for me. "You impressed me," he said. "Such an intense girl. I wanted to laugh. Even while you were looking after your poor friend. Who breathed Host air."

"Yohn."

"Anyway. Anyway." He smiled. "It's the end of the world and you're here why? You think I can help?"

"I think you can tell me things."

"Oh believe me," he said, "no one in that castle wants me to know anything. They keep me as out of it as they can these days. I'm not saying I've no ins at all—there are those who keep an old man in gossip—but you probably know at least as much as me."

"Who's Oratees?" I said. He looked sharply up.

"Oratees?" he said. "It really is? Oh. Well. Christ Pharotekton." He smoothed down his shirt. "I did wonder. I thought maybe that must be it, but . . ." He shook his head. "But you doubt. You can hardly believe it, can you?"

"Oratees isn't a person," Bren said. "They're a thing. They're junkies."

"Everything that could happen has happened sometime," he said. He leaned towards me. "Where are the failed Ambassadors, d'you think, Avice?" It was so shocking a question that I held my breath.

"If I put it to you outright, you wouldn't imagine, would you, that *every single one* of the monozogs the Embassy raises is suited to Ambassadorial duties?" he said. "Of course not. Some doppels don't take—don't look enough like each other to be fixed, have quirks, can't think enough alike, despite all the training. Whatever.

"You'd have known that without being told if you let yourself think about it. It's not exactly a secret. It's just not thought. You know that doppels retire, when the other dies." He raised his hands, slightly, indicating himself. "You've never been in the

Embassy crèche, have you? There are those who never get out
of it in the first place. If you've been grown and raised and
trained for one job, and you can't do it, what's the profit in
letting you out? That could only cause trouble."

Little rooms of rendered twins, mouldering. Slack and separate doppels gone bad, one whole, one like a melted image; or
perhaps both wrong; or neither wrong in any physical way but
with some bone-deep meanness; or just not able to do what they
were born to.

"And if you're already out," Bren said, "by the time you
realise you hate your job or your doppel, or whatever? Well.
Well." He spoke gently, breaking something to me. "When he
died, my . . . it was an accident. It's not as if we were old. People
knew us . . . me. I was much too young to disappear. They tried
to *entice* me to the rest home of course. But they couldn't force
me. So what if my neighbours don't like me? So what if they
see something crippled? No one likes a cleaved showing off
their injury. We're stumps." He smiled. "That's what we are.

"There are trainees who can *never* speak Language. I don't
know why. Just can't speak in time no matter how they practise.
That's simple: you don't let them go. But there are harder cases.
They might look like any other pair. It's happened before, to vary-
ing degrees. We had a colleague, when I was training. WilSon.
Whatever joined-up mind it was behind their Language, for the
Hosts to understand, it must have been a little out. A tiny bit.
Nothing I could hear, but the Hosts . . . well.

"We were doing exams. We'd been tested by other Ambassadors and Staff, and in our last practical we had to speak to a
Host. It was waiting. I don't know what it thought it was doing,
how they asked it to help. *Hello*, WilSon say, when it's their turn.

"Straightaway we can see something's wrong," he said.
"From how the Ariekes moves. Every time they talk to us, they

taste our minds, and we're *alien*. So it's heady stuff. But if the two halves of an Ambassador aren't . . . quite enmeshed enough? Not two random voices: close enough to speak Language and for them to get it. But wrong? Broken?" I said nothing.

"You know what Language is to them," Bren said. "What they hear through the words. So, if they hear words they understand, they know are words, but it's fractured? Ambassadors speak with empathic unity. That's our job. What if that unity's there and not-there?" He waited. "It's impossible, is what. Right there in its form. And that is intoxicating. And they *mainline* it. It's like a hallucination, a there-not-there. A contradiction that gets them high.

"Maybe not all of them. Every Host WilSon spoke to knew something was strange, and a few of them . . ." He shrugged. "Got drunk. On their words. Didn't matter what WilSon said. *Isn't it a nice day*; *Please pass the tea*; anything. The Hosts heard it and some of them got swoony and some of *them* wanted it again and again.

"Ambassadors are orators, and those to whom their oration happens are oratees. Oratees are addicts. Strung out on an Ambassador's Language."

OUTSIDE PEOPLE ran through the streets in frightened carnival. There was the noise of fireworks. Bren refilled my glass.

"What happened to them?" I asked.

"WilSon? They were quarantined, and they died." He drank.

"Everyone respects me, but that can't stop them hating me," Bren said. "I understand that. They don't like to see my wound." He wrote his name in the air—his full name, seven letters: BrenDan. There'd been a time he was BrenDan, or more properly $\frac{bren}{dan}$. Then his doppel had died, and he'd become BrenDan, $\frac{bren}{dan}$. He couldn't say his own name correctly.

196

Bren~~Dan~~ looked at me thoughtfully for a long time. He went to a desk. "Let me show you something."

He threw me a shallow box. Inside were two links. His, and his doppel ~~Dan~~'s. I examined the filigree circuits, the wires and contacts, the carefully carved initials and silver leaves. Their clasps had been cut open. I looked at him and could see the tiny marks on his neck where his had been embedded.

"What are you thinking?" he said. "Are you thinking that I keep them so they're close at hand? Are you thinking I hide them away, to try to forget them? Avice. If I'd thrown his away and kept mine, you'd think I was clinging to my dead identity, or resenting his death. If I threw them both away, you'd see me in denial. If I kept his but not mine you'd say I was refusing to let him go. There's nothing I can do you won't do that to. It's not your fault. You can't help it, it's what we do. Whatever I do, it'll be one story or another."

(Later, the next but one time I was with him, because I did come back and after that he came to me, he said to me, "I look at that link and I hate him." I said nothing. What could I say? We were sitting on the sofa in my rooms. They were nothing like as splendid as Bren's. "I don't know when it started," he said. "For a long time I thought I hated him when he died, because he died, poor bastard. Now I think it might have started earlier. You mustn't blame me." He was suddenly plaintive. "I'm sure he hated me, too. It was neither of our faults.")

"They must have suspected what would happen, you know," Bren said. "The Ambassadors. It was always the oddballs who seemed to risk ... unplaiting ... just enough to make a few Ariekei oratees. Those were the ones they restrained. Other sorts of troublemakers went AWOL or native."

"You think they knew?" I said. "And who went *what*?"

"They must have hoped EzRa *were* a drug," he said. "So

they'd affect one or two of the Hosts and not be usable. One in the eye for Bremen. They've all been very concerned about who was calling what shots, what agendas were being forced, since they heard EzRa were coming."

"I know," I said. "But Bremen must've known too, if this has happened before. Why would they send them . . . ?"

"Known about oratees, you mean? Why would we tell Bremen about that? I don't know what they had in mind, but this, letting EzRa speak, was the Embassy's riposte, I think. Not that they expected this, though. Not like this. Language like this, right there but *so* impossible, so doping, that EzRa are infecting *every, single, Host*. All of which are spreading the word. All hooked on the new Ambassador."

OUR EVERYDAY pantheon gone needy, desperate for hits of Ez and Ra speaking together, fermenting Language into some indispensable brew of contradiction, insinuation and untethered meaning. We were quartered in an addict city. That procession I'd seen had been craving.

"What happens now?" I said. It was very quiet in the room. There were hundreds of thousands of Ariekei in the city. Maybe millions. I didn't know. We knew hardly anything, at all. Their heads were all made of Language. EzRa spoke it and changed it. Every Host, everywhere, would become hardwired with need, do anything, for the blatherings of a newly trained bureaucrat.

"Sweet Jesus Pharotekton Christ light our way," I said.

"It is," said Bren, "the end of the world."

10

THE ARIEKEI told us how it would be. I was ahead of this curve, but it didn't take long for the rest of the Embassytowners to understand that the Hosts were junkies, though they may not have known how or why. I suspect there was a power struggle in the Embassy, that some would have tried, out of habit, without rationale, to wall up information. They didn't win.

The streets of Embassytown were something between carnival and apocalypse: moods of ending; hysteria; happiness, or its giddy approximation. Constables apprehended people walking determinedly toward the edge of town, in biorigging that might let them breathe the city air.

"You're going nowhere!" the officers said. "Get that off. People are dying . . ." Some would-be city voyagers must have got through. Embassytowners wanting something from the Hosts. Pointless—the Ariekei wouldn't perceive them as people, but as the meat belongings of Ambassadors.

I was able to bluff my way back into the Embassy. Seeing the way the Ambassadors were scurrying I felt for a moment almost protective of them. They didn't question me. Even JasMin seemed to have forgotten they disliked me. One of EdGar gave me a kiss, to my surprise. I couldn't see his doppel. I saw the discomfort in Ed or Gar's eyes, from stretching their link's field.

"Where . . . ?" I said.

"Coming, coming." Being so separated must have made it hard to concentrate. We didn't say much until his doppel turned a corridor corner and joined us.

"Have you been into the city?" I said. ("Of course." "No one'll talk to us.") "D'you know what's happening?" ("No." "No.") "Where's EzRa? Where's Wyatt?" ("Don't know." "Don't care.")

"You don't know where EzRa are?" I said. "After they caused all this shit? So what, you've just left them to fucking conspire?"

"Conspire?" Ed and Gar laughed. "They won't even talk to each other."

AN ARIEKENE ship-beast came toward us over their city, in which the outline of that obscure malaise was spreading, building to building. When the flyer touched down on the pad, we rigged up something like an official welcome. It's perhaps tendentious to say "we", but I made myself part of that community then, around the Staff and Ambassadors, and I think no one resented it.

Every Ambassador I could think of was there. The Ariekei entered the hall with gusts of aeoli breath, our wind, with the gilted curtains snapping like capes around them. They walked on the altwood floor with the sound of fingernails. Not a fraction so many as had come that last pilgrimage time, but this was a more formal group. JoaQuin and MayBel stepped forward, and others shuffled behind them. Our two sides watched each other. Eye-corals craned.

The Ariekei spoke so quickly only the most fluent listeners could follow. I turned to see how the crowd were taking all this, and with shock saw my husband. He stood in the doorway, and with him was the new Ambassador.

I WAS THE FIRST, but a few other people in the room started to notice them, and there were gasps. Ra, tall and looking very tired, stood in a pose midway between hopeful and resentful.

Behind him, Ez looked at the floor. His bantam swagger was gone. His augmens were off.

Scile saw me. He met my eye, then looked around the room again. Standing where he stood, he could have been shoring EzRa up, could have been protecting them, could have been menacing them.

I recognised some of the visitors. On one fanwing I saw a moment of bird-shape in tree-shape. Pear Tree. I stared at it. The Hosts said EzRa's name.

EzRa found a reserve of dignity, and met that attention. The Ariekei spoke in a confusion, one then another, squabbling even, until at last something like sense emerged. Someone began to translate what they said.

This is how it will be.

An unqualified future tense, rare in Language. This wasn't an aspiration: the Hosts could only envisage that this was how it *would* be. They didn't allow discussion: later we would make sense of it all. They didn't raise details. They didn't present requests or even demands, not really. They expressed need. All they could say, repeatedly, in various ways, was that they needed.

We will hear EzRa speak. This is how it will be. We will hear them speak. First now we will hear EzRa speak.

I could see some Staff making calculations, muttering: the best of them could strategise even during this. I admired that. They were working out what to do, what relations could remain and how others would be saved, how we could *live*, what we would make Embassytown be. They made me hope, and I'd not expected that.

The Hosts had a simple and single priority, it seemed. I was never a fool; I'd known there must be antagonisms, camps and struggles among them, before I ever saw that bloody result of one; and now a paradox, that that memory rose in me at *that* moment, when all that was evident was one implacable agenda. *First we will hear EzRa speak.*

Ez came forward, then, grudgingly, Ra. They looked at each other with very different emotions, those two unalike men. They whispered. They spoke Language together, and brought the Hosts to rapture.

11

As they unfolded those times seemed pure chaos, but by the prodigious efforts of the better Staff, a kind of life emerged. Even routines. It's shocking how fast a whole city can be made to change.

Trade, all the moments and minutiae of exchange: knowledge, services, goods, promises and extras. Our culture. The way we lived. All of those things had to be fixed.

There was a dangerous excitement, an amoralism manifesting in small cruelties and mass indulgence, that some let take them, while others struggled to make things work. In the first weeks, if you came to the Embassy, it would probably be guarded, but perhaps not. Meeting rooms and galleries might be uncleaned, might contain detritus of parties. I didn't find much pleasure in transgressions. I knew the vomited-up red wine wasn't puked in ostentation, nor left to rot in libertine performance, but because those who partied had seen or heard about the Ariekene demand; couldn't conceive of how we could keep going or what would happen if we failed to fulfil them; so didn't know if they would live another week, and had never been so afraid.

Ehrsul did not answer my buzzes, and I was so overwhelmed I didn't pursue it or visit her, as a good friend perhaps should have. EzRa was at some parties, I heard from others, then saw myself. After a short time it was only Ez who was there, at the millennial debauches. Ra did other things.

There were assignations and the collapses of relationships.

There were many marriages. I had my own hurried liaisons. Really those first days are hard to talk about. The heroes who ensured that Embassytown wasn't swept away by insistent addicted Hosts were the clerks, who set up structures while the rest of us failed not to fall apart. A little later I became something again, something important to Embassytown: just then I was not.

In those days Embassytown felt as small as it ever had to me. Not two days could pass without me meeting, at some gathering, eager or desultory or both, people I'd avoided for thousands of hours. Burnham, a simile from back when, caught my eye from the other end of a crowd gathered because of a bullshit rumour that information was about to be imparted by the Embassy gates. He looked away as carefully as I did, as I had every time since Hasser's and Valdik's deaths, since way before this new cataclysm, that I'd bumped into him or Shanita or any of the dispersed Cravat crew.

I wandered Embassytown while civil servants took pills to stay awake and worked out plans to keep us alive. I bumped, more than once, into older friends: Gharda; Simmon, the guard. He had nothing to guard. He was terrified: his biorigged prosthesis seemed sick.

Staff too lowly had no idea what to do, and those too high were crippled by the loss of everything. So were all those Ambassadors who told people that it was the viziers' faults, that they would never themselves have let things come to this, that it had always been Staff who were the real powers and who had let everyone down. No one listened to that fairy tale any more.

It was ignored people who'd done the same thing for years who changed themselves for the sake of Embassytown, and changed Embassytown. Our bureaucratic feudalism of expertise became a remorseless meritocracy. Even a few Ambassadors proved themselves. Rarely the ones I'd have guessed. That's true but a trite observation.

One of the first of the new leadership's achievements was the defeat of Wyatt's insurgency. Simmon was key to that little war. He told me about it afterwards, invigorated again. "You saw how suddenly all Wyatt's lot got moving? They were *opening the arsenals*. I guess whatever's going on triggered some bloody Bremen emergency protocol. That's what all that chaos was, a few days ago."

I'd not noticed whatever uprising of our overpower's representatives he was talking about. There was plenty of chaos enough.

"We got wind of it—never mind how—and we were ready for them. But we had to take risks." He was drawing the plan, the actions, in schema, with his hand in the air. "We could probably just have pre-empted them, you know? But that Bremen tech they've got—we reckoned it had to be pretty damn useful. So we waited and went in *after* they'd opened the silos. We had a few officers placed with them—it's not as if we hadn't been preparing for this before. We took them with only a few casualties, *and* we got the weapons. Although honestly, they're not as useful as we'd hoped. Still.

"They didn't put up much fight. It's only Wyatt who was the problem. We've put him away. Incommunicado. There are bound to be Bremen agents still out there, and we have to make sure he can't get codes or instructions or whatever to them." I didn't tell him I hadn't noticed the drama. Even ignorant of it as I'd been, I was galvanised, hearing of it.

RA, THE DIFFIDENT half of our cataclysmic Ambassador, was allowed his solitude and whatever his little projects were; Ez was allowed his louche collapse. But they were on orders, and they were guarded. They had duties. They were what kept us alive.

"A city of brainwashed," EdGar said to me. "Stronger than us, armed. We need them hospitable."

There was no thinking or strategy from the Hosts in those first days. I who was so used to glossing all their strangeness with special pleading—*it's some Ariekene thing, we wouldn't understand*—was aghast to become convinced that they were not indulging any inhuman strategy, but mindless addict need. At first crowds of Ariekei were gathered permanently outside the Embassy. When they became agitated and their demands particularly insistent, every few hours, EzRa would be fetched, appear at the entrance, and in flawless Language say something—anything at all—amplified to carry, to the crowd's obvious stoned relief.

The second time EzRa said to them *We are happy to see you and look forward to learning together*, the oratees reacted without quite the degree of bliss they'd shown previously. The third time they were unhappy, until EzRa announced some new pointlessness about the colour of the buildings, the time of day or the weather. Then they were rapt again. "Fucking fantastic," I said to someone. "They're building up tolerance. Keep EzRa inventive."

We watched news programmes that after kilohours of trivialities now had to learn to report our own collapse. One channel sent an aeoli-wearing team with vespcams into the city. They were neither invited nor barred. Their reports were astonishing.

We were not used to seeing Ariekene streets, but there are new freedoms during a breakdown. The reporters edged into the city, past plaited ropes tethering gas-filled Host rooms, past buildings that shied away from them or rose on spindled limbs like witch-huts. Ariekei crossed our screens. They saw the reporters, stared and ran over sometimes like tottering horses. They asked questions in their double voices, but there were no Ambassadors to answer them. The reporters knew Language, translated for viewers.

"'Where is EzRa?'" That was what the Hosts said.

The reporters weren't the only Terre in the city. Their vespcams glimpsed men and women in Embassy suits moving among the skittish houses. They were routing cables and speakers—Terretech that looked jarring in that topography. They were extending a network of hailers and coms boxes. In return perhaps for our lives, the maintenance of our power, water, infrastructure, biorigging, they were getting ready to bring EzRa's voice right into the city.

"We need EzRa now," EdGar said. "They have to perform. That was our deal."

"With them, or the Hosts?" I said.

"Yes. More EzRa, though. And that means we need Ez."

He was drinking and drugging. More than once, he'd disappear at the times he was scheduled to speak Language to the Ariekei, leaving Ra speechless and waiting. I didn't care if Ez killed himself, but that he'd take us with him if he did.

"They're like normal Ambassadors in one way, right?" I said. "Recordings work? So build up a library of EzRa's speeches, then let the fucker do what he wants. Let him drink himself dead." They'd thought of that, but Ez would not comply. Even begged by Ra or threatened by Staff or guards, he would only speak with his Ambassador-colleague an hour or so at any one time. We could grab the odd snippet onto dat, but he was careful not to let them collect a store of EzRa's Language.

"He knows he'd be redundant," EdGar said. "This way we keep needing him." Even in his decline and terror, Ez thought with ruthless strategy. I was impressed.

By VESPCAM, I saw the first times that EzRa's voice was played into that strung-out city.

The buildings had been unhappy for days. They were rearing and breathing steam, purging themselves of the bio-rigged parasites they bred, that were Ariekene furniture. Look out from the Embassy, to where the city began, an organic vista like piled-up body parts, and the motion of the architecture was clear. The wrongness was endemic.

The city twitched. It was infected. The Hosts had heard EzRa's impossible voice, had taken energy from their zelles and let out waste, and in the exchange the chemistry of craving had been passed, and passed on again by the little beasts when they connected to buildings to power light and the business of life. Addiction had gone into the houses, which poor mindless things shook in endless withdrawal. The most afflicted sweated and bled. Their inhabitants rigged them crude ears, to hear EzRa speak, so the walls could get their fix.

EzRa spoke. They said anything in Language. Their amplified voice sounded through all the byways. Everywhere in the city Ariekei staggered and stopped. Their buildings staggered with them.

It disgusted me. My mouth twisted. Everything beyond Embassytown shuddered with relief. It moved through pipework, wires and tethers, to every corner of the grid, into the power stations stamping in a sudden wrong bliss. Withdrawal would start again within hours. By the edge of our zone we could feel it in the paving: a shaking as houses moved. We could track their biorhythms through our windows, could gauge how badly the drug of speech was needed.

IN THE PAST, each few months at harvest- or weaning-time, we'd send aeolied Ambassadors and barter-crews out to where Ariekene shepherds of the biorig flocks would explain different wares, these machines half-designed half-born to chance, what each did and how. Now, the Ariekei neglected their out-of-city lands. Biorigging still entered the city, and we could see by the convulsions of the enormous throats that stretched kilometres to the foodgrounds that pabulum was still coming in too. And that, with reverse peristalsis, addiction was being passed out.

"This world's dying," I said. "How can they let it go like this?"

We saw no attempts at self-treatment, no struggles. No Ariekene heroes. Ambassadors could converse with them in the hours after they'd had a hit of EzRa's voice, when they seemed to humans lucid, but only to make the shortest of plans, for scant hours ahead.

"What do you think they should be doing?" MagDa was one of the few Ambassadors working to usher in change. I'd joined them. I was trying to be part of this new team. I knew MagDa and Simmon, scientists like Southel. Mostly though it was people new to me. "There's no *equilibrium* possible." "This is chance. A cosmic balls-up." MagDa hadn't equalised. I saw broken veins beneath the eyes of one and one only, and new lines beside the mouth of the other. "This is just a glitch between two evolutions," they said. "How would they accommodate it?" "This doesn't mean anything." "They'll listen themselves to death before they'll try to change."

The Hosts had always been incomprehensible. In that one sense, nothing had altered.

The upper floors of the Embassy had become a moral ruin. A little farther down, I saw Mag and Da cajole the Ariekei who came, force them to focus just long enough that we could be sure they'd understood our requests, for materials and expertise. And in return, what was it MagDa offered?

Have it say about colour, I thought I heard one Host say.

It will, MagDa said. *You will bring us the tool-animals before tomorrow and we will make sure it describes every colour of the walls.*

"We keep going through colours for them," Mag said to me.

"They're loving it," Da said. "But eventually..." "... the *piquancy* of it's going to wear off."

After this exchange I made new sense of EzRa's little speeches to the city. Someone would generally translate. Some nodded to logic. Others were random sentences, or statements of preference or condition. *I'm tired,* subject-verb-object like children's grammars. What I'd previously thought whims of subject I realised might be gifts for particular Ariekene listeners, in return for this or that favour. Economies and politics.

In the Embassy corridors, Ra, that impossible not-doppel, joined MagDa and me. Mag and Da kissed him. His presence meant we were approached by people desperate for some kind of intercession. He was as kind to them as he could be. I'd seen too many messiahs thrown up by Embassytown. "How long do we have to go on?" one distraught woman asked him.

"Until the relief," he said. So many hundreds of thousands of hours, scratching out an interstitial living while the Hosts hankered for EzRa's sounds.

"Then what?" the woman said. "Then what? Do we leave?"

No one answered. I saw MagDa's faces. I thought of what life would be, for them, in the out.

Reliefs had arrived on catastrophised worlds before. No communications could warn; there's no outracing an immer ship. No crew could know what they'd see when their doors opened. There were famous cases of trade vessels emerging from immer to find charnel grounds on once-established colonies. Or disease, or mass insanity. I wondered how it would be for our incoming captain to emerge in our orbit, as close as she or he dared to the Ariekene pharos. If we were lucky, that ship would find a populace desperate to become refugees.

MagDa in the out? CalVin? Or even Mag and Da and Cal and Vin? What would they do? And they were among the most collected of the Ambassadors. By then most others were falling, to various degrees, apart.

"They go into the city," MagDa told me when we were alone. She was talking about Ambassadors. "Those of them who can still pull themselves together a bit." "They go in, and find Hosts." "Ones they've always worked with." "Or they just . . . stand between buildings." "And they just start to talk." They shook their heads. "They go in groups of two or three or four Ambassadors and just . . ." ". . . they just . . . they try . . ." ". . . to make the Ariekei listen." They looked at me. "We did it once, ourselves. Early on."

But the Ariekei wouldn't listen. They understood, and might even answer. But they would always go back to waiting for EzRa's announcements. The vespcams got everywhere, wouldn't let Ambassadors hide their breakdowns. I'd seen footage of JoaQuin howling, and speaking Language, and in their misery losing their rhythm with each other, so the Ariekes to which they desperately tried to talk didn't understand them.

"Did you hear about MarSha?" MagDa said. I remember nothing about their voices that warned me that they were about to say anything shocking. "They killed themselves."

I stopped in my work. I leaned on the table and looked at MagDa slowly. I couldn't speak. I put my hand over my mouth. MagDa watched me. "There'll be others," they said quietly, at last. When the ship comes, I thought, I could leave.

"WHERE'S WYATT?" I asked Ra.

"Jail. Just up the corridor from Ez."

"Still? Are they . . . debriefing him . . . or what?" Ra shrugged. "Where's Scile?" I had not seen, nor heard from, nor heard of, my husband, since the start of this ruinous time.

"Don't know," Ra said. "You know I don't really know him, right? There was always a crowd of Staff around us when we were talking . . . before. I don't even know if I'd recognise him. I don't even know who he is, let alone where he is."

I descended, passed searchers looking through a room full of papers for useful things. We were doing a lot of scavenging. More floors down, and I heard someone call my name. I stopped. It was Cal, or Vin, in the entrance to a stairwell. He blocked my way and stared at me.

"I heard you were around here," he said. He was alone. I frowned. His aloneness continued. He took my hands. It was months since we'd spoken. I kept looking around him and I kept frowning. "I don't *know* where he is," he said. "Close, I'm sure. He'll be here soon. I heard you were here." This was the one I'd meant to wake. He stared with a desperation that made me shudder. I looked down to avoid his eyes and saw something I could barely believe.

"You turned off your link." I said. Its lights were off. I stared at it.

"I was looking for you, because . . ." He ran out of anything to say and his voice got to me. I touched his arm. He looked so suddenly needful at that that I couldn't help pitying him.

"What's been happening to you?" I said. Bad enough for me, but the Ambassadors had become abruptly nothing.

In the corridor behind him his doppel appeared. "You're talking to *her*?" he said. He tried to grab his brother, who didn't take his eyes from me but shook his doppel off. "Come *on*."

They weren't equalised. As with MagDa, I could see differences. They whispered an altercation and the newcomer backed away.

"Cal." The first man, the half who had sought me out, said, looking at me. "Cal." He pointed at his brother, at the other end of the corridor. He prodded his own chest with his thumb. "Vin."

I knew his look of longing wasn't, or wasn't just, for me. I met it. Vin walked backwards to join his brother, looking at me for several seconds before he turned.

12

I TRAVELLED INTO the city with MagDa and Staff, part of a group trying to keep a paralysed Embassytown alive. Aeolius on me exhaling air I could breathe, I walked at last into that geography. We couldn't risk corvids: the systems in place to ensure safe landing were now too often not operated.

We couldn't wait—our biorigged medical equipment, our food-tech, the living roots and pipes of our water system needed Ariekene attention. And I think there was also in us something that needed to keep checking, to try to test what was happening. Like mythical polar explorers, or the pioneers of *Homo diaspora*, we trudged in formation, carrying trade goods.

The architecture quivered as we came and related to us as germs in a body. Ariekei saw us. They murmured, and MagDa spoke to them, and often they would respond in ways that suggested they hardly knew we were there. We were not relevant. We went past the speakers Staff had helped to place, and around each of them, though they were currently silent, were gatherings of Ariekei. These were the furthest gone: we were learning to distinguish degrees of addiction. They would wait there for more sound, whispering to each other and to the speakers, repeating whatever they had last heard EzRa speak.

Ra had to cajole and threaten Ez into their performances, now. One concession—because Ez was treated like a capricious child, with castor oil and sugar—was, within the limits of barter necessity, to let Ez decide what they would say. What we would hear translated into Language, then, were rambling discussions of Ez's past. If EzRa spoke during one of our trips into the city we couldn't escape listening to them. Christ knows what Ra thought as he spoke these platitudes that Ez wanted his audience to get drunk on.

. . . I always felt different from the others around me, the Ariekei listeners would repeat. We would walk past a patchwork of Ez's ego in scores of voices. *She never understood me . . ., . . . so it was my turn . . ., . . . things would never be the same again . . .* It was almost unbearable to hear the Ariekei say these things. Ez, I realised, built up an arc over many days. These weren't disparate anecdotes: it was an autobiography. *And that,* I heard in an Ariekene voice, *was where the trouble really started, and what happened next you'll have to wait to hear.* Ez was ending each session on a cliffhanger, as if that was what kept his listeners avid. They would have listened no less hard had he expounded details of import duties or bylaws on construction specifications or dreams or shopping lists.

WE WOULD MAKE our way to some nursery for the processing of bioriggage, a cremator full of memory, a residence or leviathan hearthlair or wherever, and when we found through the efforts of MagDa or another Ambassador the Host for which we were looking, there would follow careful discussion. It was a tortured business, negotiation with an exot addict. But we would generally achieve something. And in the company of a Host or with a cage full of the tool-parasites our maintenance needed, or with plans or the maps we were learning to use and draw, we would retrace our way. It was always a full day's expedition. The city would react vividly to us, walls sweating, window-ventricles opening. The ears that each house had grown would flex with expectation.

That was another reason we preferred not to be outside

when EzRa broadcast. I wasn't alone in finding the gluttony of the architecture and its inhabitants, the frantic eavesdropping of the walls, horrible.

Order was tenuous and dangerous but there: this wasn't the collapse it so might have been. The ship would come. Until then we lived on the brink. When we left, we would leave a world of desperate Ariekei crawling in withdrawal. I couldn't think about that, or what would happen after that. It would be a long time until we had the luxury of guilt.

I met the same Ariekei more than once on our expeditions. Their nicknames were Scissors; RedRag; Skully. If EzRa's broadcast sounded they would snap to as utterly as any other Ariekei. But other times they did their best with us: a cadre was emerging among the Hosts who were, perhaps, our counterparts; trying, from their side, to keep things going. Harder for them, given that they were afflicted.

IN EMBASSYTOWN we had countertendencies, now, to the drive toward collapse. Schools and crèches started running again. Though no one knew yet on quite what basis our economy worked any more, shiftparents mostly kept care of their charges, and our hospitals and other institutions continued. Out of necessity our town didn't fuss about the lines of profit or accounting that had previously driven its production and its distribution.

I mustn't give the impression that it was healthy. Embassytown was violently dying. When we citynauts returned it was to streets that weren't safe. Constables escorted us. We couldn't punish those determined to party their way to the end of the world. Besides, all of us sometimes went to their convivials. (I wondered if I'd meet Scile at any: I never did.) The curfew was unforgiving, though. Constables even left some dead, their bodies censored by pixellation on our news channels. There were fights in Embassytown, and assaults, and murders. There were suicides.

There are fashions in suicide, and some of ours were dramatic and melancholy. More than one person took what was known as the Oates Road, strapping on a mask to breathe and simply walking out of Embassytown, and on, out of sight and into the city; even, some stories had it, out beyond it; to let what would, happen. But the most common choice for those oppressed to death by the new times was hanging. According to what protocols I've no idea, news editors decided that those mostly bloodless bodies could be shown without digital disguise. We grew used to shots of dangling dead.

The news didn't report the suicides of Ambassadors.

MagDa showed me footage of the bodies of Hen and Ry, lying entangled on their bed, intertwined by the spasms caused by poison.

"Where are ShelBy?" I said. ShelBy and HenRy had been together.

"Gone," MagDa said.

"They'll turn up," Mag said. Da said: "Dead." "HenRy won't be the last." "They won't be able to hide this sort of thing much longer." "In fact, given the population size . . ." ". . . the rate's *higher* than average." "We're killing ourselves *more* than others."

"Well," I said. All business. "I suppose it's no wonder."

"No, it's not, is it?" MagDa said. "It really isn't." "Is it any wonder?"

WE DRAGOONED some of Embassytown's transient machines, uploading what 'ware we could to make them less stupid. Still they were unfit for all but basic tasks.

Ehrsul would still not answer my buzzes, or, I learnt,

anyone's. I realised how many days it was since I'd seen her, was ashamed and abruptly fearful. I went to her apartment. Alone: I wasn't the only one from the new Staff who knew her, but if any of the worst outcomes I suddenly pictured were true, I could only bear to find out, to find her, on my own.

But she opened her door to my knocking almost immediately. "Ehrsul?" I said. "Ehrsul?"

She greeted me with her usual sardonic humour, as if her name hadn't been a question. I could not understand. She asked me how I'd been, said something about her work. I let her blather a while, getting me a drink. When I asked her what she'd been doing, where she'd been, why she hadn't responded to my messages, she ignored me.

"What's going on?" I said. I demanded to know what she made of our catastrophe. I asked, and her avatar-face simply froze, flickered, and came back, and she continued her meaningless tasks and directionless wit. She said nothing to my question at all.

"Come with me," I said. I asked her to join MagDa and me. I asked her to come with me into the city. But whenever I mooted anything that would mean her leaving her room, the same stuttering fugue occurred. She would skip a moment, then continue as if I'd said nothing, and talk about something outdated or irrelevant.

"It's either a fuckup of some kind or she's doing it deliberately," a harried Embassy 'waregener told me later, when I described it to her. *You think?* I was about to respond, but she clarified: it might be an autom equivalent of a child singing *I can't hear you*, with fingers in its ears.

When I left Ehrsul's, I saw a letter in front of her door, opened and discarded. She didn't acknowledge it, even as I bent very slowly to pick it up, right in front of her, looking at her the whole time.

Dear Ehrsul, it read. *I'm worried about you. Of course what's going on's got us all terrified, but I'm concerned . . .* and so on. Ehrsul waited while I read. What must my expression have been? I was holding my breath, certainly. Her avatar stuttered in and out of focus until I was done.

I didn't recognise the name at the letter's end. I saw from the way it fluttered, minutely, when I bent to put it back on the floor, that my fingers were shaking. How many best friends had she collected? Maybe I was her uptown version, linked to Staff. Perhaps each of us had a niche. Perhaps all of us had been afraid for her.

Thinking about her made me think also of CalVin, of whatever pointless actions they were performing, and of Scile, from whom I had still heard nothing. I buzzed Bren, repeatedly, but to my infuriation and concern he didn't answer. I went back to his house but no one came to the door.

I DON'T THINK I'd understood what Ra dealt with until I was on Ez duty. We could of course have simply held a gun to Ez's head, but when we threatened too hard, he threatened us back, and his behaviour was so unpredictable we had to take seriously the possibility that he'd refuse to speak, and damn us all, out of spite. So instead we chaperoned him everywhere, at once jailers, companions and foils. That way when it was time for him to perform, he could make our lives hard, and we could let him kick us around, until, sulkily, he acquiesced.

Security was always in at least twos. I asked to join Simmon. When I met him he gripped my right hand in greeting with his left. I stared. The right arm he'd worn for years, an Ariekene biorigged contrivance of imprecise colour and texture but exactly mimicking Terre morphology, was gone. The sleeve of his jacket was neatly pinned.

"It was addicted," he said. "When I was charging it it must've . . ." He had used a zelle, like the Hosts and their city. "It was sort of spasming. It tried to grow ears," he said. "I cut it off. It was still trying to listen, even lying there on the floor.".

Ez was in EzRa's Embassy chambers. He was drunk and wheedling, excoriating Ra for cowardice and conspiracy, calling MagDa filthy names. Nasty but no nastier than many arguments I'd heard. Ra was what surprised me. He stood differently than I'd seen him do before. He whom we often mocked for his taciturnity spat back epithets.

"Make sure he's ready to speak when he gets back," Ra said to us. Ez gesticulated an obscenity at him.

"Can I at least go to a *party*? Or will you bastards try to keep me even from *that*?" Ez moaned as we followed him to the venue in the Embassy's lower floors. We stood watch, policed the drink he took, though we'd never seen excess seem to alter his abilities to speak Language. We watched him fuck and argue. The glints on his link puttered frantically, hunting for and not finding its pair, striving to boost a connection Ez was avoiding.

I could say it was depressing, that party, like a walk through purgatory, we at the end of the world rutting into oblivion and drugging ourselves idiot to autogenerated rhythms and a hammer of lights through smoke. Perhaps to those participating it was joyful. It didn't hold Ez's interest. I was as impassive as a soldier.

Ez took us to what had been an office equipment warehouse in the middle floors of the Embassy and was now an ersatz bar. He drank until I intervened, which made him delighted because then he could denounce me. The only people in this peculiar thrown-together place were ex-Staff and one or two Ambassadors. They showed no concern that he was risking our world with every glass.

"Your friends," I whispered, and shook my head. He met my eyes quite unmoved by the disgust.

Embassytowners had taken over the lower floors of the Embassy, looking for safety. Those levels had become back-alleys. Men and women, nurseries and shiftparents reconfigured cupboards and spilled out of meeting rooms, turning architecture inside-out. We went walking through these night streets made of corridors, where lights not broken had been reprogrammed into diurnal rhythms and house numbers were chalked on inside doors by which people leaned and talked while children played games past their bedtime. Embassytown had come inside.

Sotted and maudlin, Ez began to badmouth Ra. "That lanky shit," he muttered as we followed him through semiautonomous zones policed by their own incompetent constables. "Coattailing me, then coming the big I-am." Ra was the only person in Embassytown who shared Ez's colloquialisms and accent. "Don't you see what he's doing? Easy for him to play the nice boy when, with . . . he can . . ." Cheap lamps flickered above us, new stars. "I shouldn't . . ." Ez said. "I'm tired, and I want to stop this . . . and I want Ra to leave me alone."

I said, "Ez, I don't think I know what you mean."

"*Please* stop *calling* me that! *Fucking* stupid, stupid . . . It's . . ."

I knew his former name. He was the man who had been Joel Rukowsi. I looked at him in the rubbish-specked hall. I wouldn't call him Rukowsi, or Joel, and when I repeated his name *Ez* he slumped and accepted it.

Simmon and I rescued him from the fights he provoked.

When it was time eventually for him and Ra to perform their dawn chorus, the first speech of the day, he insulted us as we led him back up through the changed building, through new fiefdoms, embryonic slums, where new ways of living were incubating. At the chamber I reached for the door, and Ez halted me with a touch and without speaking asked me for a moment. That was the only time that night I felt anything from him other than scorn. He closed his eyes. He sighed and his face went back to drunk and ornery.

"Come on then, you bastard," he shouted, and shoved open the door. Ra and MagDa were waiting. They disentangled while Ez mocked them.

We watched EzRa fight. When Ez made some prurient cruel comment about MagDa, Ra shouted at him.

"What do you think you *are*?" Ez laughed back. "What do you think this is? '*You leave her out of this!*'? Are you serious?" Even I had to bite back a bit of laughter at that unexpected imitation, and Ra seemed a little shamefaced.

"Here," said Ez later, as sound engineers and bioriggers prepared him for broadcast. Ra read the paper Ez handed him.

"Not going to go over that stuff from yesterday?" Ra said. His voice was suddenly and surprisingly neutral.

"No," said Ez. "I want to keep on. I think I left it at a good moment, let's keep things going." *They don't care!* I wanted to shout. *You could describe the fucking carpet, the effect would be the same.*

Ra asked questions about cadence and timing, wrote notes in the margin. Ez had no copy: he'd memorised what he wanted to say. When they spoke I wasn't looking at them but over the city, and it twitched as the first hit of language came, as EzRa continued with their stories of Ez's youth.

13

CYNICALLY, WHO WERE WE? Not many, a gathering of no ones, floakers, dissident Staff, a handful of precious Ambassadors. But our numbers were growing, and our edicts weren't completely ignored. Embassytowners had begun to do as we suggested, asked, or ordered.

We—MagDa above all—worked hard at our few Ariekei contacts. We worked hard full stop, too hard for me to feel just then whatever it was I ultimately probably would, from Ez's abuse, from reading Ehrsul's letter. MagDa even persuaded some of the most contained and coherent Ariekei into the corridors of the Embassy, not simply on eager pilgrimage to EzRa, but on new business. She might reward them with a snip of unheard recording of EzRa, one of our rare stolen buggings.

"Some of them know this is a problem," said Mag. "The Ariekei. You can tell."

"Some of them," said Da. ". . . there's some kind of debate, some kind of . . ." "Some of them want to be cured."

Like fucking fungus, rumours spread. Our cams still gusted through the city. Some were intercepted by the antibodies the houses secreted, which came up like segmented predators. But when their investigations left them satisfied that the cams were no threat, they left them unmolested. The footage taught us more about our Hosts' city than we had ever known: too late. And every little half-seen movement, everything we saw out there, the what-and-where of which we couldn't identify or clarify, gave traction to stories about missing secrets, fifth columns, Staff self-exiled, old grudges.

In the farmlands, huge flocks of biorigging spawned in irregular harvests. Foods and tech came from those stretches by biotic ways. Addiction was chemical: there was a slow stream of it from the city to the kraals and the rural Ariekei. They began to neglect their charges and come to the city, for the sound they suddenly needed without ever having heard. Their deserted manors grew sick, wheezing and hungry. Herds of rigged equipment, medical tech and building tools, girdered and rhino-sized spinners of protein and polymer foundations, went feral.

When their shepherds reached the city there was no one to meet them. The country Ariekei saw their worst-afflicted compatriots lying by speakers and starving to death, waiting for the next sentence. Their bodies lay unhonoured. If the buildings around them were still healthy enough their dog-sized animalculae would break the corpses down: if not, the slower processes of internal rot would smear them gradually into the road.

Fights were common. Withdrawal and Ariekene need meant aggression. The afflicted would tear into things on sudden searches for EzRa's Language. A less affected Ariekes, usually from the country, might frill its fanwing in formal pugnacity, but the more addicted had no time for traditional displays and would simply hurl themselves hooves and giftwings at their startled opponents. Once I saw footage of EzRa's broadcast start in the middle of such a battle. The combatants slumped against each other immediately and coiled together as if in affection, still bleeding their blood.

"Things are getting worse again," Da said. We were going to infect the entire planet.

"That's not the only thing we have to contend with." It was Bren.

He stood in the doorway. A suspiciously perfect pose, all framed. "Hello Avice Benner Cho," he said.

I rose. I shook my head at him. "You prodigal *bastard*," I said.

"Prodigal?" he said.

"Where have you *been*?"

"Prodigal extravagant?" he said. "Or penitent?" A little cautiously, he smiled at me. I didn't quite smile at him for a minute, but then, fuck it, yes I did.

"How DID YOU get in here?" someone said, so newly promoted by circumstance that they added "Who are you?" to hisses of embarrassment. Ra shook Bren's hand and tried to welcome him. Bren waved him away.

"It's not just these Ariekene refugees we have to contend with," Bren said. "Though they'll certainly complicate matters." He spoke with monotone authority. "There are other things."

Of course he couldn't speak Language since his doppel had died, but there were some Ariekei—you might sentimentally and misleadingly call them old friends—that came to his house and told him things.

"Do you think none of them want this to change?" Bren said.

"No, we know," Mag said, but he continued.

"You think there are no Hosts who are horrified? They're thinking through a fug, true, but some of them are still thinking. You know what they call EzRa? The god-drug."

After a silence I said carefully, "That is a kenning."

"No," Bren said. He glanced around the room, gauging who

knew that old term for the compound trope. "It's not like a bone-house, Avice." He thumped his chest, his bone-house. "It's more straightforward. It's just truth."

"Huh," someone said shakily, "that's religion for you . . ."

"No it is *not*," Bren said. "Gods are gods and drugs are drugs but *here*, here, there's a city not only of the addicted but of . . . a sort of faithful."

"They don't *have* gods," I said. "How . . . ?"

He interrupted me. "They've known about them ever since we got here and told them what they are and what they do. They couldn't talk about voidcraft or trousers either, before we arrived, but they find ways now. And there are some Hosts who'll do anything to stop this. That might not be much yet, maybe, until they can get themselves free enough to try to free themselves more. But if they do, well. They'll end it however they can. You should think of all the ways a few determined Ariekei might try to . . . liberate . . . afflicted compatriots."

He joined me again, in private, that night, in my rooms. He asked me where was my friend Ehrsul and I told him that I didn't know. That was almost all I said that night. Bren himself didn't have much to say, but he had come, and we sat together while he said it.

I LEFT THE CITY. Three times.

Seeing those immigrant Ariekei from the outlands gave us ideas. There were some which hadn't yet left their homesteads but had started to yearn for EzRa's pronouncements. We went to them.

Our craft had ventricles through which I could put my head and look down as we flew. It exuded air in its belly-bridge, pressurised enough that the bad atmosphere couldn't push in. I took breaths, then put my head out to watch the ground.

A kilometre below, the demesnes of the Host city. Plateaus and cultivation and simple massive rocks, fractured, their fractures filled with black weedstuff. Meadows crossed with tracks and punctuated by habitations. More grown architecture: rooms suspended by gas-sacs watched us as we flew, with simple eyes.

Leaving Embassytown and then the city felt as dramatic as entering immer. It might have been beautiful. Swaying through fields, even now during the breakdown, farms ambled hugely after their keepers if they still had them, or alone. Symbionts cleaned their pelts. The farms would birth components or biomachines in wet cauls.

Orchards of lichen were crisscrossed with the gut-pipework that spanned out from the city, still looked after in places by tenacious Host tenders. A long way off were steppes where herds of semiwild factories ran, which twice each long year Ariekene scientist-gauchos would corral. We hoped to find a few of these cowboy bioriggers left, to trade their creatures' offspring.

There was I; Henrych, who had been a stallholder and now had joined the new committees; Sarah, with just enough knowledge of science to be useful; BenTham the Ambassador. The Ambassador were unkempt, bewildered and resentful. Unlike several of their fellows, though, they had still enough decorum to ensure that they were exactly equally dishevelled.

We landed and from the hillside came the distress call of grass, as our vehicles began to graze. In our aeoli masks we gathered equipment, made camp, called in to Embassytown, established a timetable. Checked once more over the orders and the wish list. "I don't think this tribe exchanges many reactor pups," I said, down the line to home. "Talk to KelSey. They're with the wetland cultivators, aren't they? That's where they'll get them, along with some incinerators." So on. We divided hunting duties between the various crews beyond the city.

Our spancarts were skittish, their foreparts stretched in rippling caterpillar motion. We stacked them full of datchips, all sound-files. Some were stolen, some made with Ez's grudging consent, when this system had been formulated and mooted to them.

I was almost certainly not as calm as this telling would imply. I'd been looking down onto the surface of the country I was born in, grew up in, returned to, that was my home, and that, *that* view beyond Embassytown, had been impossible for me till then. So there was that, and there was what I was doing, and the stakes of it. I was looking into a season and a surface without cognates. I'd been into the out, but in homily fashion, my own planet was the most alien place I'd seen.

Things like crossbred anemones and moths froze as we passed, waved sensory limbs behind us. Our cart rutted toward settlements and animals like rags of paper flew in the hot sky. The farmstead at the end of knotted man-thick tributaries of the pipework was as restless as most architecture. A squirming tower laid young machinery in eggs. The paper-shred birds picked parasites from it. Its keepers started when they saw us, then galloped for our company. The farm lowed.

So far out, the addiction seemed weaker or different. Ben-Tham could communicate our desires and understand theirs. They knew that we might have something they could hear, and they clamoured for that, unsatisfied by the degraded remnants of fix that backwashed down the arteries from the city whenever EzRa spoke, or what they half-heard from the nearest speakers, kilometres away, or what previous barterers had offered.

We showed our wares, *voilà*, like a peddler in the hills in old books. I played a datchip, and from it, in Language, EzRa said, *When my father died I was sad but there was a freedom in it too*. The Hosts reared and said something. "They've got this

228

one," BenTham said. They'd played it many times, and it had no more effect: they at last heard it for its content, and they didn't care about Ez's father.

We offered other bits from his history, clichés of diplomacy, idle thoughts, weather reports. We gave them for free. *We are very happy about the increased opportunities for technical assistance*, and tempted them with the first few phonemes of *I broke my leg when I fell out of a tree.*

"They're asking if we have the one about unacceptable levels of wastage in the refinement industry," Ben or Tham said. "They heard about it from neighbours."

Husbanding carefully, we gave them enough to buy the bio-rigging we needed, and some expertise, some explanations. Doing so we spread the addiction, too: we knew that. We brought out pure product, EzRa speech, and these as yet only half-affected outlanders would succumb.

I made a similar journey twice more after that first time. Soon afterwards, another of our buoyant dirigible beasts didn't return.

When at last our cams found it they reeled back to us footage and trid of it dead and strewn in burnt-out flesh and a slick of guts across the countryside. There drowned in it and shattered, all dead, were our people. Ambassador; navigator; technician; Staff.

I'd known Ambassador LeNa slightly, one of the crewmembers well. I held my mouth closed with my hands as we watched. We were all affected. We fetched back the bodies and honoured them as well as we could with new ceremonies. Our crews searched the mouldering wreckage.

"The ship wasn't sick, I don't think," our investigator told us in committee. "I don't know what happened."

*

IN EMBASSYTOWN we did our best to stand in the way of warlordism, but we small band of ersatz organisers could only slow a degeneration toward that kind of rule. More Ambassadors were joining us, terrified into organisation, inspired by MagDa. Others of course remained useless. Two more killed themselves. Some deactivated their links.

Ez seemed ... not calmer perhaps, but more broken, I thought, when I chaperoned him again. Delivering him finally to Ra, though, they argued even more viciously than before. "I can make things bad for you," Ez kept shouting. "There are things I could say."

When we went into the city, we had to pass the corpses of houses and Hosts. The death breakdown of biorigging designed and bred to be immortal contaminated the air with unexpected fumes. We heard more Ariekei fighting around speakers. Some of their dead had died from the violence of the desperate; some, those without enough of the new sustenance they needed, just died; and in some places there were more organised brutalities, cadres exerting new kinds of control. The living grabbed what datchips we gave them: these were rewards for these new tough local organisers, in crude concert with which we were just managing to maintain a tenuous system.

One evening as we returned to Embassytown, I lagged behind my colleagues, shaking the mulch of rotting bridges from my boots. I looked back into the Ariekene city, and I saw two human women looking at me.

They were only there a second. They stood one to either side of an alley mouth, metres away, looking at me gravely, and then they were gone. I couldn't have described them well, probably not even recognised them again, but I knew that they had had the same face.

*

IT WAS ONLY LATER, when things went wrong all over again and these new routines were made bullshit, that I realised I'd come to expect us to muddle through until the ship came and flew us all away.

One scheduled evening we could find neither Ez nor Ra at the time of their broadcast. Neither would answer our buzzes. That was like Ez, but it wasn't like Ra.

Ez was in none of his preferred places. We searched the dangerous corridors of the Embassy: no one had seen him. We tried to buzz Mag or Da, who were often with Ra, but they wouldn't answer either.

We found the four of them in MagDa's new rooms, high in the Embassy. There were several of us, constables and new Staff like me. When we turned onto a last stretch of hallway we saw a figure huddled by the apartment door. We levelled our gun-things but she didn't move.

It was Da. As I approached I thought she was dead. But then she looked up at us, with despair.

Into the rooms and to a dreadful scene. Still as a diorama. Mag on the bed, in the same precise pose as Da outside, the wall between them. She looked up at us too, and back at the dead man on the bed with her. It was Ra, quite ruined with blood. A handle emerged from his chest, like a lever.

Ez sat a way off, rubbing his head and face, smearing blood on himself, blubbing. ". . . I really didn't, it wasn't, oh, God, it was, look, I, I'm so, it . . ." he said, and so on. When he saw us, among other emotions I swear I saw shame broader than for one dead man: he knew what he'd done to all of us. My hand kept twitching as if I'd take the thing out of Ra.

Later we found out that at first the argument had been, ostensibly, about MagDa. That was the marshalling of un-convincing, rote things to express other deeper terrors and

231

resentments. The surface specifics didn't really matter. This wasn't about whatever they shouted as they fumbled and implements turned deadly.

We weren't very used to murder. It wasn't me who closed Ra's eyes but it was me who held Mag's hand and led her away. There wasn't much time to just grieve: the ramifications of the situation were obvious. I was already thinking of the tiny stock we had of EzRa prerecorded on datchip.

When I returned the others were hauling Ez away and taking Da to join her doppel. I secured the scene. I was alone for some minutes with Ra's corpse.

"Did you have to?" I said. I think I whispered out loud. I was trying hard to keep myself together and I succeeded. "Couldn't you have backed down?" I put my hand on Ra's face. I looked at him and shook my head and knew that Embassytown and I and all the Embassytowners would die.

Part Five

NOTES

14

We hid the death for days. We were miserable with secrecy. There'd be panic when Embassytown knew. I couldn't convince myself panic in three days' time would be much worse than panic now: still we hid it, like a reflex.

We had only a few recordings of EzRa. Ez had been careful. Once we risked repeating a speech that the Ariekei had heard before, but the footage we saw of consternation, the fights we spurred among outraged listeners, frightened us. We didn't try that again. We had perhaps twenty days of broadcasts. When we played them to the city we kept them as brief as we dared.

New hierarchies were asserting among the Hosts, from what we could tell. We didn't understand them.

After the murder, MagDa equalised again, for the first time in days. They entered the committee room where we were meeting, smart and unsmiling and precisely identical. I couldn't tell if it was a good or a bad reaction. In any case it didn't last.

They accepted some condolences. They'd lost no authority, remained our de facto leader, listening, debating, and offering their thoughts and almost-orders. Obeying MagDa, and out of some prurience, I became Ez's keeper.

He wanted to talk. He maundered through self-justification, self-disgust, anger, regret. I'd sit in the room where he was held and listen. At first I tried to glean the specifics of what had happened. "What was it?" I asked MagDa once. They looked weary. One of them shook her head and the other said, "That's really not the point." This outcome had been waiting for a long time.

Plenty among us advocated simply ending Ez. I and others argued against it. MagDa took our side, which was what settled it. They calculated that an excess of mercy, ultimately, would work for them better than vengefulness. Even at that time when none of us really believed we had a future, MagDa were planning for it.

I pitied Ez, though I despised him too, of course. I felt that as shocking an act as he'd committed should change someone; that he should emerge either better or fully a monster. That he could kill someone and remain the pathetic figure he was previously shocked me. He was idiotic with resentment. He responded to all my questions with a child's churlishness. He wanted to continue telling me about his life, as he had the Hosts, with Ra, in Language. He picked up where they had left off.

He didn't come clean about much. He didn't tell us whatever his original task had been, that I was sure he'd had, his—and Ra's—intended role to undermine Embassytown's power. His motivations for this secrecy were obscure: all motivations are.

I don't know how the news of Ra's death—that he had, I suppose, technically, become Ra—got out, but word of his death, and therefore that of EzRa, did spread. A guard; a rogue vespcam; an Ambassador; a doppel saying it to a momentary partner, just because it was something that could be said. The knowledge just seemed to well up in Embassytown. On the fourth day after Ra's death I woke to church bells. Sects were calling their faithful. Soon, I knew, the mere knowledge that there was nothing we Staff could do wouldn't stop the crowds from marching on us to demand we did anything.

Embassytown would fall, perhaps even before the craving Ariekei came for us. In the time that was my own, for various reasons, foremost among them a sudden urgency, a sense that he might understand all this from his weird perspective, might help me or want help, I started hunting again for Scile.

After what CalVin had done with Scile's collaboration, I'd tried to avoid finding out which other Ambassadors were complicit in $\frac{surl}{tesh\ echer}$'s execution. I couldn't face thinking about it. Cowardice or pragmatism, I don't know. In these later days that ignorance was a relief: it was hard enough to live in Embassytown right then without relating to my new colleagues with that murder in mind. I did at last meet CalVin, at a gathering of Ambassadors, both those on MagDa's committee and those too dissolute or afraid to be. I went straight to them. "Where is he?" I asked Vin. "Scile." This time I didn't mistake him for his doppel. Neither of them answered me.

BREN BUZZED ME. "People are being attacked. In Carib Alley."

A corvid took constables, MagDa and me to the flashpoint in Embassytown's outskirts. Bren was there already, on the ground, waving us down, torch in his hand: it was night. Down a small street Ariekei were clamouring outside a block. A small group of Terre were inside. They hadn't joined the exodus from this area. "Idiots," someone said.

The Ariekei were hurling things: rubbish, rock, glass. They each gripped the door in turn, frustrated by its mechanism. They were shouting in Language. *EzRa's voice. Where is it?* "This lot are the weakest," Bren said. "They're too far gone to be satisfied with what we give them now." We were increasingly parsimonious with the recorded god-drug. "They know there are Terre here, must think they're holding EzRa's voice, on datchip or something. Don't look like that. This isn't about logic. They're desperate."

Vespcams gathered. We watched their feeds. What do you

feel, witnessing the end? In my case it wasn't despair but disbelief and shock, endlessly. There, stepped into red mud by the hooves of the Ariekei, was a Terre body. A pulped man. I wasn't the only one who cried out at that sight.

The cams darted closer. One was slapped from the air by an irate giftwing. Constables touched their weapons but what, would we attack the Ariekei? We couldn't retaliate. We didn't know what that would invoke.

Officers reached the rear of the buildings, made surreptitious entrances, got the terrified inhabitants away. We watched in split visuals: them with their charges; the Hosts clamouring as they attacked the house. There was more motion. Ariekei newcomers were approaching.

"There," said Bren. He wasn't surprised by what he saw.

There were four or five new arrivals. I thought they were coming to join the attack on the house, but to my great shock they shoved in a wedge into the crowd of Ariekei with their giftwings whipping. They reared and slammed hooves into their fellows, shattering carapaces. The fight was fast and brutal.

Ariekene blood sprayed, and there were the calls of Hosts in pain. "Look." I pointed. The cameras flitted and gave me another moment's view of some of the new attackers. "Do you see?" They were without fanwings. They had only stumps, flesh rags. Bren hissed.

The traumatised human inhabitants made it to our flyer, joined us watching that new fight. The attackers killed one of the other Ariekei. Seeing it die made me think of Beehive. The Host lay there red with hoofprints in familiar gore: its attacker had slipped in what remained of the Terre man.

"So . . . we have Ariekene protectors, now?" I said.

"No," Bren said. "That's not what you just saw."

*

WE MOVED the last people from the edges of Embassytown, into blocks we could guard with constables and rapidly inducted militia. Some holdouts we forced to leave. Ariekei gathered at the ends of streets and watched their human neighbours go. We timed a broadcast of EzRa to coincide with our evacuation: the double-voice called and the Ariekei reeled and stampeded to the speakers and left us alone.

Between the ruining city and the centre of Embassytown was a deserted zone: our buildings, our houses without men and women in them, valuables taken and only the shoddy and dispensable left behind. I helped supervise the exodus. Afterwards, in the thin air at the edge of the aeoli breath, I walked through half-empty rooms.

Power was still connected. In some places screens and flats had been left on, and newscasters talked to me, describing the very removals that had left them alone, interviewing Mag and Da, who nodded sternly and insisted that this was necessary, temporarily. I sat in empty homes and watched my friends dissemble. I picked up books and trinkets and put them down again.

Ehrsul's rooms were in this zone. I stood outside them, and after a long time I buzzed her. I rang her doorbell. It was the first time I'd tried her in a long time. She didn't answer.

The Ariekei began to move into the emptied streets. A vanguard of their most desperate. With their pining battery-animals, and followed by slow carrion-eaters they would have bothered to kill as pests before, the Hosts searched the houses, too. They pressed with incomprehension and care at computers, their random ministrations running no-longer-relevant programs, cleaning rooms, working out finances, playing games, organising the minutiae of those missing. The Ariekei found no

Language to listen to. The absence of their drug didn't wean them off it: there was no cold turkey for them; EzRa's speech had insinuated too deep into them for that. Instead, more of the weakest of them just began to die. Among the Terre, Ambassador SidNey committed suicide.

"Avice." Bren buzzed me. "Can you come to my house?"

HE WAS WAITING for me. Two women were with him. They were older than me but not old. One was by the window, one by Bren's chair. They watched me as I entered. No one spoke.

They were identical. They were doppels. I could discern no differences. They weren't just doppels, they were equalised. I was looking at an Ambassador, an Ambassador I did not recognise. And that, I knew, wasn't possible.

"Yes," Bren said to me. He laughed minutely at my face. "I need to talk to you," he said. "I need you to keep quiet about something. Well, about . . ."

One of the women came towards me. She held out her hand.

"Avice Benner Cho," she said.

"Obviously this is a shock," her doppel said.

"Oh no," I said finally. "A *shock*? Please."

"Avice." Bren said. "Avice, this is Yl." I learnt the spelling later. It sounded like *ill*. "And this is Sib."

Their faces exactly those of each other, heavy and shrewd, but they wore different clothes. Yl was in red, Sib in grey. I shook my head. They both wore little aeoli, unhooked and resting in our Embassytown air.

"I saw you," I remembered. "Once, in . . ." I pointed at the city.

"Probably," said Sib.

"I don't remember," said Yl.

240

"Avice," Bren said. "YlSib are here to . . . They're how I know what's going on."

YlSib—what an ugly name. I knew as he said it that they'd once been Ambassador SibYl, and that this recomposition was part of their rebellion. "YlSib live in the city," Bren said gently. Of course they did. He'd hinted to me of such hidden. I realised he was saying my name.

"Avice. Avice."

"Why me, Bren?" I said. I said it quietly enough that it was as if intimate, though Yl and Sib could hear me. "Why am I here? Where's MagDa, where are the others?"

"No," he said. He and Sib and Yl glanced at each other. "Too much bad blood. History. YlSib and that lot were on opposite sides for a long time. Some things don't change. But you're different. And I need your help."

I was staring into something opened up. Fractures, rene-gades, guerrilla Ambassadors, unquiet cleaved. What the hell else was out there? Who? Scile? Shiftfather Christmas? Back came stupid tales, now not so stupid. I remembered unanswered questions, I wondered who'd gone from Embassytown, who'd turned their backs on it, over years, and I wondered why.

"Embassytown's dying," Yl said. She gestured at the window, and Sib at the soundless wallscreen. The worst, most Language-starved Ariekei were coming. They shambled in unnatural bursts like toys. Troops of the collapsing, falling apart variously, claim-ing our streets without intent, with only oratees' despair, but killing as they came, us and each other. We could no longer walk the outermost of our streets: there were too many attacks, too much Ariekene rage.

Cams showed those in their dotage instar wandering with pendulous food-bellies, some stumbling by their random ways into Embassytown. No Ariekei tended them. It was shocking.

There were rumours that in periods between EzRa-word highs some Ariekei were eating these unstruggling elders, as evolution intended but their culture had abjured.

Even as things fell apart I was desperate to ask YlSib where they'd been, what had happened, what they'd done since they absconded, years ago. They'd lived so close, maybe in some biorigged dwelling that sweated air at them inside. Did they consult? Had they worked for the Ariekei? Were they independent? Trading in information, go-betweens in informal economies of which I'd never known a thing? There was no way, I thought, such a hinterland could have been sustained without the patronage of some in Embassytown.

"You said they weren't helping us," I said. "Those mad Ariekei that came and attacked the others."

Bren said, "They weren't."

YlSib said, "Factions are emerging." "Some Ariekei can't even think anymore." "They're dying." "Those are the ones tearing up the outskirts." "Then there are some trying to keep some kind of order. Live in new ways." "Manage their addiction." "They're trying all kinds of methods. Desperate stuff." "Repeating phrases they've heard EzRa say, to see if they can give each other fixes." "Trying to take control of neighbourhoods." "Trying to ration out the broadcasts." "Organise different listening shifts for different groups, to keep things more . . ." ". . . organised." "And then there are dissidents who want to change everything."

"We have sects," Bren said. "So do they, now. Not ones that worship a god, though. Ones that hate it."

"They know the world's ending," said YlSib. "And some of them want to bring in a new one." "They *despise* the other Ariekei." "That's what you saw." "Their word for the addicts was . . ." They said a word together, in Language. "They used to call them that," Sib or Yl said, "although they can't anymore."

242

"It means 'weak'." "'Sick'." "It means 'languid'." "Lotus-eaters." "They're going to start a new order."

"How . . . ?" I remembered the stubbed and ruined fanwings. *They can't call them that anymore*, because they can't hear, or speak, they've no Language. "Oh, I . . ." I said. "Oh, God. They did it to themselves."

"To escape temptation," Bren said. "It's a vicious cure but it's a cure. Without hearing, their bodies stop needing the drug. And now, the only thing they hate worse than their afflicted brethren is the affliction."

"Or, to put it another way, us," said YlSib.

"If they'd seen you . . ." ". . . they'd have killed you faster than they did their own."

"There's not many of them," Bren said. "Yet. But without EzRa to speak, without the drug, they're the only Ariekei with a plan."

"The only Ariekei," Sib said. "We've got one too, though." "We have," said Yl, "a plan."

15

In the out, I'd learnt that our Embassy isn't a huge building. In countries on many planets I'd seen much larger: taller, aided by gravity-cranes; more sprawling. But it was large enough. I was only slightly surprised to discover that there were whole corridors, whole floors that by convoluted design I'd not only never been into but had never suspected were there.

"You know what to do," YlSib had said to us. "You need a replacement." "Open the damn infirmary."

That was the basis of their idea, the plan that Bren relayed to MagDa's committee, as if it were his own. I wasn't clear on why he'd introduced me to YlSib, but he was right to trust me. Close to the top of the Embassy, in a set of infolding rooms and halls, was the separated-off zone. I followed those who knew the way.

The Ambassadors and Staff of the committee looked horrified at Bren's suggestion. He insisted, with references incomprehensible to those of the committee ignorant of the infirmary he mentioned. I pretended to be one of them.

"There could be others in there we can use," Bren said.

"And how are we supposed to know?" said Da.

"Well, that's a difficulty," he'd said. "We're going to have to have a test subject."

Only streets away, the anarchy of desperate Ariekei grew worse, and more of our houses fell. Embassytowners still foolishly near the city would turn corners into those ravenous things, who rushed at them and in Language begged them to speak, to sound like EzRa sounded. When they didn't, the Ariekei took hold of them and opened them up. Perhaps in rage, perhaps in some hope that the wanted sound would emerge from the holes they made.

I couldn't believe what we were planning. We'd gone by foot into the city, in a snatch squad. Smoke and birds circled above us. Micropolitics were everything in Embassytown by then, groups of men and women enforcing their wills in territories of two or three streets, armed with wrenches, or pistols or pistol-beasts crudely rigged, that they shouldn't have had to use, that clenched them too tight, drew blood from the weapon hand.

"Where's EzRa then, you fuckers?" they shouted when they saw us. "Going to fix everything, are you?" Some of those posses shouted that they would attack the Hosts. If they did they might take down one or two of the weakest, but against those aggressive self-mutilated they'd have no chance.

Into the ring of Embassytown we had lost, where the Ariekei had been followed by pet weeds. They were already shaggy or crustlike over what had recently been our architecture. The air here was tainted by theirs.

We kept our weapons up. Ariekei saw us, and now it was they who shouted, came forward, ran away. *EzRa, EzRa, the voice, where is the voice?*

"Don't kill unless you really have to," said Da. We found a lone Ariekes, turning, pining for words.

Come with us, MagDa said.

EzRa, the Ariekes said.

Come with us, MagDa said, *and you will hear EzRa.*

We buzzed a corvid. It was antique, metal and silicon and polymers: entirely Terretech. We were chary of using our more sophisticated machines now: they were built with a compromise of our traditions and local biorigging, and as addiction spread, they might be tainted. For all we knew they might gush that need if we flew them, in their exhaust, perhaps in the tone of their drone.

THE ARIEKES who came with us was called $\frac{shoash}{to\ tuan}$. It was confused and overcome by need for the god-drug's voice. It was physically starving, too, though it didn't seem to know it. We gave it food. It followed us because we made promises about EzRa. We took it with us to that infirmary. I wasn't the only ex-commoner on the committee, who hadn't known the wing existed. By a series of counter-intuitive corridor turns and staircases we arrived at a heavy door. There was even a guard. Security, in this time when all officers were needed.

"Got your message, Ambassador," he said to MagDa. "I'm still not sure I can . . . I . . ." He looked at us. He saw the cowed Ariekes with us.

"We're in martial times, Officer," MagDa said. "You don't really think . . ." ". . . that the old laws apply." "Let us in."

Inside, uniformed staff met us and made us welcome. Their anxiety was palpable but muted compared to everyone else's. There was a pretend normality in those secret halls: it was the only place I'd been for weeks where rhythms didn't seem utterly sideswiped by the crisis.

Carers went with drugs and charts in and out of rooms. I got the sense that this crew would continue with these day-to-day activities until word-starved Ariekei broke through their doors and killed them. I suppose there were other institutions in Embassytown where the dynamic of the quotidian sustained— some hospitals, perhaps some schools, perhaps houses where shiftparents most deeply loved the children. Whenever any society dies there must be heroes whose fightback is to not change.

The infirmary was infirmary and asylum and jail for failed Ambassadors. "As if it would work every time you tried to make two people into one," Bren whispered to me, in scorn.

Ambassadors were bred in waves: we passed rooms of men and women all the same generation. First through the corridor of the middle-aged, incarcerated failures more than half a megahour old, staring at the cams and at the one-way glass that kept us invisible. I saw doppels in separated chambers, unlinked I suppose or linked loosely enough that the wall between them caused no discomfort. Looking into room after room I saw faces twice, twice, twice.

Some cells were empty and windowless and spare, some opulent with fabrics, looking out over Embassytown and the city. There were inmates secured or limited by electronic tags, even straps. Mostly the infirm, as one of the doctors who guided us called them, said nothing, but one of those buckled in constraints screamed inventive filth at us. How she knew we were passing beyond the opaque glass I don't know. We saw her mouth move, and the doctor pressed a button that for a few seconds let us hear her. I disliked him for it a great deal.

Everything was clean. There were flowers. Wherever possible over double rooms was the printed name of those inside, with honorific: *Ambassador HerOt, Ambassador JusTin, Ambassador DagNey*.

Some had simply never had the empathy they'd needed, to pretend to share a mind, had only ever been two people who looked the same, despite training, drugs, the link and coercions. Many were insane to different degrees. Even if they had facility with Language, they'd been left unstable, resentful, melancholic. Dangerous. There were those who'd been made mad through cleavage. Who hadn't, as Bren had, been able to survive the death of a doppel. They were broken half-people.

There was a huge variety of the failed. Many more than there were Ambassadors. I was horrified at these numbers. *I never knew*, I told myself. We were too civilised to end them: hence this polite prison where we waited for them to die. I knew enough Terre history to assume that some of these failed must be counted so because of political refusals. I was reading every nameplate we passed, and I realised it was for names I recognised, like DalTon—those of dissidents of whom only bad citizens like me spoke. No sign.

Past an extreme section, men and women older than my shiftparents baying like animals and those talking with careful civility on coms to their carers, or to no one. "Christ," I said, "Christ Pharotekton."

In its withdrawal, $\frac{shoash}{to\ tuan}$ unthinkingly defecated. It realised what it had done and said something in shame: the action was as taboo for the Hosts as for us.

I think the doctors deliberately took us a long way to our destination, a room where we could hold our auditions. So we were voyeurs on chamber after chamber. We passed walls painted in brighter colours, where screens were uploaded with playware, and God help me the aesthetics were so incongruous that it took me seconds to understand. This was where they brought Ambassador-young, some just 50 kilohours old. I didn't look through the windows in those doors, and I'm glad I didn't see the unfixable children.

IN A LARGE ROOM, we asked $\frac{shoash}{to\ tuan}$ to pay attention. One by one the doctors brought in what they thought the most likely candidates, all of them under guard.

Those who'd never mastered Language were no good to us, nor those too unstable. But some pairs held almost all their lives had been incarcerated for nothing but that there was something lacking when they spoke Language, a component we couldn't detect. Many of them retained a startling degree of sanity. Those were the people we tried.

An aging duo stood before us, men without any easy Ambassador arrogance. Instead they seemed inadequate to the courtesy we gave them. They were named XerXes. The Ariekes entranced them: they'd seen no Hosts for years. "They could once speak Language," a doctor told us, "then suddenly they stopped being able to. We don't know why."

XerXes had a polite and uninquisitive affect. "Do you remember Language, Ambassador XerXes?" Da said.

"What a question!" "What a question!" XerXes said. "We're an Ambassador." "We're an Ambassador."

"Would you greet our guest for us?"

They looked out of the window. Sectors of the city were listless and discoloured in withdrawal, overrun by wens.

"Greet them?" said XerXes. "Greet them?"

They muttered together. They prepared, lengthily, whispering, nodding. We got impatient. They spoke. Classic words, that even I knew well.

"$\frac{suhail\ kai\ shu}{shura\ suhail}$," they said. *It's pleasing to greet you and have you here.*

The Ariekes snapped its eye-coral up. I thought, because I wanted to, that it was like the motion Ariekei made when they heard EzRa speak. $\frac{shoash}{to\ tuan}$ peered slowly around the room.

It was just looking because there had been a new noise. It might have reacted the same had I dropped a glass. It lost interest. XerXes spoke again, something like, *Would you speak now to me?* The Ariekes ignored them and XerXes spoke again and their voice fell apart, degraded, the Cut and Turn each saying half of a different entreaty. It wasn't pleasant.

I don't quite believe there was no Language in it. I think there was something, a remnant, in what the Ariekes heard. I've thought back to what I saw, to the way it moved, and I don't believe in fact it was exactly as it would have been to random noise. It made no difference, wasn't enough, but there was, I think, in XerXes and I don't know how many others, the ghost of Language.

Ambassador XerXes were taken back to their rooms. They went tamely. One looked at us with I swear apology as he shuffled to his imprisonment.

Others: older first; younger; then, appallingly, two sets of adolescents desperate to please us. Some were equalised and dressed the same; some were not. A pair about my age, FeyRis, attempted cold defiance, but still tried desperately to speak Language when we asked them to. $\frac{shoash}{to\ tuan}$ stared at them and recognised something, but not enough. FeyRis were the first of our candidates to curse us as they were taken—dragged— away.

I stared at MagDa. I liked them, I admired them. They'd known about this.

WE MET SEVENTEEN Ambassadors. Twelve sounded to me as if they were speaking Language. Nine seemed to have some kind of an effect on the Ariekes. Three times I wondered if we had found what YlSib had hoped we might, what we were looking for, to take EzRa's place and keep Embassytown alive. But whatever they had wasn't enough.

If EzRa's Language was a drug, I thought, perhaps some other Ambassador's, one day, would be a poison. We played

$\frac{shoash}{to\ tuan}$ one of the last datchips. It slumped and shuddered at EzRa's meanderings about the biggest tree Ez had ever climbed. There was nothing in the infirmary that could help us.

"You can't replicate that," a doctor said. "These . . ." She indicated the imprisoned mistakes beyond our room. "They have *imperfections*. That's not what there was in EzRa. Two random people should not be able to speak Language. You won't find anything like that. It wasn't just unlikely that we'd find EzRa the first time: it was impossible. How do you propose to find it again?"

No wonder EzRa couldn't survive. The universe had had to correct itself. We sat in committee. "We have to close this place," I said.

"Not now, Avice," MagDa said.

"It's monstrous."

"Not *now*, Christ!" "There's not going to be anything to close . . ." ". . . or any of us to close it, if we don't bloody think."

So, silence. Once every minute or so, someone around the table would look as if he or she was about to say something, but none of us had anything. Someone was sniffing as if they might cry.

MagDa whispered to each other. "Get what researchers you can in here," they said at last. "Riggers, bios, medics, linguists . . ." "Anyone you can think of." "This Ariekes." "$\frac{shoash}{to\ tuan}$." They looked at each other. "Do what you have to." "Test it." "Take it apart."

They waited for dissent. There was none.

"Take it apart and see if you can find out what's happening." "Inside. In its *bone-house*." They glanced at Bren and me. "When it hears EzRa." "See if you can find out anything." "Maybe we can synth it that way."

Like that, by that leadership, we would murder a Host. Not even in self-defence but calculation. Embassytown became something new. I was in awe of Mag and Da for their bravery. It was a dreadful act. MagDa had known it had to come from them.

I don't think any of us thought we'd discover in the Ariekes's innards any secrets to its addiction, but we'd try. And, too, we were all going to die soon, and it was time for new paradigms, and MagDa gave us one. They took it on themselves to tell us what it meant to be at war. They gave us a dirty hope. It was one of the most selfless things I've ever seen.

16

THE VIVISECTION on the addict in the infirmary told us nothing.

Within days Embassytown knew that the committee had tried to stave off what was coming, to create a new EzRa, and had failed. Word spread because word will spread. Stories and secrets fight, stories win, shed new secrets, which new stories fight, and on.

Mag and Da had us go to war. Too late, those of us not despairing put up barricades. We'd surrendered the edges of Embassytown. Now some streets in, we hauled out the contents of deserted houses, broke them up and threw them across our streets. Earthmovers cut trenches and piled up the ruins of our roads and the Ariekene earth below them into sloped revetments. We hardened them with plastone and concrete, stationed shooters, to protect the remains of our town in the city, from Ariekei in need.

Buildings became gun-towers. We'd always had a few weapons, to which we added those taken from the Bremen caches, and engineers and riggers made new ordnance. We checked all our technology for biorigged components, destroyed it at any sign of addiction. We burned the tainted, squealing machines in autos-da-fé of heretic technology.

All this was too late, we knew. Ambassador EdGar hanged themselves. EdGar had been on the committee. Their suicides shocked us all over again. Ambassadors were suicide pioneers, and other Embassytowners copied them.

Men and women would suit up by the barriers at our borders, aeoli breathing into them, holding knives, clubs, guns they had made or bred. They'd trudge over our fortifications and into territory that had recently just been the street, was now badlands. They left us, swivelling at side streets, weapons out in manoeuvres copied from the forays of our constables and the Charo City-set policing dramas imported in the miabs. Sometimes, at the limits of our vision, the Ariekei would wait for them, by sickly indigenous buildings.

We didn't try to stop these one-way explorers. I doubt they thought they would escape Embassytown's fate by walking into bad air, into an exot city gone bad. I think they just wanted to do something. We called them the morituri. After the first few, little crowds began to come, to cheer them as they went.

The Ariekei were horrifying now. All were sick, and starving. They were thin, or strangely distended by hunger-gases; their eyes were unfamiliar colours; they jerked, or dragged limbs that didn't behave. Their fanwings quivered. Some still tried to work with us. They strived against their addiction. They gathered at the base of the barriers, ostentatiously not attempting to breach them, to prove goodwill. They would call us. We would fetch MagDa or RanDolph or another Ambassador on the committee, and they would attempt to parley.

Sometimes the Hosts left us energy, fuel, miraculously untainted biorigging. We gave them the food or medicines they were no longer able to make. We promised them EzRa's voice, which was all they begged for. Whatever inklings they had about how lies worked, about the nature of our promise, they showed no suspicion. They waited hopelessly. Often they dispersed only when driven away by their less-controlled siblings.

The most desperate oratees, incapable of planning, would come full tilt at the barricades, leap far and fast up them, grabbing with giftwings, shouting in Language. We repelled them. We killed them when we had to. I've seen Ariekei shot, blown apart by explosives, burnt by the caustic sputum of biorigging, cut with blades. When anyone killed their first Ariekes, a life of conditioned respect would break: gunners would weep. The second time not.

ANIMALS INFILTRATED the lost streets. Altbrocks, foxes, monkeys moving curiously down wheel-ruts. Truncators climbed drainpipes and worried at loosening windows. Once in a while some depressive guard would shoot one and the beasts would scatter, but it quickly became bad luck to kill a Terre beast. It became instead a sport to take out the fluttering, tottering, strangely walking Ariekene animals that also came. No one was sure whether truncs, neither Terre nor indigene, were targets or not, and they were left alone.

We avoided thinking about our inadequate stocks of food, of energy, of the stuff we needed. A narrative went up with our walls of torn-up rubbish, of last stands and resistance, the onslaught of hordes. It helped. In the evenings, people gathered in the little neighbourhoods left to us. I was surprised at what gave us comfort. Artists plumbed our archives, digital archaeology, back millions of hours, to the antediasporan age. They pulled up corroded ancient fictions to screen.

"These ones are Georgian or Roman, I gather," one organiser told me. "They talk early Anglo, though." Men and women bled of colour, in clumsy symbolism, fortified in a house and fighting grossly sick figures. Colour came back, and protagonists were in an edifice full of products, and sicker enemies than before relentlessly came for them. We read the story as ours, of course.

*

WE KNEW THE Ariekei would breach our defences. They entered the houses that edged our zone, found their ways to rear and side doors, large windows, to holes. Some came out of the front doors into our streets and tore apart what they found. Those with remnants of memory tried to get to the Embassy. They came at night. They were like monsters in the dark, like figures from children's books.

There were other dangers: there were human bandits. A rumour circulated that one group of criminals included Kedis and Shur'asi, as well as Terre. There was no evidence. Still, when, by what was certainly human action, a Shur'asi was found dead by our main barricade, the excuse was whispered that it had been part of that predatory gang. They only died by violence or mishap, and for that race the death—every Shur'asi death— was an abomination as epic as the Fall.

Not all the Ariekene corpses we cleared were killed by us, nor by the random brutality of other afflicted Hosts. Some were destroyed with what seemed a more deliberate alien savagery.

"That's those we saw," Bren told me. "Without their fan-wings. We're worrying about the addicts, but we need to think about them, too."

"Where are YlSib?" I said.

"They're not lunatics, you know," he said. "There are ways of being in the city. Yl, Sib . . . and others. You know ambassading doesn't always take."

"That place has to close, Bren. Christ. Those people can't be kept like that."

"I know."

I stayed the night with him, for the second time. We said even less than we had the first time, but that was really alright, as alright as it got that night. "Do you think there are languages made up of three voices?" I asked him at one point.

"It's a big out," he said. "Sure. And four, and five."

I said, "And places where exots speak Anglo in ways that mess up human heads."

We stood naked by his window, his arm over my shoulder and mine around his waist, and listened to fires, shouts, shattering.

BREN GOT A BUZZ early the next morning. He would not say from whom, to my anger. He raced us to the border. A tide of Ariekei were coming. They galloped at the barricades in a wave, an invasion organised with last gasps of sentience. *I very much stress that I wish to hear the voice of EzRa please,* the Ariekei shouted as they came to kill us. *Is there a possibility that we could hear EzRa speak?*

The guards were calling for backup. MagDa, our comrades and Staff came. With animal-guns fast-bred without ears, with rapidly machinofactured bullets, with hurled clubs and polymer crossbows firing quarrels made of reclaimed stair-rods, we staved the Hosts off. Ariekei burst, screaming their polite requests, *we most sincerely ask.* Zelles scuttled up our barriers and we shot them too. Kedis were with us. There were Shur'asi playing out electrified wires. I saw Simmon firing expertly with what had once been his off arm.

With only the tiniest organising the Ariekei would have taken us, but they were drugless and incompetent. They had to clamber over hillocks of their dead. Scavengers came: wild house antibodies. Our own birds tasted the air over the carnage and arced away again. My eyes were watering from acrid Ariekene innards. There was a commotion from side streets. Something was slamming into the Hosts. I shouted for Bren's attention. It was a mass of those other, self-mutilated Ariekei. They'd come hidden among the others, a fifth column. Bren watched them without expression, while the rest of us gaped, as they dispersed our junkie attackers brutally.

"Bren was the first here," Da said quietly to me. She looked over to where Mag spoke to him. "With you. He knew this would happen, didn't he? How?"

I shook my head. "He knows people."

"Do you?"

I wasn't going to mention YlSib. Da was no fool: it wouldn't have surprised me if she was aware of everything, including relevant names. "Come on," I said.

"What do you know, Avice?"

I didn't answer but I met her eye, to make sure I didn't seem embarrassed or ashamed; so if she could tell I was holding back, she knew it was because I was trying to show respect for something. I was buzzed right then, from an ID I didn't recognise, sound only, no trid or flat. The voice was muffled beyond recognition.

"Say that again," I shouted. "Who is this? Say that again."

Whoever it was did and that time I heard. I held my breath and hoped I was wrong and put it to speaker, so Mag and Da and Bren could hear. But I was right. The words came one more time, much clearer.

"*CalVin's dead.*"

ALL WE FOUND in their rooms was the detritus of drink and of sex. There was no answer on CalVin's buzz. We went to clubs they'd been known to visit, where to my disgust a last fervent few were still trying to blot out the end of the world. They told us CalVin hadn't been there for days. The last time, they'd been accompanied by some uninterested man.

Down to other bars, and nothing and still nothing. I knew abruptly who had been with CalVin. We took a route to where

I'd once lived, where Scile had once lived, and to which now that I'd gone, he'd returned. My key still worked. Scile's stuff was everywhere, the flat was all his now, but he was absent. There was a note from him, to me, on the bed that had once been ours. It had been opened already. I unfolded it just enough to read the line *This is to say goodbye*, and stopped.

CalVin were in another room. The message had been wrong: CalVin wasn't dead. Vin was dead. He dangled. Cal was watching him move pendulum-precise. I saw another note, on another mattress.

Cal looked at me. God knows what he saw in my face right then. "I didn't feel it," he said. "I didn't know. I . . ." He touched his neck, his link. "It was . . . but we turned it on again. I should have known. I didn't know. How could . . . I didn't know."

He sounded bestial with loss. "How?" he shouted. "Who *is* this?" He threw out his hands at his dead doppel, his brother, impossibly alone dead.

Part Six

NEW KINGS

17

I HELD SCILE's letter for hours, and I don't think I even knew it. It was I who ended up alone with Cal, after we'd taken him to the Embassy and given him drugs to calm him.

"Did you cut him down?" he said.

"We took care of him," I said.

"Why are you here?" he said to me as others came and went.

"MagDa'll be here in a minute," I said, "they're just organising some—"

"I didn't mean . . ." He didn't speak for seconds. "I wasn't complaining, Avice. Vin's gone . . . Why are you here with *me*?" Even now it was hard to acknowledge something we'd known for months, the fact of disparity. After a long time I just shrugged.

"I just didn't know." He spoke with wonder. "I had to . . . we separate sometimes now, we have to, a little bit. And . . . I was just . . . He and Scile were working, I thought, and . . ."

He put his own note, from his doppel, on the bed. He let me pick it up. People brought food and murmured in sympathy: CalVin had collapsed fast into selfishness, as others fought to fix the world, but Cal, and CalVin, had been central enough beforetimes to retain something. CalVin had been a leading Ambassador. Tipped to head the Embassy when JoaQuin retired. For many of the committee, their failure hadn't been a failing but a sickness, and this was its dreadful result. I unfolded Vin's message.

I'm not like you. Forgive me.
Tell her something from me.
Please forgive me. I'm not so strong. I've had enough.

Perhaps I'd expected or hoped for something like that second line.

"You see my orders," Cal said. "So what shall I tell you?" And though he tried to make it unpleasant, I couldn't bear the break in his voice. I looked at the other paper, Scile's letter. "I think it was . . . Vin found that just before . . ." Cal said. I hadn't heard MagDa and Bren come in. I realised they were there when Cal said something like, "Avice Benner Cho and I are just comparing our valedictories."

Dearest Avice, I read.

Dearest Avice,
This is to say goodbye. I am walking. Out. I hope you can forgive
me for this but I cannot stay, I will not do life here anymore—

And then I stopped, refolded the thing. Even Cal looked at me with a bit of sympathy.

"He was something, once," I said. "I won't indulge this." *This isn't the man I married*, I could have said, and I shocked them by laughing coldly. I pictured the visionary enthusiast I'd loved traipsing through Embassytown to find a place to end himself. I wondered when we would find him.

MagDa took the note from me. Da read it, handed it to Mag.

"You should read this," Da said.

"I'm not going to read it," I said.

"It explains things. His . . . theories . . ."

"Jesus fucking Christ Pharotekton, MagDa, I'm not going to read it." I stared them down. "He took the Oates Road. He's gone. I don't care about his fucking theologies. I can tell you

264

what it says. Language is the language of God. The Ariekei are angels. Scile's their messenger, maybe. And now it's the fall. Our lies corrupt them?"

Bren's expression was fixed. MagDa shifted and couldn't deny the accuracy of what I said.

"You think you're the only one suffering?" they said. "Get over yourself and do it now, Avice." "It was when he read *this*"—Mag or Da shook Scile's letter—"that Vin did himself in, do you realise that?"

"What were they *doing*?" I said. "What was Vin *thinking*? So does Scile say what . . . ?" I regretted asking.

"Just that he can't bear it here anymore," Bren said. "So he's gone. And the reasons why. The ones you said."

THE FANWINGLESS, self-mutilated Ariekei were murdering more of their neighbours. Bren sent vespcams searching. He followed vague directions I was sure came from YlSib and other contacts. We saw the deafened Ariekei's raids, had camswarms enter the corpses of houses and the holes where dwellings had uprooted or sublimed. I didn't know what we were searching for. He'd given us no idea of which direction he'd walked away to die, and I repeatedly imagined the lenses finding Scile's body. They did not.

Where there was the new breed without their fanwings, they were bunkered down in ruins, touching each other's skins, and pointing. If they caught our cams they destroyed them. They hunted the oratees.

There were Ariekei not so far-gone as the addict-living-dead, nor so enraged as the marauders: in biorigging nurseries or their skeletons, they talked frantically in Language so fast Bren found it hard to follow. "I've not heard talk like that," he said. "Things are changing."

They were trying to live. They shouted for EzRa's voice, and built encampments around the speakers that had been silent for days now. They cleaned them like totems. They tended what few young survived, and protected the post-sentient oldsters, also addicted, though they didn't know it. We saw a stand-off between a tiny group of these at least residually civilised, and the walking ruins, who looked at the mindless elders and made mouth-moves of hunger.

On my own I watched other things. Grubbing through border-cam footage from the night we found Vin—no one knew I was doing it—I found at last a few seconds of my husband, on his walk, out of Embassytown. One more change of shot after abrupt change, and I was watching him descending one of our lower barricades.

He glanced up, at what must have been another cam, the stream from which I couldn't find, so I never saw his expression full-on. I could tell it was Scile, though. He went, not walking slowly nor with obvious depression. He walked into the danger-ous street like someone exploring, in those seconds I saw, before the signal stuttered, and there was just the street and he was gone.

DURING THE WEEKS of his incarceration, Wyatt, Bremen's redundant man, had repeatedly demanded to talk to us. At first, in a nebulous sense of due process, the committee had agreed. All he'd done was shout in panicked bullying, denounced us. We stopped coming.

Some people speculated that he had managed to send an emergency flare to Bremen: even if he had, and even if it was well programmed, it would be months before it reached them, and months again until they sent any response through the immer. Too late for us to be saved, even as mutineers.

I didn't think much about it when MagDa first told me Wyatt was demanding to see us again. We'd been keeping him in solitary, in case of those imagined other Bremen agents in Embassytown to whom he might give orders. "He's finally heard about Ra," Mag said. "He knows he's dead." Incommunicado or not, I was surprised it had taken so long for word to get to him. "You should hear this, actually." We watched the feed from Wyatt's cell.

"*Listen* to me!" He addressed the cameras carefully. "I can stop this. Listen! How long has Ra been dead, you *idiots*? How can I help if you won't tell me what's happening? *Bring me to Ez.* You want to rule, you can rule, be a republic, I don't care, I don't give a *shit*. It doesn't matter. Whatever you want, but if you want there to *be* an Embassytown at all then for God's sake let me out of here. I can stop this. You have to take me to Ez."

We'd seen him wheedling, and blustering, but this was new.

At our perimeter, oratees and their Ariekei enemies came at us incessantly. At the start of what looked like our last defence campaign, MagDa, Bren, the best of the committee and I went to see Wyatt.

EMBASSYTOWN JAIL was still staffed by a few guards who, out of helplessness as much as duty, didn't disappear. Wyatt had refused to explain anything to us until we took him with us—under guard—to see Ez. We watched the half-Ambassador in his cell, in a dirty prison uniform. "What did you think?" Wyatt muttered. He was speaking to us while he stared at Ez. "How did you think that worked?" he said. He nodded and added, "Hello, Avice."

"Wyatt," I said. I didn't know why he singled me out.

"Two strangers, two friends, just so bloody happened to get a score like that on the Stadt Empathy test? Christ Uploaded, are you stupid?" He shook his head and held up his hands in apology—he wasn't trying to fight. "Listen. This didn't just happen: this was done. Understand?" He pointed at Ez. "Scan that bastard's head."

His insinuation was that whatever he wanted to explain might change things, might give us a fingerhold of hope. If that was true, Ez must have known it too, but had done and said nothing. He'd pissed away even his own hope.

"Scan it," Wyatt said. "You'll see. He was *made*." Made by Bremen. "My eyes only," Wyatt said. "You might still be able to get the orders off my datspace, if you haven't destroyed it. 'Ez.' Operative Joel Rukowsi. I'll give you the passes."

Rukowsi had had a certain facility, a predisposition for mental connection unachievable for most of us: but it was generalised, not directed. He wasn't a twin: he had no close friends with whom he'd achieved any particular intuitive bond. They didn't have language to give his talent an accurate name, so they misrepresented it calling it empathy. It wasn't that he felt as others felt, though: his ability manifested in nasty parlour tricks.

He'd been an interrogator. Virtuoso—knowing when a subject would break, what to press for, what to promise, whether they were lying, how to make them stop lying. He was recruited young, and they'd honed his strange skills, with exercises, ways of focusing, and with more invasive methods, too. They'd left him different.

Some among our little group were murmuring, interrupting Wyatt. I clicked my fingers to shut them up. "What?" I said. I waved my hand at Wyatt, *Go on*. "They made him . . . what . . . ? A mind reader?" Ez sat beyond our sound with his head down still. I wished the guards would hit him.

"Of course not," Wyatt said. "Telepathy's impossible. But

with the right drugs, and implants and receivers, you can get brains into a certain phase. Enough. With a sensitive like him—" I sneered at that and Wyatt waited. "You know what I mean. There's not many of them, but someone like him, when they've worked on him, and get him to train with someone else with the right hardware plugged in . . ." He tapped his head. " 'Ez' there can make himself read like that person." He waved his hand sine-wave style. "Same output. It's related to linktech but it's much stronger, works on heads bugger-all like each other, *so long* as one of them's . . . Well, a quote sensitive unquote.

"At first they were thinking about totally other stuff, under-covers for id-readers, get agents out of scans—mimic brainwaves and whatnot. Then something occurred to them. You know," he continued slowly, "supposedly they once tried growing their own doppels? Back in Charo City? When the colony started." He shook his head. "Didn't go so well. Story goes they sink years into it, without any Ariekei to listen to to keep the skills up, with no sense of Embassytown on the ground—miabs being even less frequent then—and end up with . . . well, pairs of people who are dysfunctional in Bremen." He indicated twoness with his hands. "And everywhere. Hardly reliable.

"But then here's Rukowsi. The thinking was it might be a way to solve an old problem."

The mystery of what it was the Hosts discerned in our Ambassadors' voices remained unsolved: all that Charo City had ascertained was that after implants, augmens, chemicals and hundreds of hours of training, Joel Rukowsi and his fellow agent, linguist Coley Wren, codename Ra, had been able to score astonishingly on the Stadt scale.

No one had known whether it would sound like Language to the Ariekei—but Stadt was the only test anyone had for that, and the operatives looked, at least, to have passed. If in fact it hadn't worked, if it had failed in the ways the paymasters had imagined it might possibly fail, if EzRa had spoken and elicited polite incomprehension, then nothing would have been lost. Two career agents would have a long and dull assignment, until the next Bremen-bound ship. But what if they succeeded?

"None of you lot are fools," Wyatt said. "Why would you think we are? You think we didn't get all your provocations, your fake meetings, your secret agendas, your disobedience, your tax-skimming, your doctoring of biorigging, keeping the best, or making it so no one but Embassytowners can make it work? You think that's been invisible? For Christ's sake, we've known for hundreds of thousands of hours that you've been building to independence."

The silence after he said that would have meant a declaration of war, shortly before. In these new times it was only a silence. What he said felt not like a revelation but like something impolite. Wyatt rubbed his eyes.

"It's just history," he said. "It's adolescence. All colonies do it. We can set our fucking clocks by you. This is my fifth stationing. Before this, I was in Chao Polis, on Dracosi, on Berit Blue. Does that mean anything to you? Christ, do you people not read? Don't you upload the dat that comes in the miabs? I'm a specialist. They send me in where outposts are spoiling for a fight."

"You quash secession," said Bren.

"God, no," Wyatt said. "You may be the mysterious old man here, but I'm from the out, and you can't hide your ignorance from me. Berit Blue *did* secede, with only the tiniest war." He held thumb and forefinger minutely apart to show how small the war had been. "Dracosi's independence was totally peaceful. Chao Polis is midway through thrashing out a plan with us for regional autonomy. How crude do you think we are, Bren? They are free . . . and they're *ours*." He let that sit.

"But there are exceptions. You're too far from Bremen, too hard to reach, for easy management. And you're not ready. You weren't going to be getting independence soon. It's the fault of Language: that's what's confused you. You think you're aristocracy. You *thought*, I should say. And that this colony was your *estate*. And you had a kind of point: unlike every other aristocracy I've ever seen you really are indispensable. Were. So you've been choosing your successors since forever. Congratulations: you invented hereditary power.

"But every one of you, every Ambassador and every vizier, every member of Staff in Embassytown, is a Bremen employee. 'Ambassadors': get it? Who do you think you speak for? We can hire, and we can fire. And we can replace."

EZRA HAD BEEN a test. An operation to strip our Ambassadors of power and hobble self-government. Their success would have changed everything. In two, three ship-shifts, the social system of this outpost would have been overthrown. If those other than our Ambassadors could speak Language, apparatchiks, career diplomats and loyalists could be sent to Embassytown for a few local years, and soon we'd rely on Bremen for survival. Our Ambassadors would die slowly half by half, doppel by doppel, and be mourned but not replaced. The crèche would close. The infirmary would empty as death took the failed, and there would be no others.

It would have been a bloodless, elegant, slow assertion of Bremen control. How could we have asked for independence when our contact with the Hosts who sustained us relied on Bremen staff? All Embassytown had had was its monopoly on Language, and with EzRa, Bremen had tried to break that.

A world-destroying mistake. Not a stupid one: only the very worst luck. A quirk of psyche and phonetics. It made sense that they would try. It would have been an elegant imperial manoeuvre. Counter-revolution through language pedagogy and bureaucracy.

"Biorigging's . . . good," MagDa said. "It's invaluable." "And, minerals and stuff from here's useful too. And a few other things." "But still." "Come on." "Why all this?" *We're a backwater,* they were saying. There was no false pride or denial. Most of us had wondered at some time why Embassytown wasn't just allowed to die.

"I'd have thought it would make sense to some of you," Wyatt said. "That you'd realise exactly what's going on." And he looked up, straight at me.

I stood and folded my arms. I looked down my face at him. Everyone turned their gaze to me. At last I said, "Immer."

I'd been to towns in hollowed rocks and a planet threaded with linear cities like a filigree net, to dry places with unbreathable air, ports, and places about which I could say nothing. Some were independent. Many belonged, free or not, to Bremen. "They never let a colony collapse," I said. We'd all heard it. "Never." No matter if the cost of transportation outweighed the prices of trinkets and expertise shipped back, they wouldn't let this town go, so long as we were theirs.

My companions were nodding slowly. Wyatt was not.

"Jesus, Avice," he said. "What do you sound like? 'It is a foundation of our government . . .'" There was a strange glee in him, a functionary's dissidence, giving the lie to lines he'd spoken many times. "You know how many colonies *have* been cut off? You've seen the charts, the gravestone symbols in the immer." I knew the stories of planets studded with human and human/exot ruins, where high-rises sank into alien muck.

Found landscapes deserted by design, failure, and in one or two instances, mystery. They were an immerser cliché. I felt reproached by all that empty architecture: that, knowing of it, I could still have repeated my government's lines.

"If it were in Bremen's interests," Wyatt said, "we'd let you go, and send me to oversee it. We didn't go to this effort because we *'leave no colony behind.'*" He looked at me expectantly again. *Have another go.*

I thought of the charts. I looked up, as if through the ceiling, at Wreck. I knew more about the immer than anyone else there, including him. I remembered conversations, the shy enthusiasms of a helmsman unaware he hinted at any secrets.

"We're on the edge," I said to my colleagues. "Of the immer. They're exploring. Embassytown was going to be a way station."

"All the biorigging and so on," Wyatt said. "It's nice." He shrugged. "Nice to have. But Avice Benner Cho's right. You've had more attention than a little place like this deserves."

None of us looked at Mag or Da. We all knew now what several of us had suspected before, that their lover Ra had been an agent, had betrayed them, and us. It was no surprise he'd had an agenda, but that it was something so inimical to Embassytown shocked me. And that Ra, in the days of crisis when everything had changed, had not said. Though, I didn't know what MagDa knew.

I missed the immer. The way the mess and mass of it gushed by ships on their way to impossibly far parts of the everyday universe, immersed in that infinitely older unplace. I imagined being an explorer on pioneering ships built for ruggedness, buffeted by currents through dangerous parts, through schools of immer-stuff sharks, repelling random or deliberate attack. I didn't believe in the nobility of the explorer, but the thought, the project, compelled me.

"They'd have to build fuelling stations," I said. "And it's a hard place to emerge: they'd have to put more markers in place." Buoys that jutted half in immer, half in the quotidian void, with lights and immer-analogues of lights to guide incomers. The night over Embassytown was to have glimmered with more than just Wreck. It would have been strung with little colours. And while ships stored up on fuel, supplies, chemicals for life systems, and uploaded the newest dat and immerware, Embassytown would be where crews waited and played. "They want to make us a port town," I said.

Wyatt said, "Last port before the dark."

Embassytown might come to be a kilometres-wide sprawl of bordellos, drink, and all the other vices of travellers. I'd been to many such places in the out. Then we might have had our own street children, harvesting food and mutating the rubbish on town dumps. It wouldn't be inevitable. There are ways of providing port services without the collapse of all the civic. I had been to more salubrious stopover cities. But it would have been a struggle.

To control a source of beautiful half-living technology, of curios, of precious metals in near-unique molecular configurations might have been desirable. To control the last outpost, a jumping-off to an expanding frontier, was non-negotiable.

"What's out there?" I said. Wyatt shook his head.

"I don't know. You'd know better than me, immerser, and you don't know at all. But something. There's always something." There was always something in the immer. "Why's there a pharos here?" he said. "You don't put a lighthouse where no one's going to go. You put it somewhere dangerous where they *have* to go. There are reasons to be careful in this quadrant, but there are reasons to come—to pass through, en route somewhere else."

"They'll come," MagDa said. "Bremen." "To see how they're doing." "Ez and Ra, I mean. To check on them." They looked at each other. "We might not have so long to wait." "As we'd thought."

"More than five bloody days is too long, now," someone said. "We're at the end."

"Yes but . . ."

"What if we—"

Wyatt was a clever man who had misplayed his hand, and was trying to salvage something: his life, at least. He'd told us everything, and not out of despair as it might seem, but as a gamble, a strategy. We looked at the glass that separated us from Ez. Ez raised his eyes to ours, to all of ours, as if he knew we stared.

18

GROUPS OF ARIEKEI were on their rooftops, between dead buildings, roaming in armed gangs: all strategies to protect themselves from the mutilated rampagers. Ariekei dead were everywhere, and here and there the remnants of Kedis, and Shur'asi, and Terre, dragged by Ariekene murderers for reasons beyond our reason. Packs of zelles wandered, hungry for food and EzRa's speech, deserted by their erstwhile owners and gone incompetently feral.

It wasn't a city anymore, it was a collection of broken places separated by war without politics or acquisition, so not war at all really but something more pathological. In each holdout, a few Ariekei tried to be the things they remembered. But they could concentrate only for hours at a time, before the equivalents of delirium tremens overtook them. Their companions would whisper words they'd heard EzRa say to whichever of their company was succumbing, trying to imitate the Ambassador's timbre. They were just words, just clauses. Sometimes those convulsing would return to half-mindfulness: enough to remember that something needed rebuilding.

Between those remnant settlements were the truly mindless that didn't even know that they shook when they did, and only hunted for food and for the voice of EzRa, and were hunted by each other. The self-mutilated, though, were suddenly rarer. I wondered if they were dying.

In places we had to haul our barriers back, abandon sections of Embassytown to the oratees. At the same time, there was an unexpected exodus of Hosts—we still called them that, sometimes, in unpleasant humour—from the city. Ariekei in small but growing numbers found the mouths and orifices where industrial guts linked the city to the meadows of biorigging and wild country. They followed them out.

"Do they think they'll find EzRa out there?" We didn't know where they were going, or why. I thought perhaps they simply couldn't bear to live any more in a slaughterhouse of architecture, amid what had been their compatriots. Perhaps their need for quiet deaths was stronger than their need for EzRa's voice. I tried not to experience too much relief, or even hope, at that notion, at the possibility that more would leave; but, cautiously, I felt some.

WE EXHUMED Ra. I didn't see it.

We thanked Christ that he'd not been cremated or rendered biomass. It was MagDa who'd saved his body: he'd had no faith, but his family's listed tradition was Unitarian Shalomic, which abjured those usual local methods, and in an effort at respect MagDa had had him interred in a small graveyard for those of such heresies.

We waited like parents-to-be while doctors worked with the schematics Wyatt provided. They removed from Ra's dead head the implant, the hidden booster of his ordinary-seeming link. It was the size of my thumb, sheathed in organics, though it was all Terretech. It made me wonder if, had the Bremeni designers used Ariekene biorigging, the implants themselves would have become infected like the Hosts, and the thing that let Ez and Ra be EzRa would have become hooked on their voice. What theology that would have been, a god self-worshipping, a drug addicted to itself.

*

THE COMMITTEE dragooned scientists from wherever they still worked: the stumps of hospitals; rogue-ministering in the streets; of course from the infirmary. We begged and forced others to start work again. Southel, our scientific overseer, organised the researches. They moved fast.

. I believe Joel Rukowsi, Ez, thought himself a consummate game-player. He thought how broken he looked was a front, I think. We asked him why he'd said nothing about his hidden, embedded technology, why he'd have gone to his death with the rest of us rather than do something that might keep us all alive. He implied some hidden agenda but I don't think he had an answer. He was just eaten by his own secrets.

He didn't understand the mechanisms, could only truculently describe how it had worked for him. He looked at the insert we had dug out of Ra, warm in my hand.

"I don't feel anything," he said. "I just knew . . . how he was feeling, what to say. I don't know if it was that thing made it easier, or what."

The researchers had teased apart the filigrees that enmeshed it into Ra's mind with disentangler techzymes. Its nanotendrils dangled from it like thin hair, twitched in my hand in vain search for neuro-matter. It mimicked the theta, beta, alpha, delta and other waves detected from its companion piece in Joel Rukowsi, coordinated the two feeds into impossible phase. Whatever the brain-states, the output would seem shared.

"It's an amp, too," Southel told us. "A stimulant. Pumps the anterior insula and anterior cingulate cortex. Emp centres." She took the thing away and learnt it, tried to uncover what it was and did, to take it apart and build another. MagDa spent hours with her, focused her energies on the project.

"They're up to something," Bren said to me. "MagDa. You can see they've had an idea."

Ez never said he'd help us, but we didn't give him any choice, and his only resistance lay in sulking. He would obey us.

"Will you do it?" I said to Bren that night. I spoke quietly. He looked away. It was at these times that I felt we could speak, when he was naked and I watched the night lights of the city now made carnival with biofires glaze him through his windows, his aging athlete's body.

"No," he said. "I don't want to. I'm too old, too stuck. I don't even think I could. I know there aren't many choices. I wouldn't be any good at it: I'd say the wrong thing the wrong way. Whoever does this needs very very much to want to live, and I don't, enough. Don't be offended. I've no death wish but nor do I have the necessary . . . verve.

"Yes, I know. Ez is Cut, it has to be a Turn-speaker. Well, we can always go to the Ambassadors and find someone desperate enough to cut themselves off from their doppel. That might not be so hard now. I'll lay you money . . ." He laughed at that, at how silly money had become. "I'll bet there are some new cleaved for us to pick from. And some'll be Turn. But you know, anyway, who we're going to choose." He turned to me. "It has to be Cal."

Neither of us spoke. I didn't even look at him.

"What do we know about Ez and Ra? They weren't doppels. But maybe what they did share was important. Hate. We're not training a new Ambassador, we're distilling a drug. We have to replicate every ingredient we know about. We need the Turn to *hate* the Cut. A voice tearing itself apart. Alright, Ez came and ruined the world. So, sure, why wouldn't the Ambassadors hate him? Why wouldn't I?" He smiled at me, beautifully. "But I'm tired of this place and I don't hate Joel Rukowsi enough, Avice. We need someone who does. Cal hasn't just lost his world, he lost his doppel. He hates Ez enough. Me, I'd be weak tea. My question is, do you think Cal knows he'll do it, yet?"

Probably, I thought. He must know what his duty would be: to become symbiont with the man who had destroyed his history, future and brother.

BEFORE HE WENT into surgery the committee gathered for what we all knew was a valedictory-in-case. Cal was like some foul-tempered birthday boy. He sought me out.

"Here," he said. He was right up in my face, and I stepped back and tried to say something neutral, but he was shoving something at me. "You should . . . have this," he said. Sometimes you could hear him pause like that, waiting for Vin to finish a clause. He gave me the letter Vin had left. "You've read it," he said. "You know what you meant to him. This is yours, not mine." Sort of to punish him for various things I didn't shrink back but actually took it.

"What the hell were you doing with Scile, all that time?" I said.

"You're asking about this *now*?"

"Not back *then*," I said, coldly. Folded my arms. "Not at the Festival of Lies. I know perfectly well what you did then, Cal."

"You . . . have no idea . . ." he said slowly, "why we did what we . . . had to—"

"Oh Pharotekton spare me," I interrupted in a rush. "Because I think I have in fact a pretty solid fucking idea why—if you don't know what's happening to Language how do you know what'll happen to *Ambassadors*, huh?—But in point of fact even if that's not your whole story I do not care. I don't mean then, I mean now. Since all this started. Surl Tesh-echer's long gone, but you were spending time with Scile since EzRa arrived. And everything went . . . What've you been doing? You and, and Vin?"

"Scile's always full of plans," he said. "We did a lot of planning. He and I. Vin ... got something else out of it, I think." He regarded me. It was when he'd read Scile's note that Vin had taken his own life. Irrespective of what Scile was in himself, what he wanted, Vin had found a community with him—of some grief or loss or something. A fraternity of those who'd once loved me, or still did? My stomach pitched.

WHILE CAL was under anaesthetic, Ez began to panic and insist that he wouldn't do anything, that he wouldn't help us, that he couldn't, that it wouldn't work. I heard from one of the guards how MagDa had arrived in the middle of his little meltdown. Mag had stood by the door while Da walked over to where Ez was sitting, and leaned over and punched him in the face. Her knuckles split.

She'd said "Hold him," to the guards, and brought her bust-up fist down on him again. He'd shouted and wriggled, his head cracking side to side. Joel had stared up at Mag and Da in the utterest astonishment, bloodily whooping with pain. Mag had said to him in a quite flat and calm voice, "In fact you *will* speak Language with Cal. You'll learn how, and you'll do it fast. And you won't disobey me or any other Staff or committee members again."

I wasn't there but that's how I was told it happened.

19

THE STRATEGYLESS onslaughts on our barricades continued. Our new town edges smelled bad, of Ariekene death. Our bricks rubbled around Host corpses. Our biorigged weapons were hungry and dying. Our Terretech ones were failing. Within days we'd be fighting hand-to-giftwing.

It was the usual siege-stuff that would finish us: the ending of resources. No food came through the dedicated loops of colon that linked Embassytown to our subcontracted farms, now, and our stores were hardly infinite. We had no power from the Ariekene plants, and our own backups would fail.

I'd never been able to convince myself that there was no harm to it, but I couldn't stop nostalgia. Just then, looking down streets with angles not as we'd have built them, which terminated or twisted in ways that still seemed almost playfully alien, toying with our teleologies, there was no way I couldn't remember when I'd stared down them in my early life and systematically populated that out-of-sight city with every kind of child's impossibility and story. From there followed a quick run-through of everything. Learning, sex, friends, work. I'd never understood the injunction not to regret anything, couldn't see how that wasn't cowardice, but not only did I not regret the out, but nor, suddenly, did I the return. Nor even Scile. When I unhitched my attention and let it wander down out-of-reach streets—which have been clocked before as yantras for reminiscence—it wasn't that I thought well of my husband; it was that in those moments I remembered what of him I'd loved.

I was spare with all that, rationed it. We tended our aeoli. The poor things had been relocated, their fleshly tethers cut and cauterised, with as little trauma as possible, but they were suffering. We had no Terretech that could replace them, and our air-gardeners frantically protected the biomes of them and their companion things, which shaped currents, sustained our rough air dome. They strived to keep them safe, unhearing, charged by unaddictable technologies, as protected as possible from cross-contamination, but despite all efforts we knew we might not be able to keep our breath-machines from addiction or sickness, and no Host savants would help us now.

As the aeoli wheezed, so would we, and the Ariekei would breach our defences and walk in. When they'd finished with us we would lie with the dead's traditional lassitude, and the Ariekei would prod us and ask us forlornly to speak like EzRa. Either they would all die, then, or new generations would be born and start their culture again. They would perhaps construct rituals around our and their parents' bones.

These were the bad dreams we were having. It was into this landscape that god-drug EzCal arrived.

I'D LEFT BREN and MagDa and others to the task of bullying and nurturing our last hope. I'd preferred to oversee other duties, the movement of supplies and weaponry. Despite knowing that Cal was waking, that he was being reintroduced to Ez, that they were making their first attempts, that they were sitting the Stadt test, that the results were being calculated, I didn't ask what was happening. I even avoided Bren.

Rumours spread that something was being made, that an autom had been perfected that could speak Language, that the Ambassadors and their friends were preparing a miab, would risk immer, to escape. We didn't leak the truth because it seemed too tentative. When EzCal did emerge into our newly nightmared town, I realised another reason we had said nothing: for the performance of it. A promise fulfilled may be a classic moment, but prophecies mean anticlimax. How much more awesome was an unexpected salvation?

I couldn't avoid picking up information: when Cal was woken, when he was healed. Though I avoided what details I could, I knew before he and Ez emerged into the Embassy square that they would do so, and I was there ready. Everyone in Embassytown seemed to be there, in fact. There were even Kedis and Shur'asi. I saw Wyatt, flanked by security, to both guard and secure him. There were automa too, Turingware struggling, so some of them expressed inappropriate bonhomie. I couldn't see Ehrsul. It was only with disappointment that I realised I'd been looking.

We were close enough to the borders of our shrunken town to hear the gusting of Ariekene attacks on the barriers, and the missiles and energies of repulses. Officers kept Embassytowners back from the Embassy's entrance. It struck me that I must have chosen to cut myself off from what had been happening in the hospital so that I could experience this as nearly as possible a member of the crowd. I looked up at the other committee members, who were parting, and stepping forward was Cal, with Ez behind him.

"EzCal," one of the official escort shouted, and Christ help me someone in the crowd took it up and it became, briefly, a chant.

Cal looked like something horrific, made worse in the moving glare of lights. His head was shaved, his scalp the palest part of his pale skin, the link on his neck shining. I think he was kept alert by some concoction of drugs: he moved in little insect bursts. His skull was crossed with dark sutures: big physical stitches, a crude technique, supposedly dictated by dwindling supplies of nanzymatic healers, but one that so exaggerated the spectacle I wondered how medically necessary it had really been. He stared into the crowd. He stared right at me, though I'm certain he didn't see me.

Joel Rukowsi was Ez again. Physically he was unmarked, but of the two he seemed the less alive. Cal spoke to him harshly. I couldn't hear the words. It was Ez who was the empathic, the receiver, who had to make this work.

"So I lost everything," Cal said into the crowd at last. Amplifiers carried his voice and everyone was quiet. "I lost it all and I went down, into that lost place, and then when I realised that Embassytown needed me, I came back. When I realised it needed us..." And he paused and I didn't breathe, but Ez stepped forward and said in a voice that was, unlike his face, strong, "... we came back."

Applause. Ez looked down again. Cal licked his lips. Even the local birds all seemed to be in the plaza, watching.

"We came," Cal said, "and let me show you..." and after another heart-stopping pause Ez muttered, "... what we'll do."

They looked at each other, and I could suddenly see an echo of what must have been hours of preparation. They watched each other's eyes and something happened. I imagined the pulses of the implants, hot-synching them, pumping out into the universe the lie that they were the same.

Ez the Cut-speaker and Cal the Turn counted each other in and opened their mouths and spoke Language.

When we heard them, even we, humans, let out gasps.

$$\frac{\textit{a sohrash kolta qes esh}}{\textit{burh lovish sath}} \cdot$$

I went away a time and now I've returned.

*

THE CITY WOKE. Even its dead parts shuddered. We all bloomed like flowers, too.

Through the wires below our streets, past the barracks and barricades, at the speed of electricity under brick and tarmacked roads empty of Terre and picked through now by Ariekei suddenly still, into the kilometres of rotting architecture, the house-beasts waiting for death, up and through the speakers. From scores of loudhailers came the voice of the new god-drug, of $\frac{ez}{cal}$, and the city came out of hermetic miserable withdrawal into a new high.

Thousands of eye-corals craned; fanwings that had been slack suddenly flapped rigid and strained to capture vibrations; mouths opened. Flights of collapsed chitin stairs raised in tentative display, suddenly stronger with the onrush of chemical fix that came with that new voice. *I went away a time and now I've returned*, and we heard the creak of reinflating skin, of flesh responding, metabolisms far faster than ours sucking on the junk energy it drew from the dissonance of EzCal's Language. All the way to the horizon, the city, its zelles and its inhabitants, rose and found themselves wherever in their walking death they'd stumbled.

Ariekene towers and gas-raised dwellings woke over the edges of Embassytown, looked down at us, opened their ears and listened. The addicted city came out of its coma of need. Our guards and gunners shouted. They didn't know what they were seeing. Their quarries, the oratees, were suddenly still and listening.

There was to be nothing more about Joel Rukowsi's life, it was clear. This was Cal's script, not Ez's. In several different ways, varying the shape of the sentences so the Language wouldn't lose its efficacy, he and Ez repeated that EzCal had come to speak. Embassytowners were crying. We knew we might live.

We would have to re-establish ways of communicating our needs to the Ariekei, and working out what we offered. Somewhere in that city now trying to rouse itself there must be those Hosts with which we had established understandings, which might now be able to take some kind of control again, with which we could deal. It wouldn't be a healthy polity. A few in control of their addiction would rule over those not, compradors at our behest: a narcocracy of language. We'd have to be careful pushers of our product.

Bren was on the stairs, and I waved, pushed through the crowd to him. We kissed, believing we wouldn't die. EzCal were silent. Elsewhere, out of my sight, hundreds of thousands of Ariekei stared at each other, high but coming lucid for the first time in a long time.

"Hosts!" we heard from the barriers. There were only a few minutes before they began to gather, to clear away their dead.

For one moment, simultaneously in every quarter, every Ariekes listening and their revivifying rooms stiffened again, in an aftershock of feeling. I saw it on the cam, later. It happened when, without looking at each other, according to I don't know what impulse, Cal and Ez leaned forward and with flawless timing, spoke the staccato Cut-and-Turn Language word that meant *yes*.

Part Seven

THE LANGUAGELESS

20

I WAS A TRADER AGAIN. I went with others in corvids to the country. Business. Now in this reign of EzCal, god-drug II, we could leave again.

MayBel was our speaker on this trip. They could say that name: $\frac{ez}{cal}$.

In the weeks since I'd flown out last, the landscape had raggedly changed. By the jut of rocks there were skeletons, where biorigging had come to die. The meadows were torn up by the tracks of stampeding machines, the new routes of refugees into the city in search of the god-drug voice, and later refugees out, in that exodus we still didn't understand. The city had been depleted, by more than the numbers of dead.

We came down where there were farmlands worked, newly, differently from before. A society was starting. It wasn't strong. The farmers were addicts again, of a new drug, but it was better than being the mindless starvelings they had been. We had no choice but to be dealers.

We went with our datchips beyond the reach of the speakers. We found Ariekei who still thought EzRa was the ruler and voice of Embassytown, and had unaccountably been silent these past days. Despite MayBel's articulacy it wasn't clear they understood what had changed, until with eager giftwing fingers, they played the files, and heard the voice of EzCal.

I want more of the other one, a farmer said. It tried to remember the way we used to trade: the haggling Terre had taught the Ariekei when our predecessors first arrived. Clumsily it offered us more of the medical rigging it had grown if we would give it another of EzRa's chips. We explained that we had none. Another, though, preferred the newcomer. It indicated several of its chewing beasts, which would defecate fuel and components: it would give us more than ever before, if we would give it more of this new EzCal.

Were those Ariekei who preferred EzCal more measured? Was there a calm, a focus to them, contrasting with a febrile air to those who still hankered for EzRa? Certainly, after ecstasy and before withdrawal, the composure between the Ariekei's necessary fixes seemed easier for us than they had been before. This EzCal version of Language left the Ariekei clearer-headed, a little more like the Hosts we had grown up with.

We tried to intervene, to shape what structures were emerging. We tried to re-establish conduits for our necessaries. I imagined Scile dead in all the landscapes I passed—in the city, huddled where his aeoli had failed; in the first downs beyond.

We overflew desolate remnants of farms, vats dedicated by old agreements to the production of our foods: nutrient-rich pabulum; crops in Terre-air bubbles; food animals and sheets of meatcloth. Fallen and falling, there were parts though that were restorable. Our crews did what they could, coaxed airglands to fill chambers, restarted traumatised birth-pens. We found local Ariekene keepers, and with snips of EzCal's speechifying we restored them to mindfulness and gave them delight, coaxed them back to the farmsteads to help us. They cured the buildings, fixed the cityward flow of what we needed. Cells of food jostled like corpuscles on their way to Embassytown.

With those peristalses of imports, we might have more or less ignored the city, now that its inhabitants weren't attacking us anymore. We could have just broadcast the god-drug's announcements to its convalescing boroughs to make its inhabitants pliant.

We didn't, of course. Most of us felt concern, even responsibility, for the biopolis. Nonetheless, we weren't expecting what turned out to be the vigorous interventions of EzCal. Really, of Cal. Cal, and with him the other half of the god-drug, didn't merely broadcast or make careful forays into the streets, to find a new Ariekei government: EzCal paraded.

The committee could have tried to stop them. Ez was our prisoner. When sometimes he tried—always obviously—to make his own plans, to turn a situation to an advantage, he was cackhanded. At first, mostly, he did as we told him; then he did what Cal told him. Cal disturbed me: his fever of importance. What we said was he was ours, that we decided what he did, and Ez with him, and it was true for a few days, until he'd remembered the minutiae of ruling.

"No, let's not go slowly," he said to us after that—to me, in fact, after I'd said that the city was still dangerous, and that with the systems we'd put in place we maybe didn't need to deal too closely with it yet. "Oh yes we do," he said.

EzCal's recitations were quite different from EzRa's. Cal put a transmitter in front of the Embassy, where he could be seen when he Languaged. He would turn up early for the broadcasts and wait, arms folded or on his hips, looking at the square, and to our surprise, it wasn't only him who did so: Ez would be there, too. He barely spoke except during these performances, in Language, and if he did, his mumbles and monosyllables made you think he was barely with you. But he never made Cal wait.

Cal wouldn't look at Ez except as he had to. It was easy to see he hated him. He found a way, though, to make himself into this new thing, using Ez as a tool.

All you who listen to me, $\frac{ez}{cal}$ said. It was the third Utuday in the third monthling of October. I didn't look at the feeds but I know what I'd have seen if I had: clutches of Ariekei throughout the city ringing the speakers and clinging to each other. I wasn't aware I was listening to EzCal's words until I reacted with shock to a promise I'd not known I was translating.

I will come and walk among you tomorrow, EzCal said. I swear I heard noises from the city when they did. Faintly, over the membranous walls. That reaction was a revolution of a kind. I'd never seen any Ariekes understand or pay attention to the specifics of what EzRa had said—their voice had been nothing but intoxicant. Where listeners had liked one banal or idiotic phrase over another, it was as abstract and meaningless a preference as that for a favourite colour. This was not the same. Some in the city, even tripping on EzCal's voice, had understood the content of those words. I wished Bren had been there with me when that happened.

"What in hell are you doing?" I went and said to Cal. At first he didn't seem to notice me. Then his expression went from bewilderment to irritation to uninterest in less than a second. He walked away, and Ez followed him, and Ez's guards followed them both.

LIKE THE KING in a story, EzCal climbed up the barricades and down again into what had been our streets, and into a mass of hundreds of waiting Ariekei. They were motionless and silent. They moved out of EzCal's way with little hoof-steps.

EzCal's retinue of nervous men and women scrambled down the plastone-set rubbish and rubble behind them. No path was cleared for us; we had to weave very tentatively between the Hosts. There were plenty of us, viziers insisting that they were indispensable, I, MagDa and others from the committee after them and trying to issue orders or just watching, collating. I had a sense I couldn't quite articulate that *of course* Cal, EzCal, had known that their words wouldn't only fulfil and fuel Ariekei cravings, but would communicate specifics.

The effortlessness of it. EzRa's audience had fugued as much at agricultural reports as at the narratives Ez had seemed or pretended to think caught them up. Now the stories Ez told had real audiences, but they weren't his stories anymore. The Ariekei kept their fanwings flared, listening hard. Cal walked as if he and Ez would keep on to the edge of historic Embassytown and into the city. They had no aeoli, so this was pure theatre. Ez kept up with him.

Listeners, EzCal said. They were amplified by tiny point-microphones on their clothes. Cal hadn't been looking at Ez, I'd have put money on it, but they spoke together. EzCal waited so long I might have expected the hold of their voice on the assembled to ebb. It had only been a single word, not even a clause, with the grammar that seemed particularly succulent to the Ariekei. But they waited.

Listeners, EzCal said. *Do you understand me?*

The Ariekei told them *yes*.

Raise your giftwings, EzCal said, and the Ariekei did. *Shake them*, they said, and again, immediately, the Ariekei did.

I'd never seen anything like this. None of the watching Terre looked anything but stunned. If Ez was excited or surprised he showed no sign of it at all. He just looked out at all these addict-obedient. *Raise your giftwings to listen*, EzCal said. *Listen.*

They said the city was ill, that it must be healed, that there was very much to do, that there were plenty of hearers in the city who were still dangerous or endangered, or both, but that things would be better now. To the Ariekei, these political platitudes, in this voice, might be revelations. They listened, and they were transported.

I didn't see any pleasure in Cal's expression. The grim strain of his face, the muscles clenching—it looked to me as if he had no choice but to do and be this, now. *Listen*, EzCal said, and the Ariekei listened harder. The walls strained. The windows sighed.

WHEN THEY REGREW the city the Ariekei changed it. In this rebooted version the houses segmented into smaller dwellings and were interspersed with pillars like sweating trees. Of course there were still towers, still factories and hangars for the nurturing of young and of biorigging, to process the new chemicals the Ariekei and their buildings emitted when they listened to EzCal. But the housescape we overlooked took on a more higgledy-piggledy aspect. The streets seemed steeper than they had been, and more various: the chitin gables, the conquistador-helmet curves newly intricate.

The old halls were still there, and that architecture revived enough by EzCal's voice to fail to die, but not quite to rise. The tracts of decayed city between new village-like neighbourhoods were dangerous. The prowling grounds of animals and of Ariekei so far gone they'd never fully woken. They would crowd isolated loudhailers during announcements and gain enough from EzCal's voice to give them aggressive need, but not enough to give them mind.

"We'll clear them out, when we can," Cal said. In the meantime the city was scattered fiefdoms, with each of which we tried to establish protocols. I found out something of their specifics—"that one's run by a little coalition of the not-very dependent; that one's too risky to go into right now; the Ariekes running that place there, around the minaret, it was a functionary before the fall"—from Bren. Bren learnt them from YlSib.

"MagDa won't push you on it," Bren said to me. "But . . ."

Bren saw the expression on my face. "You can see what's going on," he said finally. "They're not running things now, they're not in a position to close the infirmary . . ."

"You think they would if they could?"

"I don't know and just now I don't care. Cal certainly won't. You saw what happened when EzCal spoke. If MagDa needs to know anything you know, please tell them. We need them clued in. They're smart, they must know the sort of source you're getting information from, but they won't ask. They have plans, I'm sure. They've been spending time in Southel's lab. Have you seen them talking to her?"

It wasn't as part of an official group, committee business, that I went back into the city, when I did. I went with Bren, to meet his friends again: YlSib, that secret rogue Ambassador.

OUR AIR-SHAPING was weak enough now that we had to wear aeoli within what had recently been Embassytown streets. So far as we could Bren and I were careful to avoid vespcams, though I knew if we were seen we'd only be a rumour among many. We stationed ourselves in the ruins. From a balcony in an apartment where children had lived (I trod over the debris of toys) we saw EzCal go again among crowds of Ariekei that listened and obeyed their instructions.

"Next time they're going to head into the city," said Sib. I hadn't heard YlSib enter. "So . . ." Sib pointed out of the window at EzCal. "Language works differently with this one."

"We should have called them OgMa, not EzCal" Bren said. We looked at him for an explanation. "A god," he said, "who did sort of the same thing."

YlSib wore biorigged pistols. Bren and I had cruder weapons. YlSib moved with vastly more facility than the halting citynauts with whom I'd made earlier forays. They didn't hesitate on the way to where brickwork in ruins became biology. The air changed on our way. The way the currents went over me wasn't like the wind in Embassytown. We were in a place full of new sounds. Small fauna claimed areas. Ariekei in the streets didn't stop for us, though some raised eye-corals and stared. There were pools overhung by bladderwrackish polyps that dripped reactions into the liquid. I wondered if they were foundations, deliberate town planning.

I looked down an avenue of marrowy-trees to Embassytown. An Ariekes near us startled me, asked repeatedly in Language what we were doing. I raised my weapon but YlSib were speaking. *I'm* $\frac{yl}{syb}$, they said. *These are*— and then they said something that wasn't our names. *They are coming with me. I'm going home.* $\frac{koh\ taikoh}{uresh}$, YlSib said, and they put stress in their formulation by making it a personal. *I, homegoer*, was what they said, so I wondered if going home was a powerful thing to the Ariekei too.

"They know us," said Yl. "These days some are too gone to remember, but if we meet any who can speak, we should be alright." "Although," Sib said, "I guess there might be new allegiances. Some of them might have . . ." ". . . reasons to not let us pass."

In fact some Language we heard on that journey made little sense. Phrases spoken by wrecks of speakers out of nostalgia for meaning. YlSib led us finally to a shredded clearing. I gasped. There was a man waiting for us. He leaned below a column of metal that recurved over his head very like a streetlamp. He looked transplanted from an old flat image of a Terre town.

They nodded, muttered to Yl and Sib and Bren. They made sure I couldn't hear them. The man reminded me of no one. He was nondescript and dark-skinned, in old clothes, an aeoli of a kind I didn't recognise breathing into him. There was nothing

I could have said about him. He left with YlSib and Bren came back to me.

"Who the fuck is that?" I said. "Is he cleaved?"

"No," said Bren. He shrugged. "I don't think so. Maybe his brother's dead by now, but I don't think so. They just didn't like each other very much." Of course I knew this counterworld of exiles existed now, of misbehaving cleaved, Staff unstaffed, bad Ambassadors; but to see its doings astounded me. How had they kept going during the days of collapse, before god-drug II?

"Do you speak to any of the similes still?" Bren said.

"Jesus," I said. "Why? Not really. I saw Darius at a bar, ages ago. We were both embarrassed. I mean Embassytown's too small for me not to run into them sometimes, but it's not as if we *talk*."

"Do you know what they're doing?"

"I don't think there's a 'they', Bren. It's all ... disbanded. After what happened. Maybe some of them still meet ... But that scene was ruined ages ago. After Hasser. Can you imagine now? No one cares about them anymore, including their speakers. Language ..." I laughed. "It isn't what it used to be."

YlSib returned, scraping decaying city-stuff off their clothes. "That's true," Bren said. "But it's not true that no one cares anymore. You don't know where we're going: your company's been requested."

"What?" I had not thought that this infiltration was about me, that I was a task to be fulfilled. YlSib led me to a basement-analogue and ushered me in, into the biolit presence of Ariekei. "Avice Benner Cho," YlSib said. They spoke my names perfectly simultaneously, at the same pitch, so though it was two voices it sounded to me like one.

The room smelt of Ariekei. There were several. They were making noises, speech and mutterings of thought. One approached me out of the half-dark and spoke a greeting. YlSib told me its name. I looked at its fanwing.

"Christ," I said. "We've met."

It had been a close companion of Surl Tesh-echer, $\frac{surl}{tesh\ echer}$, the best liar in Ariekei history. It was the Ariekes I'd once called Spanish Dancer. "Does it remember . . . ?"

"Of *course* it remembers, Avice," Bren said. "Why do you think you're here?"

BREN AND YLSIB gave to the gathered Ariekei a clutch of datchips. They took them quickly, their limbs and digits betraying agitation. "Do EzCal know you're recording them?" I said.

"I hope not," Bren said. "You've seen? They're trying to do what Ez did when he was part of EzRa—make sure we can't build up a stock of recordings to make them redundant."

"But you have."

"These are just their public recitations," he said. "They can't stop people tapping those, and why would they? They think because it's been *said*, because it's out there, the Hosts've heard it, and it's lost its thing."

I looked one by one around the other Ariekei there. There were other patterns on other fanwings I thought I had seen before. "Some of these were in Surl Tesh-echer's group as well," I said. I looked at Bren. "They were its friends."

"Yes," Bren said.

"What they can do is lie," Bren said. "Not that any of them's anything like as virtuoso as Surl Tesh-echer was. It was . . ." He shrugged. "A harbinger. On the edge of something."

"Your husband was right," YlSib said. "To stop it. In his terms he was right. It *was* changing everything." There was a silence. "This lot have had to carry on without it since. It's slow." "They do what they can."

Every Ariekes took a datchip, each to a different part of the room. Each in similar elegant motion draped its fanwing over it. Their membranes spread. They withdrew, hunched into sculptures, made the room a drug-house. With the volume very low, they ran the sounds. Responded instantly as I watched, trembling, judders of bio-ecstasy. I could see lights of speakers through taut fanwing skin, hear the muffled chirruping of audio: the soul of EzCal, or its spurious fabricated semblance.

"How the hell can those recordings still work?" I whispered. "They've already been heard."

"Not by them," Bren said. "They wait. Bloody willpower. They fold up their wings when they know EzCal's going to speak. They were already doing it with EzRa. They make themselves *hold out*. They're trying to go longer and longer without."

It was hard to imagine that the shuddering figures represented a resistance to the reign of god-drug. Still. "They can take these now because they didn't take them before," Yl said.

One by slow one the Ariekei rose. They looked at me. A strange reminiscence. We seemed to pick up where we'd left off. Spanish Dancer came up to me: its companions circled me. They said the succession of sounds in Language that were me. I had not heard myself spoken for a long time.

They said me first as a fact. *There was a girl who was hurt in darkness and ate what was given her.* Then they began to deploy me as a simile. *We now,* Spanish Dancer said, *when we take what is given in god-drug's voice, we are like the girl who was hurt in darkness and ate what was given her.* The others responded.

"SURL TESH-ECHER was more than just the best liar, you know," Bren said. "It was sort of a vanguard. It was never just about performing lies. Why would they be so interested in *you*, if that was all, Avice? How do lying and similes intersect?"

What other things in this world, one of the Ariekei was saying, *are like the girl who was hurt in darkness and ate what was given her?*

"It's been hard," Bren said. "They were all scattered by the war." The war of not-enough drug. The war of Ez killed Ra. The war of the walking dead. "Now they've tracked each other down, they're going to keep going. They didn't worship Surl Tesh-echer. But it was sort of a figurehead."

"Prophet," Yl or Sib said.

"Why can't you tell MagDa, and even Cal . . ." I said, then trailed off because of course the group in this room was a conspiracy. Striving to limit the power of the god-drug. Cal would try to sabotage it. I wished I didn't believe that. Bren nodded, watching me think.

"Yeah," said Bren. "Now, MagDa are different. But there's only so much they'll risk. They want to get out, now, and they can only see one way to do it, and that's hanging on. They won't risk anything else. They might even scupper it."

"Scupper what? What are you trying to do?"

"Not *me*," Bren said.

"All of you. You, you," I said to YlSib, "these Hosts. What are *you plural* trying to do?"

"MagDa's way won't work," Bren said. "Just to stave things off. That's why they won't take on Cal. It's not enough to try to keep everything going until the ship gets here. We have to change things." While he spoke, the Ariekei moved around me like flotsam in a current, and they said the phrase I was and tried to make it into new things, to think of new things they could insist that it, I, my past, was like.

"EzCal's not the only one we have to be careful of," Bren said. "You have to keep this quiet." I remembered the parting of Ariekei when Hasser had come and killed $\frac{surl}{tesh\ echer}$.

"You're worried about other Ariekei," I said.

"These speakers were dangerous before," Bren said. "Scile *was* right about them, and so were their . . ." He shrugged and shook his head so I would know whatever phrase he used was inexact. "Ruling clique. And I don't know where *they* are now, yet, but I bet EzCal have an idea. Or Cal does. They've done business before. Why do you think he's so keen to get into the city?"

I'd thought Cal's eagerness was newly visionary fervour. But back then, there in the Festival of Lies, Cal, and Pear Tree, looking at me. "Jesus Pharos." Scile had watched too. A conspirator then, Scile would approve of EzCal now. Their priorities, like CalVin's before them, were power and survival; Scile's were always the city and its stasis. Those had overlapped once, but history had left Scile behind. Hence his hopeless walk.

"Cal might already have found his friends again," Bren said. "This lot . . ." He indicated the room. "They were a threat once. You saw. Now . . ." He laughed. "Well, everything's changed. But they might still be a threat. Different: but maybe even more. Cal might not know this group still exists. If he ever knew. But the Ariekei he worked with before do. So if he finds *them*, this lot here had better keep very quiet. So we have to, as well."

"*How* are they a threat?" I said. "I never understood. Why are they doing this? Whatever it is they're doing."

Bren struggled. "It's hard to explain. I don't know how to say."

"You don't know," I said. He bobbed his head in a half-yes-half-no.

"How's your Language, Avice?" said one of YlSib. They spoke to Spanish Dancer and it answered. I could follow some, and when I shook my head Yl or Sib would translate a few clauses.

It's not good that we are this. We wish to be other than this. We're like the girl who was hurt in darkness and ate what was given her because we imbibe what is given to us by EzCal. There was a long silence. *We want instead to be like the girl who was hurt in darkness and ate what was given to her in that we want to be* . . . and then there was silence again, and Spanish Dancer shook its limbs.

"It tried to use your simile twice, contradictorily," Sib said. "But it couldn't quite manage."

Now, Spanish Dancer went on, *it's worse. We didn't expect this. It was a bad thing when we were made intoxicated and helpless by the god-drug's words, lost ourselves, but now it's different and worse. Now when the god-drug speaks we obey.* Yes, it said that with modulations that meant nothing to me, but no matter how alien the Ariekene mental map, sense of self, I thought that must be truly terrible. I'd seen the crowds respond instantly to EzCal's instructions, choiceless about it. *We want to decide what to hear, how to live, what to say, what to speak, how to mean, what to obey. We want Language to put to our use.*

They resented their new druggy craving and their newer inability to disobey. This conclave could hardly be unique in that. But it dovetailed with what they had always wanted to achieve: their longtime striving for lies, to make Language mean what they wanted. That older desire seemed to make them execrate their new condition even more than other conscious Ariekei.

"We promised to bring you here," Bren said. "Said it like a Host." He smiled at the child's oath. "They were adamant they had to see you. I better get you back before you're missed, then YlSib will have to go on. Other drops. These people aren't the only ones trying to find a different way."

What a dangerous circuit, through rebel cells in the collapsed, regrowing city. I'd always stressed, as I'd had it stressed to me, how incommensurable Terre and Ariekene thinking were. But I thought about who it was had told me that, those many times. Staff, and Ambassadors with a monopoly on comprehension. It was giddying to feel suddenly that I was allowed and able to make any sense of Ariekene actions. What I saw there was dissent, and I understood it.

I saw only these liars, these fervent attempters to change their speech. Bren and YlSib might go from them to others trying to eradicate all their cravings and live Languageless; from there perhaps to those fighting to disobey EzCal's casual orders; then to others who were maybe searching for chemical cures. I wasn't even really participant on this trip, the first visit, though I was present and Bren trusted me. He hadn't brought me out of camaraderie—I was there because I was a simile, and these dissidents wanted me for strategic purposes, as another group might request a piece of 'ware, or a chemical, or explosives.

Embassytown in its crisis was throwing up fervour. Give me three days, I thought, and I'd find people who believed that EzCal, or Ez, or Cal, was the messiah, or the devil, or both; that the Ambassadors were angels; or devils; that the Ariekei were; that the only hope was to leave the planet as fast we could; that we must never leave. So with the Ariekei, I thought, and felt hopeful and depressed at once. Language was incapable of formulating the uncertainties of monsters and gods common elsewhere, and I was abruptly convinced that these gatherings were the Ariekene cargo cults. Was I at a Ghost Dance? Bren and YlSib were patronising the far-fetched, millennial and desperate.

I watched Spanish Dancer struggle to express me, to make me mean things I'd never meant before, try to force similes into new shapes. *We are like the girl who was hurt in the dark and ate what was given to her because we . . . because like her we are*

... *we are hurt* ... It circled me and stared at me, and tried to say ways it was like me.

"Why won't MagDa's plan work?" I said. "I know, I know, but ... just say to me once why we can't just keep going until the ship."

Bren, Sib and Yl looked at each other, to see who would speak. "You've seen how EzCal's acting." It was Sib. "You think it's safe for us to carry on like this?"

"And, among other things," Bren said, sounding, if I'm honest, disappointed, "even if it did work, you saw what happened to the Ariekei when EzRa ended, without their ... dose. So what about when the relief gets here? When we leave?" He indicated Spanish Dancer. "What happens then, to them?"

21

ANOTHER OF OUR FLYERS disappeared. It had been doing rounds of farmsteads close to the city, as per EzCal's orders, asking for—insisting on—what we needed: it wouldn't be hard for us to dismantle the speakers if what we required wasn't forthcoming, and the Ariekene farmers knew that. The coms broke off and weren't re-established. We released vespcams.

Squads were subduing the last independent zones on isolated floors of the Embassy, where squatter-chiefs and their groups had refused amnesty. I was out at a barricade, a mass of broken furniture, odds and sods of houses, unneeded machines; but coagulated here, unusually, not with plastone but a quick-setting polymer, a resin poured all over and set hard as brick and glass-clear. The detritus was visible, like rubbish floating in water, frozen in a moment. We weren't at war anymore, and machines were cutting a V-trench walkway through the barrier, an excised wedge with perfect flat faces through the tough transparency and the crap within. The pass's edges were randomly punctuated with sectioned debris.

I was with Simmon. We were watching the gusting staticky visions of vespcams on his handscreen. "What's that?" I said. It was the lost corvid. It was dead. The ground around it was scorched. There were heaps that might be human bodies.

WE CAME FAST and armed over the wild, over paths made by Ariekei and their animals and zelles, perhaps by wild outsider humans, exiles from Embassytown, in outland farms. We hadn't established contact with all of them. I was surprised by a brief and strong sense of loss for floaking, of all things. I tried to tell myself that this, what I was doing, was heir to that tough going-with-the-flow, but I was hardly taken in.

The airship was spread across the ground. We descended into a terrible aftermath. Eventually we went to work. The closest thing we had to a specialist took samples from what might be bite-marks or burn-marks on all the corpses. They were everywhere.

"Oh God," said our investigator. There was Lo, of Ambassador LoGan. His chest was caved and cauterised. "That's not a crash injury. That's *not* a crash injury."

Vizier Jaques was there, and the edge of his wound, his missing arm, was neither shorn clear nor burned, but a rip from which he'd bled out. He'd died in excruciation, it looked like, scrabbling for his flung-away limb. The microbes the group had brought inside them had started the job of decay, and the Ariekene landscape in which they worked made for chemical oddness, so the rot wasn't like rot in Embassytown.

Everyone was dead. The expedition had included a rare Kedis functionary. A mature hermale I hadn't known. "Oh Jesus, it's Gorrin," someone said. "The Kedis are going to be . . ."

We went slowly from body to body, putting off each as long as we could. The wind was cold as we picked through the remnants of our friends. We tried to gather them: some fell apart; others we wrapped to take home.

"Look." We were trying to reconstruct what had happened, following the scraped earth, reading it, it and the dead become hieroglyphs. "This was brought down." A hot toothed missile had burst into the flyer's side.

"There are no predators like that . . ." someone started to say.

"But it came down slow enough for them to get out." That was me. "They came out and then they were . . . they were hit outside."

We found remnants of biorigging eggs, from a recent barter trip, smears of yolk and foetal machines. The crew had been returning. The aeoli we wore made our own voices loud in our ears, as if each of us was alone. Carrying our dead we flew with carronades ready, looking for the ranch where our compatriots had been. It was announced by smoke. Outlying dwellings were ruined, the nurseries mostly gone. There was one hutch that seemed still just alive, and in distress, but we had no idea how to provide it a coup de grâce, and could only try to ignore its pain.

There were no Ariekene dead. The kraal was empty. Dust-coloured animals ran away, and our arrival sent up rag-paper scavengers, flocks that moved like thinking smoke.

Someone fired and we all dived for the floor shouting. The gun howled: it was of one of Embassytown's treasures, an old banshee-tech gun cobbled into a form humans could use. The officer had shot it at nothing—a movement, a scuttling of tiny fauna. Ariekene young had been abandoned, and floated in a broth of dead. There were bodies of their elders. Hoofprints were everywhere. We set cams to follow what we thought might be trails.

Body-thick arteries emerged from the farm, entangled in the earth and the tube that went over the rockscape toward the city. The pipeline was burst. The matter of it was spewed by a sabotage blast, the ground a quag of dirt and amniotic fluids.

"What's this?"

In a hollow were organic discards. Frameworks like splayed fish ribs; skin in webbing between tines; a nest of intricate bones. These were remnants of fanwings. We gathered the little trophies. Behind us we heard the distress call of a last building left alive.

We'd put speakers in the farms with which we'd made contact, and the ongoing supplies of EzCal's voice should have guaranteed us what we needed, but we'd had trouble before. Now we knew why. We sent crews and cams along the supply pipes, and found other ruptures. We lost another flight, and then the officers we sent to find it.

EzCal went to the centre of the city to broadcast. Their journey there from Embassytown was as extreme in its pomp as we could do, then. There was pressure on those of us in the committee, still ostensibly Ez and Cal's organisers, Ez's jailers, indeed, to attend and wear smart clothes. Wyatt came with us. His reward for birthing EzCal was that he was freed, kept under watch but made committee. He was expert in crisis politics, and he wasn't a Bremen agent anymore, or not just then. Whatever happened later we'd deal with later.

"If he could get away with a goddamn canopy, he would," I said quietly to MagDa. The god-drug walked in the city, Ez looking down and unsmiling, Cal, his head still shaved in the style he now maintained, his stitches gone but new tattoos mimicking them on his scarred scalp, looking up, occasionally glancing at Ez with energy and hate. "They'd have us carrying them on our fucking shoulders."

MagDa didn't smile. We were in the middle of that daily promenade from Embassytown, behind EzCal, surrounded by Ariekei who followed their instructions and shouted sort-of cheers. Mag and Da were stricken. *Wait*, I wanted to say to them. *It's alright. There are others. There are people and Ariekei looking for ways out.* I wouldn't betray Bren, and I knew he was right: there was too much risk that MagDa might be unnerved by these plans.

"I don't know . . ." said MagDa to me. "I don't even know what we'll do." "When the ship comes."

"We have to guard our resources," Cal said, after their performance, looking at footage of ruined farms. EzCal insisted that the rations of Embassytowners be reduced. They ordered squads of constables to the nearest plantations, and to those that provided our most needed pabulum. The attacks were becoming more frequent. Each group of officers that went out was accompanied, as they had to be for communication with those they were sent to protect, by an Ambassador.

"It'll be fine," PorSha said to me, preparing. "It's not the first time." "We're used to it." "We had to go out to haggle, before, didn't we?" "Out of the city." "It's the same."

It wasn't the same. Before, with Embassytown and the world collapsing, they, and all the better Ambassadors, had kept us alive with their desultory trades. This time they followed orders. I had originally thought that Cal would do as little as he could when he became part of god-drug II. I was used to being wrong.

EzCal DID FIND Pear Tree, the erstwhile leader of that once-powerful Ariekene faction. Perhaps Cal had his own investigators. Not all the city-dwelling Embassytowner exiles would share Yl and Sib's perspective: they might have enemies, of whom some were perhaps agents for EzCal.

What had happened was that during one of their speakings in the city plaza EzCal had been suddenly in the middle of a small group of Ariekei retracting and extruding their eyes and staring. EzCal hadn't been afraid. One of the group had been Pear Tree.

It accompanied EzCal on their following performance, walking with them all the way from a meeting in Embassytown.

There were other Ariekei with them, some closer to EzCal than any humans, Staff, committee or Ambassador. My memory was unreliable, but watching the trids—I played hookey from my accompanying duties—I suspected at least two others might have been among those that had stood aside to let Hasser murder $\frac{surl}{tesh\ echer}$. I held my breath: I was on a side in a secret war.

That time, EzCal didn't speak for a while. They rationed their words. When they did, they announced that $\frac{kora}{saygiss}$—Pear Tree—was chief of this township. That this area was chosen from all the scattered remnant parts of the city, to be EzCal's node, and that its regent there was $\frac{kora}{saygiss}$. EzCal couldn't speak except as the god-drug, and the words they said were always compulsions. This wasn't like a momentary order to raise gift-wings: it was a ruling, and when EzCal finished speaking, the Ariekei who had heard them remained ruled by $\frac{kora}{saygiss}$. The Ariekei were very quiet, and then did not complain.

For all I knew $\frac{kora}{saygiss}$ might already have been head of what-ever clutch of streets it frequented. EzCal might have changed nothing—except that by saying it, they changed it. There was now a collaboration, an allegiance, between Embassytown and this new heart of the city. I had just seen the tasks of Bren, YlSib and their comrades, get harder.

I think I had been avoiding thinking about what Cal, EzCal, really was, and were. Whether it was design, buffoonery or luck that underlay our new politics, I was not safe.

ARIEKEI FROM the new township EzCal had inaugurated left the city with PorSha, KelSey and the constables. These were now joint operations. KelSey came back, but PorSha did not.

We had receivers and cams around all the farm grounds. They flagged us when anything beyond their expectation-algorithms occurred, which is how it was that all of us in the committee were buzzed instantly, and the footage relayed direct to our rooms, at the next attack.

Corvids headed out. They wouldn't arrive in time, but we had to act, even pointlessly. I was with Bren. We scrolled as fast as we could back and forth through chaotic images. Scenes of tending, of interaction with farmhands. PorSha, a pair of tall diffident women, communicating necessities to the Ariekei. Convulsions as the tube passed goods that would be shat out in Embassytown. Snatches of conversation in Anglo-Ubiq. The time-counter skipped. This datspace was fritzing. "We need Ehrsul," Bren said. "Do you ever . . . ?" I shook my head. A constable was standing with mud across her. She stared anxiously not at us but over our shoulders, attempting to report.

"*Sergeant Tracer at . . . ,*" she said. There were violent noises. She watched something off-screen. "*Under attack,*" she said. "*Groups of . . . hundreds, fucking hundreds . . .*"

Her transmission ended, the picture spasmed and was replaced by a view rapidly diminishing as the cam flew up. Tracer was lying on her back, among human dead. She tugged off her aeoli mask, an unthinking spasm of dying fingers. Images strobed. A great company of Ariekei, moving quite unlike the farmhands. They galloped, they swung giftwings, they trailed blood, liquid drizzled from weapons, a spray of dust. None of them spoke — they shouted wordlessly, voicing only attack-meanings, without Language.

They beheaded a minor Staff-man I'd once known a bit. I held my mouth closed. One kicked him down, gripped him with its giftwing, another swung a blade worked out of some coralline stuff. They had biorigged weapons they turned on the farm walls. One Ariekes shot our women and men with a carbine, wielding the Terre weapon with surprising precision. We saw them murder Terre without weapons at all, send jags of their own bone into human innards, or yank masks away, suffocating our people in alien wind.

Bren sped up the footage. He brought us up to live shots. Carnage was ongoing. The officers were vastly outnumbered. They were trying to reach the corvid, and were taken down. PorSha was shouting Language to the attackers. *Wait, wait, no more of these actions*, they said. *Please, we ask you not to do this—* We lost that cam, and when it came back PorSha were dead. Bren cursed.

All the speakers we had placed in the farmland started suddenly to shout, in EzCal's voice. The god-drug had found each other, here in Embassytown, and were yelling down the line. *Stop!* they said, and things stilled. I leaned towards the crude picture. The carnage, all the motionless Ariekei.

"Jesus," I said at the numbers. I held up my hands. Bren said, "What are they doing?"

Stand still, the god-drug shouted across the kilometres. *Come forward, stand in front of the dead Ambassador.*

For seconds there was no motion. Then an Ariekes stepped out of the crowd, took careful hoof-steps into the cam's view. The others watched it. Its back, its extended fanwing, stretched open, listening to the voice from the speaker, turning into and out of the light as it listened to EzCal's voice.

There were no other fanwings in the crowd of killers.

"That's a farmer," it's said. "It's not one of them."

A large Ariekes slapped two of its companions with its giftwing and pointed at the enthralled on-comer. It arced its back to display a wound. EzCal continued to speak.

"They saw the buildings hearing, and that one," I said. "That's why they stopped. Not because they had to."

One by one at first, then countless at a time, the murder-squad of Ariekei arched their backs. I saw the quivering of scores of fanwing stubs. I heard Bren whisper, "God." The Ariekei displayed their wounds. Some made wordless sounds I'm certain were of triumph.

"They know we can see them," I said.

Following speechless giftwing-jabbed instructions from their larger comrade, self-mutilated Ariekei stood either side of the entranced farmhand, and held it. It didn't even notice. *Stop what you are doing, release your grips*, we heard EzCal say. Their Language petered out. The farmer raised and opened its giftwing repeatedly, obeying the instruction not intended for it. Those it was intended for ignored it, did not hear it, kept hold of their quarry.

The big Ariekes tugged the biorigging-farmer's fanwing. I winced. It twisted. Its victim screamed doubly and tried and failed to get away. Its tormentor's giftwing moved like a human hand uprooting a plant. The fanwing wrenched free: roots of gristle and muscle parted and with a burst of blood came finally away, pulling fibres out of the quivering back, trailing them.

Fanwings are at least as sensitive as human eyes. The traumatised Ariekes opened its mouth and fell, stupefied with pain. It was dragged away. The deafener held up its grotesque dripping bouquet. It made a loud wordless noise. Triumph or rage.

EzCal were speaking again, I realised. They issued orders and were ignored.

22

THAT WAS THE START of open war. We called it the First Farm Massacre though it was the only one we then knew of—a horrible perspicacity. It took us days to understand what was coming.

That final mutilation, by one Ariekes of another, was a recruitment. If the victim survived the shock and pain, it was made another soldier, on the enemy side. "How does it receive orders?" I said, but no one could answer me. Perhaps there were no orders, only rage stripped of language. *Can they think? If they can't speak, can they think?* Language for Ariekei was speech and thought at once. *Wasn't it?*

We didn't know whether to roll back our presence from the outlying farms or bolster it, so we tried both. More visceral pipelines blew. The pictures were the same in different settings: in a copse of trees like organs; in a dustbowl; in scree; each time a burst of flesh and a litter of ruined cargo. Our stores depleted.

Infrastructure wasn't the only thing attacked. After the Farm Massacre the fanwingless swept into an encampment defended by other, hearing, Ariekei: this became the Cliff-Edge Incident. We had troops there with them equipped with rare out-tech, and they were able to shoot several of the attackers. But half our officers were killed by the time the marauders suddenly left, galvanised by some signal we couldn't understand. Perhaps by an empathy to tides we couldn't sense, like birds circling and become one organism.

We didn't become inured to the footage. EzCal called the committee together, and brought $\frac{kora}{saygiss}$, Pear Tree, with them.

EzCal told us they were making changes in the way the city was administered, as if that might help. Cal talked about making allegiances against "bandits". I tried to listen, to understand the shape of politics now. From Bren's scorn I knew that where there wasn't anarchy or secret renegacy in the city, there were strange comprador authorities like that of $\frac{kora}{saygiss}$.

We had to witness absurd joint patrols. Under EzCal's orders, our constables policed outlands beyond the city accompanied by Ariekei dragooned into militia. An Ambassador had to be present, of course, to transmit instructions, on what EzCal stressed was god-drug authority. They took weapon training: career bureaucrats attempted to transform themselves.

The missions disaggregated, failed, as orders relayed by disorientated Ambassadors were interpreted differently by Ariekei and Terre. The Ariekei were not even resentful, so far as I could see—and I knew now that there was such a thing as Ariekene resentment—only bewildered. The first three such patrols achieved nothing and the fourth was attacked. When we reached the site the rescue squad found our Terre people dead and their Ariekei colleagues mostly gone, inducted no doubt by brute surgery into the rebels. The joint patrols were ended.

"WHAT IF THEY don't want to fight? Even after they've had their fanwing taken? Or what if they want to fight the ones that took their fanwing?" I, traitor, was at the secret liars' club in the city, again, so Spanish Dancer's comrades could consider me. They contemplated urgently. As urgently as Bren had brought me back through the city. Spanish Dancer itself wasn't there.

"A fanwing isn't just an ear," Yl said. She and Sib looked at me. "It hears, yes." "It's the mind's main doorway." "More important than sight." "Their physiology's nothing like ours." "If they've got no fanwing, they hear no sounds at *all*." "And with

317

no sound, they can't hear their own speech." "Which means an Ariekes can't speak." "So it can't speak Language."

Perhaps there was no sense of truth left for them, or thought. Those rebels must be a fractured community, without speech, if they were a community at all. Language, for the Ariekei, was truth: without it, what were they? An unsociety of psychopaths.

"So even if they didn't want to be part of the rebellion," I said, "with their fanwings taken, they're . . ."

"Insane." "Or something like it." "Maybe some *don't* take part." "Maybe they drift. Get lost." "Maybe they die." "But they're not what they were." "It's no surprise that most of them join." ". . . The bandits." YlSib smiled without humour at EzCal's absurd terminology.

"They can't all have been press-ganged," I said. The key cadre of that army was surely those that had deafened themselves. That despairing, literally maddening act of revolt had perhaps been performed independently, risen up in hundreds of Ariekei; perhaps a gathering had agreed together, and in a mass act of self-inflicted agony, between EzRa's meaningless pronouncements—because we realised these dissidents had been attacking us, if in more disorganised fashion, before the reign of god-drug II—had made themselves an organising core. There might be a room somewhere littered with rotting fanwings, the birthplace of this millennial mass.

Each trapped in itself. God knew how many of them, a strike-force of the lonely and lost. How did they move together? How did they coordinate their assaults? I thought again that they must be gusted by instinct and some deep-grammar of chaos: they could not plan. Maybe each strike wasn't a careful raid but just a sharp edge of the random. I remembered, though, what had looked like interactions among the self-deafened during the First Farm Massacre, and was perturbed.

"They've started coming into the city in squads," Sib said. It wasn't a city, just tribes of junkies and thralls where a city had been. "What they used to do was *kill* the other Ariekei." "If you've broken free from something like god-drug..." "...maybe they thought those who didn't were disgusting." But they weren't killing them now: they were recruiting. YlSib made simultaneous plucking motions, twisting imagined fanwings from their anchorings.

I shuddered and turned it into a headshake, and told them I wanted to see Spanish Dancer, as if it was a friend. I wanted to understand it, to make sense of its strategy for emancipation. YlSib were pleased. They took me to the grotto under eaves fringed like fingers where the Ariekes lived. For quite a long time, we all sat silently.

A HAMLET OF houses in the suburbs, gently regrowing, were taken suddenly down with biorigged weapons of serious power, crossbred from existing strains. Informer Ariekei working with the god-drug told us that something terrible was coming.

All who live in the city and all who live in Embassytown must stand against these attackers, EzCal said, with $\frac{kora}{saygiss}$ beside them. No matter how assiduously the compelled Ariekei tried to obey them, those words were too nebulous to mean much. EzCal never spoke an intoxicating order making all Ariekei obey $\frac{kora}{saygiss}$: they must have been afraid of unintended consequence.

I wanted to return, as often and for as long as I could, to the liars in the city straining to meet $\frac{surl}{tesh\ echer}$'s challenge. I was trying to learn how to get there—the route and strategies for the route—but still could only go when YlSib and Bren came with me. After that dramatic attack on the remains of the city, Spanish Dancer and the other gathered Ariekei were distressed (I recognised it). One of their number had left them.

YlSib listened. "They argued with it." "It told them . . ." "It said it was ashamed." Bad enough when the first god-drug had pushed them into trips: so much worse now they could see their tripping selves made to obey. "It . . . oh." "It plucked itself."

"No," I said.

It wasn't just, I thought, the loss of their—what, friend?—to self-savagery, of mind as well as body, so it could not hear nor speak again, that must hurt them. They wanted to be a hope, against the revolutionary suicide of those that tore out their social mind with their fanwings, became nihilist revenge. Were there ranks among the Languageless? Were those that made themselves an aristocracy above those attack-recruited? I looked at Spanish Dancer's many dark-point eyes, which had seen its companion tear its fanwing like trash, after their years of work, their project that had started long before this end of the world.

By our barricade gates, in rump street-markets, quickly tolerated, an economy of recycled necessities, people began to talk again about the relief. When it would come, where we would go, and what life would be like for Embassytowners exiled to Bremen.

Our now wild cameras inhabited the plains. Many broke down or their signals degraded. But some still got footage to us.

Some were a long way into country not punctuated even by farms, beyond the transport ducts. I heard rumours of certain footage before I saw it. I scorned the idea that it existed but was being kept from me—wasn't I committee? But though it failed, I discovered that there had been an effort to do just that. I shouldn't have been shocked. An internal split, a craven and conniving column reporting direct to the god-drug. There wasn't even any reasoning. Secrecy was just a bureaucrats' reflex. There was no way they could contain these files: a day after the first stories about them started circulating, the rest of us got to see them.

A group of us uploaded them to committee datspace. Bren was agitated. I was taken aback by his impatience, that he so obviously had no idea if the whispers about what we were to see were true. I was so used to him knowing things he didn't tell me. I teased him about it, in a rather brittle manner. We watched the cam's memories. Plenty of kilometres away but hardly in another country. The viewpoint swept through narrows: I swayed to avoid overhangs the recorder had ducked days before. Some fool at the back said something like "Why are we watching this?"

Through a nook in rock the cam went to a valley of pumice-coloured earth, burred birdlike suddenly tree- then tower-high over the slope, focused where a river had been. We gasped. Someone swore.

There was an army. It marched in our direction. There were not hundreds of Ariekei but thousands, thousands.

I heard myself say *Jesus, Jesus Christ*. We knew now why the city seemed depleted. *Pharotekton*, I said.

The microphones were crappy but we heard the noise of the march, the percussion of hard feet walking not in time. The amputee Ariekei shouted. They must not even know, not even hear their own constant catcalls. Machines among them walked at the wordless correction of keepers. The Ariekei carried weapons. This was the only army on this world and it was marching on us.

The cam went close, and we saw thousands of stumps of thousands of fanwings. Every Ariekes there was a soldier, not obeying orders but trapped beyond society in soundless solipsism, unable to talk, hear, think, but still moving together in that mystery fashion, sharing purpose without speaking it. They couldn't have a unified intent but we knew they did, and what it was, and that we were it.

23

AS WELL AS THE Languageless and the SM, for self-mutilated, at first we called the incoming army the Deaf. Embassytown's human deaf objected hard to that; they were right and we were ashamed. Then someone named the attackers according to an antique language. It meant that same word, *deaf*, but rendered *the Surdae* any insult seemed diluted; particularly because, fast bastardised or misunderstood, the term became *the Surd* and then misprisioned into *the Absurd*. Hosts, coming to kill us for sins we'd committed, if at all, without intent.

Above all it was their discipline that was absurd, impossible, the way without words groups would peel off from the main slow body, coordinated into snatch squads that tore through strange country and took apart our rangers, or recruited new Ariekei troops by ripping their flesh. Eventually and abruptly transmissions to us ended, cams batted out of the air by breakdown, wind or the sudden irritation of the enemy. We sent more of course. Plans began.

As our spies gusted out to search, we were breaching old agreements and habits of isolation. The cams showed us the coast, the gently toxic sea. We had a country, on which the city sat, in which was Embassytown. We weren't used to seeing that. I'd used cartographic 'ware in the immer, but not these charts. We had a continent. It would have been hard for me to trace the outlines of Embassytown, harder to draw the city, and I wouldn't even have recognised the shape of the landmass on which we were such a tiny point. Now we needed them it wasn't hard to break those taboos and pull up maps. They'd never been forbidden, as I'd seen in the out in some unsubtle theocracies: only inappropriate, and old politenesses were dead. Our cams uploaded directions so we could trace the Absurd.

Their few, their first, the pioneers had also learnt the specific violence to make unspeaking comrades of their victims. How had it been? They had spread out of the depleting city, claiming farmers, on past any urban gutwork into the wandergrounds of nomads, claiming the nomads, the gatherer-hunters of unneeded or escaped technology, building. Someone might one day write the history of that trek, the recruiting crusade.

There were more than all those stolen and violently cured rural addicts. I imagined these crazy figures emerging from wilderness like prophets; those distant Ariekei already alarmed or enraged at what they heard of their cousins in the city reduced to zombie-ecstatics or the craven desperate, might, even if far-off enough to have avoided the affliction, not have needed coercion to join the Absurd. Perhaps there'd been a while before the army went in with regular, remorseless violence, and instead there'd been debates about endeafening among the not-yet-recruited, in some settlements. Articulate, last-ever uses of speech to argue for its eradication.

I made Bren come with me into the city. It was easy to leave, though our borders were supposed to be controlled. Routes in and out weren't hard to learn.

"They'll be here within two weeks," I said. He nodded.

"You see they're all in prime instar?" Bren said. "They're not protecting the old or looking after the young."

The young, though, might soon enough be grateful to them. Even uncared for, a few in each Ariekene litter must survive, and when they emerged to their adult form, woke into Language, they would find a city purged of us. Without god-drug. The Absurd would martyr themselves to that future. They'd put themselves beyond the reach of any compromise or agreement.

We stuck to the safer sub-regions of the city. I found my way—my own, this time, leading Bren—to where Spanish Dancer and its friends practised lying, and I tried to help them find new ways to speak me.

"WE'RE FORMING an army," Cal said. We were as disdainful as we could be at that. *Gather many of you in the square and be ready to fight*, EzCal broadcast to the Ariekei. They told them to put forward soldiers. They demanded $\frac{qura}{mashi}$ volunteers. $\frac{qura}{mashi}$ was the biggest aggregate of units with a name, and meant anything more than the largest exact number for which terminology existed, $\frac{qura}{spa}$, 3072. $\frac{qura}{mashi}$ translated usually as "countless". EzCal were demanding as large a force as the Ariekei could give.

Cal waved his hand. Beside him, Ez was like a ventriloquist's doll, existing only when he spoke, or was spoken through. Wyatt watched Ez like an anxious relative. I wondered how many Ariekene soldiers the god-drug would get, and whether the process of building that force would be violent. The natives in all the little villages left in the city, islands between zones of the deadly mindless, would try to obey, in various ways. They knew the Absurd were coming. The locals ruled or "ruled" or whatever by $\frac{kora}{saygiss}$, those over which EzCal had given $\frac{kora}{saygiss}$ aegis, would surely provide most of the soldiers.

". . . one main force of Ariekei to guard the city, stationed at all the weak points we have, and there'll be a couple of . . . well, of special squads prepared," Cal said, at the committee meeting. I couldn't listen to this, these desperations disguised as strategy. I couldn't look at anyone else in the room. There was nothing we had that could hold off the oncoming army. When we were dismissed I got my stuff together slowly, and after a moment realised it was only I, Ez and Cal left in the room. I don't know how that happened. I wouldn't rush. I couldn't look at them. I was their enemy, and I had secrets that were mutinous.

Cal slouched, looking tired. He looked shrunken, far off by the wall. A moment's illusion and the chair seemed to dwarf him like a throne would a boy-king. Ez stood like a surly courtier. They must be waiting to practise their necessary proclamations.

"Do you miss my brother, Avice?" Cal said.

"Do I . . . ? Vin? I . . . Yes." It was some way true. "Sometimes I do. Do you?"

Cal watched me from under his brow.

"Yes. I was angry with him. Before he died." He paused. "I was angry with him before that, then worse after. Of course. But I miss him."

I tried to work out if I could glean any advantage on any axis by keeping him talking, but I could think of nothing to say. "*Please*," he said angrily, not to me. Ez looked up.

"I'll . . ." Ez said, and walked out. It was the first word I'd heard him say for himself, for many days. Cal didn't watch him go.

"Vin missed you," he said.

"Did he?"

Whatever had happened to Cal, whatever he'd become, I was sure that he saw me as I saw him through a window of memories that included mornings, evenings together, nudity, of fucking, sometimes beautifully. What could I do but remember the last looks Vin had given me? I'd seen that need that could perhaps have been given another name, and that perhaps Cal resented. Because he thought his brother's affections were a zero-sum, and that I'd stolen from him? Because he didn't have it to give himself?

I, to my utmost shock, choked and had to close my eyes. A great big diffuse grief, not just for Vin, but some for him. I thought about the months I'd spent as CalVin's lover. I tried to recall a time when both of them had moved with me at once. I could not. Had they both touched me at once, ever, or had it always been one, then some languid time later, as I'd imagined, assumed, the other? I looked at Cal. Had he merely tolerated his doppel's desires, all that time?

I thought, *Have you and I even been together?*

"Waking without him. I don't get used to it." He spoke rapidly. "I'm not supposed to. Truth is there are times it's not bad. The silence isn't always unwelcome." I looked away from his awful smile.

"Truth is, Avice, I can't tell you if I miss him. That's not true, I can tell you and I do, but it isn't as *clean* a feeling as that. To have to say *everything*, like I do—or did . . . Well, it's bad and it's good and it's bad. I've been to the retirement homes where cleaved are. Normal ones, not like Bren, making trouble. I don't know, is that me now?"

He jerked his head at the door through which Ez had left. "That bastard, eh? It can be ugly how things go. I was going to say . . . I don't know what I was going to say. I'm doing what I have to."

"What is it you're doing, Cal? Why d'you have to?" I said that though I'd not intended to respond, or involve myself in whatever this was. "We tried this once before, Cal; you made armies and it was a disaster . . ."

"Avice, please." He shook his head, and hesitated, as if he was trying very hard to think how to communicate something.

"It was joint patrols that didn't work. You'll see what we do now. This is different. Anyway, what would you rather? We can't just leave them to come in . . . And haven't you seen?" He gesticulated again after Ez. "I can make them do anything I want."

"Well . . ."

"Well, anyway that's not really the point. I do, we do want protections around the city, we need it, but that's not the real point. The real point is the squads that go *out*. I've been thinking a lot." He waved a hand at his throat, his voice. "About this. I've been thinking how to use it. I know why the first patrols went wrong: we just ordered them to *patrol*. That was much too vague. Tasks, though, that's different. Specifics. With beginnings and endings."

"What tasks are you going to set them, EzCal?" I said. The slip, calling Cal that, wasn't deliberate.

"You'll see. And you'll be impressed, I think. I'm not operating like you think I am. I know what you think I am, Avice."

I walked away. It was just unbearable.

I DIDN'T WATCH CAL, with Ez, inspect his Ariekene troops—what a pantomime. I heard he made MagDa his assistant, had them talk for him. EzCal couldn't do it: it would have created a comedy of overwhelmed squaddies mindlessly attempting to obey every word, whether it was an order or not.

There were, in fact, $\frac{qura}{mashi}$—some thousands. An unprecedented gathering. Through MagDa, Cal organised them into ranks, and squadrons, and units, each with its own commander. There wasn't as much of the chaos as I'd expected when our new defenders went to their outposts.

They weren't enough. The Absurd army outnumbered them by several times. I didn't yet understand—had ignored him telling me—that this warcraft and panicked pomp was a minor part of Cal's intentions. I didn't even notice that MagDa were gone for two days, alongside others, part of a squad I imagine EzCal gave some carefully chosen name. While they were, without knowing they were, I went again with YlSib to Spanish Dancer, as the army of Absurd approached. I'd had enough of inevitability. In the city, outside Embassytown, it felt, even illusorily, as if more than one outcome was possible.

EzCal summoned us to a lecture hall. I went to that meeting, as I did to all of them, feeling like a spy. Not wholly misleading. The committee was depleted. In steeply banking rows of chairs we looked down at EzCal in the centre. I sat by Southel and Simmon. MagDa was with EzCal, their faces scuffed with injuries. By them was $\frac{kora}{saygiss}$, and there were other Hosts in corners.

"We'd like to start with a silence," Cal said, "for officers Bayley and Kotus, who gave their lives on this mission, for the sake of Embassytown." We waited. "Let's make sure it wasn't in vain. Bring them in."

There was a commotion. We gasped and swore and drew back. What the guards entered and brought before us were enemies. Two deafened Absurd. They were held in cuffs. They eyed us, their eyes in polyp motion. Their legs and giftwings shook in constraints. They tested their tethers with cunning.

We watched them. Cal circled the captives, pointing out the injuries of the wilderness, the flanges of the ripped-out fanwing. He pointed at each thing he described with a long thin stick. He was like a picture of an ancient lecturer, in some pre-diaspora centre of learning. The attackers made noises as he rounded them. Calls that sounded like halloos, like calls to gods. $\frac{kora}{saygiss}$ and the other Ariekei in the room watched them and kept up their own constant movement, twitches in a disgust-echo of the prisoners' strainings.

Our people had tracked a group of Absurd broken off from the main oncoming army to raid an isolated settlement. There'd been a fight. There'd been deaths on both sides. At last, Cal said, after unprecedented cooperation between the Terre and our Ariekene allies we'd subdued and taken these Absurd alive.

"We need to understand them," Cal said. "So we can defeat them."

We were here to take notes, to learn Languageless behaviour. By experiments before cams in sealed rooms; by interactions gbetween the Absurd and our allies, that would not be interactions but actions from $\frac{kora}{saygiss}$ and its coterie, and ignored by the Absurd; or if responded to in such ways that they were not discernible to us as reactions at all.

The solipsism of those that had torn out their own fanwings seemed impenetrable. Perhaps some on the committee believed Cal's assertion that we were preparing to defeat them, but seeing him cajole $\frac{kora}{saygiss}$ —speaking through MagDa again to avoid the tedium of repeatedly enthralling the Ariekes ally—to speak to the Absurd, which they pointlessly attempted, making MagDa try it too, I think there must have been many who knew, as I did then, that his hope was to negotiate.

But they were thousands who'd closed all windows in and out of themselves, cut off Language, become monads full of murder. No knowledge we had could make much difference. With the scrags of Wyatt's arsenal and Cal's Ariekene force we might kill some, but the city was still shrinking, inhabitants dying, self-mutilating, running to nearby settlements where speakers would broadcast the god-drug voice. There were more Absurd than Ariekei that would fight by us.

MagDa spoke in Language; then one or other would say, "They can't even fucking hear us," while the Absurd snarled.

"So show them," Cal said. "*Make* them understand." And this exchange would continue and mutate, upsetting and pointless. The whole Ariekes would repeat its words: MagDa and the other Ambassadors would make gestures with their hands. Our enemies came closer. The Languageless pulled against their bonds. They watched their interlocutors, ignoring overtures and focusing on actions. I saw sudden shared moments of attention, responding to idiosyncrasies of $\frac{kora}{saygiss}$'s motion invisible to me.

The Absurd glared at each other. They made noises without knowing it. They got each other's attention with spread-out eyetines, made motions to indicate things to notice. To the extent that they could, they moved, taking up positions while Cal and Ez flashed up images on screens, played vibrations to them through the floor. They walked, triangulated, parted.

I didn't say anything fast enough, but when they suddenly tried to attack an Ariekes guard I realised I'd known it was about to happen. They were subdued before they could use their own strapped bodies as ungainly bludgeons, but the synchronicity of their movements astounded me. It sent me back to my husband's books.

"How do you say 'that' in Language?" I asked Bren. "Like *that* one." I pointed. "Which glass do you want? *That* one."

"It would depend." He looked at the glass by his counter. "Talking about that one, I might say . . ."

"No I don't mean any specific one, but in general, *that* one." Pointing. "Or *that* one." Moving my hand. "Thatness."

"There's nothing."

"No?"

"Of course not."

"Thought so. So how would I distinguish that glass and that one and that one?" I tallied them with my finger.

"You'd say 'the glass in front of the apple and the glass with a flaw in its base and the glass with a residue of wine left in it.' You know this. What are you asking? They taught you these basics, didn't they?"

"They did," I said. I was quiet a while. "Years ago." I spoke in years again, not kilohours. "But if you were translating an Ariekes saying, 'The glass with the apple and the one with the wine,' to *me*, you'd probably just say, 'That glass and that one.' Sometimes translation stops you understanding. I'm not fluent. Maybe that's helping me right now."

"Translation always stops you understanding," he said. "What is it you're thinking?"

"How many days before they get here?" I said. "Can you get hold of YlSib? And others? Any you can?" He narrowed his eyes but nodded. "We need to go. Get YlSib or whoever to contact Spanish Dancer and the others. I'll—" I stopped. "I don't know," I said. "I don't know whether . . . Maybe I can tell Cal."

"Tell *me*," Bren said. "I thought you'd despaired."

"I did too."

"What, then? Tell me."

I told him. Revelation was spoiled for him, but I can retain it here, for you.

Bren nodded, and listened to what I can't call a plan—it was hunch and hope—and when I was done he said, "No, we can't tell Cal." He touched me under the chin, and put his arms around me, and for a moment I let him take my weight and it was lovely. "Of course we can't."

"But we're trying to fix things," I said. "You know EzCal aren't stupid . . ."

"It's not about whether they're stupid," he said. "It's about who they are, and what they represent. Maybe Cal would see reason. Maybe. But I don't think so, do you? Want to risk it, really?"

"If we go, he'll find out."

"Yes. And see you as an enemy. And he'll be right. Don't think he—they—won't find time to try to stop us."

"Alright then," I said. "I'll be an enemy."

He smiled at me. "What else are we going to do, Avice?"

We turned arm-in-arm to look at the screen on which the captive Languageless tried to shuffle, alone in their room, watched by cams. It was a quiet moment for our banishing, as we got ready to exile ourselves. We saw the two Ariekei our rulers held moving not quite like two things unconnected, but according to something else; not a plan but a knowledge of each other; a community.

24

I WAS STILL OF some cultural interest. So was Bren~~Dan~~, the free cleaved, troublemaker, licensed dissident. If we disappeared together people would notice. And we might already be watched. That was why the next time, the last time, I went into the city alone.

While the committee fretted and Cal took what power we'd had, Embassytown streets got on with things. Walking through my shrunken town with my aeoli and supplies, I was surprised to pass more than one outdoor party. Some shiftparents of the playing children saw me watching and caught my eye, and even the poignancy of that, of knowing together that this was a last game to keep those children occupied, didn't detract from a moment's pleasure.

There were constables on the streets but not much for them to do except wait for the war: they didn't police with fervour. They didn't clear out the proselytisers, the, I don't know, Shakers, Quakers, Makers, Takers, each with their own theology damning or rescuing us. They weren't treated, even the most brimstone of them, as threats or pests, but as performers. People teased them, while they remained doggedly devout.

I wanted to stop, to ask someone to join me at a café where they were giving away free drinks or accepting the little IOUs we proffered in polite charade. The usual lament: *I may be some time*. The wistfulness of we who are about to leave. I got out of Embassytown close to where Yohn and Simmon and the others and I had held our breath and where I'd touched a tether. I exited through the corridors of a border house, alone.

On my chart were marked various colonies of city Ariekei, each annotated, the latest information Bren could gather. *1: Heartland.* $\frac{kora}{saygiss}$. *Loyal.* To my left. *2: Status uncertain. 3: Contributed to troop but dispute with* $\frac{kora}{saygiss}$. *4: Communalistic? 5*, and on. I knew the displayed boundaries were all porous. As the Absurd approached, those little polities got more insular, their between-fix politics and cultures more divergent, the streets that separated them much worse. I wasn't at all safe.

The first few hundred metres altbrocks had ambled, I'd heard bird wings and been with insects. Now I was in the territories of local fauna, with at least two names: our vernacular; their markers in Language. I stood still for a dog-sized thing we called a browngun, which the Ariekei termed $\frac{kosish}{rua}$ or $\frac{ter}{sethis}$ depending on a taxonomic distinction we never understood. It crossed my path with an urchin frog-tongue gait. Overhead passed the scraps and biorigged machines, wild, or carrying Ariekei.

I could navigate immer but this geography nearly defeated me. It was dangerous in no-person's-lands, and it would be more so at the settlements, where I'd be threatened not by the random rages of the mindless but by the guarding of borders. With this new tribalism inhabitants of different areas sometimes fought. More than once I had had to hunker beyond a house-bone or a trash pile, watching such violence.

My breath was short with fear. Around a convolute, half-hearing the diaphragmatic burr of this neighbourhood, I stopped abruptly. There were two men in front of me.

They saw me and raised rifles. I couldn't see their faces through the visors of their aeoli. The incongruity of Terre figures right there stopped me for a dangerous moment but I moved, just before they fired, and bullets thumped into the ventricle or alley where I'd been. I ran. I heard them behind me. I shoved beneath underhangs, lost myself. I grit my teeth, my heart slamming.

I wasn't panicked. My thoughts were precise. I turned fast at another noise. Someone human was reaching for me from a doorway like gills. I staggered back but he put his finger to his mask, in a *shhh* face, and beckoned. I went to him and he pulled me into a chamber. We sat, listening. I stared at him, but he wasn't memorable in any way. I scanned him like I might decode him.

"Are you alright?" he whispered.

"Yes." I started to say *Who are you?* or *Who were they?* but he shook his head. He listened again.

"Come with me," he said at last. I tried to ask again who he was, but he still didn't answer. He didn't owe me any explanation, I supposed, after all. I let him lead me, creeping.

At the end of a long detour, Yl and Sib were waiting. They greeted him tersely. The three of them confabulated too quietly for me to hear. The man turned and raised his hand to me briefly as he left.

"His name's Shonas," Sib said. "He was a vizier once. He's been in the city for about eight years." We headed cautiously back toward my original intended route.

"Why's he here?" I said. "And who shot at me?" A lintel arced to let us in.

"He came here after a breakdown between him and an Ambassador," YlSib said. "It was a bit of a scandal. He disappeared. You were in immer probably. In the out." "You wouldn't remember." As if. "The other two were DalTon."

I don't remember being surprised. Those dashing dissidents I'd assumed dead, cleaved, or incarcerated in that terrible infirmary. "They went away." "They went weird." "Shonas came into the city to stop them, and . . ." ". . . Well. He's on our side." "Against Am*bass*ador DalTon." "We hadn't heard from those bastards for a long time until all this started, don't know what they've been working on." "They're pigs in shit, now." "They must love all this." "They got wind of your plan."

A parallel economy of narratives, counterfights and revenge. "How do they know what I've got planned?" I said.

"Word gets out."

"What the fuck does that mean?"

"Come on. Stories get *out*." "They might not know anything except *you're coming to the city*. Which would mean you have a plan." "Which whatever it is they're against."

"Are they working with Cal? With EzCal?"

"What? Because they tried to stop you?" YlSib glanced at me. "Just because Cal would try to stop you too?" "It's hardly the same thing." "DalTon have their own reasons for every-thing."

"Which are?" I said.

"Oh there are so many reasons out there," YlSib said, exhaustedly. "Who can keep track of them all?" "Pick one." "They aren't your friend." "Won't that do?"

"No."

"They're tired of all of it." "And you're not." "And you're trying." "How's that?"

Dal and Ton, nihilist since the crisis and before. It was a vindication that they thought me worth attacking. Ask Cal if he'd rather Embassytown be destroyed or survive without him, he'd claim the latter and mean it: but he'd go to his grave, and all our graves, to stop me, when he knew my plan, because it would undermine him. DalTon wanted to stop me because I wanted to save the world. I'm sure it made much more and coherent sense to them, with their long, furious self-exile. There were kilohours of story there I'd never know. DalTon were against me, Cal was against me, DalTon were against Cal, Shonas was against DalTon, Shonas was for me but not against Cal, and so on. I never, in Embassytown, the immer or the out, had the constitution for intrigue. Floaking, I'd hoped, was a way around it. But politics finds you.

"How many are there?" I said. "Outcasts. In the city."

Yl and Sib said nothing. My plans to save Embassytown were briefly part of what happened to DalTon and Shonas, and the drama of the revenge of the ex-Ambassador and their one-time vizier had happened to me. I was grateful to Shonas for my life.

"It's on its way," YlSib told me. "What do you call it? Spanish Dancer."

"I know, it's rude of me," I said. "I'll stop using that name."

"Why?" "It doesn't care and neither do we."

The room was small. Windowless of course, illuminated by fronds that glowed.

"There's power," I said.

"No." "The light's emitted by a necrophage in the walls."

"Come *on*," I said. The building was dying and we were lit by that. I could only laugh.

I asked again, but YlSib wouldn't tell me what had sent them hundreds of thousands of hours ago out of Embassytown, to live behind aeoli masks in that exile microculture. We waited. "More city-Hosts are leaving," YlSib said. "And plenty of them are going to join the Absurd." "There won't be many left to guard, even if they're prepared to."

"They won't have any choice. EzCal'll order them to."

"What's your plan?" "What is it you want to do?"

"You know what," I said. "Bren told you." The truth was I

didn't know to explain it. When Spanish Dancer arrived, I said, "Look. I'll show you."

I remembered the way the captive Languageless had moved. The Absurd were closing in and there was no point waiting for Bren. With YlSib's help, their careful translation, very slowly at first, we started. I, against every inclination I'd had for many years, had no choice but to take control.

I DON'T THINK urgency is a bacillus that can cross exotypes, but it was as if the Ariekei understood that something in me had changed. They and I fervently engaged. I remembered them in The Cravat, fascinated in me and all the other similes.

"You want to lie," I said to Spanish Dancer. I spoke quickly: "Show me what you can do. How close are you? Let's start again." I spent hours listening to it and its group perform their little untruths, through YlSib's translations. I made notes and strained to remember how $\frac{surl}{tesh\ echer}$ had done what it had done. That seemed to me the key.

I'd talked about it with Bren. Often $\frac{surl}{tesh\ echer}$ had wordplayed, eroding qualifying clauses until what was left was a sudden surprising lie. But that method, however well done, was a sideshow. $\frac{surl}{tesh\ echer}$'s theoretical focus had been on me.

It had seen us—us similes made of Terre, not merely us similes—as key to some more fundamental and enabling not-truth. Its signature mendacity, spoken with dandy élan though only a word-trick, hinted at that shift born of contact. *Before the humans came we didn't speak so much of certain things. Before the humans came we didn't speak so much. Before the humans came we didn't speak.*

Through a dissembling made of omitted clauses it laid out its manifesto. Before the humans came we didn't speak: so we will, can, must speak through them. It made that falsity a true aspiration. $\frac{surl}{tesh\ echer}$, insisting on a certain might-be, changed what was. It had learnt to lie to insist on a truth.

"So," I said to Spanish Dancer, and the companions that had joined it. "Let's follow Surl Tesh-echer." YlSib translated. The Ariekei reacted. "It pointed where to go. You know me. I'm the girl hurt in darkness who ate what was given to her. Tell me what I'm like, and we'll get to what I am."

I gave them their nicknames. Spanish Dancer, Toweller, Baptist, Duck. I'd say their names and point and even smile — you never know, you don't know what they have or haven't clocked. Their battery-beasts skipped about as we worked. All these Ariekei could lie, a bit. They were followers of the greatest liar in their history. I helped them leave things out, whisper clauses, with wilful misdescriptions.

Before the humans came. I had YlSib repeat $\frac{surl}{tesh\ echer}$'s claim. The Ariekei failed: the lie code-jammed their minds. "What colour?" I'd say, holding up rags or plastic. They would bud and unbud their eyes.

After hours their attention went. Duck was shuddering, Toweller was humming and emitting piping sounds. I understood. We had no datchips. The Ariekei had to go to the street to wait for the loudspeakers. Inside, we couldn't hear the broadcast but we felt the house quiver. Yl and Sib and I looked at each other, and I think we were all imagining our students stampeding to the nearest voice-point, perhaps fighting off the mindless, perhaps beating each other in their need, as EzCal spoke.

"How come you're behind this?" I said to YlSib. "I mean, if it works, it changes things for you . . ."

"What do we lose?" "An expertise?" "And what's gained? By everyone?" "What's our expertise done for us?" They looked down again. Bren had told me he'd hated his doppel, with a quiet hate. The sight of YlSib's exhaustion, how they didn't look at each other, made me wonder if that was the condition of all Ambassadors.

When the Ariekei returned they were calm again. *Continue*, one said. I nodded exaggeratedly and said "Yes." I said it again, slowly. What I was trying for was a break, a rupture, a move from before to after. A tipping point that, like all such, could only be a mystery.

"WHAT AM I LIKE? What's like me?" YlSib rendered my question and the answers.

"You're the girl who was hurt in the dark and ate what was given to her." "The scavengers that come to our houses' latrines to feed are like the girl eating what was given to her."

"Charming." I willed them to strive for poetry. Closed my eyes. They asserted similarities. I didn't let them stop. After quite a time their suggestions grew more interesting. They overreached: the conversation was full with stillborn similes.

"The rocks are like the girl who was hurt in the dark because . . ."

"The dead are like the girl who . . ."

"Young are like the girl who was hurt in the dark and ate . . ."

Finally and suddenly, Spanish Dancer spoke. "We're trying to change things and it's been a long time and through our patience knowing it'll end we're like the girl who ate what was given to her," YlSib translated. "Those who aren't trying to change anything are like the girl, eating not what she wanted but what was given to her."

I opened my mouth. The tall Ariekes leaned over me, multiple unblinking. "Oh, my God, it knows," I said. "What I'm trying to do. Did you hear?"

"Yes." "Yes."

"It made me two different, contradictory things. Compared them to me."

"Yes." They were more cautious than me, but I smiled till they couldn't not smile back.

WE BROKE OFF LATE, when the Ariekei grew so needy for the god-drug voice they couldn't work anymore, withdrew into shaking confusion. I slept uncovered on the slightly giving floor, until Yl or Sib shook me awake and gave me some inadequate breakfast. I could tell by the translucence of the tower-skin that it was day again. My pupils were there, better: EzCal had given their morning broadcast.

YlSib told me EzCal had discovered I was gone. They were searching for me. Squads were in the city. "You aren't just out alone anymore," they said. "You're on the run." "You're hiding." They didn't have to say *One of us.*

All day we worked at the inadequate similes of the Ariekei. It got me exhausted and impatient. As it grew dark I heard the moist opening of the room, and Bren came in. I took hold of him passionately, and he kissed me but held me back. I broke off when I saw what followed him. He had with him one of the Absurd.

"It's been a bastard journey." He laughed very shortly.

The thing was weak. Bren had it at the end of a rigid prod and shackles that coursed constantly with current. Otherwise it would easily have overcome him. The Languageless thing was wounded from that constant burning. Its giftwing was strapped to it, its legs were hobbled. I'd known this was the plan, but I couldn't believe Bren had succeeded.

"Christ," I said. "How did you *do* it? Oh, Jesus, look at it. This is horrible. You look like a torturer."

"Yes it really is," he said.

Spanish Dancer and the other Ariekei surrounded it. It strained and failed to reach for them. They tottered back, came forward, morbidly curious, it looked like.

"How is it in Embassytown?" I said.

"They're afraid," he said. "They probably think you and I are working for the enemy. Or they're saying they do."

"The Absurd?" I said. "That's . . ."

"Absurd, yes."

"It's crazy."

"You know how they are," he said. People would say it even as they knew it made little sense. They were right to be afraid. The Absurd were coming.

"How did you get it?"

"In all the ways you can imagine," Bren said. "False papers, bribery, misdirection, intimidation. Creeping at midnight. Violence. All that."

"Now we can actually test things," I said.

Bren took datchips from his bag. "Here," he said. "This lot can have a bit of control over themselves. So you're not totally beholden to the broadcasts. We can get them out of here."

"Why exactly *do* you want them to lie?" Yl or Sib said. I stared at them. They hadn't understood at all. They'd thrown their lot in with a plan just because it was a plan.

"It's what the lying means," Bren said to them. "Why do you think we're leaving the city?" They shrugged.

"It's about how symbols work for them," I said. "I never thought we could shift that. But you know what made me change my mind? That there are already Ariekei who've done it." I pointed at the captive. "They've managed to do what Surl Tesh-echer and Spanish Dancer and this lot have wanted to do

343

for years. They've got new minds. And they're using them to kill us."

IT WAS THE freakish precision with which the Absurd coordinated attacks that had started me thinking. They were communicating: there was no other explanation for such efficient murder. Languageless, they still needed and made community, though they might not have known that's what they were doing: each probably believed itself trapped in vengeful solitude even as the violence they committed together disproved it.

I'd seen them gesticulate. Their commandos or commanders indicating with their giftwings. The Absurd had invented pointing. With the point they'd conceived a *that*. They'd given the jag of the body, the out-thrust limb, power to refer. That *that* was the key. From it had followed other soundless words.

That. That? No, not that: that.

Each word of Language meant just what it meant. Polysemy or ambiguity were impossible and with them most tropes that made other languages languages at all. But *that*ness faces every way: it's flexible because it's empty, a universal equivalent. *That* always means *and not that other*, too. In their lonely silent way, the Absurd had made a semiotic revolution, and a new language.

It was base and present tense. But its initial single word was actually two: *that* and *not-that*. And from that tiny and primal vocabulary, the motor of that antithesis spun out other concepts: me, you, others.

The code they'd created was quite unlike the precise mapping they'd grown up knowing. But it was Language that was the anomaly: this new crude thing of flailing fingers and murderous stamping was closer by far to what we spoke, was at last cousin-tongue to those of sentients across the immer.

"We could never learn to speak Language," I said. "We only

ever pretended. Instead the Absurd have learnt to speak like us. The Ariekei in this room want to lie. That means thinking the world differently. Not referring: signifying. I thought that was impossible. But look." I pointed at the thing that wanted to kill me. "That's what they've done. Every time they point, they signify. So far the price is way too high. But now we know Ariekei can do it. And teaching this lot that without taking their wings means teaching them to lie.

"Similes start . . . transgressions. Because we can refer to anything. Even though in Language, everything's literal. Everything is what it is, but still, I can be *like* the dead and the living and the stars and a desk and fish and anything. Surl Tesh-echer knew that was Language straining to . . . bust out of itself. To signify." That's why it had, with so strange a strategy, come at lying through us. I hadn't brought Scile's books with me but I'd gone over them many times, learnt from and argued with them, and I knew what I needed to. "I had to be hurt and fed to be speakable, because it had to be true. But what they *say* with me . . . That's true because they *make* it.

"Similes are a way out. A route from reference to signifying. Just a route, though. But we can push them down it, even that last step, all the way." It became clearer to me as I spoke. "To where the literal becomes . . ." I stopped. "Something else. If similes do their job well enough, they turn into something else. We tell the truth best by becoming lies."

Not paradoxes, I wanted to say; these weren't paradoxes, they weren't nonsense. "I don't want to be a simile anymore," I said. "I want to be a metaphor."

Part Eight

THE PARLEY

25

WE HEARD STRANGE SOUNDS, and saw vessels rising, heading out of Embassytown and the city. Most were corvids crossbred of biorigging and bloodless tech. There were spiny church-sized hulks among them, older than Embassytown.

"I can't believe they got those things up," I said.

"They're not as fierce as they look," Bren said. "They were survey ships once. It's all theatre. Even with the, whisper it, Bremen arsenal, we don't have a hope."

Bren had once, with his doppel, been party to hidden arrangements. They'd debriefed spies and double- and triple-agents. "Wyatt was clever," he said. "He did exactly the right amount and kind of not talking about what he had access to to make it scary. But it was nothing."

The fleet lumbered away on their doomed sorties. Taking off my aeoli in the sealed air-breathing room, seeing the Ariekei wait for me, I was exhausted, and had to close my eyes.

OUR OWN FLIGHT from the city was complicated: between four Terre and the Ariekei we were able to push and pull our Absurd prisoner with us, but not easily. It had berserker strength. We had to administer charges to it often, and tug it hurting from the punishment.

"Let's leave it," said Yl.

"Can't," said Bren. He was the most assiduous of us in trying to communicate with it, whenever we stopped. He got nowhere.

It hardly looked at him, focused its enraged attention on the addicted Ariekei.

"They're going into battle," Bren said, indicating the sky. "It's pointless but I respect them for it a bit. EzCal are going to fight." Efforts at negotiation were stillborn and the Absurd came closer. Refugee Terre from arable outposts were trekking to Embassytown. The journey overwhelmed many of them, and left their bodies to degrade from within in suits and biorigging, into mulch that wouldn't fertilise this soil. "EzCal are wondering if they can just fight their way out of all this." As if pugnacity could outweigh the simplicity of numbers.

"I'll give them this," Bren said. "EzCal will be on the field. It was Ez who insisted. The bloody convivials are over. Back home it's . . . bad." I'd left only a few tens of hours ago, but now it was the day after the parties. Poor Embassytown.

WE TOOK EVASIVE ways but there were too many of us to be really secretive. We relied on the chaos that Embassytown and the city were accelerating in each other. We crawled through tunnels between bones, and waited and shocked our captive into stupor when we saw patrols of Ariekei, humans, or both, clearing the streets, shooting the mindless.

It was difficult, peering across skin plateaus to where constables of our race and Ariekei enforced a brutal order. YlSib had repeatedly to whisper *You must be quiet* to Spanish Dancer and its companions. I made frantic arm movements to hush them, which of course they didn't understand. More flyers went over our heads. We hid from regiments on the way to the front.

I kept up efforts to teach. We tried to shield our Ariekene companions from the sounds of the speakers when EzCal's (now prerecorded) utterings began—we holed up and they listened instead to the datchips we'd brought, dosing themselves in small triumph, defeating the tyranny of god-drug's rhythms while their fellow-citizens stampeded for the voice. I don't know how they kept track of which chip each of them had heard and was therefore spent to them.

Our prisoner could see what they were doing, as they hunched, fanwings spread. I imagine that it looked with disgust. Certainly it strained in its shackles.

We quickly had our catechism. I drew it from what Spanish Dancer had said. I whispered it in Anglo-Ubiq; YlSib spoke it in Language. Bren, I saw, mouthed the simile of me that he'd first spoken a long time ago.

"You're trying to change things," I said. YlSib repeated in Language. "You want change like the girl who ate what was given her. So you're like me. Those who aren't trying to change anything are like the girl who didn't eat what she wanted but what was *given* to her: they're like me. You're like that girl who ate. You are the girl who ate. You're like the girl. You are the girl. And so are the others, who aren't like you."

The first time YlSib moved from *you are like* to *you are* the Ariekei started very visibly. That succulently strange lie *you are*, born out of the truth, *you are like*, that they'd already asserted. And its contradiction, too, their enemies as like me as they were. We showed them how their own arguments came close to making liars of them.

ADDICTED VEHICLES galloped by us into the wilderness. In the morning YlSib took us to a transporter. It was blunt and ugly but full of breathable air. We rode an unseen pillow of vented particles following the tracks of the Embassytown-and-city troops.

In empty suburbs were scattered gangs of zelles, their Ariekei dead, looking forlornly for things to power. Bren drove our mongrel conveyance. It was nowhere near as fast as the military craft that had gone out, but it exceeded our walking pace, punted on its way by swinging side-limbs like gondoliers' poles. Through hollowed-out window-eyes I watched the city recede. At first there were outskirt dwellings and warehouses descending into muck, but they ended and the sky came down to meet us.

We raised dust. Spined bushes shuffled out of our way, so paths opened for us in the fields, stretching for many metres ahead then began to fracture, to branch off in the possible directions we might take. The Ariekene battery-beasts moved around my legs. Behind us the shrubs crawled back to their previous positions. The city was a line of towers, rotund halls like unplanted bulbs. It receded.

I looked at it a long time. I shielded my eyes as if that made for magic binoculars, but I couldn't see through it to the smoke or Terre towerblocks of Embassytown. I wondered if there were travellers among the Ariekei, and where if anywhere were other cities from which and to where they might go. I couldn't believe I didn't know.

The zelles grew restive before their owners: they were less able to fight their addiction. Over the hours, the Ariekei huddled as low as their intricate bulks allowed against the pipes and lights in the vehicle. One by one they enfolded their fanwings over datchips.

YOU ARE LIKE *the girl, you are the girl. They are like the girl, they are the girl.*

" $\frac{qeshiq}{malis\ inna}$," YlSib said to them: *Repeat it.*

We are like the girl, the Ariekei said. *You are the girl*, YlSib said, and the Ariekei scuttled, an excitement that pleased me. They couldn't do it but understood, in some alien abstract, what they were trying to do. *The girl . . .* some said, and some *. . . we*

... or ... *us* ... or ... *it's like* ... Poor YlSib, poor Spanish. I was relentless.

"What's that?" I'd seen something scatter a trail kilometres behind us. There was another motion mark, to the west, and soon overhead was another tiny gusting machine. A very few other transports followed us, got closer and visible. A many-wheeled cart on liquid suspension; a truck all Terretech but for biorigged weapons; one-person centaurs, headless equine frames at the front of each of which sat an aeolied woman or man. A glider climbed thermals. Bren stopped us. YlSib got out as the exodus approached.

Other vehicles slowed too. Other drivers and pilots peered out of their windows. Behind me, hidden in our machine, the Absurd hissed, unhearing its own self. The escapees were like YlSib: city exiles. Runaway Staff, I imagined, as well as those not fleeing such grandiose pasts. The glider landed and Shonas leaned out. I wondered where DalTon were. The city-dwellers were wary, but they mostly knew each other, greeted each other and swapped brief information about the Absurd, and the Embassytown and city forces.

When we drove on again, we did so together in a little entourage. The glider overhead signalled to us with its wings and wing-lights. "Tell Spanish to come here," I said to YlSib. "Tell it what I say." I pointed out of the chariot's eyes. Spanish Dancer didn't look in the direction of my gesture. "Look out and upward at the machine above us," I, then YlSib, said. Sometimes when I spoke for the Ariekei, I unthinkingly mimicked the precision of Language as translated into Anglo-Ubiq. "The vessel overhead, the colours on its wings, the way they move—it's telling us things. It's talking to us."

Spanish Dancer looked with some of its eyes at the plane, with some of them at YlSib, and with one at me. I stared at that eye. *YlSib've told you, but do you* know *it's me speaking?* I thought.

"It doesn't understand," Yl or Sib said. "It can tell I'm not lying, I think, but it can tell that the plane's not talking to us either."

"But it is," I said.

WHEN DAWN CAME we veered, to avoid EzCal's force, to bypass the camp.

"Come on, come on," Bren said to himself. We were desperate to reach the Absurd before the combined troops did. "They're in no hurry," said Bren. "We'll overtake them. They don't want to fight anyway—they're going to try to negotiate."

"The problem is," I said, "they can't."

I could still see the glider. The other craft were behind, close enough for us to wave at their drivers. By midmorning gas-trees filled the plateau ahead, a canopy of thousands of house-size fleshbags bobbing in breezes, straining at the ground. One by one the other craft peeled away from behind us. "Hey," I said.

"They can't come through here," Bren said. Only the three centaurs were with us now. YlSib looked nervously at each other.

"Bren," said one. "They're little, we're not." "We can't go through here either." "Not secretly." "We'll leave tracks . . ."

"Have you not been listening?" he said. He yanked at the controls and if anything accelerated. "We don't have any time. We have to get there fast. So please get to work. You should be teaching. Because it isn't enough for us to get there: we have a job to do when we do."

But it was impossible to concentrate as we approached the forest. Some of the trees moved weakly out of our way, hauled by roots, but most were too slow. I braced. The carriage's jutting legs scythed through rope trunks. In our passing trees soared straight up, dangling their broken tethers. We left a line of them accelerating skyward as we cut into the woodland. Through the rear windows I saw the centaurs carrying their riders over the coiled stumps we left behind. There wasn't much debris: it had flown away.

"Beyond this forest and then a few kilometres," Bren said, voice shaking with our motion. "That's where the armies are."

Bloated treetops buffeted each other above. There were darks and shadows of layered variety around us, in which, I abruptly thought, there might be anything: Ariekene ruins, such impossible things. In our wake was a wedge of sky into which the dislodged trees rose in strict formation until they reached wind and scattered. It was because of that gap in the forest that I saw the plane twisting in dogfight turns.

"Something's happening," I said. We craned to see it curve up and the weapons below its nose flare, against another, attacking flyer.

"Fucking Pharotekton damn," Bren said.

We couldn't hide. Wherever we veered we'd announce our route in soaring trees, so we did nothing but try to increase our speed, the centaur-riders jabbing rifles behind us. Detonations sounded and from the tops of explosion clouds bobbed trees and their ragged remains tugging tails of smoke-matter and vegetation.

Shonas, in his glider, fired. For a moment I thought we were being chased down by his enemy DalTon, that I was collateral in someone else's drama, but the attacker flew jack-knifes no human could have piloted. EzCal had ordered an Ariekene vessel to take us, to stop us reaching the army they must realise was our destination.

The centaurs scattered into bladdery undergrowth. I heard YlSib jabbering Language. They were telling Spanish Dancer what was happening.

"Maybe I can . . ." Bren said, and I wondered what plan he had. The glider caromed across our field of vision into the ground, burst in a splash of rising trees. Yl and Sib howled to see Shonas's death.

I hadn't believed, not really, that EzCal would spare a craft for this, for us, now. I screamed and the ground under us burst.

I WOKE TO NOISE. I coughed and cried out and looked into the many eyes of an Ariekes. Above it I saw our ripped-up chassis letting the sky and swaying vegetation through. Beside me was the motionless face of another Ariekes, dead. I thought for moments I was dying. I pulled my aeoli mask up, as the living Ariekes tugged me with its giftwing and pulled me from the overturned vehicle, through a big rip.

It wasn't many seconds since we'd been wrecked, I realised. I stumbled and leaned on Spanish Dancer. We were in a crater, edged by vegetation stretching up on frayed stems.

There was more than one Ariekene dead. The living were hauling out of the hollow, dragging Bren and Yl and Sib with them. The Absurd stumbled disoriented, and one of the wounded Ariekei shoved it, sent it towards us, jabbed its giftwing in our direction. We heard a gasp, and up from the forest at the edges of our brutal clearing went another tree, this one dangling a tangled man, one of the centaur outriders, whose mount had thrown him. He clung, but he was tiny-high very fast, and whatever had snared him gave and he abruptly fell, without a cry I could hear as the plant kept rising. We didn't see him land but he couldn't have lived.

I stumbled over wrecked biorigging. By the time the murderous flyer was back above the bombsite it would have seen no life. We watched it from our hide a few metres of forest in. It circled several times and headed out, toward the Languageless army.

26

"WE HAVE TO WALK," Bren said. "A couple of days, maybe. We have to get through the forest." The Embassytown army were ahead, but we knew they would delay engaging, and we still hoped to reach the attackers before them. Everything, though, depended on whether we could teach the Ariekei what we had to. Every couple of hours we stopped on our limping, blistered way, and repeated a lesson or tried a new one. Neither the Ariekei nor their batteries seemed to tire. I don't know if or how they mourned their companions. Even our captive tramped before us stolidly, subdued by the environs or the attack or something.

Bren guided us with some handheld tech. I was conscious of the forest's darkness, coloured by the bruisey flora. The wood was full of noises. Things of radial and spiral form moved around us. We bewildered the animals—we didn't read as predators to the prey nor vice versa, and they were neither afraid of nor threatening to us. They watched us quizzically, those with eyes. Once one of the Ariekei said something dangerous was near us. A $\frac{kosteb}{floranshi}$, big as a room, opening and closing its teeth. It would surely have attacked the Ariekei had they been alone, but its confusion at the sight of us aliens, uncoded in its instinct, stilled it, so we saved them.

They'd rescued a clutch of the datchips, but not all. They would have to husband them. One by one, as they had to, the Ariekei took themselves into the privacy of the wood and listened hard to EzCal's voice, catching us up, a little high but clearer-headed.

We kept on into the evening, and the forest got sparse, until it was tree-flecked grassland under the glimmer of Wreck. We granted ourselves a little sleep: mostly, though, my priority was to teach.

YOU ARE LIKE *the girl, you are the girl.*

"Sweet Jesus," I said. "Just fucking *say* it." Their urgency, in fact, I'm as certain as I can be, was at least as great as mine.

"YlSib," I said. "Ask them this. Do they know who I am?" Language. The Ariekei murmured. *She's the girl who was* . . . I interrupted. "Really know, I mean. Do they know what a girl is? They know I'm a simile, but do they know that the *girl* is *me*? What do they think *you* are, YlSib? How many?"

"You know what she's asking," Bren said. "Tallying Mystery." Did the Ariekei think an Ambassador one person or two? Staff had always told us it was a pointless, untranslatable, impolite question.

"I'm sorry but I need them to understand that you're two people because I need them to understand that I'm one. That these bloody squawks I make are *language*. That I'm *talking to them*." The Ariekei watched one meat-presence emitting noises more quickly and loudly than usual to the others.

After a silence Bren said, "It's never been something Ambassadors have been exactly keen to make clear."

"Make it clear," I said. "Ambassadors don't get to be the only real people anymore."

I don't believe we could have overturned generations of Ariekene thinking, even with so avant-garde a group as this, had they not known somewhere, to some degree, that each of us was a thinking thing. Spanish and its comrades responded at first as if *of course*, so what; then slowly as YlSib pressed the point many times, with growing fascination, confusion, or what might be anger or fear. At last I saw what I hoped was a fitting sense of revelation.

She is speaking, YlSib said to them. *The girl who ate what was given to her. Like I speak to you.*

"Yes," I said, as the Ariekei stared. "Yes."

Language was the unit of Ariekene thought and truth: asserting my sentience in it YlSib made a powerful claim. They told them that I was speaking, and Language insisted then that there must be other kinds of language than Language.

"Make them say it," I said. "That what I'm doing is speaking."

Spanish Dancer said it. *The human in blue is speaking*. The others listened. They struggled, but one by one managed to repeat it.

"They believe it," I said. This was where it began to change.

"Translate," I said to YlSib. "You know me," I said to the Ariekei. "I'm the girl who ate, etcetera. I'm like you, and you're like me, and I'm like you. I *am* you." One of them shouted. Something was happening. It spread among them. Spanish Dancer stared at me.

"Avice," said Bren in warning.

"Tell them what I say," I said. I looked at Spanish. I met its almost-eyes as urgently as if I were talking to a human. "Tell it. I waited for things to be better, Spanish, so I'm like you. I am you. I took what was given to me, so I'm like the others. I am them." I shone a torch on myself. "I glow in the night, I'm like the moon. I am the moon." I lay down. "They know how we sleep, yeah? I'm so tired I lie as still as the dead, I'm like the dead. I'm so tired I *am* dead. See?"

The Ariekei were staggering. Their fanwings flared, folded and opened. They reached for me with their giftwings, making Bren gasp, but they didn't touch me. They said words and noises.

"What's happening?" Yl or Sib said.

"Don't stop translating," I said. "Don't you dare." The Ariekei sounded together, a moment's horrible choir. They retracted their eyes. "Don't stop. I'm the girl who ate blah blah. What have you said with me all this time? Everything you said's like me *is* me. You've already done it. It's all just things in terms of other things." I stood before Spanish Dancer. "Tell it its name. Say: There were humans a long time ago who wore clothes that were black and red like your markings. Spanish dancers." I heard YlSib neologise "$\frac{spanish}{dancer}$." "I can't speak your name in Language, so I gave you a new one. Spanish Dancer. You're like, you *are* a Spanish dancer."

One by quick one the Ariekei shouted then went silent. Their eyes stayed in. They swayed. No one spoke for a long time.

"What've you done?" whispered Sib. "You've driven them mad."

"Good," I said. "We're insane, to them: we tell the truth with lies."

Like sped-up film of plants in the sun, Spanish's eye-coral at last budded. It started to speak and said two trickles of gibberish. It stopped and waited and started again. Yl and Sib and Bren translated but I didn't need them. Spanish Dancer spoke slowly, as if it was listening hard to everything it said.

You are the girl who ate. I'm $\frac{spanish}{dancer}$. *I'm like you and I am you.* Someone human gasped. Spanish craned its eye-coral and stared at its own fanwing. Two eyes came back to look at me.

I have markings. I'm a Spanish dancer. I didn't take my eyes off it. *I'm like you, waiting for change. The Spanish dancer is the girl who was hurt in darkness.*

"Yes," I whispered, and YlSib said "$\frac{shesh}{qus}$," *Yes.*

Other Ariekei were speaking. *We are the girl who was hurt.*

We were like the girl . . .

We are the girl . . .

"Tell them their names," I said. "You move like a Terre bird: you're Duck. You drip liquid from your Cut-mouth, so you're Baptist. Explain that, YlSib, can you? Tell them, tell them the city's a heart . . ."

I'm like the liquid-dripping man, I am him . . .

With the boisterous astonishment of revelation they pressed the similes by which I'd named them on until they were lies, telling a truth they'd never been able to before. They spoke metaphors.

"God," Yl said.

"Jesus Christ Pharotekton," said Bren.

"God," said Sib.

The Ariekei spoke to each other. *You're the Spanish dancer.* I could have wept.

"Jesus Christ, Avice, you did it." Bren hugged me for a long time. YlSib hugged me. I held onto them all. "You *did* it." We listened to the Ariekene new speakers call each other things in unprecedented formulations.

There were two poor bewildered remnants that could not, no matter what I said, that stared at their companions uncomprehending. But the others spoke in new ways. *I'm not as I've ever been*, Spanish Dancer told us.

MUCH LATER, when we'd been hours in our camp, I took a datchip, slowly, mindful of how long it had been since a fix, and played it. It was EzCal saying something about the shape of their clothes. Those two still unchanged, Dub and Rooftop I'd called them, which hadn't shifted with the others, responded with the usual addict fervour to the sounds.

None of the others did. I looked at the Ariekei and they at us. They took slow steps, at last, in all directions. *I don't feel . . .* one said. *I am, I am not . . .*

"Play another," Bren said. EzCal spoke thinly to us about some other nonsense. The Ariekei looked at each other. *I am not . . .* another said.

I picked up another and made EzCal mutter the importance of maintaining medical supplies, and still only those two reacted. The others listened with nothing more than curiosity. I tried more, and while Dub and Rooftop stiffened the altered Ariekei made querying noises at EzCal's ridiculous expositions.

"What happened?" YlSib stuttered. "Something's happened to them."

Yes. Something in the new language. New thinking. They were signifying now—there, elision, slippage between word and referent, with which they could play. They had room to think new conceptions.

I threw the chips to them, laughing, and they began to go through them. Our clearing was filled with overlapping voices of Ez and Cal.

"We changed Language," I said. A sudden change—it couldn't undo. "There's nothing to . . . intoxicate them." There only ever had been because it was impossible, a single split thinkingness of the world: embedded contradiction. If language, thought and world were separated, as they just had been, there was no succulence, no titillating impossible. No mystery. Where Language had been there was only language: signifying sound, to do things with and to.

The Ariekei sifted the datchips, listening with disbelief at how they heard what they heard. That's what I think. Spanish Dancer remained bent, but its eyes looked up at me. Perhaps it knew now, in ways it could not have done before, that what it heard from me were words. It listened.

"Yes," I said, "yes," and Spanish Dancer cooed and, harmonising with itself, said: "$\frac{yes}{yes}$."

27

ONE BY ONE as the night went on the Ariekei withdrew, and one by one they began to make terrible sounds. I fretted about the noise, but what could we do? Spanish Dancer, Baptist, Duck, Toweller, all but Dub and Rooftop, which looked on without a scrap of comprehension, went through what sounded like agonies. They didn't all call out or scream, but all of them in different ways seemed as if they were dying.

YlSib was alarmed, but seemed neither Bren nor I were surprised by what we heard: the noise of old ways coming off in scabs. Pangs of something finishing, and of birth. Everything changes now: I thought that very explicitly, each word. I thought: Now they're seeing things.

In the beginning was each word of Language, sound isomorphic with some Real: not a thought, not really, only self-expressed worldness, speaking itself through the Ariekei. Language had always been redundant: it had only ever been the world. Now the Ariekei were learning to speak, and to think, and it hurt.

"Shouldn't we . . . ?" Yl said, and had nothing with which to finish it.

The said was now not-as-it-is. What they spoke now weren't things or moments anymore but the thoughts of them, pointings-at; meaning no longer a flat facet of essence; signs ripped from what they signed. It took the lie to do that. With that spiral of assertion-abnegation came quiddities, and the Ariekei became themselves. They were worldsick, as meanings yawed. Anything was anything, now. Their minds were sudden merchants:

metaphor, like money, equalised the incommensurable. They could be mythologers now: they'd never had monsters, but now the world was all chimeras, each metaphor a splicing. The city's a heart, I said, and in that a heart and a city were sutured into a third thing, a heartish city, and cities are heart-stained, and hearts are city-stained too.

No wonder it made them sick. They were like new vampires, retaining memories while they sloughed off lives. They'd never be cured. They went quiet one by one, and not because their crisis ended. They were in a new world. It was the world we live in.

"YOU HAVE TO show the others," I said to Spanish Dancer. Rudely interrupted its birth. It deserved a different passage but we had no time. It listened in its queasy awe and newness. "The deaf ones. You can talk to them. They think they're beyond language at all, but you, you can show them what they've done." *Language was never possible. We never spoke in one voice.*

In the sun, we saw figures kilometres off. Humans rattling slowly towards us. Small ships went overhead, heading back toward the city. "Look," Bren said. "That one's wounded."

As we got closer we could see that there weren't many Terre, maybe thirty or forty, hauling equipment or urging on slapdash-looking biorigging, rocking in cars. We saw them see us, and for a moment they seemed to be preparing weapons. Then they calmed.

"They must have seen this lot first," Bren said of the Ariekei with us. "Thought it was an attack. But with us here they think we're an Embassytown squad. They're plantation staff." Wilderness dwellers who had only now cleared their homesteads and outland farmfactories. They'd been in the path of the Language-less army and lost their nerve as the Absurd came at their lands killing all the humans they met and tearing their houses to the ground, murdering or recruiting the country Ariekei alongside which the Terre had lived.

More boats went overhead. They would probably not look long enough to see the Ariekei in our party, or that we were heading in the wrong direction. In fact they wouldn't notice us at all: they were busy returning to the city. Several of the vessels, I could see, were bleeding.

Spanish Dancer whispered, called the humans things it couldn't have called them before. It was paying close attention, as it had for hours, to our captive.

We avoided the refugees. "Depending how fast the Absurd are going," Bren said, "we'll reach them tomorrow or the next day. Probably the next day—what is that, Muhamday, Ioday?" None of us had any idea.

"What about the Embassytowners?"

"We've avoided them. I think we went past them. They'll still be stationed. Especially—" He pointed at the sky. "You saw the boats. The scouts've been wounded. EzCal knows they can't win. They'll have Ariekei and Terre at the front trying to negotiate."

"Yeah, they're not going to succeed, though," Yl said.

"They won't," Bren said. "How can they? They don't think the same at all."

"Spanish understands what we have to do," I said. "Have you seen how it's being with the captive? It knows they *are* thinking the same, now. That they're both *thinking*."

IT WAS A VERY new ecosystem to us, there with the sparse trees, where we watched Spanish and the other Ariekei work. Here the key predator was not the $\frac{kosteb}{silas}$, with its big, nearly immobile body and limbs that could reach fast and far through trees, but fast $\frac{delith}{hi\,ki}$ that hunted by night. Vaguely related to the Ariekei themselves, the rear two limbs of the bipedal $\frac{delith}{hi\,ki}$ were ferocious weapons, as, of a more manipulable kind, was the arm that corresponded to the giftwing. $\frac{delith}{hi\,ki}$ fanwings were immobile. They peered through the dark with eyes attuned to motion. They were social hunters. They worked in concert to corral the dog-sized prey-animals of the plain.

We were too large for them to come for us, but they still watched. Flying things skittered at our torches: burrowing eaters of phosphorescent rot, used to honing in on glowing ground, emerged and gnawed confused at the pooled light.

We didn't take the leash off our prisoner—we didn't trust it or know how to decide if it became trustable. But we'd been treating it with less fear for days, and did so with even less now. The new ex-Host liars regarded it, and whispered to each other in words they'd used countless times, that now did very different things. By early morning something was changing. The Ariekei were circling the captive. It wasn't gasping or lunging at them, or at me, or Bren or YlSib: it was watching us, and watching the other Ariekei.

28

SPANISH DANCER and our captive circled. The others ringed
them. Every few seconds one of the two would shove out its
giftwing like a knife-fighter looking for an opening. It would
sketch out some outline in the air: there would be a pause and
the other would follow suit. Spanish's fanwing frilled open and
shut. The Languageless's stub trembled.

The gesticulations were information, motion telegrams.
Talking. They didn't understand each other but they knew there
was something to understand. And that was liberation. When
they did make communication—something ridiculous, Spanish
throwing a pulpy bud then pointing into the muttering wildlife
where it lay, and the Absurd picking it up—their euphoria, even
alien, was palpable.

Signifying Spanish could speak through gesture now. For
our captive that no longer had a name, perhaps the strangeness
was greater. It had thought that without words, it had no
language. Its comrades communicated with each other, never
knowing they did, not across the chasm with untorn Ariekei;
and mostly what they expressed to each other was the very
hopelessness that made them believe they were incommunicado.

But in the panic of the attack and our escape, it had
understood shove-and-point instructions to flee. It had watched
Bren, YlSib and me speak and listen to each other with gestures
for stress and clarity. The rest of the Absurd army never had to
reflect on these behaviours. Spanish had learnt it could speak

without speaking: the Absurd had learnt that it could speak, and listen, at all.

"They were yanking it around," Bren said. "It was impossible for it not to know what they meant: they were shoving it and pointing the same way. They *made* it obey them. Maybe you need violence for language to take."

"Bren," I said. "That's crap. We were all running the same way. We were *all* trying to get out. We had the same intentions. That's how it knew what we were doing."

He shook his head. Formally, he said, "Language is the continuation of coercion by other means."

"Bullshit. It's cooperation." Both theories explained what had happened plausibly. I resisted, because it felt trite, saying that they weren't as contradictory as they sounded.

"Look," I said. Pointed above the horizon. There was smoke, stains in the sky.

"IT CAN'T BE," Bren said, as if to himself, as we moved as fast as we could. "They were going to wait." He said it more than once. When specks appeared far off on the lichened downs, we pretended that there were many things they might be, until we came too close to deny that they were bodies.

We looked down an incline to the aftermath of war. Thousands of metres of remains. I was breathing very hard, through my aeoli, in horror. At this distance the specificities of carnage were hard to gauge. I was trying to estimate Terre versus Absurd, but the death was too tangled. In any case, many of the Ariekene corpses I saw must be EzCal's forces, like the humans with which they lay.

We led our not-quite-captive. It was in its collar but we hadn't shocked it for kilometres. Spanish Dancer drummed its hoofs. It looked at me and opened its mouths. It pointed at the ruination. It opened and closed its mouths and said to me:

« toolate »
toolate

"Yes."

« toolate »
toolate ·

"Yes. Too late." We had not taught it that.

« too.late »
too.late ·

STRUNG OUT, artificially, druggedly alert, there was an unpleasant drag to my senses, as if things I saw or heard left residue when I turned from them. My aeoli mask in a rare reminder of its biorigged life shifted, uncomfortable at the smell of the dead. Everywhere were men and women burst open. There were Ariekei dead with fanwings and without, strewn together. Innards evolved on opposite ends of space alloyed in compound decay. There were corpse-fires and rubbish.

Wrecks. The aftermath was scored by lines of char culminated in craters, where fliers had come down. Bren sifted through junk, hands wrapped in rags. I copied him. It wasn't quite so hard as I'd expected.

This had all happened perhaps two days before. These scenes made me careful and cold. I didn't look too close at the faces of the scores of Embassytowner dead. I was too certain I'd see one I knew. Picking through remnants between those smoke pillars I tried to learn the history of the fight. There were many more Embassytown-and-city dead than Absurd. Fighters lay mid-action, in mouldering stasis, hands and giftwings and weapons still on each other. We read these corpse dioramas for the stories of their creation.

"They have corvids," I said. Strategising without speech, the Absurd were driving biorigged weapons. "Jesus," I said. "Jesus it's an *army*, I mean it's an *army*."

Shockingly few combatants were left alive. A few mortally

wounded Ariekei cycled their legs in the air, craning eyes. One cried out in Language, telling us that it was wounded. Spanish Dancer touched its giftwing. The Absurd moribund were dying with too much focus to notice us. On some I saw the bleed from fanwings newly excised—there were new recruits to that force even among the dying.

Pinioned under Ariekene dead was a woman still just alive, her broken aeoli wheezing oxygen into her. She looked at Bren and me as we tried to calm her and ask her, "What happened here?" But she only stared, terrified or air-starved out of speech. At last we laid her back down and gave her water. We couldn't move her; her aeoli was dying. We found two others alive: one man couldn't be woken; the other was conscious only of his impending death. All we got from him was that the Absurd had come.

Bren indicated ripped uniforms. "These are specialists." He pointed at runnels out of the battlefield. "This wasn't . . . These were outriders, this was a guard group, around something, that came in first."

"The negotiators," I said. He nodded slowly at me.

"Of course, yes. The negotiators. This was supposed to be a bloody parley. They gave it a try. My God." He looked at the remnants around us. "The Languageless didn't even slow."

"And now they're heading for the rest." For the main mass of the Terre-Ariekei army.

WE HAD TO double back. We took an abandoned vehicle, cleaned the mess of war out of it. We sped along the cut through the marks of thousands of hooves. I was pressed against the Ariekei. Spanish and Baptist were crowding around the Absurd. They were sketching marks in the air, and the captive, if I could still describe it so, was doing the same.

It wasn't long before we saw a line of figures. Bren stiffened. I knew how weak our plan was, but we had no choice. "It's alright," I said. "They're Terre."

A big, dirty derelict band, dressed like penitents, a trudging little town. There were children among them. They looked at us through their masks. They were as intense as monks, too. Some backed away, muttered among themselves. A few temporary leaders came closer, and a few soldiers, refugee from that ruination, in scorched uniforms.

The Ariekei stayed back. They kept the self-deafened close, disguised its injury. The humans told us they'd run from the depredations of the Absurd, from pioneer homesteads and bio-rigging farms. This was everyone running: they'd found each other. Been joined by the AWOL and soldiers from defeated units. They were behind their attackers now, were following them to the city, like those prey-fish that seek safety in their predator's wake. They had no plans, only the vague sense that this might keep them alive a few days longer. Their passage in the tracks of the enemy was a despairing homage to their own defeat.

A militia-man told us, "We were with Ariekei. Leaders. The most eloquent, I suppose. There to communicate. We were there to protect them, the negotiators, give them space, time, when they were trying to get through to . . ." The soldiers had been instructed to do whatever was necessary while the Ariekene speakers struggled to make the Absurd understand them. "They were trying to *talk* to them."

"How?" I said.

"No how." I thought he'd said *know-how* and didn't understand.

"There was no how," he said. "We wondered. We could see the Absurd coming; they had fliers and weapons and vehicles, and there were thousands of them. We wondered what it was the Ariekei were planning. What they'd cooked up. It was only, Jesus . . . They got ready by listening to EzCal on datchip. A couple of us in the unit understand Language . . ." He paused at that inadvertent present tense. ". . . They told me what EzCal was saying, in the recordings. 'You must make them understand.' Again and again. In all different ways. 'You must speak to them so they understand you.'" The man shook his head. "That's what they got high on. When the Absurd came, they shouted at them through loudspeakers."

"But they're deaf," I said. He shrugged. The wind sent his greasy hair rippling from under his battered helmet.

"We sent some of them out to meet . . . the enemy . . . close. Their plan must have been . . . Well, the Absurd just came through them. To us." There'd been no plan at all. I looked at Bren. There'd been no secret strategy: only the knowledge of what had to happen, with no idea how.

"They tried to do it by fiat," Bren said. The god-drug had hoped their ineluctable instructions would carry this. What despairing deity.

"Jesus," I said. "Do you think they thought it would work?" There were a lot of dead back there. "Where are the rest of your army?" I said. "EzCal's army?"

The man shook his head. "Most of them . . . us . . . never wanted to fight," he said. "They wanted to beg. But they can't even. Beg. Can't make them hear. They're retreating back to the city. Getting behind the blockades." He shook his head slowly. "Those won't stop them," he said. There was nothing between the Absurd army and the city, and Embassytown.

The refugees watched us go. Told us it was in the wrong direction and shrugged when we ignored them. They gestured goodbye and good luck with a kind of dead politeness, a strange courtesy. At the edges of the mass, those most monkish ones watched us with hostility I'm certain most of them couldn't have explained.

We travelled in their hoof-churnings, and stalked the Absurd from just beyond their sight. From thickets, from behind rises. It rained. We sprayed muck. It didn't seem to get very dark that night; it was as if the stars and Wreck were shining unnaturally, so I could lean against Spanish Dancer and watch it sketch hand signs with the Ariekes that was no longer a prisoner, and I could see the grey landscape.

When dawn came, there were a few cams around us, gadding spastically. Intel-gatherers for the army, still transmitting. Our sound and motion attracted them, and they paced with us in a flitting corona. I looked straight into the lens of one, through the air to someone watching in Embassytown.

We could hear the Absurd, now. They were just one segment of landscape over. The cams swarmed suddenly away, over flora and geography. A corvid flew close overhead on some frantic wartime job, and we had to hope it had not seen us, that we wouldn't be eradicated, so close.

THERE WERE NO secret ways we could ensure a smaller group of Absurd would find us, no ways we could split one section of their expedition from the others. Each Languageless thought itself alone, though we knew that wasn't true. The closest this huge vengeful mass would have to generals would be its unspeaking vanguard. We passed their flank, hidden by landscape, and made our way to a place they'd find us.

Finally, stinking in our suits, we left the vehicle. I was strongly conscious of what a scene we must have been. Four

Terre. Me at the front. Behind me Bren, tense and ready. The marks of the journey had made YlSib easy to tell apart. They stood beside each other, each with a weapon poised.

The Ariekei. Ranged in a curve around us, as if they made up our group's fanwing. Spanish Dancer was closest to me, and watched me with several of its eyes.

At the centre of the group stood the untethered Language-less. The thing that was no longer our enemy looked from one to another of its Ariekene companions. It made a motion with its giftwing. One by one most of the other Ariekei responded in a similar way. It made me a bit breathless to see.

There were two that didn't. Dub and Rooftop watched the motions of their companions. Nothing they could understand was occurring.

Spanish Dancer said to me: "$\frac{they\ come\ now\ we\ will\ see}{they\ come\ now\ we\ will\ speak}$." I stared a while, and at last nodded. "You will," I said. "We will. They will."

"$\frac{let\ me}{let\ me}$," it said. Two noises came out of it that meant nothing to me. It said something rapidly in Language, and its companions, and Yl and Sib and Bren looked up sharply. $\frac{spanish}{dancer}$ tried again. "$\frac{thank\ you}{no\ thank\ you}$," it said to me. I was silent. What could I say?

THE FIRST OF the Absurd came. Fliers squalled over the country, must have seen us, but perhaps decided that we were too nothing to be blown away. A loose, fast-moving posse of tireless Absurd became visible, moving toward us. We braced. Someone said something about *the plan*.

Those at the front of the army, the groups a kilometre or so ahead of the main force, saw us. They stampeded up the scree and at us, pointing giftwings, directing segments of their own crowd, which peeled off into wedge-shapes, flanked us, in the unsaid strategy they thought merely rage. I could hear their hoofbeats. Then I could see the shades of their skins, the craned forks of their eyes, the flanges of their fanwing stubs, as they raised weapons.

"Now," someone said, and I truly couldn't say if it was me.

Spanish said something too quiet for me to quite hear, that I don't think was in Language. It walked forward with the other leaders of its revolutionary group and the Absurd came with them. It went farther, stepped out and raised its giftwing and the stalk of its fanwing, so its injury was plain. It waved them like standards. It announced its status—*I'm one of you*—and urged its comrades to stop, gestured to all the incomers, *wait, wait, wait, wait*.

The Absurd army didn't slow at all. I felt sick. "*Courage*," Bren said, in French. I did not smile. The inchoate motion language the fanwingless spoke was camouflaged by shared purpose. From their untidy ranks came a shot.

"Jesus," I said. Spanish Dancer, $\frac{spanish}{dancer}$, spoke with its voice and hands as its once-fellows approached to murder or brutalise it. I wondered what would happen to it if it were deafened now, now that language was different for it. Spanish's and the Absurd's motions registered to the enemy as little as windblown plants.

They're not ignoring, I thought. *They don't know*. They didn't know that these minds weren't like the others they'd finished or changed, how could they? I dug among our packs.

"Show your fanwings!" I shouted to Spanish. "Show them you can hear!" YlSib began to translate, but Spanish was already unfurling, and the others were copying it, except for Dub and Rooftop, who did so only when Spanish told them to in Language. Another missile came close. "Tell Dub and Rooftop to get in front," I said.

I made a datchip play, and the thin voice of EzCal exhorted us to something or other. But every one of the Ariekei had already heard that speech so did not react to it, and I cursed and threw it away.

"Oh," said Bren. He understood. I fumbled again while the Absurd came close enough that I could hear their murder-croons. I spilled a handful of chips and finally got another to sound. EzCal said, *We are going to tell you what it is that you must do . . .*

We Terre heard it as sound. Spanish Dancer and the others heard it too, now, as sound: they just cocked their fanwings quizzically. But Dub and Rooftop were still addicts. They snapped upright, shuddered so elementally it was as if gravity took them toward the source of the voice. They glazed.

"Yes," said Bren.

I played another. Dub and Rooftop were swaying, recovering from EzCal's first words; jerked giddily they were caught up again. Rooftop shouted at what was, I realised, EzCal's descriptions of trees.

Our self-defeaned Ariekes kept waving at the others, and Spanish and the others mimicked it, their own fanwings opening and closing, and in the middle of them all Dub and Rooftop lost themselves. I kept the sound going. "$\frac{stop}{stop}$," said Spanish, and I could think how horrible the sight of that powerless staggering must be to it, reminding it what it had been, making it watch its friends suffering in compulsion, but I wouldn't cease.

As the first of the Absurd crested our rise and came towards us, weapons up, first one, then more, then many, hesitated. I pressed another chip and heard Bren say *yes.*

Every army has one soldier at its very front. A big Ariekes, its Cut- and Turn-mouths open as if it were howling, picking its feet high as it came for us. I was holding out a datchip as if it might stop it. Its eyes spread in all directions, one for each of us, watching Spanish, and the Ariekes that had been our captive

378

jerking its arms as the Absurd did to each other, and Dub and Rooftop stumbling. If I was thinking anything I was praying. It was very close.

Abruptly the soldier stopped. It lowered its sputtering mace. It involuted its eyes, opened them again and *watched* us. I was still playing EzCal's voice. It wasn't the only motionless one, now. As if I were merciless, I made Dub and Rooftop dance their addiction. The Absurd gripped each other, gestured or stood still, watching.

"Don't stop," said Bren.

"$\frac{stop}{stop}$," said Spanish, and Bren said again, "Don't."

"What . . . ?" said Sib.

"What is it?" said Yl.

The army of hopeless and enraged had been driven to murder by their memories of addiction, and the sight of their compatriots made craven to the words of an interloper species. That degradation was the horizon of their despair. I'd made them see the motions of their ex-selves hearing their god-drug—there was no mistaking that tarantella—but that other Ariekei had fanwings unfurled, could hear, but were unaffected.

There wasn't supposed to be such a thing as uncertainty in the minds of the Absurd. Its sudden arrival arrested them. Our ex-captive waved its giftwing and its stump. *Stop*, it was saying, and many in the army that faced us knew that it was saying so, and were stunned to know that they knew it.

Poor Rooftop, I thought, poor Dub. Ariekene dust coiled around me and I blinked. Thank God they never learnt to lie. We'd needed real addicts, to prove that the others were free, and the rage of the Absurd therefore misdirected. I kept Dub and Rooftop moving. I made them sick on god-drug. Spanish Dancer watched them, fanned its fanwing. I was shouting.

*

INFORMATION MOVED desperately slowly among the Absurd—even their quickest thinkers still had only a tenuous understanding that they *could* transmit information. What they said to each other at first with their waving and upheld limbs was simple: *Don't attack.* Following that: *Something is happening.*

The information was discombobulated with distance, moving backwards through the rank. At the front, gestures got close to: *They can hear but are not addicted.* Farther back, ranks of the Absurd told those behind them simply: *Stop.*

"$\frac{stop}{stop}$," said Spanish. Our Deaf went to the front of the army, and Spanish went with it. With the Absurd generals watching, the two of them—ostentatiously, in wing signs and sigils scraped in the earth, ideograms that startled me—started to talk.

THERE WERE MANY many hours, two days and nights of frustration and silences, while the army waited. Hesitated. Individuals kept coming up from the ranks to see what was happening. Every one that did was astonished: unaddicted Ariekei; Terre waiting respectfully; the process of slow dawning between hearing and Absurd, as we still questionably called them; scrawls in dirt.

Those with a little knowledge became agents of patience among the others. We could see their influence, by whatever gestural persuasions, when, toward the end of the second day, human refugees approached from the army's flank, easily killable, but the fanwingless didn't assault them.

The Terre must have realised that the Absurd had stopped, wondered at the strange calm and come to find its source, and the Languageless had let them. The refugees set up camp a way away from us, and watched.

It took a time before the boundary of comprehension between Absurd and $\frac{spanish}{dancer}$'s group, the New Hearing, was more fully breached, but nothing like so long as I'd once have expected.

We weren't teaching the deafened to communicate: we were showing them they already could, and did. It wasn't incremental but revelatory; and revelations, though hard-won, are viral.

"We need EzCal here," I said.

"They won't come if they know what's happened," Bren said. "If they know that they've lost."

Even if it means the end of the war? But I knew he was right. "Well then we can't tell them the truth. We see any vespcams we smash them. They can't know what's happened."

TOWELLER AND BAPTIST understood the mission we gave them. They wouldn't have done a few days before. They returned to the city in a flyer with the Absurd.

"They know what they have to do?" I said to Spanish Dancer.

"$\frac{yes}{yes}$." They'd sneak back in the wounded ship, take on the roles of loyal addict-soldiers, bringing news of a breakthrough. They'd tell EzCal that the Absurd had stopped, were just waiting, and that the god-drug and their entourage must come. It couldn't occur to EzCal that they were being lied to. That was what we were relying on. How could it? They would, after all, hear it from Ariekei, in what they would think was Language. Say it like a Host.

"They know what to do when EzCal speaks to them?"

"$\frac{yes}{yes}$." They knew to seem as if it swept them over.

"They know to ask for them to speak, if too long goes by without?"

"$\frac{yes}{yes}$." They knew to mimic the addiction. They knew what they had to do.

The two different tribes of post-Language Ariekei shared symbols. The human refugees made no attempt to come closer. "Did we do it?" I said.

Surrounded by semiosis, Dub at last juddered and abruptly achieved change and withdrawal, apropos of nothing I saw, gasping and speaking newly. Its companions watched its unexpected transcendence or fall. Rooftop, though, couldn't reach it. It dosed itself with the last of the datchips. It was the only addict left among us.

I don't know what the parameters of friendship were among the Ariekei, but I think that they must all have been sad. And Rooftop, $\frac{sagg}{leav\ veth}$ as its name was, must have been lonely. It watched the scratch-and-gesture conversations around it, and I thought that being surrounded by the changed must be, for it, like a mild hell. *You did save us*, I thought at it. *Without you we'd have died.* As if that could comfort it.

EVERY DAY Spanish told me of the progress. When I consider what it was that actually happened, what the Absurd and the New Hearing achieved, it took no time at all. I don't know how many days of camping among these silent discussions it had been when I realised that there were cams watching us, eddying nervously in the wind. But I knew we were past ready.

"Jesus," I said, and pointed them out to Bren. "Christ Pharotekton." I stood below the cams, gesturing at them like newly expressive Ariekei, beckoning them.

They were scouts from a school around EzCal's ship. It couldn't be far: they'd come, following the directions and promises of Toweller and Baptist. Some vespcams seemed to want to shy away; others focused on us. It was too late for the god-drug to turn back now, block transmissions, pretend ignorance, even if they understood what they were seeing. The feeds from those little lenses were being watched not only in the oncoming ship, but by thousands of Embassytowners.

"Listen," I shouted, and was aware of many Ariekene eyes

on me. The lenses scudded, anxious midges, came a little lower. "Listen to me," I said and grit my teeth in the wind. "Listen to *me*."

"They must've been wondering what the delay was," Bren said. "What was keeping the Absurd. How long have they been waiting? Hiding, waiting to die, wondering what's the hold-up."

"*Listen*," I said. "Get them here. *Get EzCal here now.*" I pointed at Spanish Dancer, at the fanwingless to which it spoke, and first Spanish, then one by one all the hundreds of Absurd, pointed at me. The cams buzzed, changing positions, and I kept my eyes on one fixed point, as if the little swarm were one entity into whose eye I stared. "Get them here now. EzCal . . . Can you see me, EzCal?" I jabbed my hand. "Cal, get here now and bring your fucking sidekick with you.

"You get to live, so spread the word. Embassytown, can you hear me? *You get to live*. But you better get here and find out what you have to do, EzCal. Because there are some *conditions*."

29

I'LL GIVE EzCAL THIS. When they didn't speak, when they stood to look out over the ridge down kilometres of country and the camp-town of the Absurd, they looked epic. They didn't deserve it.

They'd come to affect baroque: perhaps it was a comfort to some Embassytowners. There were trims of glitter on Cal's clothes, a crest on his aeoli mask. Even Ez wore purple.

In silence their failings were transmuted, or camouflaged at least. Cal's sneer passed for regal: Ez's sulking a thoughtful reserve. They had a small entourage: people who had recently been my colleagues. Some greeted me and Bren when their flier landed. Simmon shook my hand. Southel had come, and MagDa. I couldn't describe their expressions. Wyatt was with them, still guarded, it seemed, but consulted, great operator, prisoner-vizier. He didn't meet my eye. Baptist and Toweller stepped down, back from Embassytown, greeted their companions. Greeted me. The Embassytowners watched them, in what must have been great shock. This journey hadn't turned out as expected.

The officers who'd come had weapons. I know that if the situation had been a little different, EzCal might have tried to have them kill us, as they'd tried to kill us when we travelled. Now, though, the remnants of the Staff in their pointless retinue and the officers and even JasMin, who were there, wouldn't let them. By now everyone in Embassytown had seen the incoming army, and my transmission, and everyone knew that we had stopped them. All Cal had for a last few hours was the pretence that he ruled.

Those Terre refugees had come closer day on day: they were mingling with us now, though mostly all they did was watch our interactions with the Absurd. Ez looked into the sky, and back across the distance toward Embassytown.

Much later I'd hear stories of his actions during my travels: how he'd contrived to test Cal's patience; the plans for what could only be considered a coup, which Cal had crushed more in contempt than anger. Ez eyed us. I could see him calculating. *Jesus do you never stop?* I thought. I didn't give a shit about his story. To Embassytown and the Languageless, Ez and Cal's squabbles were vastly less important than that they were EzCal.

I stood with delegates from the Absurd army, twenty or thirty thrown up from the ranks. "So it's you I'm talking to, is it, Avice Benner Cho?" Cal said coolly. "You speak for . . ." He indicated the fanwingless closest to me, our erstwhile captive.

"Theuth," I said. "It goes by Theuth."

"What do you mean 'it goes by Theuth,'" he said. "It doesn't go by anything. . . ."

"*We* call it Theuth," I said. "So that's what it goes by. I'll show you how to write that down. Or better, Theuth will."

BAD ENOUGH to be defeated, isn't it? Even now you'd try to take us out, Cal: me, Bren, the rest of us. Because the way we saved Embassytown means the end of your reign, as it has, look, ended; and even though your whole damn prefecture was a function of despair and collapse, you'd rather lose it on your terms than be saved on ours. That was what I wanted to say.

There were Absurd with Theuth and Spanish, those most adept at the generation of the ideogrammatic script they were inventing, the most intuitive at the reading and performing of gestures. It wasn't a stable group. Even a few brave Ariekene addicts had arrived, too, come all the way from the city subsisting on pilfered datchips, to see the historic agreement, the change. Rooftop was there, playing its own sound files to itself in sadness. Human runaways squatted on overlooking ledges coloured with Ariekene mottled moulds, and watched the negotiations. They came and went as they wanted.

Cal, perhaps Ez too, tried to depict what was happening as protracted discussion. Really it was just a slow process of explaining facts, and receiving orders, in a nascent script. What took days was making sure the Absurd understood, and understanding what they wanted us to do about it.

You've no authority, I could have said to Cal. This is a surrender. You'd love a bit of pomp: that way in later years you might invoke end-of-empire ghosts. But you're just here because I told the Absurd you were the one they'd have to tell what to do. And the humans watching, the refugees scowling under their cowls, are going to remember how it's obvious that you don't know what's happening. You're doing a lot of *hanging around* during this particular change of epoch, because you're only a detail.

CAMS WENT EVERYWHERE. There were a proliferation of independent home-rigged kits, or those hijacked or gone rogue and uploading their feeds to whatever frequencies they could. Embassytown was watching on the other side of all the lenses.

At night the Ariekei surrounded my party. We asked them to: I still wasn't certain EzCal wouldn't attempt revenge.

"What's going to happen?" MagDa said. They looked at me with wariness and respect.

"It'll be different," I said, "but we will be here. Now they know they can be cured it changes everything. How is it in the city? And in Embassytown?"

Panic and expectancy. Among the Ariekei it was still mostly confusion. There was fighting between factions—they'd seemed united under EzCal's proxy $\frac{kora}{saygiss}$, and obeyed EzCal's orders, but now they fought for reasons difficult to make sense of.

"We'll—they'll—do everything they can to spread this," I said. "No more fixes necessary. We're trying to work together. Theuth mostly speaks for the Languageless now. Spanish is talking to us—to YlSib, obviously, but it can even . . ." MagDa hadn't seen Spanish and me in the evenings: talking, haltingly. "But I have to tell you something," I said to her quietly. "I've heard how people are describing what this is, and it's wrong. There is no cure. Spanish and the others . . . they might not be addicted anymore but they're not *cured*: they're changed. That's what this is. I know it might sound the same, but do you understand that they can't speak Language, anymore, MagDa? Anymore than you ever could."

IT WAS A MORNING, very cloudless. In the lower lands around me, among the filamented undergrowth of the planet, I knew there were agents of script, disseminating the new skill, the concept of it, among the Absurd. Already there were deviant forms from those first suggested, dissident renditions of ideograms, specialist vocabulary created by the semiogenesis of scuff-and-point.

It wouldn't be long before some Ariekene reader reproduced the ground-scratch writing in stain, on something they could hand over, rather than trying to remember and replicate it. Maybe we'd show them how. I imagined a pen held in a giftwing.

The leading cadre of the Absurd stood still. The Embassytown entourage were as smart as they could manage in these circumstances. Various of the human refugees were watching. Theuth and Spanish stood close to me, looking at the cams.

Spanish attracted my attention with its giftwing. "$\frac{you\ are\ ready?}{you\ are\ ready?}$" It spoke to me softly. I hesitated and it spoke again. "$\frac{are.you?}{you.are}$"

EzCal faced me. They looked like kings again. Ez's face was blank: Cal's was swollen with anger.

"Listen. Do you understand?" All the Embassytowners could hear me easily, but it was EzCal I was speaking to. "Do you understand how it's going to be?

"The Absurd are coming back to the city, and so are we. We'll set things up together. They'll have some ideas. I tell you, if I were Kora-Saygiss, your little quisling, I'd be careful. It was smart of you not to let it come. We'll work out the details. We'll be there, in Embassytown."

Until the relief. Everything's different, forever, I thought. I glanced at my notes. "They were going to kill us because we were the source of god-drugs. They knew it was too late for them, they were lost, but they were going to make a totally new start for those after them if they got rid of the problem. Us. You understand how selfless they were? It wouldn't help *them*. It was for their kids. This generation would either be deafened, dead or dying in withdrawal.

"But now they know the addicted can be cured." I ignored MagDa's stares and pointed at Spanish: it pointed back at me. "And if they can be cured then we're an irrelevance. That is why we get to live. See? But they have to *be* cured. That's the condition. Otherwise we're still a sickness. And it takes time to cure oratees." I gestured at Rooftop, still untouched by metaphor. Everyone looked at it. It looked back. "And there's plenty of them. So your job is to keep them going in the meantime, EzCal, till they don't need you anymore. Without you to tide them, the addicted'll start to die. Too quick to be cured, or even deafened. So you have to keep them alive."

"$\frac{it's.love}{it's.love}$," Spanish said. There were gasps from all the humans, who'd never heard it speak its doubled Anglo-Ubiq. Spanish was explaining again why the Absurd would have killed us all and mutilated their compatriots, and why they would now let us live. The Ariekei loved the Ariekei. That verb of ours was the only one that came close. It wasn't flawless, but that's in the way of translation. It was as much a truth as a lie. The New Hearing and the Absurd loved the addicted, and would cure them one of the two ways out, induct them into one group or the other.

"None of you have been ambassadors for a long time," I said. "Who've you been speaking for but yourselves? And now you're not a god or a fix or a functionary, EzCal—you're a factory. The Ariekei have a need: you fulfil it. And believe me, the content'll be policed." Ez's face didn't move. Cal's twisted. No chance to issue orders that could, literally, not be disobeyed. "The city'll be full of Absurd. So if you try to stir things, put instructions in what you say, even restart the war, they'll stop you. If we're too much trouble to bother with, we're gone. They don't want to take the fanwings of all the addicted, deafen every single adult Ariekei in their cycle, now there's another way: but they will if they think they have to. Do you see?"

There's nothing else for you to do, I thought. You have no choice. Those officers, the ones you brought with you, will hold weapons to your heads and demand you speak Language if necessary. And I'll be with them. Spanish and the Absurd would spread the two cures. Recourse to the knife wasn't the existential catastrophe it had been for all those here, who'd thought it ended thought. It would never be relished, but for those who couldn't get clean, it might be considered.

Every day, out of love for their afflicted fellows, the Ariekei would make EzCal speak. We were a temporary necessity. Cal looked so stricken I almost felt pity. *It won't be so bad.* There were many ways we might live, until the ship came.

"Do you understand?" I said, to Cal, to EzCal, and to everyone listening, on the plateau and in Embassytown. I loved the sound of my voice that day. "You see why we're even alive? You have a job to do."

" $\frac{like.me}{all.to.be.like.me}$," Spanish Dancer said. Somewhere there was a series of human gasps, and I heard someone say, "No."

Spanish spread its eye-coral. Ez looked up, Cal turned.

A figure came at us from higher on the hill. A dark-cloaked man. He was followed by a few frantic refugees, shouting. His cape gusted. Curious Absurd parted for him, watching what he was doing, and I shouted *no* but of course they didn't hear. I gesticulated for them to close ranks, but they were new to Terre gestures, and I didn't have time to make them understand.

The man pulled out a weapon. Through his stained old aeoli I could see it was Scile.

MY HUSBAND AIMED a fat pistol at me. We were all too slow to stop him.

Even as he came I stared and as I tried to think how to stop what he was going to do, somewhere below that I was working out where he'd gone, and how, and why, and what he was doing now. I stared at the nasty pouting mouth of the gun.

He changed his aim as he came, pointing at Bren and Spanish Dancer. I tried to push the Ariekes away, but Scile wasn't aiming at it now but at Ez, and then at Cal, and Cal began to turn his eyes to me. Scile fired. Calls and screaming started in Terre and Ariekene voices, as in a plume of blood where energy took and opened him, Cal fell away, staring at me, and died.

Part Nine

THE RELIEF

30

THIS IS WHAT $\frac{\textit{spanish}}{\textit{dancer}}$ said.

It was in a plaza in the city, a big square made bigger by cajoling the buildings. I remember it very well. Bren stood by me and whispered a translation but I could make almost perfect sense of it all.

I remember the weather, the houses, the air and the crowd of Ariekei. Thousands, addicts jostling to the edges of the opening. Some must have expected EzCal, wanted their god-drug fix. This is what Spanish Dancer said.

> Before the humans came we didn't speak so much of certain things. We were grown into Language. After history we made city and machines and gave them names. We didn't speak so much of certain things. Language spoke us. The words that wanted to be city and machines had us speak them so they could be.
>
> When the humans came they had no names, and we made new words so they would have places in the world. They didn't do as other things do. We spoke them into Language. Language took them in.
>
> We were like hunters. We were like plants eating light. The humans made their town in our town like a star in a circle. They made their place like a filament in a flower. We spoke the name of their place, but we know it had another name, sitting in the city like an organ in a body, like a tongue in a mouth.
>
> Before the humans came we didn't speak so much

393

because we were like this one, who years ago was the girl who was hurt in darkness and ate what was given to her. We were like her. You decide why we were like her and why we were not like her. Why she's like herself or is not. We've been like all things; we left the city during the drugtime and speak more now.

Before the humans came we didn't speak. We've been like countless things, we've been like all things, we've been like the animals over Embassytown in the direction of which I raise my giftwing, which is a speaking you'll come to understand. We didn't speak, we were mute, we only dropped the stones we mentioned out of our mouths, opened our mouths and had the birds we described fly out, we were vectors, we were the birds eating in mindlessness, we were the girl in darkness, only knowing it when we weren't anymore.

We speak now or I do, and others do. You've never spoken before. You will. You'll be able to say how the city is a pit and a hill and a standard and an animal that hunts and a vessel on the sea and the sea and how we are fish in it, not like the man who swims weekly with fish but the fish with which he swims, the water, the pool. I love you, you light me, warm me, you are suns.

You have never spoken before.

That was what Spanish Dancer said to its gathered people. It said more. It was much less clumsy with them than I'd been when I changed it: it understood much better the psyches it wanted to alter, and its words were surgery.

At first those in the square listened, not knowing what for. As its words grew more outlandish and impossible, there were brayings of consternation. They were raucous, as they would be at any virtuoso lies, then something much more. There was a hysteria of admiration and concern.

As Spanish spoke, Ariekei shouted in more than astonishment. These were the sounds of crisis. I remembered them from when I'd taught Spanish Dancer to lie. I was hearing minds reconfigured. Deaths: old thoughts dying. I saw the upthrown giftwings and fanwings of ecstasy, ecstasy in an old sense, not without pain and terror, of visions, and then the silence of the adult Ariekei new-born.

There were only a few that first time. Most who listened were left terrified perhaps, tremulous, having glimpsed something. When at last they calmed, some eventually clamoured for EzCal again, their need making them forgetful.

But there were others who tipped over, became new things, learnt language, at what Spanish Dancer said. I understood almost every word it spoke.

Sometimes when Spanish Dancer is talking to me in my own language, it doesn't say $\frac{metaphor}{metaphor}$ but $\frac{lie.that.truths}{lie.that.truths}$, or $\frac{truthing}{lie}$. I think it knows that pleases me. A present for me.

31

Poor Scile.

How do I tell this?

Most mornings I go to Lilypad Hill. The adjutants and I discuss plans. "Anything yet?" I say, and every morning so far they've checked the readings and shaken their heads, "Not yet," and I've said, "Well, soon. Be ready."

Can I say *Poor Scile*, after everything? I can. His actions disgust me—there are dead friends who'd be alive if it weren't for him—but could you not feel pity to see him?

He's in the jail we made from the infirmary. His neighbours are those failed Ambassadors still too broken to walk out of the doors when we opened them. Scile knows he's alive because, criminal as he is, he didn't do anything so very bad, so unforgivable as to warrant execution. We've decided we don't have the death penalty just for murder.

I go to see him sometimes. People understand. It's pity, concern, curiosity and the ghost of affection. He can't believe what's happened. He can't believe he so failed.

It was pandemonium when he killed Cal. I'm surprised he wasn't shot in turn, that we were able to take him alive.

"You will *not* do this," he said. Cal still twitched on the ground. Scile swung his gun at Spanish Dancer. "They will *not* be like you." We stopped him before he fired again. Spanish smacked his pistol away. Grabbed Scile's shirt and said to him "$\frac{why}{why}$?" Scile put his hands over his ears and called Spanish Dancer a devil.

It hadn't been a suicide walk but a pilgrimage. He'd gone to find the Absurd army, to walk behind them a witness and apostle while they—what, cleaning fire, holy avengers who'd rather cut themselves than be tainted by lies?—purged the ruined Ariekei, got the world ready again, a nursery, for unborn pure-Languaged young.

It had been a brutal hope but it had been hope. I'm sure Scile heard when EzCal was born, no matter where he was. I don't know how word could have reached him but word does. He must have known EzCal and their oratees couldn't withstand the Absurd. But he didn't reckon with me and Bren and Spanish Dancer. The horror he must have felt to see us and what we did, from the camps, beside the army. He was patient, waiting until the god-drug arrived before doing his holy work.

He sacrificed himself, he must have thought, for the Absurd. Perhaps he had in mind the child Ariekei that would one day walk through empty Embassytown, think of explanations for its ruins, and say them in Language. Scile was ready for us all to die.

He wasn't quite wrong: there had been a fall. The Ariekei are different now. It's true that now they speak lies.

Poor Scile, I'll say it again. He must think he's fallen among Lucifers.

RECENTLY A MIAB incame to Lilypad Hill. We were no longer the people to whom it had been sent. I think that's why I felt what I can only call *naughtiness*, opening it. I felt what only I would recognise as the faintest immerdamp around it. Like bad children we pulled out treats. Wine; foods; medicine; luxuries: there were no surprises. We opened our orders, and Wyatt's sealed instructions too. He didn't try to stop us. They were no surprise either.

*

THE NEW ARIEKEI can speak to automa, and can understand them.

"I don't want to go in," I said.

"It's fine, it's just . . ." Bren nodded.

He and Spanish Dancer took longer than I expected. I waited in the street, watched hoardings move. The products they advertise aren't sold anymore.

They rejoined me. "She's there," Bren said.

"And?"

we.spoke.to.it
we.spoke.to.it ·

"And . . . ?" I said. "Did she speak to you?" I said to Spanish. It and Bren looked at each other.

i.don't.know
i.don't.know ·

I looked up at her building. There must be cams at points; there are cams everywhere, and my friend had always been part of her surroundings. I didn't wave.

"*Ehrsul I know that you can understand the words I'm saying,* Spanish said," Bren said. "In Anglo. And she doesn't even look back. She goes: 'No, you can't speak to me; Ariekei can't understand me.' 'Avice would like to know how you are,' it says. 'What you've been doing.' She says, 'Avice! How is she? And you can't speak to me. You don't understand me, and you can't speak anything but Language.'"

WE PASSED an avenue of outdated trids, a grassroots market, while I said nothing, and Bren did not insist. In the command economy of our reconstruction, our basics are provided, but extras, luxuries, throw up such barter. They make me think of markets in other cities, on other places.

The blockades have been taken down. Some city-dwellers say that as they can breathe our air but we can't breathe theirs, the Embassytown atmosphere should be extended over the whole city. Where there are new additions being grown, Ariek-ene buildings are subtly unclassic. Here a spire; an angled window; a familiar kind of buttress: our Terre topography's become fashionable.

$\frac{kora}{saygiss}$ CAN'T BE FOUND; and DalTon can't be found: or no one who knows where they are, human or indigenous, will say. Of course their disappearances made me suspect club justice. But I'm in informing networks as good as any, and if something like that has happened, it's been very quiet. Which is no way to *encourager les autres*. I think probably either that they were some of the many killed and effaced by the war, or that one is or both are hiding—it's not as if you can't still do that in the city—waiting for whatever. I suppose we'll have to be vigilant.

DalTon's one thing, as far as I'm concerned. As for $\frac{kora}{saygiss}$, though, I don't think revenge of lynch or any other kind is what most New Ariekei want, if they even say they lived under $\frac{kora}{saygiss}$. No Ariekei I know have been able to answer my questions, about what it was like, about whether they remember how they thought, before. About Language. Spanish Dancer's first speech, about that change, was as much infection as exposition. I don't say they don't remember; I say that they can't tell me how it was if they do.

No one knows why some Ariekei are immune to metaphor. No attention from Spanish or its growing number of deputies, its proselytisers, altering their listeners with careful, infectious, ostentatiously lie-filled sermons, works on all of them. Each meeting there are successes: Ariekei staggering out of Language, into language and semes. Others come close, to go next time or the next. And there are those who refuse to; and those that, like Rooftop, sick with purity, just can't. They still can't speak to me, only to Ambassadors. They only understand a dying Language.

Now we have the drugs, the voices, to keep them alive, and no more gods.

EzSey, I heard one oratee tell YlSib, was its favourite, because the tremor occasioned by their voice was . . . and there, vocabulary, mine and its, failed us. Others prefer EzLott, or EzBel, according to the high they give.

Scile was usually a better thinker than his last murder would imply. He knew how we'd created EzCal: he should have thought we could just do it again. We unhooked the mechanisms from inside Cal's head, and they were safe, but even had they not been, we never faced another end.

"I've got something," MagDa had said. "Southel's been putting together a few prototypes for weeks." "Boosters." "We've had volunteers. We're ready to go."

While we'd pursued ours, that had been their secret plan. A stockpile, against Cal and EzCal, whose power lay in their uniqueness. MagDa's and my and Bren's treacheries dovetailed. Scile had brought no narrative to a conclusion. He killed Cal and very little changed.

At first it was the cleaved Turn who volunteered, shaved their heads and had sockets implanted, tried out boosters like clawed tiaras, hooked into links and let gun-prodded Ez, Rukowsi, read them, and speak with them. Lott was the first to take on the role while her doppel, Char, was still alive.

Some are afraid to, but many Ambassadors have powered down their own links. They don't equalise. They don't speak Language much anymore. There's not much call. I don't think they all dislike each other. Bren says he disagrees, but I tell him he can't think beyond his own history, which is understandable.

We keep Joel Rukowsi safe because we need him and his freakish empathic head, but even that I think will change. We'll find others like him. In the meantime we work him hard, and stockpile hours of drugtalk. We can afford to be generous to the exodusers.

It's two cities now—one of the addicts, one of all the others—that intersect politely. The Absurd and the New have much more in common than either do with the oratees. Hearing's nothing: the Absurd and the New *think* the same.

Spanish exchanges politenesses with Ariekei at every corner, with the Terre, with the fanwingless too, by the touchpads they carry, our Terretech contribution. I'm learning to read and write their evolving scrawl, like a young Ariekes. As soon as they awake into their third instar, now, like some rough ritual they're hard-trained out of their instincts. They have only a few liminal days of pure Language, when word is referent and lies are uncanny, between animal instar and consciousness. Afterwards, the young New Ariekei know their city wasn't always this way but can't imagine it other.

Of those that can't unlearn Language, some are deafening themselves, knowing it'll cure them, that it's not the cutting-out of speech and mind they might once have thought. Others, like Rooftop, are preparing to leave. We'll never visit their autarchic communities. They won't be linked by pipework to the city. We'll hand over many many datchips, enough to last a long time. The exiles will live out their addiction and raise a new brood, never let them hear the chips, until their children speak Language too, but unafflicted and free. Humans—vectors of addiction—will be banned and taboo: the city, where they speak differently now, they'll explain, will be taboo. For the next little future, it's not humans but the New Ariekei that'll ambassador between the city and the settlements.

I know how it'll go, though. A New Ariekes will come to trade: they'll speak to it, Language to language, and they'll think they do, but they won't understand each other. Some of the young'll be intrigued by this odd stranger, and a few adventurous Language-speaking young will make their way to the city gates. That'll be the story. Doubtless there'll still be addicts here—outcasts, holy fools or whatever their status then—and the newcomers will hear the drugtalks broadcast for them, and instantly be addicted too.

THE SHIP'S CREW will have weapons, of course: Bremen weapons, more advanced than ours. But we're very many and they'll be few. Besides, we mean them no harm. We'll have an honour guard.

"Welcome, Captain," I'll say as the doors open onto Ariekene soil. "Please come with us." They'll be guests as much as prisoners.

That's tendentious. They'll be prisoners, but we'll treat them well.

According to Wyatt's instructions, our next relief is due to deliver to Embassytown several new Ambassadors of EzRa's kind. They've improved their empathic techniques. EzRa was the test: next was supposed to come Bremen's coup.

Too late. We got our coup in first. Instead, the new Ambassadors will have a job pushing product to addicts.

$\frac{\text{welcome captain}}{\text{welcome captain}}$, Spanish Dancer will say. It'll gesture politely with its giftwing to the armed Embassytowners waiting. $\frac{\text{you will please come with us}}{\text{you will please come with us}}$.

THE NEW ARIEKEI were astounded to learn that Terre have more than one language. I uploaded French. "I, *je*. I am, *je suis*," I said. Spanish Dancer was delighted. It said to me, $\frac{\text{je.voudrais.venir.avec.vous}}{\text{I.would.like.to.come.with.you}}$.

That's not its only innovation. They don't speak Anglo-Ubiq here, but Anglo-Ariekei. I'm a student of this new language. It has its nuances. When I asked Spanish if it regretted learning to lie, it paused and said, "$\frac{i.regret.nothing}{i.regret}$." A performance perhaps, but I envy that precision.

I wonder if Spanish Dancer ever mourns itself. If it lets me read what it's writing, which I'm almost certain is the story of the war, I might find out.

It did tell me another story. When Baptist and Toweller returned to Embassytown, pretending to be oratees, to persuade EzCal into the wilderness where we were waiting, the god-drug wouldn't see them. EzCal told them instead to relay their message through one of their regular Ariekene entourage, which saw and recognised them as followers of the controversial $\frac{surl}{tesh\ echer}$.

It knew something was wrong: it could have given them up. Baptist and Toweller, in an instant and bravura moment of decision, admitted to their contact the true situation: that new, better times were coming, for all of them, *if* EzCal could be enticed out.

Knowing that like their prophet they might be liars, it still decided to believe them. Given hope for the first time in a long time, that functionary went and told EzCal exactly what Baptist and Toweller had been about to. But they were New and it wasn't. It knew the truth, and it had never lied before. It had had to dissemble, in Language, managing with Herculean effort and luck to get out words that sounded like grunts to itself. That was the real hero of the war, Spanish Dancer told me, that nameless Ariekes, telling the only lie of its life.

IT WOULDN'T BE that hard for Bremen to destroy us. But I think we can make it worth their while not to. War across immer isn't cheap. We have to make sure we're useful. We know what our use can be. Look at us here, on the dark edge of the immer!

There will be the port they wanted. Within a local decade. We'll be the last outpost. That was always our intended role, only now we know it, and while it won't be quite what our metropole had in mind, we can run ourselves.

Welcome to Embassytown, the frontier. I know how fast the stories'll come. I'm an immerser: I've heard them. Just beyond our planet's shores will be, people will say, El Dorado immer lands; deserted ships long lost; Earth; God. Alright then.

I know what chancers'll come, what pirates. I know the likelihood that Embassytown will become slum: but we'll moulder and die or be eradicated by Bremen shivabomb if we have no use. Scile in his visionary stupidity, trying to save the Ariekei, would have damned them: if they killed us, when the relief came it wouldn't forbear genociding them in return. I remember Scile's not from a colony when he fails to think of such things.

So we're to be ravaged by speculation and thrill-seekers. We'll be the wilds. I've been to deadwood planets and pioneer towns: even those way stations have their good things. We'll open up the sky. We'll have knowledge to sell. Uniquely detailed maps. Immer byways only locals like us can find. We have to establish our credentials as an explorocracy; so to survive and rule ourselves, we have to explore.

We'll soon have one immership in our little navy, and at least one captain. When the next Bremen delegation comes to see what to make of us, we'll have something to offer.

Immersion's never safe. This far out, at this edge, we're back to the dangerous glory days of *homo diaspora*. I don't have any hesitation. I've gone out, I've come back, and it's time to go again, in directions and for distances no immerser has gone. In kilohours, I might be meeting an exot I'm the first Terre ever to see, working tongueware, trying to make a greeting. I might find anything.

I've been studying navigation and immerology, techniques that I, the floaker, had always avoided. "You've never floaked in your life," Bren told me, brusquely, when I said that to him. I've started to dream of how Embassytown will look, from the ship. That's why I'm at Lilypad Hill every day. Because I can't wait.

"Good morning, Captain. You'll come with us." And I and my crew will take the skiff to orbit, to the ship.

"Ready," I'll say, and set the helm beyond *void cognita*. I'll push the levers that set us out. Or perhaps the gracious thing will be to allow my first lieutenant to do it. We don't know how the passage will affect such crew: I've warned them that. They're still insistent.

So perhaps it'll be Lieutenant Spanish Dancer who'll instigate that indescribable motion from everyday space through the always. We'll immerse, into the immer, and into the out.

IT WOULD BE foolish to pretend we know what'll happen. We'll have to see how Embassytown gets shaped.

By Embassytown I mean the city. Even the New Ariekei have started to call the city by that name. $\frac{embassy}{town}$ they say, or $\frac{town}{embassy}$, or $\frac{embassytown}{embassytown}$.